THE CHRONICLES OF BRAWLOXOSS, BOOK TWO

A PRINCESS IN TRADE

J.R. KNOLL

ARTWORK BY SANDI JOHNSON

ISBN: 1452813043
ISBN-13: 9781452813042

A few dedications...

This is for everyone who has dared to love when everything and everyone said it is impossible.
For my sister Lisa, who is the model for Le'ell,
Mariah who helped along with the editing process,
Joyce and Clifton Knoll, two parents who never let me give up,
My Grandmother Sybil Lee and my late Grandad M. M. Lee,
For everyone who dared to believe in this story when even I lost faith that it would ever happen,
And my loving wife Tami, who continues to tolerate me and for some reason loves me, even against all odds.

CHAPTER 1

EARLY SPRING, 989 SEASONS

All at once the crisis seemed over, and two unicorns reveled in their freedom once again. The land, it seemed, would return to its state of order and balance, but these unicorns had stepped beyond what they had always known, yet never knew existed. One would be changed for the rest of her life by the horror of witnessing the capture of her stallion, her own pursuit, and the chance encounter with an enemy of her kind, a dragon, who would turn out to be nothing of the like. In her uneasy alliance with him, she had seen through the eyes of another species, been a female of the humans, a woman, and learned their ways. She would learn love again, of friendship and of another who would be her mate. Despite her self-doubts the tethers of the forest held her firm, calling her home even when doubts made her question who she was. Freed from this world by her enemy and ally, and in turn coming to his aid, she returned home, seeing each detail of the Abtont Forest as if for the first time, and with new eyes. Her life would begin again. The innocent young mare who only days before had frolicked in the forest and meadows would return with experience and knowledge that no other unicorn had possessed. This would forever change and torment her, as what she had been as a human lingered stubbornly within.

Her mate and stallion walked at her side, haunted by his own experiences in the human's world. As their prisoner, he had learned a new appreciation for the freedom he had so long taken for granted. Now, back in the forest with his mare and true love at his side, he sought to put the ordeal and its memories forever behind him, though he would never truly be rid of them.

The journey back into the forest would take over a day, but in each other's company the time seemed not to exist at all. Aching bodies seemed to heal quickly and their spirits soared with each sight of the other. Happiness had truly returned to them both.

They knew their herd would already be gathered at the Spagnah River and the rich grazing near its banks. There, new foals would be born and their herd would join others in what could only be described as a celebration of spring for the unicorns. This was the only time of the season they gathered in such numbers. It was part of the order and balance of the land.

Or, so it should have been.

The balance had already been corrupted by the humans, though their taint had never before reached this part of the forest. At this time of season, predators, even us dragons, rarely ventured so deep into the thick of trees near the Spagnah River, nor were we interested in the fields of lush grasses and grains that would draw many a grazer. With unicorns there in such numbers, even briefly, game would be difficult to come by and very well protected, so most predators would seek their meals elsewhere. Again, this would be something affected by the humans.

With many of the grazers hunted out to the North, some predators would indeed venture into this area forbidden to them by their instincts. To a hungry enough creature, even the formidable unicorns would seem viable prey.

Others, however, did not come looking for food. They had another purpose, a sinister one.

So nearly home. The two unicorns almost arrogantly walked in the open on one of the roads cleared through the forest by the humans. Their fear of humans seemed diminished, especially the mare, and their thoughts whirled around returning to their herd.

The bay stallion stopped suddenly, his long black mane flailing on the breeze as he did. Intense eyes stared almost blankly ahead.

Stopping beside him, his snow-white mate also stared ahead, though she lacked the experience to be able to sort out what it was her essence had found.

"Vinton?" she timidly said to him.

He remained silent, his breath coming more deeply.

She reached out further with her essence, touching many unicorns and finding fear among them, and one in pain. Panic was there. They were running toward the river from two different directions. Several were already there, including the one in pain, the one wounded at the shoulder near the neck.

The stallion raised his head and tested the air, finally saying, "Our warning of the human hunters is too late. They have found the herd." His eyes narrowed. "They are not pursuing. They've injured one and they know right where to find her, but they...." His flanks heaved, his breath coming heavy with deep whickers as his eyes widened. "Oh, no."

"What is it?" she asked nervously.

Slowly, he shook his head. "Shahly, a drakenien has also found the herd. That's why the humans are not pursuing."

"A what?"

"Drakenien. It's like a dragon, but far more primitive and far less intelligent."

"Should we help drive it away?"

He looked to her. "Unicorns can't drive them away. We have little defense against them."

"But our horns and essence."

"Shahly, it isn't a dragon. Our essence will not harm it and our horns may not even penetrate its armor."

The mare looked behind her, scanning the forest with her essence. "This is just not a good time. We are supposed to announce our joining to the herd today. Are these drakeniens very fast?"

"They can run down any horse or unicorn in the open."

Her essence touched something and she smiled, then looked to her mate and announced, "I have an idea. Come on!"

As she bolted forward, the stallion protested, "Wait! What are you doing?"

"We're not in the open, Vinton. We can lead him away."

"Away where?" he demanded as he caught up to her. "What did you sense?"

"You said they're not very intelligent. I think we can outsmart him."

"Shahly, you don't know what you're up against."

She whinnied a laugh. "Neither does the drakenien."

They burst from the forest onto the river flood plain where they abruptly stopped, staring at the huge beast less than a hundred paces ahead of them that stalked toward their herd.

It was a fearsome creature, over seven human's heights long. Its head was over two heights from the ground. It's thick upper body and heavily muscled forelegs gave way to shorter, stout rear legs and a declining rear body. A short, blunt tail, less than a quarter of its total length was heavy with muscle and stiff looking, though it clearly could be used as an effective weapon against rivals. Its neck was also thickly muscled, giving way to a broad head and a snout full of long, thick pointed teeth. Blunt dorsal scale ridges, ending in sharp edges and points, ran from between its eyes to the end of its tail. Flanking each were bronze colored plates of armor scales that draped over half of its neck, body and tail. Each armor plate ended in a dark red spike. The longest of these—half a human's height long—were at its shoulders. Truly, this was a creature to be reckoned with in the Abtont Forest. It did not come from the forest; rather it was a warm blooded creature from the Northlands and the West where its kind can be found mostly in rugged areas, plains or tundra. No, this was not a creature well suited to the forest at all. It was too big and awkward among the trees, a fast and distant runner but not at all agile.

The unicorns watched for a moment as the sight of this awesome predator sank in. What to do now eluded the mare and she found herself instinctively hesitant to act. They both wanted to run, but as they watched it stalk toward the river with panning eyes and flaring nostrils, they also noticed the small group of unicorns a hundred paces away—directly in its path!

One of the unicorns, a cream white mare with long white mane and tail, lay on her belly near the river, a human's arrow buried deep in her shoulder and a long stream of blood running from the wound. Her head was down and her eyes closed. Her breath came labored as she clearly fought the pain of her injury. A silver-gray unicorn with white mane and beard tended her injury with his horn, spraying his light blue essence from its tip. He concentrated on his work, but was wary of the predator and braced for flight. Another mare, this one of a blond color with a white mane and tail stood between the drakenien and the other unicorns. She, too, was braced for flight, her head held low as her eyes were locked on the predator.

Shahly could sense the deception the blond mare offered the drakenien, yet it still stalked toward them, following its nose straight to the injured mare. It was less than forty paces away from the injured mare, and soon the two unicorns aiding her would have to flee, lest they be taken as well.

The bay looked to his white mate and asked, "What are you going to do?"

"Uh..."

"Shahly..."

The mare looked behind her, reaching out with her essence. The presence was still there. She looked back to the big predator and snorted.

The drakenien turned his attention to them.

Vinton raised his head, his ears perking up as he pressed, "Now would be a good time to do something!"

Shahly's eyes narrowed. "We need to get him to chase us."

The drakenien turned toward them, baring his teeth.

"I think that will be the easy part," the stallion said flatly.

They turned together and fled, looking back to see the drakenien in pursuit about sixty paces away.

"Well, he's chasing us," Vinton observed. "What now?"

"We have to keep him close enough to keep his interest."

"I don't think that will be a problem, Shahly. Can you tell me what we're doing?"

"We're leading him away from the herd."

"And then what?"

She looked behind her, seeing the drakenien growing closer. "Vinton, what is the one thing a big predator would be afraid of?"

The roan looked to her. "What are you talking about? There is nothing in the forest..." He looked ahead again, mumbling, "Oh, you can't be serious."

The mare looked behind her again. "Oh, yes I can."

Vinton snorted, then easily leaped over the large fallen tree in the path.

Shahly didn't see it.

She tumbled over the log, rolling to a stop in the leaves and pine needles that littered the trail. She lay on her side, not moving for long seconds, then she whickered her disgust as she slowly raised her head. Heavy footfalls caught her ears and she looked behind her, then rolled and sprang to her hooves, darting for the trees.

The drakenien was upon the unicorn and lunged toward her with gaping jaws, also not noticing the fallen tree in his path.

Shahly stopped just inside the trees and swung around, almost smiling as the drakenien stumbled and fell to his side, his bulk rolling to the forest floor.

Yes! She thought. She had outfoxed him, outmaneuvered him. Her heart thundered. Exhilaration was where fear should have been. She liked this feeling. This one small victory was wonderful! Yet, it was not enough.

As the drakenien struggled to right itself, Shahly emerged from the trees, standing well within striking distance as she watched the huge predator.

He got his feet under him and looked right at her—and froze.

Shahly stepped toward him, bringing their noses less than her own body length apart.

They stared at each other for long, tense seconds.

The drakenien snarled.

Shahly's eyes narrowed and she laid her ears back, snorting.

More tense seconds passed. The drakenien did not seem to know what to do, but finally figured it out. He roared, and lunged to his feet, his gaping jaws swinging toward the unicorn.

She bounded aside, barely avoiding the teeth that slammed together well within touching distance. As he tried to regain his senses, Shahly ducked and ran beneath him, sprinting to her waiting stallion who stood watching from fifty paces away.

He swung around and ran to her side as she reached him and together they resumed their chase down the path.

The drakenien was quickly in pursuit, angrily roaring behind them as he slowly closed the gap between himself and his prey.

Vinton glanced at his smaller mate and asked, "Have you gone insane?"

She whinnied a laugh and replied, "No."

The forest blurred by. The path opened onto the riverbank, then wound back into the forest, snaking along the trees, then suddenly opened into a large, grass covered meadow. Dragon-scent finally prevailed over the pines and green things of the forest and the two unicorns veered toward the form lying in the center of the meadow.

Scarlet scales sparkled in the sunlight and, as Shahly whinnied, the dragon raised its head, opening its amber eyes, which were clearly heavy from sleep. This was a sleek creature, its horns sweeping gracefully from above and behind its eyes. Dorsal scale ridges running from between its horns all the way down to the end of its tail grew erect as the dragon saw the drakenien. The dragon's eyes widened and it sprang up, staying on all fours and opening its wings to half of their full span. Its muscular body was very tense and betrayed the curves of a female, and as the drakenien and the unicorns he pursued drew closer, she opened her jaws and trumpeted a warning to the other predator.

Shahly and Vinton stopped and wheeled around to see the drakenien had also stopped and was roaring back, much deeper and much more frightening. His teeth were bared and his jaws gaping as he held his ground, boring into the scarlet dragoness with his angry eyes. He rose up, arching his back and somehow looked even larger as the spikes on his body flared out, adding to his size.

The dragoness responded in kind, spreading her wings as she thrashed her tail and trumpeted at him again.

The drakenien advanced, his teeth bared and his snout wrinkled behind his nostrils as he roared at the dragoness.

She retreated. Though longer than the drakenien, she was far smaller in body and clearly no match for him.

The unicorns backed away toward the dragoness as the drakenien advanced.

Vinton snorted as he stared up at the gigantic predator before him. "I was actually hoping…"

"So was I," Shahly admitted. "Can we protect Falloah?"

"Like we protected the herd?"

The dragoness trumpeted loudly in a long, high-pitched burst that echoed through the forest.

The drakenien hesitated, then snarled and stalked forward again, a long growl escaping him. He had issued his final warning.

The unicorns retreated nearly to the dragoness and the bay glanced back at her, asking, "Can you belch fire?"

"No," she growled, irritated and frightened.

"We're running out of ideas," he observed.

Shahly stopped retreating, then lunged forward and reared up, boring into the drakenien with her essence and suggesting a horrible threat.

He turned his attention to her, baring his teeth. He was not intimidated and had clearly never encountered a more powerful foe in his adult life.

Shahly laid her ears back and retreated as he advanced again, realizing that the threat had been empty to him and her bluff had failed.

"Valliant try, anyway," the stallion offered.

A familiar presence swept into the clearing and a huge black dragon dropped from the sky, landing hindquarters first only twenty paces from the drakenien, then dropping to all fours and opening his jaws, roaring a deep, nightmarish roar as he locked his eyes on the drakenien. He was far larger both in length and weight and kept his wings open as he arched his back and flexed the powerful muscles beneath his armor scales, drawing his dorsal scale ridge erect from between his horns to the end of his thrashing tail. Long claws dug into the earth beneath him as enraged blue eyes began to glow red. Scaly lips were drawn back from long, white teeth and a deep growl rolled from him. Slowly he drew closer to the drakenien, directing his snout down slightly and bringing his long horns up.

The drakenien roared back, snapping his jaws.

Not intimidated, the huge black dragon growled again and advanced, opening his jaws further as his eyes, glowing bright red now, bored into his enemy.

Shahly snorted, then turned and trotted to the scarlet dragoness, flicking her tail at the drakenien as she did.

Eyeing the confrontation, Vinton followed.

The drakenien backed away, his teeth bared and his eyes locked on the dragon's.

The black dragon half stood and charged, roaring.

Roaring back, the drakenien shied away from the dragon, lowering his head as he backed away much quicker.

Striding forward with ground shaking steps, the black dragon positioned himself between the dragoness and the drakenien where he stopped his advance, stood fully and held his ground, his eyes boring into his enemy from five human's heights high.

The drakenien retreated many more steps, then turned his head away from the dragon and sniffed the ground. Half a moment later, when the dragon growled at him again, he turned and loped toward the tree line, leisurely testing the air. He was holding his head low and his back was no longer arched. The spikes on his body folded down and his short tail was held almost straight down.

Vinton looked up to the black dragon and sharply barked, "Well?"

The dragon sat catlike, wrapping his tail around him on the ground as he turned his eyes down to the unicorn and casually replied, "Well what?"

"Aren't you going to chase him?" the unicorn pressed.

"To what end?" was the dragon's answer.

Vinton huffed impatiently. "You're a predator."

"I know that."

"Predators chase fleeing animals. It's what you're supposed to do."

"Such an authority on predators, are you?"

Vinton grunted. "I've had enough experience to know."

The dragon raised his brow. "I see. So why don't you chase him?"

"I'm not a predator!" Vinton growled.

The dragon looked to the drakenien as it wandered back into the trees. "A good thing, too. You'd starve."

The bay snorted.

Shahly looked up to the black dragon, puzzling. "I don't understand, Ralligor."

"You don't understand what?" the dragon replied dryly.

"Why didn't you fight the drakenien like you did the ogre at Red Stone Castle?"

"Shahly," the dragoness started, "we only fight another predator when we have to. Ralligor had to fight the ogre to save us."

"Or when it's an easy victory," the black dragon added. "There was no need to waste the effort today. I just had to make it clear to him that pursuing a confrontation with Falloah would not be a wise idea."

"But what if he had attacked you?"

Ralligor looked back to the drakenien as it disappeared into the forest. "He wouldn't."

"But he was going to attack Falloah," Shahly pressed.

The dragoness' eyes betrayed amusement as she glanced at Vinton, then explained, "No, Shahly. He was trying to frighten me away. He might have attacked me if I hadn't left soon or if Ralligor hadn't arrived when he did, but he knows a battle with me would be costly to him even if he had won or even killed me."

Shahly tried to comprehend, turning her eyes back to where the drakenien had disappeared. "If he is frightened of you and isn't going to fight, then why did he just walk away? Why didn't he run?"

"He doesn't want me to pursue him," the black dragon answered.

"But if he doesn't run, he would be easy for you to catch. Isn't he afraid you will attack him?"

"Not if he doesn't run."

Shahly leaned her head and asked, "Why?"

Ralligor vented a patient breath. "Do you know what a hierarchy is?"

She stared up at him and just blinked.

The dragon tightened his lips. "Do you have others in your herd of higher status than the rest?"

Shahly nodded.

"As predators," the dragon explained, "I am of higher status than the drakenien because I'm stronger."

"Oh!" Shahly declared. "I understand. You are stronger, so you protect the drakenien like Vinton protects the herd!"

Ralligor closed his eyes and growled a sigh.

Vinton looked away and whickered.

Falloah also looked away, growling a soft laugh.

The black dragon looked to Shahly and advised, "Perhaps you should not try so hard to understand the workings of predators. You could hurt yourself if you think about it too hard."

Shahly wrinkled her nose and whickered, "Huh?"

Vinton raised his head, looking into the forest as he whinnied, "The humans!"

Shahly wheeled around, reaching into the forest with her essence to find her herd. Her lips parted as she stared blankly into the trees, feeling the other unicorns as they, too, sensed the approach of the human hunters. "They stayed away because of the drakenien," she said as if to herself. "And now they're going after the herd!" She whinnied and launched into a full gallop toward the riverbank where the herd had gathered. Her mind whirled. Instinct urged her to hide in the forest, but she could barely hear it. The herd was in peril.

She galloped into the middle of the clearing by the river, right into the middle of the chaos of hunting humans and fleeing unicorns. She did not hesitate long to survey the situation before a rope dropped over her head from the left and was brutally tightened around her neck. She knew from her experience before that the rope was charmed and her spiral would not cut it.

Her eyes narrowed and she turned toward the rider who pulled the rope ever tighter, baring her teeth as she saw him.

He was a dirty, bearded human, much like those who had pursued her before. Before, she did not know how to deal with them. She did now.

Boring into the horse's thoughts, she suggested a threat right in front of him, showing the image of a deadly serpent.

The horse panicked and reared up, whinnying and his rider rolled from his back.

Shahly tried to shake the rope from her, then looked up to see other humans on foot rushing toward her. She bored into their minds as well, and bayed loudly at them.

They stopped, seeing a giant white forest cat before them instead of a unicorn. In a panic, they dropped their ropes and fled.

Other humans approached, perplexed at the reaction of their comrades.

She turned toward them, not bothering to defend herself as she saw Vinton running toward them, and she whinnied a laugh as he knocked them to the ground with his shoulder as he ran by.

He stopped and turned to see the humans getting to their feet, then he galloped to his mate and locked his hooves into the ground to stop near her.

She looked to him, smiling as she whinnied, "Isn't this exciting?"

He snorted, glaring at her. He was clearly not having the fun she was.

Shahly cringed slightly, looking up at him like a foal who was about to take a good scolding, then she turned her attention to the humans who approached. "Vinton, I think we have a problem."

They looked around them, seeing that they were surrounded by about twenty humans.

Vinton snorted through his nose and growled, "Any more ideas, Shahly?" He sounded really irritated.

Shahly glanced around, knowing that all of these humans would be difficult at best to trick. "At least the rest of the herd got away."

"They might have anyway," he observed, then saw the cream colored mare still lying by the river, the silver still by her side concealing her with his essence. "Damn. We need to think of something and think of it fast."

Shahly reached out with her essence, smiling as she touched a familiar presence. "No we won't. Just stand still and act frightened."

Vinton turned his eyes to her. "I won't have to act."

The humans closed in, raising the loops of their ropes to throw.

Other unicorns watched nervously from their hiding places in the forest.

A human on horseback pointed to Vinton, ordering, "Take the stallion first."

Shahly looked to him and whickered, "Not today."

The black dragon dropped from the sky near the river, landing on all fours and he roared like something from a nightmare.

All the humans seemed to see was this massive predator's bulk and all of those teeth and they fled in all directions, disappearing into the forest.

Shahly whinnied to them, "Now go home and leave us alone!" She felt very satisfied with herself when she looked back to her stallion, then laid her ears back and lowered her head when she saw his expression.

He was very annoyed, and made no secret of it as he stared back at her. Ralligor glanced around, seeing that all of the humans were truly gone, then he stood and strode to Shahly and Vinton, his eyes still scanning the forest. "Pesky creatures, these humans," he observed.

Shahly whickered a laugh. "I think all humans are afraid of you."

"If they're smart humans," he agreed, then sat and looked down to them, shaking his head. "I was right. You *do* like being chased by humans, don't you?"

She snorted at him. "I do not. We were trying to keep them away from the herd."

He reached to her and removed the rope from her neck. "And it worked nicely, didn't it?"

Vinton grunted. "Do you see any other unicorns in their hands?"

"We found a small group leading two of your herd away," Ralligor replied. "Falloah is dealing with them." He pursed his scaly lips and loosed a burst of fire at the rope, then dropped it and watched it burn.

"Why help us?" Vinton demanded.

"Perhaps I don't want to see another talisman built," was the dragon's answer.

"And we're friends!" Shahly snapped.

Vinton snorted and looked away. "Friends with a dragon."

The old silver unicorn slowly stood, his horn glowing bright blue as his eyes were locked on the dragon. Cautiously, he paced toward the huge predator, directing his horn toward the dragon's back.

Ralligor half turned his head and advised, "Since we both know you're planning to do something very foolish I would suggest that you think hard about the consequences."

The silver unicorn froze. The element of surprise was gone.

"Or are you just determined to be ripped apart today?" Ralligor added.

The silver's eyes narrowed. "I've tangled with dragons before."

"I remember you," was the dragon's response. "You don't want to tangle with me again."

The silver looked to Vinton.

The bay shook his head. "He is no threat to the herd." He looked up to the dragon, his eyes narrowing as he finished, "Is he?"

Ralligor turned his eyes to Vinton. "Am I?"

Shahly snorted and stepped between them. "No he isn't. Now stop this!"

"This doesn't concern you, Shahly," the silver warned.

Ralligor looked back to him. "She's a unicorn, isn't she? I'd say it does concern her."

"Ralligor is my friend!" Shahly whinnied. "I trust him and so should the rest of you."

"He is a predator," the silver insisted.

"He saved Vinton and me from the humans," Shahly explained. "He drove away the drakenien and the humans today."

The silver shifted his eyes from Shahly to the dragon. "For what reason?"

"I was bored," was the dragon's reply, then he turned and looked up. "I'm no more of a threat to you than she is."

Falloah landed gracefully beside him, out of breath. She dropped to all fours and gasped, "The unicorns are running back this way. I couldn't get the ropes from them. They ran away too quickly."

"We'll deal with them when they arrive," Ralligor assured.

Other unicorns began to emerge from the forest, all on alert and all nervously eying the dragons.

The exhausted dragoness closed her eyes and slowly laid to her belly, folding her wings to her sides as she continued to gasp for breath. "I don't think I can fly anymore, *Unisponsus*."

"I know," he replied, looking tenderly down at her. "You need to eat. There is a herd of grawrdoxen up river I can hunt in the morning. Just rest here tonight."

Falloah looked around her, "I don't think we are exactly welcome here."

Shahly approached her. "Of course you are. Rest here as long as you like." She looked up to Ralligor and asked, "What is wrong with her? Why is she so weak today?"

"She hasn't fed as a dragon for some time," the black dragon explained.

"Oh," Shahly realized. "She's hungry." She glanced around and informed, "There is plenty of grass and fruit here. You're welcome to some of it."

"She needs meat, Shahly," Vinton explained. "Grass won't do her any good."

The silver snorted. "You're telling me that a hungry dragon among the herd is not a threat?"

Ralligor looked to him. "You would make a wonderful meal for her, if you weren't so old and gamy."

The silver's eyes narrowed.

"He's hunting elsewhere tomorrow," Vinton insisted, then looked up to the dragon and snapped, "Must you make your presence here so difficult?"

"Don't you have fleas to scratch?" the dragon snarled.

Vinton snorted, then looked to Falloah and offered, "You are welcome to rest here tonight among the protection of the herd. It's the least I can do for you."

"I don't want to make the other unicorns too nervous," she insisted.

He approached her and assured, "They'll be fine, as long as this overgrown lizard beside you can behave himself."

She glanced up at him.

Ralligor rolled his eyes and growled.

Falloah looked back to Vinton and smiled. "Thank you. Shahly is fortunate to have such a stallion."

He glanced aside, then whinnied a laugh. "If only you were so fortunate."

Ralligor looked to Shahly. "Your stallion is more ass than unicorn, I think."

Shahly looked away, whickering a laugh.

Other unicorns nervously approached, many of them seeing dragons for the first time.

The tension drained slowly that night, but not completely.

Shahly slept at Ralligor's side with her Vinton beside her as well. She had never felt so safe.

The other unicorns would not sleep so soundly.

Morning would bring an unpleasant awakening.

Just before sunup, as an early morning glow illuminated the clearing from the East, unicorns and some other animals began to race through the clearing. Panic was among them.

The commotion roused Shahly and she wearily raised her head, watching as several unicorns galloped by, then looked sleepily to see what they were fleeing from.

The drakenien burst from the trees, growling as he pursued the unicorns with his jaws wide open.

Shahly sprang to her hooves, whinnying, "Vinton!"

He also sprang up.

The silver ran to his side, whickering, "I thought that thing was gone!"

Vinton glanced toward the river, seeing the cream colored unicorn still lying in the grass there.

The silver lowered his head as the drakenien saw them. "She will need more time, Vinton."

The scarlet dragon raised her head, her eyes locked on the drakenien. She tensed and slowly raised herself up, growling.

The drakenien hesitated, his spikes flaring out. In the dim light, he did not recognize the huge black mass lying between the dragoness and the unicorns.

Ralligor's eyes opened slowly, his brow low between them.

Falloah backed away.

The drakenien glared at her for just a moment, then he looked back to the three unicorns who were not fleeing and stalked toward them.

The silver backed away.

The drakenien was only ten paces away when Ralligor finally raised his head. His eyes glowed red and his lips curled away from his sword sized teeth as a thunderous growl rolled from his throat.

Finally seeing the dragon, the drakenien stopped, and turned his attention to the larger predator.

They just stared at each other for long seconds.

Ralligor's long claws dug into the ground beneath him.

The drakenien's eyes shifted back to the unicorns.

Shahly snorted at him.

Ralligor growled, only provoking a look from his opponent.

More long seconds passed.

And patience abandoned the dragon. He launched himself forward with a horrifying roar and gaping jaws.

With no time to react, the drakenien backed away and tried to snap back.

Ralligor's jaws slammed shut at the base of the drakenien's thick neck, his teeth plunging through the drakenien's armor with a horrible crunch.

Screaming a roar, the drakenien tried to struggle away, retreating as best he could.

The black dragon drove his teeth in further, slamming his clawed hands into the drakenien's head and side as he continued to push his enemy backward and sideways.

The drakenien screeched and swung his tail at the black dragon, ramming the spikes into the dragon's thigh, but lost his footing and rolled to the ground.

Ralligor opened his jaws, pushing the drakenien down and pinning him to the ground.

Screeching, the drakenien struggled and kicked to free himself, then screeched louder as the dragon's teeth ripped into his shoulder.

The horrified unicorns looked on as the one-sided battle raged.

As suddenly as the dragon had attacked, he backed away.

The drakenien struggled to his feet and raised his eyes to the victor, holding his tail straight down.

Ralligor growled a warning, then approached with heavy steps and bared teeth.

Cooing submissively, the drakenien backed away, then turned and slowly limped into the forest.

The black dragon watched him disappear into the trees, then looked back at Shahly, growling, "I hate being awakened so early."

"So do I," she confessed. "Will he come back?"

Ralligor turned and faced her, seating himself as he replied, "I don't see him approaching the area again as long as he knows I'm here."

The silver unicorn stepped forward and asked, "What can we do if he does?"

"Asking an enemy for advice?" the dragon retorted.

Glancing aside, the silver unicorn huffed a breath, and would not meet the dragon's eyes. "I never claimed to be the wisest of us, and clearly the legends of your kind are not entirely true."

Falloah sat beside her huge mate, adding, "Nor are all of the legends of your kind."

"So how do we keep it away?" Vinton asked.

Ralligor answered, "Use the legends of your kind that are true, assuming they are right about you being more intelligent than other grazers."

Vinton snorted.

Shahly considered, then danced excitedly and declared, "I know how! Come on, Vinton!" She launched herself after the drakenien, disappearing into the forest.

"Shahly!" Vinton called after her, then he shot an angry glare at the black dragon and whickered, "This is *your* fault."

Ralligor raised a brow and shot back, "How do you figure?"

"She was *never* this impulsive before she met you."

Ralligor nodded. "Perhaps you're right. Perhaps I should have allowed her to remain the way she was. Of course, *you* would still be a guest of Red Stone Castle if I had."

Vinton snorted, glanced at the silver unicorn, then turned and ran after Shahly.

The silver vented a sigh as he watched Vinton disappear into the forest, then shook his head. "His bitterness is not entirely his fault. The legends of your kind are told to the youngest foals and such learning is difficult for some to unlearn."

"Shahly learned not to fear me very quickly," the dragon pointed out, also staring into the forest where Shahly and Vinton had disappeared.

Nodding, the silver admitted, "She is still very young and naïve. She has never had the burden of protecting the herd."

"She took the burden on herself when the humans came into the forest," Ralligor pointed out.

"I suppose she did," the silver admitted. "Still, Vinton is considered a leader of the herd and has much responsibility."

"Leader of the herd, is he?" Ralligor shook his head. "Your kind may be doomed, then."

The silver unicorn looked up at him, and snorted.

CHAPTER 2

There comes an awkward time in the growth of all creatures when they are no longer children, yet have not quite reached adulthood. This time of adolescence can be a confusing period, especially for those creatures capable of abstract thought, those of us who are intelligent. I have heard many stories of different species whose young could not easily make this transformation to fertile adulthood. Though difficult for many, it seems to be at its worst in dragons. Our young, especially drakes, find themselves vying for control of their own territories, hunting grounds, and finding and impressing that special mate while still too young for the task and relatively small compared to those of us who are established. Dragon hierarchies can be brutal to those of this age. How well I know this.

For some reason, this period of adolescence is unnecessarily complicated in humans. As with all primates and other lower animals, they establish their hierarchies, but unlike others they are not based on strength and experience. Some are considered born to alpha status without ever vying for the position. Sadly, most of them accept this. What it is about "royal blood" is not entirely clear, especially since many are actually weaker than those not of their bloodlines.

Often in humans, there are those who feel the need to take the responsibility of leading others. I can only surmise that this is done more for the rewards of the position than the role itself. Great and horrible wars have been fought for control of territories not their own, many times successfully, many times not. The allure that would drive humans to such lengths to control others continues to escape me as such power is always pursued by great responsibilities and often even greater enemies. Dragon Landmasters, always the strongest of us, often find themselves in life and death battles with their rivals and the enemies of dragons. Aside from massive hunting grounds and his choice of females within his territory, a Landmaster has little else to look forward to. The constant patroling of his territory and frequent battles keep him seemingly on constant alert for any threat. Lesser males, those loyal to their Landmasters, will assist in defending the territory, but the brunt of the responsibility lies with the Landmaster himself. Unlike human hierarchies, he does not rely on his offspring to take his place. He must be overthrown in battle. Rarely is this done by one of his own bloodline, though this is not unprecedented.

As with us dragons, humans often lose their territories in this manner, not in one on one combat, but with armies following a single leader. This is destructive and seems extremely wasteful, but it does serve to keep their numbers under control. These wars can start as an effort to expand territory, to settle disputes, or any of a number of pointless reasons. Kingdoms may stand on the brink of war for generations, living together in an uneasy coexistence until war tears one or both apart or one or both just fade from the land.

My words are not the simple ramblings of an old dragon. They mesh together in an incident that would mold the fates of the human inhabitants of the Spagnah River Valley. Enemies would have to learn trust. Lower humans of many species would join in an alliance of grand and unnatural proportions. War lines would be drawn across borders, across races and species. None in the valley or anywhere in the Western Abtont Forest would be immune. Visions of conquest would lead the strife, but unforeseeable variables would be waiting. Not phantom armies or vengeful sorcerers, angry dragons or anything of the like, nothing that anyone could expect at all.

Spring meant that winter's air still vied for control of the night and would cast a crisp chill and sometimes a thin white frost throughout the land until the morning sun could chase it endlessly west. An hour before sunup was not the time most humans would be stirring unless tasked to do so, which a few were. Their watchful eyes would pierce the darkness around the castle fortress, seeking any threat, any sign of invasion from their rivals.

So it was on a fateful morning that should not have been any different than the last, but for one detail: This was to be the first truly warm day of spring.

Zondae Castle was the very definition of a fortress. Half of those living within its high stone walls were warriors dedicated to its defense. Only a few walked the battlements this early morning, some manning the gates and towers to alert those within of a night attack that they thought could come at any time. They would also watch for returning patrols, but only after sunup, as no night patrols ventured from this castle.

On this crisp morning, a patrol of five was expected to depart as the early morning glow began to bathe the land from the East, but today they would be joined by a sixth. Five of them made the walk from the outer palace to the stables, four casually chatting amongst themselves. The fifth lagged a pace behind, alert to the others but with a wandering mind. Cloaks and mantles would be held close to muscular and finely honed bodies as weapon belts and other equipment were slung carelessly over the shoulders of three while the other two seemed ready to mount and ride their horses. Two were younger than the others, one eighteen seasons and the other only sixteen. Excitement brewed from the youngest as this would be her first patrol. The nineteen season old seemed calm as she lagged behind the rest, yet something calculated in her mind, something not related to the patrol to which she was attached.

As they entered the stable and lit the lamps to illuminate the inside, the firelight found the five women in good spirits. They were all very tall for human females, as tall as or a little taller than the average males of their species. Normally bronze skin was a little paler after a winter of covering against the cold. These were not women typically found throughout the land. They were much more muscular, much more aggressive, taking on roles traditionally held by men.

For the most part, their hair was dark, black, brown or auburn, but for one. Her hair was fiery red. There seemed to be no leader among them as they casually saddled their horses, strapping equipment to the animals and preparing them for the long day ahead. Their conversation continued, and only the auburn haired girl, who was only recently nineteen seasons old, seemed not to participate. She listened absently, her eyes mostly on her saddle as she worked and her mind continued to wander to other things. Girlhood still rounded the features of a face that was free of blemish or scar and very well proportioned, though she was very much a woman grown as her well made body would reveal. She was not dressed in armor, only white fur over her hips, the same white fur over her breasts, held there by thick black leather straps around her back and neck and covered by a black hooded cape. Her fur lined boots were worn almost all the way to her knees. Her arms and legs were otherwise bare of clothing, gauntlets or armor. Her long auburn hair was not restrained and was worn loosely over the lowered hood of her cape and all the way to her mid-back. Her dark green eyes showed strain beyond her age and betrayed a distraction in her thoughts, though she found herself wary of her companions.

One, a young brown haired woman of perhaps twenty seasons threw her saddle over her horse, continuing to complain about a troublesome

A Princess In Trade

woe. "I just don't understand," her exasperated voice rang out. She did not notice two of the others exchanging amused smiles behind her. "I've done everything! He just can't seem to learn and I'm getting so damned impatient with him!"

"Ren'shee," a red haired woman started, trying not to laugh at her companion, "it's a common problem. Some just take a little longer to train than others."

"I have way too much invested in him to deal with these problems much longer!"

"Just give him some time. I'm sure he'll work out."

"That would require patience, Jan'ka, and I've run out."

The auburn haired girl glanced over her shoulder at them, then smiled and resumed strapping her saddle to her horse.

A black haired woman in her mid twenties approached the brown haired girl and patted her shoulder. "You sound frustrated. Would you like to borrow one of mine to work it off?"

The brown haired girl stopped what she was doing and considered, then looked back at the black haired woman and asked, "Can we trade for a while?"

The black haired woman raised her eyebrows. "And what is in this for me?"

Ren'shee offered, "If you can train him well enough I'll let you borrow him whenever you want."

"I already have three," the black haired woman informed.

"Please," Ren'shee drawled. "Traw'linn, I'm desperate."

The black haired woman considered, then asked, "Which one would you want?"

The brown haired girl bit her lip, then finally confessed, "Maldrek is your most experienced, isn't he?"

Traw'linn smiled. "That he is, but I'm not sure you could handle him."

The others laughed.

The auburn haired girl just smiled and shook her head as she closed the flap on one of her saddle bags.

"Please, Traw'linn," Ren'shee begged. "I *need* him! Just for a few days, I promise!"

Traw'linn rolled her eyes and conceded, "Okay, okay." Something sinister took her eyes and she smiled slightly. "What if I don't want to give Jaireg back?"

Ren'shee smiled back. "Then I'll just have to keep Maldrek."

The black haired woman nodded. "Sure. Just wait and see how well *I* can train him."

🙢 20 🙠

A tall, muscular blond haired woman entered and set her hands on her hips as she scanned the stable. This was a woman near forty seasons old and quite well experienced in the art of battle. Her long hair was restrained in a pony tail behind her. She wore light plate armor beneath her dark green cloak, armor that only covered vital areas and left her with much freedom of movement. Her dark blue eyes were as stones in her strong and attractive face, her brow a little low over them as she shifted her gaze from one woman in the stable to the next, then loudly cleared her throat.

All activity in the stable stopped and the other women there turned to face the blond woman, but for the auburn haired girl, who slowly, discreetly pulled her hood over her head, and went back to tending her horse.

"Captain Pa'lesh," the black haired woman greeted.

The blond woman strode past her, into the stable to her own horse, which was already saddled, and checked the equipment there. "I was foolishly expecting everyone to be ready when I got back."

"I'm ready!" the brown haired, sixteen season old girl quickly responded.

"Sure you are," Pa'lesh mumbled. "You ladies be sure you are ready for inspection. I don't want any little incidents today."

The auburn haired girl tensed a little more.

"Isn't inspection kind of a waste of time?" Jan'ka asked, sounding a little exasperated. "All you do is nit-pick and look for the slightest thing out of place."

Pa'lesh hesitated, then, in one motion, pulled her sword and spun around, the tip of her sword stopping right on Jan'ka's throat before anyone could even blink.

The red haired young woman shrieked a breath and froze, her wide eyes locked on the sword.

Pa'lesh's eyes bored into Jan'ka and for long seconds she held her sword against the smaller woman. "You weren't prepared. In battle, you would be sucking your last breath through the gaping hole in your throat."

Jan'ka slowly raised her sheepish eyes to the blond woman's.

Ren'shee slowly approached, her eyes on Pa'lesh. "Since when should we be on our guard against each other? She just said..." She backed away as Pa'lesh turned on her.

"You missed the point entirely!" Pa'lesh shouted at her.

Everyone cringed.

"It is my job to make sure you are ready for what is out there," the blond woman explained more calmly. "You *will* listen to me and do exactly as I say, *when* I say to do it." She glanced at the other women, seeing they were clearly intimidated, especially the youngest. She vented a sigh, then conceded, "Very well. I'm releasing the burden to you. Everyone check someone else's horse and make sure your sister is ready for the field. If she goes out unprepared it will be both your fault."

"*I* will inspect yours," Jan'ka spat.

Pa'lesh sheathed her sword and turned her eyes to the red haired woman. "Fine." Then, unexpectedly, she smiled. "And when you find nothing missing or out of place, you owe me your finest bottle of wine."

Jan'ka smirked. "I'm sure I'll find something, Captain."

Nothing was found, and the patrol waited for Jan'ka to retrieve her lost wager.

As usual, they left the gate just before sunup, as the early morning glow began to illuminate the sky to the East, though it barely penetrated the tall trees of the forest and lamplight illuminated the road before the riders. No one spoke as they rode slowly, quietly into the forest.

The auburn haired girl lagged behind. Ahead, the road would fork, and she prayed the patrol would take the fork to the right today.

As they neared the fork, the sun began to climb higher, better illuminating the road and forest. This is just what the auburn haired girl did not want. Her eyes darted around, looking for a trail into the forest she could slip into. There were many of them in this part of the forest, but there was one that would take her in the direction she wanted to go. Perhaps it was just a little further. She turned her eyes to the four riders who were seven or eight paces ahead of her.

Four?

Her eyes widened and she counted again.

"Oh, no," she whispered.

"Oh, yes," Pa'lesh announced from her left.

The auburn haired girl swung her head around to see the Captain riding up from behind her. She just stared at the blond haired woman for long seconds, then turned her eyes forward again.

"Did you really think I wouldn't notice you there in the stable?" Pa'lesh asked.

"Do you really think I care?" the auburn haired girl spat back.

"If you're smart you do," the Captain retorted. "Where is it you think you're going, Le'ell?"

"Is it so unusual for someone to want to go on the morning patrol?"

"It's unusual for you, seeing as how it's a chore for you to get you out of bed before high sun lately."

Le'ell shot her an angry look, then turned her eyes forward again. "You needn't be suspicious of everything and everybody, Pa'lesh."

"Only of you lately. So what is it you are hiding?"

"I'm not hiding anything. I just wanted out of the castle."

Pa'lesh nodded. "I see. I want to see you riding in the *middle* of the patrol the rest of the day."

Le'ell's eyes slid to the Captain. "Quit treating me like a child."

"Let's get something straight right now," Pa'lesh hissed. "As long as you are on *my* patrol you will follow my orders and conduct yourself like a good little soldier—not a spoiled child—or I'll take you back to the castle right now, bound and slung over your saddle like a dungeon escapee. Do you understand?"

Le'ell turned fully to her and hissed back, "How dare you?"

"I have permission, and I have orders from the Queen to return you to Zondae at the first sign of defiance. Are we clear on that?"

Le'ell turned ahead, her brow low and her lips tight. She knew Pa'lesh meant what she said. Venting a deep breath, she finally lowered her eyes and nodded.

"Good girl," the Captain commended. "Now take up your position where I told you."

Le'ell stubbornly hesitated, then glanced at Pa'lesh and kicked her horse faster.

Truly, this was turning out to be a long, frustrating day.

About two hours passed. They had traveled less than three leagues and were half way to the Spagnah River, which was the border with their closest enemy, when Pa'lesh raised her hand and stopped the patrol. For long seconds she just stared ahead at something. All that could be heard was the wind in the trees. Not even the birds here were singing. Slowly, Pa'lesh scanned the forest, looking from one side of the road to the other, then directly down the road. She held up three fingers, then held two together and curled them in as if drawing down a bowstring as she lowered her arm.

Three of the women in the patrol took the bows from their saddles and readied arrows.

Ren'shee grasped her sword, which hung on the left side of her saddle, and gave Le'ell a fearful look.

Le'ell just nodded to her and grasped her own sword.

The boredom of the routine patrol was suddenly a terrifying exercise in patience.

Pa'lesh removed her dagger from her belt and flipped it over to hold it by the blade then kicked her horse slowly forward, her eyes panning back and forth as she rode ahead of the group.

The women with the bows pulled their bowstrings and took aim, one aiming to the left, one to the right, one straight down the road.

A long, tense moment followed as she rode about thirty paces ahead of the rest of the patrol. Her eyes never stopped moving. Finally, she stopped her horse, scanned the area once more, then held her hand up, motioning for the rest of the patrol to follow.

Le'ell and Ren'shee kicked their horses ahead of the women with the bows, never taking their hands from their swords. The other three followed.

Stopping with her horse to Pa'lesh's left, Le'ell looked to the Captain, not liking what she saw in her eyes.

"Wait here," Pa'lesh ordered as she slowly dismounted.

The rest of the patrol watched her walk to the tree line and kneel down. She examined something lying beside the road, then looked up, her back stiffening as she saw something further down. Looking back down to what was in front of her, she hesitantly reached to it, laying her hand on it, then she motioned for the rest of the patrol to advance.

Only when she saw the Captain stand and seem to relax somewhat did Le'ell feel her nerves calm.

Pa'lesh stood and turned to the patrol. Her face was a little ashen but her features were still as stone as she ordered, "Jan'ka. Take Le'ell and Tam'ree back to the castle and report to the Palace Captain, then get Blue Garrison here. Go!"

Jan'ka and Tam'ree turned their horses.

Le'ell looked behind Pa'lesh, gasping at what she saw.

"I said go!" the Captain barked.

Turning her horse, Le'ell was quick to catch up to the other women.

They were all silent for a time, pacing their horses quickly toward the castle.

Jan'ka shuddered. "What could have done that?"

Shaking her head, Le'ell stared blankly at the road ahead of her and answered, "Not something I would want to meet with only half a patrol. Keep your bows where you can shoot quickly."

The other two women complied.

Scanning the forest, Tam'ree whimpered, "What if it's still out here? What do we do if we meet it?"

"First off," Le'ell started, "just relax. Pa'lesh clearly does not think that whatever it was is still in the area."

"We don't even know what it was," Jan'ka pointed out. "Or who."

Tam'ree shook her head. "No way a person could do that to someone. There's no way."

"I've seen many horrible things people can do to one another," Jan'ka informed, "but nothing like that."

"Do you think it might have been soldiers from Enulam?" Tam'ree asked anxiously.

No one answered, but hearing the name sent Le'ell's mind back to previous thoughts.

A time later, they came upon the fork in the road that had given Le'ell pause earlier, and she paused again.

The other two women stopped a few paces down the road and turned their horses, staring inquisitively at the auburn haired woman.

Le'ell stared down the fork in the road, then looked to Jan'ka and ordered, "Go on back to the castle. I'll catch up later."

Jan'ka exchanged glances with Tam'ree, then hesitantly asked, "Do you really think you should—"

"I can take care of myself!" Le'ell snapped. "Just report back to the castle as soon as possible. I'll catch up." Without another look back, she turned her horse and kicked it into a gallop down the fork in the road.

Some time later she knew she was approaching the river. Remembering previous trips, she knew the road would open into a field of tall grass, and as if summoned by her thoughts she saw the road open. Smiling, she kicked her horse even faster, determined to chase across the field as fast as her horse would go.

Nearly there, something in the field moved, something big!

She reined in and brought her horse to an abrupt stop. The horse grew nervous and very agitated, so she gave it a few reassuring pats on the neck, her eyes locked on the mammoth beast in the clearing before her.

Even from about fifty paces away, she could see that it was over four times bigger than her horse and looked about ten times heavier. The long hair that covered its body draped almost all the way to the ground and was a deep brown streaked with silver, white near its thick neck and shoulders. As it lifted its huge head—one and a half times higher than her horse's head—it casually looked toward Le'ell, slowly chewing on a mouthful of grass. Its face was shaped much like a bull's, but its snout was blunter and very wide. Its thick, black and silver marbled horns were each about half a pace long, curved and forked at the ends where they formed sharp looking points of glossy black. Its tail reached only half way to the ground and swished occasionally as if to ward off flies.

Le'ell had seen Grawrdoxen many times and they never failed to impress her. To her knowledge, they had never been domesticated. The meat was way too tough and gamy to eat. Hunting them was perilous at best as arrows and spears could not penetrate that thick hair and hide, and being charged by an animal that was ten times the weight of a horse and nearly as fast was a little too risky for even the bravest hunters. She knew little ate them as wolves, forest cats, and even people were too small to tackle even one.

Hearing thumps on the ground, she looked to one side and saw another approaching, then noticed several more in the distance.

She jumped down from her horse and tied the reins to a tree, then slowly approached, looking for a younger one. Although she knew they were relatively docile, she made a wide circle behind the big bull in front of her, keeping her eyes on it. Its shoulders were twice as high as she was tall and it had plenty of bulk to match.

It watched her for a moment, its head moving slowly to keep its gaze trained on her, then it seemed to lose interest and returned to its grazing.

There were many of them in the field, many different sizes. One looked very old and leaner than the others and walked with a limp, favoring a front leg.

Nearby, she saw a cow and her pony-sized calf grazing together. The calf was all gray and white with shiny black nubs for horns.

Not wanting to startle them, Le'ell approached slowly, suddenly aware of the dried grass crunching beneath her boots, the shuffle of the new grass as she waded through it, and her own breathing and heartbeat.

Twenty paces away, she stopped as the cow lifted her head and looked right at her. As if responding to its mother's reaction, the calf also looked her way.

Le'ell stared back at the huge cow, desperately not wanting to provoke her.

The cow snorted and went back to her grazing.

Le'ell took a deep breath and released it slowly, then cautiously strode forward again.

The calf was still staring at her, then turned unexpectedly and snorted at her.

She froze again.

The calf raised its head and trumpeted, a little high pitched for an animal his size.

The cow looked her way again.

Glancing around, Le'ell noticed all of the Grawrdoxen looking right at her. This was very unsettling. There were easily a dozen of them in the field, possibly more in the trees. Should they decide to charge her, she was too far from the tree line and her horse to get away from them.

They all just stared for a tense, terrifying moment.

One by one, they lost interest in her and resumed their grazing, all except for the calf.

Slowly, Le'ell strode toward it again.

It barked another trumpet, rocking back and forth, then snorted and loped toward her.

Le'ell stopped again, raising her hands before her as she bade, "Whoa, boy. I don't want to hurt you."

It did not stop.

She backed away from it.

The calf charged!

Le'ell tried to dodge away, but the calf was upon her quickly and butted her hard in the midriff with its nose, knocking her to the ground. Her wits returned quickly and she found herself lying on her mantle, flat on her back with the calf standing over her.

It snorted again.

She tried to raise up on her elbows and crawl away, but the calf butted her back down with its nose, sniffed, and licked her face with its broad, wet tongue.

"Oh, ick!" she exclaimed, pushing the calf's head from her. When she raised her arms to defend herself, it licked her forearms then her midriff. Le'ell kicked at it, ordering, "Stop! That's disgusting!"

Rarely does a Grawrdox get to enjoy the taste of pure salt, and the little bit of perspiration still on Le'ell's skin was something he just could not pass up.

One hard lick on her chest pulled her top out of place and almost completely off of her. She screamed and tried to fight it back down over her breasts but the calf's tongue was relentless. Le'ell soon realized she was laughing, that is, until the calf's tongue lapped over her face again.

"That's enough!" she screamed as it licked her belly and chest again. Getting her top back on was going to be impossible, so she tried to pull her mantle over herself. Unfortunately, the calf was standing on it.

Le'ell tried to stand and get away from this over-friendly beast, but it butted her back down and started licking her back when she rolled over to protect her face and chest, and she felt the back strap of her top being worked up toward her neck.

She tried to rise onto her knees but was quickly stopped by the mantle, still fastened around her neck, so she untied it and pushed herself up.

The calf did not butt her back down this time, but it relentlessly licked her back and shoulders as she fought to get her clothing back on.

She rose up on her knees, felt the Grawrdox licking the backs of her legs and calves, and took advantage of its distraction to get dressed again. This done, she sprang to her feet, ripped some grass from the ground, and shoved it in the calf's face.

It took the grass from her and did not try to lick her this time.

Le'ell looked down at herself, seeing that her skin was glossy with calf slobber, and grimaced as she looked back to the young Grawrdox, informing, "You owe me now." She took her dagger from her belt and approached the calf again, this time grabbing a handful of its hair.

The hair of the adult Grawrdox was strong but very course. The calves, however, had hair that was almost like silk, strong but very fine and soft. This is what she sought. She measured out about an arm's length of its hair and cut a handful of it away, pulling it halfway through her belt before going for another.

As she worked on the second handful, the calf turned its head and began licking her thigh, leaving behind not only slobber but also small chunks of well-chewed grass mush.

"Oh, you disgusting little bastard," Le'ell hissed.

One of the Grawrdoxen let out a long snort.

The calf looked to it, as did many of the other Grawrdoxen.

Before Le'ell could see what was going on, the calf turned and bolted, knocking her to the ground. She lost her grip on her dagger and watched it disappear into the deep grass.

Many of the Grawrdoxen grunted.

Le'ell looked toward the adults, then sucked a quick breath, and rolled out of the way, barely in time to avoid the cow's broad hooves as she charged by. She looked to the fleeing cow, then heard many other heavy hoof beats, turned and saw another coming right at her at a full run, and rolled out of its path with little time to spare.

All of the Grawrdoxen trumpeted, snorted, and ran toward the trees, following the cow's path.

Le'ell scrambled to her feet and narrowly avoided another of the Grawrdoxen. She easily dodged two more and finally realized that they were not coming after her; they were running away from something. She also realized that she was in the path of the old crippled one. Though lagging behind the others, it was moving remarkably fast despite its limp. She backpedaled, veering out of its path.

It trumpeted and turned toward her.

She drew in a shrieking breath and retreated faster, only making a few steps before her foot found a deep Grawrdox hoof print. She stumbled, quickly lost her balance, and hit the ground flat on her back, the breath exploding from her.

Le'ell forced her wits back to her and raised up on her palms, drawing her legs to her as she saw the old Grawrdox less than twenty paces away and still charging right at her!

She had no time to react.

Something huge and black swept in fast from over the trees and slammed into the Grawrdox, knocking it over.

Le'ell shrieked a gasp as she watched the black dragon sink his long claws into the Grawrdox's body.

Pinned on its side, the Grawrdox kicked and swung its head, trumpeting loudly as it tried to get in a shot with its horns, one of them slamming into the dragon's body.

With a thunderous roar, the dragon lunged and slammed his jaws shut right behind the beast's head, sinking his murderous teeth all the way into his prey, then he wrenched his head and broke the Grawrdox's neck with a sickening crunch.

This was suddenly the most terrifying moment of Le'ell's life as she sat on the ground, watching such a large, powerful beast killed so easily. The dragon she watched was enormous and thickly muscled. His teeth, now stained crimson, were half the length of a sword for the most part. As the sun hit his black scales just right, they reflected jade green and midnight blue back. Thick, black horns swept back from behind his eyes, eyes that were pools of pale blue surrounding black-red pupils.

With his wings still almost fully extended, he stepped back from his prey and stood fully, his head looking to be at or over six men's heights above the ground and his long tail thrashing in the grass behind. Clearly a male from his size and build, his arms bulged with powerful muscles as did his legs. The armor-like dorsal scale ridges that ran from between his swept back, glossy black horns all the way down his back and to the slender end of his long, thrashing tail all ended in sharp points and stood erect as he stared down at the vanquished Grawrdox.

A long moment later, the dragon folded his wings to him, his dorsal scales folding down to his back and interlocking there like articulated armor plates. He turned and looked behind him and up, moving with the grace of a cat, and let out a terrifying roar that seemed to shake the very land she sat on.

Le'ell balled herself up and covered her ears. Seeing movement, she lowered her hands and looked to the sky where the black dragon had descended from, seeing another dragon glide over the treetops. This one was a scarlet beast with ocher breast and belly, throat and wing webbing. It was leaner with round, feminine features. Her lean arms were held to her breast as she descended toward the kill, her amber eyes locked on it. She lowered her talon-like feet and swept her wings forward in air grabbing strokes, landing gracefully just behind the black dragon, then she folded her wings and strode to the kill, looking up at the black dragon almost tenderly. She was much smaller than the black dragon, about a height and a half shorter and nowhere near as heavy. She was not bulky with muscle nor did she appear to be as heavily armored.

He watched her approach, then growled at her, or to her, and dropped to all fours, sinking his teeth into the Grawrdox and ripping its body open.

Le'ell grimaced as hair flailed and blood sloshed everywhere.

The scarlet dragon crouched down and bit into the gaping wound left by the black dragon. She tore a large piece of flesh from the kill, one that looked half as big as Le'ell's whole body, and raised her head, gaped her jaws and lunged at the meat, collecting it further into her mouth as she snapped her jaws shut again. She repeated this, then closed her lips over her teeth and swallowed it whole.

The black dragon fed the same way, though he took substantially larger mouthfuls, as large as or larger than Le'ell's whole body!

Le'ell had never seen dragons this close before. A few times she had seen them in flight, way up in the sky, but never twenty paces away, and she found herself watching them intently. She had read few scripts on dragons, as they had never really interested her, but now she found herself learning more in a few moments than in ten seasons of schooling. These dragons were sharing a kill. The male had made the kill and actually summoned the female to it, then bade her to feed. This was incredible! To Le'ell's knowledge, no one else had ever seen dragons do this—perhaps with good reason.

With a thunderous growl, the black dragon raised his head and turned toward Le'ell, looking right at her with his scaly brow held low over his eyes.

Now, *this* was the most terrifying moment of her life.

Le'ell knew she could never reach the trees in time, knew she could never get away from such an awesome predator. She knew their eyesight was as keen as a hawk's, that they could smell and hear beyond any other animal. Terror coursed through every part of her as she stared back into those piercing eyes, and yet she felt more overwhelmed with a sense of awe, a respect she had never before felt. She no longer felt as the person she had been, now merely something of interest to this awesome predator before her. She felt she owed him homage and knew the rest of her life was completely up to him.

One of the dragon's scaly brows cocked up, then he looked back to his kill and ripped another huge piece from it.

The scarlet dragon casually glanced at Le'ell, then resumed feeding herself, clearly not interested in a mere girl with such a big kill before her.

Slowly, Le'ell stood and backed away, each step sounding horribly loud, even over the ripping and crunching of bone of the feeding dragons.

The black dragon looked toward her again.

Le'ell froze.

A rustling in the forest behind her drew her attention and she looked over her shoulder, her entire body going rigid as a drakenien emerged from the trees, his eyes locked on the dead Grawrdox. She was unable to move as she watched him slowly stalk toward the kill, appearing to limp slightly as he favored a front leg. He was thankfully angling away from her, trying to maneuver behind the dragons and never taking his eyes from the Grawrdox. Praying he was more interested in a large animal to eat than hunting a human girl, Le'ell remained perfectly still, terrified of drawing his attention and keeping hers locked intently on the big predator.

As he neared the dragons, Le'ell noticed that the black dragon was watching him, and when the dragon turned and bared his teeth, Le'ell feared an epic confrontation between super predators would take place right before her. Amazingly, a growl from the dragon had the drakenien stop in his tracks and look up at his rival.

The scarlet dragon looked over her shoulder, then turned fully when she saw the drakenien.

Nothing happened for long seconds. They all just stared at each other.

The black dragon gaped and roared loudly at the drakenien through bared teeth.

The drakenien roared back, but lowered his head and backed away when the dragon advanced, then he laid to his belly, watching the dragon approach. With the dragon upon him, the drakenien turned his head and trumpeted in a rather higher pitch than one would expect from a beast this size.

It seemed time to fight, and yet the drakenien did nothing as the dragon clamped his massive jaws shut around his snout. Le'ell waited for the sickening crunch of bone and armor, but the dragon never really bit down. His teeth did not even penetrate. With the drakenien held firmly in his jaws, the dragon growled one last warning, then released him and turned back to the kill, grunting something to the scarlet dragon as he neared her. And to Le'ell's amazement, they casually resumed feeding on the Grawrdox again as the drakenien just lay there on his belly looking on. Clearly, the dragon had made his point and there would be no further clash of predators today. This was somewhat unfortunate, seeing as how the drakenien was only about twenty paces away. At least if he was locked in battle with the dragon she could escape unnoticed. Now, she would have to take her chances.

Slowly, she took a step back, then another. The predators did not seem to take notice and she backed away further. She had to force herself just to breathe, her eyes shifting back and forth from the dragons to the drakenien and back. From the few scripts she had read, she remembered *never* to run from a predator, especially a dragon, as this would only provoke it into giving chase, and she had no chance at outrunning these predators. Turning the way she was walking, she saw her horse at the tree line. It seemed leagues away.

What felt like a lifetime later, she reached her horse, staring at the reins as she tried to untie them. This was difficult as her hands were shaking so badly.

Finally, the reins were free and she mounted her horse and dared another look back at the dragons, her mouth falling open as she saw the drakenien staring back at her.

Le'ell steered her horse into the forest, riding just inside the tree line as she kept a close eye on the dragons and drakenien, which had not fed and was watching her intently. She hoped beyond hope that her horse could outrun the drakenien in the forest, and that it would not have to. Halfway there, the drakenien turned his attention back to the dragons, who did not seem to take notice of her as she slowly made her way around the meadow.

She found the path on the other side and directed her horse to the middle of it, then stopped her horse and looked over her shoulder, wincing as she found herself in full view of the dragons.

Seated beside her huge mate, the scarlet dragon casually stared back at Le'ell. The black dragon continued to feed and the drakenien continued to watch him.

"Slowly," Le'ell commanded as she kicked her horse down the road.

When the dragons were out of sight, Le'ell kicked her horse's flanks, sending it faster down the road, then faster yet, and once she was at a full gallop, dared a look back, then turned her eyes forward. She tried to forget about the dragons, knowing she never, ever would.

The road widened, allowing the sun to come over the trees.

Le'ell loved this time of the season, when winter yielded ever so slowly to spring. She breathed in deeply, then shook her long hair out as the wind passed through it, enjoying the warmth of the sun coupled with the slight sting of the lingering winter air on her bare skin.

Some distance later the road opened into another clearing, this time a river floodplain.

She stopped her horse and looked over the slowly moving water.

A thin blanket of fog hung over the water's surface, telling her there must be a warm water spring feeding it.

Perfect.

She jumped down from her saddle and led her horse to the water's edge, allowing her to drink, then she untied the blanket from the saddle and rolled it out onto the lush grass, weighing it down at the corners with stones. She looked over the water again, sat in the middle of the blanket, pulled off her boots, then stood and undressed fully. This would be an ideal time to wash off that calf's slobber.

She rolled her clothes up and tossed them onto the blanket, then sprinted to the water and dove in where it looked nice and deep.

The water was not quite as warm as it appeared to be.

With the chill of the nearly freezing water penetrating quickly to her bones, Le'ell surfaced and screamed, "Oh my Goddess!" as she found air, then quickly swam to the shore and ran out of the water, finding the air to be even colder.

Shivering and with her arms crossed over her chest against the cold, she ran to the blanket and kicked her clothes off of it, then sat huddled in the center of it in the warm sunshine. Soon, she lay down and closed her eyes, enjoying the warmth of the sun as she allowed herself to dry.

Some time later, she realized that it would not be such a good idea to be caught naked and napping by the river, so she dressed, loaded the blanket back on the saddle, mounted her horse and rode down river, toward the shallows where she could cross.

Another hour passed before she paused again, scanning the area for a time. The forest had changed over the winter and she did not exactly know where she was. The Spagnah River should have been nearby and she expected to already be there. Venting a sigh, she kicked her horse forward again.

A league or so later she saw something lying in the road, something that looked frightening like a young woman, and as she grew closer her fears were confirmed. About ten paces away, Le'ell stopped her horse and jumped down, running the rest of the way to the thin, dark haired girl.

The girl's tattered white clothing had been torn half from her, telling Le'ell that she had been attacked and left for dead.

As she drew closer, Le'ell could see that the girl was still breathing, a good sign.

Then she saw the iron bracelets that were riveted around the girl's wrists. Perhaps she was an escaped slave from Enulam.

She knelt down beside her and gently turned her over, then placed her fingers gently on the girl's throat to check the strength of her pulse.

Suddenly, the girl's eyes flashed open, locking on Le'ell.

Startled, Le'ell tried to stand and back away, but the girl grabbed her wrists and shouted, "I got her!" When Le'ell tried to pull free, the girl clung to her stubbornly and pulled back hard.

Le'ell looked around her, her eyes finding several men emerging from their hiding places in the forest, and she felt the first real surge of panic course through her.

The men who quickly approached were dressed in wool and leather and did not have the builds of warriors, though they were all armed with swords. None had shaven for some days, as was required of the men at Zondae, nor were they groomed well, their long, matted hair hanging from their heads like vines.

Le'ell's heart felt as if it was trying to ram its way through her chest and she found herself frozen where she knelt.

One of the men seized her arms from behind and said in a gruff voice, "I have her."

When Le'ell felt her wrists released, she sprang up, rammed her head into the man's face, then jerked an arm free and torpedoed her elbow into his gut with all of her strength. Hearing the air explode from him, she pivoted the other way and caught him hard on the side of the head with her fist.

As he staggered and fell, Le'ell spun back and found the girl coming at her. She seized the girl's forearm, easily half turned her and delivered a solid punch to her side right at the base of her ribs, then kicked the back of her knee and pushed her back by the arm, sending her backward to the road.

She wheeled back around and assumed her battle stance as another man charged her and reached for his sword. Before he could free it from its sheath, Le'ell kicked him hard in the jaw, knocking him out cold. Spinning the other way, she kicked another charging man hard in the midriff, then spun and kicked him hard with her other foot, connecting perfectly with the side of his head.

Three down, she thought as she sidestepped and turned toward the other side of the road, seeing four more coming right at her, two very close. She reached for her dagger, finding the sheath empty, and turned panic stricken eyes to the men closest to her.

The first to reach her was the smaller of the two and she dispatched him with a quick kick under the chin, then kicked at the second.

He easily knocked her foot aside.

She backed away, her eyes a little wide as she looked up into his. He was thicker in the arms and chest, leaner in the midriff and his face betrayed fighting experience the others clearly lacked.

He waved his hand and the two men who were still standing backed away. Another slowly rose from the ground, rubbing his face, his eyes locked on Le'ell in a spiteful glare.

She only glanced at them all, then turned her eyes back to the largest of them.

His eyes narrowed as he pulled his jerkin off, revealing a substantially built chest and abdomen, then he threw the jerkin from him, beckoned to her and bade, "Come at a warrior, girl."

Drawing a deep breath to regain her bearing, Le'ell assumed her battle stance, glaring into his eyes as she spat, "Do I face all of you cowards at once again?"

He smiled with one corner of his mouth and shook his head, answering, "You have only me to worry over, vixen."

She shifted her weight, demanding, "And when I beat you?"

"Not a real warrior, little girl," he assured.

"Wait," one of the other men bade. "We'll not be needin' her injured."

"Quiet!" the large man barked, still staring at Le'ell, then he beckoned to her again, prodding, "Come at me, girl."

Hesitantly, she kicked at him, not entirely surprised this time when he blocked her strike, but he dodged her second, one which he should not even have known was coming, and Le'ell retreated a step.

When he struck back, she spun away from his hand and kicked at his side.

He was ready and knocked her foot away still again.

This strike, dodge, and parry continued for a few moments. He was far better trained than she was, and he was just toying with her.

Fatigue began to take its toll and Le'ell finally jabbed at the big man's throat, a mistake she realized too late.

He seized her wrist and twisted her arm sharply, then slammed his fist into her abdomen.

She cried out as he struck. Suddenly, breathing was impossible and the pain from that single blow made her legs collapse and she dropped to her knees. He threw her wrist from him and allowed her to double over and sink all the way to the ground.

As Le'ell fought to remain conscious, she soon realized there were many men standing over her. She was pushed down to her belly and her arms were pulled behind her and her wrists bound tightly with what felt and sounded like leather straps. Something wound around her ankles, then her knees.

"Good day's work," one of the men said.

"This one's more trouble than she's worth," another sneered as if he could not breathe through his nose. "I don't trust that she'll do any better on the ride back."

"She'll bring a hefty enough price," still another assured, sounding as if he could not move his mouth well.

"I did good!" the bait girl insisted. "Didn't I do good?"

"Of course ya did," the large man assured.

"Treacherous wretch," Le'ell hissed. This girl was like a dog or one of the men at Zondae, loyal to her masters, obedient, and craving approval, and Le'ell felt sickened by her.

The big man knelt down beside Le'ell, grabbed her hair and jerked her head back, asking spitefully, "You gonna give me more problems, wench?"

She turned her eyes on him and snapped, "Your problems haven't even begun, dog."

He nodded and released her, reaching for something on his belt. "Aye, you are a spirited one." He produced a broad leather strap and wound it around her throat, right under her jaw, then pulled back on it hard.

Le'ell sucked one more half breath, then nothing could get by the strap, no air at all. She instantly felt pressure in her head, her hearing dulled to almost nothing, her vision seemed constricted by red. She struggled to breathe, fighting back against him as much as she could, fighting to free her wrists and twisting to free her legs. Her lungs burned horribly. Then, blackness.

CHAPTER 3

This *had* to be a conspiracy. Absolutely everything had gone wrong so far, and now this.

Prince Chail stood over a head height taller than an average man and was far heavier. Built like a titan, his thick arms bulged as he crossed them over his massive chest, and he watched as his reflection in the full length mirror he stood in front of ripped the seams out of one of his best shirts, a full sleeved white silk shirt that was ideal for riding when the air was still cold. His brow was low over his dark brown eyes as he glared at the ripping seams, and as he tensed, the seams ripped more.

He abruptly turned from the mirror, his shoulder length brown hair flailing as he did. He tore the shirt from him, revealing muscle that bulged from every part of his chest and midriff, balled the shirt up in his powerful hands and threw it in the corner with several others, grumbling, "I cannot believe this!" His voice was very deep for a man of only twenty seasons. "What the hell else is going to go wrong today?"

Someone knocked on the door, very daintily.

"Come in," he sighed as he strode past his huge bed and to the wardrobe on the other side of the room.

The door opened and he looked toward it, seeing a small woman enter the room. She was wearing a short white top that left her midriff and shoulders bare, and a short skirt of the same material and color that showed off her slender, shapely legs. Her red hair dropped to her upper back and was restrained behind her. Her brow was arched high over her green eyes. She held onto the edge of the door, clearly reluctant to enter further, and finally said, "My Lord, I have news from the stables."

Chail turned fully. He knew from the look on her face that it was not going to be good news. Drawing a deep breath, he folded his arms and said, "Be gentle."

She glanced away, clearly afraid to tell him.

"Go ahead," he prodded. "Everything else has gone wrong today, one more thing cannot make things that much worse."

She took a deep breath and reported, "Your horse, my Lord."

Chail's features hardened and he nodded. "Came up lame, didn't he?"

The woman timidly looked away and said, "I am sorry, my Lord."

He released another long breath and shook his head, then assured, "No, it's my own fault. Damn. My shirts don't even fit any more, damn winter battle training."

"May I mend something for you, my Lord?" she asked hopefully.

"No," he answered grimly. "I just need new ones."

She looked him up and down, smiling slightly as she said, "I do not think you need a shirt at all, my Lord."

He smiled at her. "You always know just how to bring my spirits up out of the well." He raised his brow. "Unfortunately, it is a bit cold to be riding without something. Go and tell the Stablemaster to saddle one of my father's horses."

"A black one like the last?" she asked.

"Perfect," he confirmed, then turned back to the wardrobe. "Now, a shirt."

He heard the slave woman approach and stepped aside as she pushed by him to the wardrobe. She spent a moment rummaging through his clothing, finally producing a light gray swordsman's shirt and his black cloak, then she turned and handed them to him.

The Prince examined them, then he looked down to the woman and confessed, "I really wanted to wear white."

"This looks good on you, though," she countered.

He nodded and said, "Thank you."

"I will go and inform the Stablemaster of your wishes," she said softly, then bowed to him and hurried from the room.

He watched her go, then shook his head and slipped into his shirt and cloak. He checked himself in the mirror once more, running a hand over his long hair, then he turned and proceeded out of the room himself.

On his way through the sparsely decorated, lamp lit corridor, he saw ahead of him the woman he had just sent to the stables, cornered by two fat castle guards dressed in maroon tunics, leather boots, tight fitting leggings and helmets. Palace guards were palace guards mainly because they could not make it as Enulam warriors for one reason or another, and all too often they took this out on the women around the castle. This never failed to ignite Chail's temper and he stopped where he was, waiting for just the right moment to intervene.

"I do not see what that matters!" one of the guards shouted. "I will not be back-talked by a slave wench!"

Crying, she tried to explain, "But Prince Chail told me—"

"Quiet!" the other shouted. "You were not told to speak, wench!"

The woman turned her eyes down, sobbing.

Chail started forward.

The first guard seized her throat and slammed her against the wall, ordering, "Stop that blubbering at once or you'll taste the back of my hand!"

Chail was about five paces away.

"I am sorry, my Lord," she sobbed.

An arm's reach away, the Prince stopped.

The guard holding the woman growled, raising his hand as if to strike her.

Chail folded his arms and snapped, "If you want me to break that arm then go ahead and follow through."

Both guards looked at him, then backed away from the woman.

The Prince looked to the slave woman, asking harshly, "Have you sent my orders to the stable yet?"

She shook her head and admitted, "No, my Lord."

"Go," he commanded, and as she fled, he approached the guards, looming over them like a father who was about to administer a good beating to two disobedient boys. "Would you two care to explain yourselves?"

They just glanced at each other.

"The women around the castle do their work so much better when they are not in fear for their lives," Chail explained. "I am sure you would, too."

One of the guards raised his chin and informed, "We perform our duties as good as or better than any."

The Prince seized his tunic, turned him, and slammed him against the cold stone wall, glaring down at the guard as he growled, "How well will you perform your duties after I've beaten you senseless?"

The guard swallowed hard and did not answer.

"That is what I thought," the Prince growled. "Now both of you listen and remember because I am not fond of repeating myself. You will never again raise a hand against a woman who is not coming at you with some deadly weapon. Do I make myself clear?"

The guard nodded.

Chail looked to the other one.

He also nodded.

The Prince released the guard and turned down the corridor, saying as he left, "Just remember that a little compassion goes a long way, and a little cruelty may just get you both on my bad side."

Chail never delighted in correcting anyone, but he was not the kind of man who could stand idly by and watch cruel acts carried out against another, slave girl or not. He was not yet King, but he was not bashful about using his size, his strength, and his title of Prince to right wrongs and come to the aid of those less fortunate than himself.

The incident was quickly from his mind and he strode outside, stopping to watch the activity that never seemed to stop so long as there was sunlight.

To his right he saw young warriors training for their futures and the future of the kingdom. He had spent many an hour training with them and helping the instructors, who often told him that his presence was of great help and inspiration to the boys and young men who had to spend so much time on the training field.

Six mounted soldiers on his left caught his eye and he watched them charge out of the gate. Patrols came and went several times an hour and Chail would occasionally go with them, but not today.

On his left, about sixty paces away, were the stables and the beginning of his journey this day.

Two men led a horse out of the first stable and into the sunlight, one kneeling down to examine a front hoof.

The man kneeling was clad in leather chaps and a thick belt that had many tools hanging from it. His leather apron was very dirty, much like his hands and very thick arms, and was held in place by the belt. He had no hair on his head or face, save for his bushy black eyebrows.

The other man was well dressed in blue and white, a thin man with thinning hair and fair skin, a full beard and high black boots that were very shiny. He was talking with the Stablemaster, no doubt about the horse, and shaking his head.

Since it was Chail's horse they were examining, the Prince decided to approach as unnoticed as he could and hear what they were saying.

The Stablemaster leaned back on his heels and shook his head; his eyes still on the hoof as he said, "King Donwarr is going to have somebody's head for this, and I'll be damned if it is going to be mine."

"You are the Stablemaster," the other man scolded. "You're supposed to be tending these animals' hooves."

The Stablemaster looked up to the well-dressed man and countered, "Can I help it if he rides them too damn hard?"

Chail rolled his eyes up. He knew the Stablemaster was right and had been warned by him more than once about this.

"He's a growing lad," the thin man defended.

"He's twenty seasons old, for God's sake," the Stablemaster growled. "He ought to know better than to take these horses out so damn fast over the rocks."

"I know I ought to," Chail confessed as he finally walked up on them.

The Stablemaster stood, finally betraying his true size. This was a massive man, much taller than the Prince and even bulkier, though his form resembled a thick tree trunk with broad shoulders. He glared at the Prince and folded his thick arms.

The thin man turned and backed away a step.

Prince Chail glanced at the huge stallion and asked, "So what is wrong with him?"

"He has cracked a hoof," the Stablemaster reported, almost spitefully. "He'll not be ridden for at least three weeks."

The Prince nodded and looked down to the horse's hoof, mumbling, "Well, it figures. I suppose I was a bit hard on him yesterday." He looked to the Stablemaster and asked, "Can you have another ready in about a half hour?"

"And let you lame it up, too, you lunatic?" the Stablemaster shouted. "I already have the problem of reporting this one to King Donwarr!"

"I'll make it worth your while," Chail assured.

Tight lipped, the Stablemaster set his fists on his hips and raised an eyebrow, glaring down at the Prince.

"I know," Chail offered, "I'll make you head blacksmith."

"I'm already over the head blacksmith," the Stablemaster growled.

The Prince looked him over and suggested, "How about a new apron? I could have one special made for you."

"I like my apron."

Chail nodded, then raised his brow. "I could get you a woman."

"I have two."

"Oh." Chail looked to the thin man in blue and grimly said, "There is just no pleasing him."

The Stablemaster brutally grabbed the horse's reins, startling it somewhat, then pointed his finger at the Prince and growled, "You start goin' easy on these animals or I'll take you out back of the stable and teach you to respect them better, Prince or not!" He turned and led the horse back into the stable, grumbling the whole way.

Few men in the world actually intimidated the Prince, and as he watched one of the few storm away, Chail looked to the thin man and observed, "He seems a little irked with me."

The well-dressed man shook his head and informed, "He almost always seems a little irked with you, Prince Chail."

The Prince nodded, then turned and strode back toward the palace, confessing, "Yes, I realize that. Perhaps I should take his advice before he can make good on his threat."

The thin man caught up to him and asked, "Why these lone rides into the forest, especially so close to Zondae?"

"Why not?"

"It is just not wise," the thin man explained.

"I know, Ralk," the Prince sighed, "but you must remember that I am a grown man and am capable of tending myself. I have proven so on many occasions."

"Those barbarian women nearly captured you twice last season," Ralk reminded. "You were just fortunate there was a patrol in the area."

"Nearly is such a relative word," the Prince countered.

The thin man sighed, shaking his head. "I just do not understand why you do not take these matters more seriously. You could have been killed out there last season. Or worse. And your sword being unmatched in the kingdom is—"

"Thank you," Chail interrupted, smiling, then he stopped and turned to the thin man, assuring, "Look. If my father asks of me, just tell him that I have gone for a ride and will be back around dark, and not to worry."

Ralk shook his head. "You realize he is going to whip me to death if anything happens to you."

Chail laughed and patted the thin man's shoulder, assuring, "Then for your sake I will see to it nothing does."

"My Lord," came a woman's voice from behind.

Chail tuned and saw the woman he had sent to the stable running toward him.

"My Lord," she called again.

"Yes," he responded.

She reached him, glanced at Ralk, then timidly looked up to the Prince, and hesitantly informed, "The King has sent word that you may not go out riding today."

"What?" Chail roared.

She cringed, reporting, "He had a stable hand waiting to meet you, but you never came inside the stables."

"Damn," the Prince growled as he wheeled around and strode back toward the palace.

The slave woman trotted to his side and assured, "His Majesty is just concerned about you, Highness."

"His Majesty was not even supposed to know!" Chail bellowed.

Ralk ran abreast of him and met his pace, also looking up at him as he tried to calm him. "He may just have some task for you to perform, or battle training with him. You have the only sword arm in the kingdom that matches his, after all."

"Where is he now," Chail growled.

"In his study, my Lord," the slave woman answered.

"Probably to add another hour or more to my waiting," the Prince grumbled. "Ralk, you must make certain that I have a horse saddled and waiting when I come back down."

"But," the thin man protested, "his Majesty's orders."

"You just let *me* take care of his Majesty and have my horse ready when I return."

Ralk and the slave woman did not follow him into the palace.

Tapestries and paintings, small furnishings, wooden doors and wall hung weapons blurred by as the Prince strode with purpose down the corridor, up a flight of stairs, deep into the castle, up another flight of stairs and to the end of another corridor. His objective was there.

A waxed and polished timber door stood in his way. With one mighty kick from the Prince, the latch surrendered, its pieces dancing across the marble floor as the door swung open and Chail exploded through it.

The King's study looked much like the rest of the castle, the stone walls decorated with bookshelves, swords, shields, battle-axes and tapestries. His desk, which directly faced the door five paces away, was huge and made of dark wood. It was well organized, assorted piles of parchments, maps, and documents in their places and several feather pens in their inkwells. Two simple wooden chairs sat on the side of the desk facing the door.

Slowly, the King's dark brown eyes looked up from the parchment he was studying and to his son, who strode at him, glaring. Like Chail, the King was a large man, heavily built in his arms and shoulders. His long hair was brown, streaked with silver, as was his full beard. This time of the day was unusual for him to be dressed so casually, just wearing his red bathrobe, loose fitting silk trousers and black boots.

Prince Chail stormed toward his father, kicked one of the chairs aside and slammed his fists down onto the desk, his eyes boring into the King's as he demanded, "Why won't you allow me to take my ride?"

"Good morning, Son," was the King's answer. "You look a little miffed."

"Why?" the Prince shouted.

The King nodded. "My morning is going very well. Thank you for asking."

"Quit evading me!" Chail ordered. "Why can't I take my ride?"

King Donwarr tossed the parchment down onto his desk, replying, "Yes, I could have slept better. I suppose I just have a lot on my mind."

Chail's lips tightened.

"Like," the King continued, "why my son insists on these lone journeys into the forest, especially so close to the border."

The Prince pushed off of the desk and folded his arms. "Perhaps I just want to be alone for awhile."

Shaking his head, King Donwarr leaned back in his chair also folding his arms and asking, "What are you hiding?"

"Nothing," Chail growled.

The King nodded, then vented a deep breath and said, "I see." Another deep breath, then, "I am a little concerned with you, Son. You don't stay around the castle much, you don't ride on patrols like you used to, and you and I do not spend the time together that we once did."

"There is nothing for you to be concerned about," Chail assured, looking away. "I just want to ride, and I want my solitude. That's all. You need such simple pleasures yourself from time to time."

The King looked down to his desk and nodded, admitting, "Yes, I do, occasionally. But that is not what is concerning me."

"Then what?" Chail growled.

King Donwarr vented a deep breath, then looked back up at his son. "Chail, when I was your age I already had several women."

The Prince rolled his eyes, grumbling, "Not that again."

"Yes, that again," the King grumbled back. "I don't understand why you don't take an interest in women the way other men do. I mean, it just is not healthy not to appreciate them."

"I have plenty of appreciation for women," the Prince sighed.

King Donwarr raised his brow. "You hopefully don't have such an appreciation for men."

Chail shot a look of infuriation at his father and barked, "That's insulting!"

The King smiled and laughed, "Finally! A spark of manhood."

The Prince leaned on the desk, his lips pursed as he glared at his father.

Smiling, King Donwarr leaned forward in his chair and folded his hands on the desk, asking, "Still bent on this ride?"

Chail looked away from him.

"I see," the King said softly, nodding. "Very well, Son. I'll not try to stop you further, then."

Chail slowly looked back down at him. "If?"

The King raised his brow. "Always suspicious of me, aren't you?"

"With good reason," the Prince countered.

King Donwarr smiled and bade, "Go ahead with your ride, Chail. But first, I want you to go to the stockyard and take a look at the woman I purchased for you a short while ago."

Chail closed his eyes and vented a deep breath, shaking his head as he groaned, "Not another one."

Laughing under his breath, the King assured, "Oh, I think you will like this one. She is a tall, well made vixen, muscular and darkly sunned. Has dark eyes that will melt you down to your bones in a hurry." He raised his chin slightly. "Spirited, too, something you seem to like in a woman. And, if you like what you see, you may have her."

The Prince nodded, conceding, "All right. I'll go and take a look at her." His eyes darted back to his father and he added, "But if I do not like what I see I am going on my ride."

The King smiled. "If you don't like what you see, then you and I will have to have a long talk. As far as your ride, you won't want to go."

Chail nodded, then pushed off of the desk, turned, and strode for the door, countering, "We'll see."

CHAPTER 4

L e'ell had seen many auctions take place at Zondae. Men and animals were sold like this every few days. She had never participated, much less been actually on the auction stand and sold.

She shared an iron cage with five other women, all of whom were dressed in skimpy white outfits and comfortable looking sandals. The cage was ten paces square with a wooden bench on each side but one, where the only door was. The other five women sat close together on one of the benches, involving themselves in quiet, casual conversation as if to pass time. Le'ell glanced at them only occasionally as she paced from one end of the cage to the other, watching the ground and occasionally kicking at it, her arms folded tightly.

Enulam men would stop at the bars of the cage with annoying frequency to leer at the women inside and Le'ell knew she was their favorite target.

She stopped in the center of the cage and looked around her.

On one side was a stone structure, obstructing her view of the palace. On the other side were the stables. Behind the cage was what appeared to be a work area where women washed linens, oiled boots and other leather pieces, and performed other menial tasks. She turned and paced toward the front, looking to the stage where she had been taken and sold to the highest bidder. The huge crowd of men had thinned and only a few women waited off to the side to be sold. None looked happy to be there.

The only door of the cage was not locked and escape would be easy if not for the two large men who stood right outside of it, watching the auction.

When several men approached the door to the cage, Le'ell backed away, raising her chin and slowly lowering her arms to her sides. Her eyes were locked on them as they entered, but she only got a glance from most of them. They looked to the bench and one beckoned to one of the women.

She stood, bowed her head and approached him, looking toward the ground. When she reached him, he took her arm and led her out.

The other women watched them leave and were silent for a moment after, then resumed their casual talking.

Le'ell shook her head and resumed pacing.

A short time later, more men approached and she turned, seeing four of the men who had captured her greeting the guards at the cage. Seeing them infuriated her. *They* were responsible for her being held in this place.

The large man met her eyes.

She stared back coldly.

The cage door was opened and the four men entered, the large man beckoning to her.

Defiantly, Le'ell raised her chin, refusing to budge as she stared back at him.

He beckoned again.

She just glared back at him.

His lips tightened as he glared back at her for long seconds, then he strode to her, stopped about an arm's reach away, and said, "When I do this," he beckoned again, "you come. You do like you are told and speak when you're spoken at. Understand me, wench?"

"I don't obey pigs," Le'ell spat. She knew fear of the big man, but refused to show even a hint of it.

The other men laughed.

"You should watch that sharp tongue of yours, wench," he advised with a noticeable tone of warning. "You might just have it clipped."

"I can do some clipping of my own," she countered, her lips curled.

He slapped her, swinging her half around.

She wheeled back and decked him.

The other men laughed hysterically as he went down.

Rubbing his jaw, the big man looked up at her, glaring, then pointed to her and shouted, "Get her, you fools!"

His companions and one of the guards rushed forward as he scrambled up.

Le'ell managed to kick one of them solidly in the chest, but was quickly overwhelmed by the rest of them. Her arms were pulled brutally behind her and tied there. Another man held her at the knees while the guard wrapped a leather strap around her ankles and tied it.

Le'ell fought hard against them, but stopped struggling as she saw the large man walking up to her, his eyes locked on hers. At this point, she felt herself trembling and could not stop the fear from coming through her eyes.

He stared down at her for long seconds, then raised his hand to strike her.

She closed her eyes and turned her head, cowing away from him. When she did not feel him strike her, she slowly looked up at him.

He was nodding, and said, "You are finally learning, vixen." He knelt down and butted his shoulder into her, just below her belly, then wrapped his arms around her legs and stood, picking her up like a sack of grain.

Unable to resist at all, Le'ell draped over his shoulder, finally realizing that she had made a big mistake in striking him.

The Enulam men who were outside the cage cheered as Le'ell was removed.

She could not see where she was going, but soon realized that he was taking her into the stone building that was not far from the cage.

Once inside, she was taken to the center before she was put down.

The timber door closed. She was trapped inside with the four slave hunters.

It stank here, like hot metal and leather, sweat, and unkempt men. The air was still, hot, and sticky. The two lamps that hung on the wood pillars in the center of the room offered barely enough light to see outside of their glow. A thick rope dangled from a beam that ran across the pillars about a height and a half from the ground. At the end of the rope was a leather strap, dangling there as if waiting for its next victim. An iron ring protruded from the ground, right beneath the beam.

Two of the men took her arms and drug her toward the pillars. This was not unlike how many of the men at Zondae were punished. For the first time, Le'ell would find herself on the receiving end of what she had seen administered so many times.

Once between the pillars, her ankles were lashed to the ring in the ground while another of the men untied her wrists.

Fear crept along Le'ell's spine, along all of her limbs. She just stared straight ahead, her eyes finding a table about five paces in front of her that had many devices of torture laying on it, which appeared to include several types of whips, a few knives, and serrated instruments. In the dim light, she could not be sure, but they were terrifying nonetheless. Beside it was a cauldron full of glowing hot, smoldering coals with three iron rods stabbed into it, each glowing a little red near the coals.

No wonder it was so hot in here.

Her wrists were freed and held behind her by one of the men. She half turned her head as if to see him, then looked forward again.

One of the men stepped in front of her; a dirty, thin man dressed in leather and a fur jerkin. He smiled, revealing brown, rotted teeth and said, "Don't give us no problems now, vixen, aye?" His breath stank of ale.

She refused to look at him, but her eyes narrowed and she hissed, "Do nothing you'll regret and I may not."

He huffed a laugh and informed, "I like breakin' a woman with a lot of spirit."

Her eyes shifted to m and she countered, "Perhaps you will not mind if I break you a little, first." She jerked one of her hands from the man behind her and slashed her fingernails across the dirty man's face, ripping his cheek open. As he yelled and backed away, she half turned and slammed her elbow into the abdomen of the man behind her, jerking her other hand free.

He clutched at her, trying to get her back under control.

Desperately, Le'ell slammed the back of her head into his face, then wheeled around to finish him off, but with her legs anchored to the ground, she lost her balance.

One of the men caught her before she fell far. Another took her arm and twisted it behind her. The man behind her took her other arm.

She screamed like a forest cat, trying desperately to twist free, then was still as her eyes found the dirty man she had scratched. He was standing right in front of her, blood dripping from his face. His brow was low over his eyes and his lip was curled up ever so slightly.

Le'ell felt her jaw trembling horribly.

He glared at her for long seconds, then hit her hard across the face, snapping her head around.

Her body was drained of strength and her mind of her wits for some time. By the time she recovered her senses her wrists were tightly bound in front of her and were pulled up toward the ceiling. Breathing was difficult as her hands were pulled higher and her body was pulled taut.

The dirty man stepped toward her, grabbed her hair and jerked her head back. He moved his face close to hers and sneered, "You gonna fight like a man, you gonna take it like a man." He looked to one of the other men present and ordered, "Pull her tighter."

Le'ell heard the big man laugh and felt her body jerked even tighter. The bindings around her wrists and ankles felt as if they were cutting into her and her joints felt as if they were being pulled apart as her feet were lifted slightly from the ground. She winced, tightly closing her eyes against the pain, but would allow no other sound from her. She refused to let them know they were hurting her, refused them the satisfaction.

Somehow they seemed to already know.

Still holding her by the hair, the dirty man smiled fiendishly and licked his cracked lips, then said almost playfully, "No, vixen. It ain't even started yet. I'll have you beggin' for me to kill ya soon." He ran his hand over the scratches on his face and sneered, "Gonna cover your back with these."

She turned her eyes from him, fear creeping along every part of her.

"Better," he commended. "Why don't ya beg me real nice fer mercy, eh?"

Her eyes snapped to him and she hissed, "I'll see you in Hell, first."

He huffed a laugh and pushed her head from him, nodding as he admitted, "Aye, that you might, vixen, but now I give you some hell." He turned and approached the table of knives and whips, the big man following.

Le'ell watched fearfully, barely able to breathe as they discussed which instruments to use on her. They seemed to take forever; each second was another step through a hellish fear of what was to come.

"You have any grog in here?" one of the men behind her asked.

"Pitcher over there," another answered.

She looked up to her wrists, trying to struggle out of the leather binding. It was hopelessly tight.

The two men finally made their choices.

The large man strode toward her, making certain she got a good look at the knife he had chosen, one that was curved with a very sharp point and serrated blade.

The dirty man approached and stopped, staring at her with a smile on his lips and a short whip in his hand. The whip had many lengths of leather half an arm's length long that looked wet and heavy; some knotted near the end.

"It's called a can-o-nine-tails," he informed. "Don't want to cut you up too bad to start with, aye?"

Le'ell forced herself to breathe as he slowly walked behind her. Her heart was thundering and she could feel sweat starting to trickle down her arms and face, her body and legs. She flinched as he cut the whip through the air behind her; the full realization of what was about to happen finally dove home.

He cut the whip through the air again and said spitefully, "Weren't real nice of you to scratch me face like that."

She half tuned her head and spat back, "You had it coming, dog. Now cut me down before you do something you will really regret."

A few seconds of silence followed, then all of the men laughed hysterically.

This was a bad sign. They were not taking her seriously.

"I mean it!" she barked, trying to sound commanding. "You mark me just once and it will mean war!"

They laughed again.

The dirty man grasped the back of her neck, still laughing as he said, "I don't fear war from a trussed up girl on the business end of my whip."

She raised her chin just a little, asking, "Don't you know who I am?"

He shook his head and replied, "Afraid not. Why don't you tell me?"

Her eyes narrowed as she said, "I am Princess Le'ell, heir to the throne of Zondae, and I promise that you will die a horrible death if you mark me even once."

He nodded, then looked to the men behind him and laughed, "I've never broken a princess before."

"I haven't either," another laughed.

Another added, "A real princess would have brought more at the auction."

The big man stepped around in front of her, still holding the knife, and folded his arms, leering at her as he said, "Princess, are you?" He stepped toward her, and raised the point of the small knife to her throat. "I think you are nothing more than an insolent little girl who is in way over her head."

Le'ell raised her chin, trying to back away from the blade. She had to think and think fast. Finally, with her eyes locked on his, she curled her lips and asked, "Do you intend to kill me after selling me to that other dog?"

He ran the blade down her throat, stopping at the strap to her top as he growled, "I do not like your tone, wench." He hooked the blade under her strap and cut it easily with one pull.

Le'ell swallowed hard, feeling the steel of the blade sliding down her chest. She had to make them believe her. Still staring into the big man's eyes, she drew a shaky breath and insisted, "I can prove I am who I say I am."

The big man hooked the knife under her top, his eyes on it for long seconds, then he looked to her eyes and asked, "How?"

Finally! "Take me to Zondae," she instructed. "I will arrange for you to meet with my mother, the Queen. She may even reward you for bringing me back."

He pursed his lips, then shook his head and said, "I could see that you're from Zondae, but I'll not be goin' there. Me and my men would be killed as soon as we stepped through the gate."

"Not with me escorting you!" Le'ell insisted.

He jerked on the knife, cutting Le'ell's top at the front, then he reached behind her and pulled it from her, saying, "You are no Princess. You are but a slave wench." He turned and strode behind her.

Le'ell watched him as far as she could. She felt the knife slide between her hip and the fur that covered her. As he cut away the last of her clothing, she desperately cried, "Stop this! Stop at once!"

The dirty man ordered, "Quiet!" and the whip struck her between the shoulders.

The pain was worse than she had imagined. The leather on the whip was salted.

She threw her head back and flinched, shrieking a breath then clenched her teeth and shut her eyes tightly against the pain.

"You speak only when you are spoken at," the dirty man continued, striking her between the shoulders again.

Her body jerked as it stung right through her and she sucked a hard breath, grasping the rope that held her arms up.

"You understand me?" he asked. When she did not answer, he struck her again and demanded, "Cry out, wench. Tell me you'll be a good little vixen."

Now it was personal. After a few deep breaths to collect herself, she spat back, "You will get no such satisfaction from me, dog."

"Oh, I think I will," he corrected, then struck her again, and again.

The pain was unbearable. Still, she clung to her dignity.

His sixth blow struck her lower, his seventh her mid-back.

She whimpered, tears streaming from her eyes.

"This one's got too much pride," one of the men observed.

Another laughed. "Maybe she likes it."

"No," came the voice of the dirty man. "If she likes it so much she'd be screamin'. Come on, vixen. Scream for us." He struck her lower back this time, then again. "Show us you like it."

She whimpered, burying her face between her arms. It was becoming too much to bear.

"Go on," the dirty man prodded, striking her back again. "Lets have a little scream."

Nothing happened for long seconds.

"Want me to stop?" he asked, cutting the silence.

Le'ell would not answer. She stared at the cauldron of coals, forcing herself to breathe normally. The pain from the lashes was still with her, stinging with every heartbeat.

"So you don't want me to stop," the dirty man said, almost sounding amused by this. He struck her between the shoulders again, adding, "Makes me no never mind. Got all day to keep at ya." He struck her side very hard, just below her ribs.

This stung horribly and she threw her head back and drew a shrieking breath, her entire body going rigid.

"Ah," he drawled. "Ya like that." He struck her there again, then the other side.

His fifteenth blow struck her hip, his sixteenth her buttocks, and his seventeenth.

Le'ell found herself weeping and, try as she may, she just could not stop. When she heard the dirty man approach her and felt him stroking her hair, she refused to look at him, and tried harder to regain her composure.

"Come now," he urged in a gentle voice. "Just give me a little shout. Beg me nice and I might just stop doin' this."

With her teeth clenched, Le'ell hissed, "I promise you will die for this."

He backed away a step, then the whip struck the backs of her knees.

This time, a scream exploded from her.

"Good!" he commended, then struck her there again, and again. "Beg me, now. Beg me to stop."

Another hesitation. Anticipating when she would be hit made the whole ordeal that much worse. The room was quiet and all Le'ell could hear was her own shameful sobbing.

"Gonna beg me?" he asked loudly, his voice almost echoing.

She clenched her teeth, raised her chin and stubbornly shook her head.

"I don't hear ya," he shouted, striking her legs again.

"Stop," she finally cried.

"Well, now," he drawled. "Ya can talk after all. Can ye beg?"

"Stop," she sobbed, resting her forehead against her arms. "Just stop."

"Can't hear ya beg me!" he yelled, striking her lower back.

The pain began to rip through her entire body and she screamed, "Please stop! Please!"

He seized the back of her hair and jerked her head back, sneering, "I see ya got manners, too. Ye learn slow, don't ya, vixen? Need another lesson, I think."

"I don't," Le'ell assured desperately. "Please stop!"

He brutally pushed her head from him and corrected, "Sure ya do." He took a few steps away from her and ordered, "Gimme a cup of that brine."

Le'ell felt something cold splash against her back, something that almost instantly began burning the whelps left by the whip. It felt like fire against her and she screamed wildly and struggled hard against her unyielding bonds. Never in her life had she felt such pain.

Her next realization was her own sobbing. She just hung there, limp and powerless, her head resting against her arms as she wept. The burning the brine did to her had subsided, but her back still burned horribly. Her wrists were sore and felt raw from the leather strap she had been struggling against.

The whip sliced through the air behind her again.

Le'ell shrieked, her whole body jerking as if it had struck her, though it did not. This was it. Pride and dignity abandoned her. Nothing remained within her but pain, anxiety, fatigue. She closed her eyes and cried shamelessly, praying they would just stop torturing her.

"Gonna do like you told, now?" he asked harshly.

Le'ell nodded, her eyes closed tightly as she softly answered, "Yes." Her voice was more like a little girl's now, tiny and afraid.

The dirty man approached and ran a hand over her hair, asking pitifully, "Now, was that so hard?"

She drew a stuttering breath and shook her head.

"Course not," he drawled as if trying to sound sympathetic. "You a good girl, aren't ya?"

Hesitantly, she nodded again.

Someone seized her hair and jerked her head back and she looked into the face of the large man.

His eyes narrowed as he looked into hers, then he shook his head and said, "I'm not convinced."

"She'll be a good girl," the dirty man assured.

"We'll see," the large man growled, then ordered, "Cut her loose."

Le'ell felt her ankles freed first, then her boots were pulled from her as another of the men untied the rope that held her arms up. It felt good to have her arms down and she almost collapsed as she allowed her still bound hands to fall before her.

The big man grabbed the back of her neck and turned her to the door, ordering, "Outside!"

As he pushed her, she stumbled, but kept her footing as she was led to the door by her neck. Humiliation waited outside, but she didn't care. One of the men opened the door as she was pushed toward it and the sunlight burned her eyes. She tightly closed them and turned her face away, then blinked them open again to see that she was being taken toward an area between the holding cage and the stage where she had been sold at auction.

Fingers tightening around the back of her neck and pulling back was her signal to stop, and she did.

"Wenches of Enulam," the big man summoned.

Suddenly, many eyes were upon them, men and women alike. All activity seemed to stop.

"This little vixen thought she could fight like a man," the big man announced. "She thought striking a man would win her respect. Look at her now!" He grabbed her hair and jerked her head back, smiling as she winced. "Anything to say, vixen?"

She hesitantly turned her eyes toward him.

He jerked on her hair again and shouted, "Are you deaf? I think you want to say something!"

Her mouth quivering, Le'ell whimpered, "I'm sorry."

"Can't hear you," he shouted.

"I'm sorry," she strained to say louder.

He threw her to the ground and took the whip from the dirty man, then looked around him and sneered, "Does she look so strong now? Did she sound so strong when she screamed in the cottage?"

Le'ell looked around her, seeing pity in the eyes of the women who stared back, and some of the men.

"The big man looked back down at her, his lip curled back as he growled, "Let's see if she's learned her lesson."

As he raised the whip, Le'ell balled up and screamed "Please, no! I'm sorry! Please no more, please!"

He smiled. "That as nice as you can beg?" He brought the whip down hard.

Le'ell screamed and turned her face into her hands, but the whip never reached her.

His arm was caught half way down and he was swung around to face another man, one who had approached unnoticed.

A very tense moment followed.

Le'ell looked fearfully up to the huge, broad shouldered man who had just arrived. He was noticeably bigger than the large man and wore a loosely fitting shirt of light gray, his long, dark hair tied behind his head and dropping below his shoulders.

"Give me that!" the huge man barked, taking the whip.

The large man backed away a step, then held his ground.

The new arrival just glared at the large man for a moment, then looked down to Le'ell, his eyes glancing over her back, then he looked to the other men and ordered, "Help her up, and be gentle with her."

Le'ell felt her arms grasped and she was pulled from the ground. Every movement hurt and she made no secret of it, whimpering as they helped her up. Glancing at the huge man in gray, she saw that her feeble complaint had provoked the desired response in him, and she almost smiled.

His eyes were as stones, his brow low over them as he turned to the large man and growled, "Who told you to beat this woman? Did you not know she was just purchased by the King?"

"I knew," was the large man's response.

"She is a gift for his son," the huge man informed, "a gift for me."

The large man raised his chin, folding his arms as he snarled, "So?"

The Prince's eyes narrowed. "You knew, and yet you saw fit to beat her for your amusement, anyway."

"She had it coming," the dirty man defended from behind.

"True," the large man confirmed. "She struck me in front of my comrades as if she was a man. That is something no woman will get away with."

"Or man?" the Prince countered, his words sounding like a challenge.

"Or man," the large man said sternly, hammering his words through.

The Prince turned his eyes down, looking to the whip in his hands as he nodded. He waited a few long seconds before he spoke again. When he did, his words were soft, reminding Le'ell of a gentle breeze that glides through right before the fiercest storms. "I see. So, I am to just allow you to treat my women any way you please?"

"If you are smart, boy," came the large man's answer, a certain authority in his voice.

"Prince or Highness," the man in blue reminded, still staring down at the whip.

"I have no loyalties to your throne, boy," the large man informed sharply. "Be glad I do my business here."

The Prince slowly turned his eyes to the large man.

Le'ell raised her chin and whispered to the men holding her, "Perhaps we should step back."

They did.

The whip dropped to the ground.

The Prince's hand could barely be seen moving as the back of it slammed into the large man's eye, knocking him backward a few steps.

As the Prince advanced, the large man wheeled back and struck him.

Le'ell winced as the Prince's head was snapped around and she watched anxiously as he stepped back and reached for his mouth. She knew the large man's strength, as she had felt it herself, though this prince had just taken a much harder blow than she ever had.

"Consider that your first lesson, boy," the large man growled.

"And my last from you," the Prince countered as he kicked the large man hard in the abdomen.

Le'ell watched as the two men fought, a slight smile fighting its way to her lips as the Prince seemed to overwhelm the large man. He was the larger of the two, both stronger and quicker. Le'ell knew first hand that the large man had considerable skill as a warrior, but even here he appeared to be no match for the Prince, yet still he would not yield.

The Prince took a fist right in the belly, then, growling like a forest bear, he pushed the large man's shoulder, cocked his arm back and turned all of his body into the swing, connecting with his enemy's jaw with such force that it snapped the large man's head around with an unnatural crack.

The large man turned fully, then fell forward to the ground and moved no more.

Staring down at his vanquished foe for just a few seconds, the Prince then turned his attention to the dirty man and beckoned with his finger.

Seeming more like a terrified rabbit than a man of authority now, the dirty man hesitantly approached the Prince, his eyes shifting from him to his fallen comrade and back again.

The Prince stared down at him for long seconds, then seized his throat hard, gripping like a hawk.

Unable to breathe, the dirty man wrapped his hands around the Prince's wrist and hand, trying in vain to pry the powerful hand from his throat, and finally sank to his knees.

With a gleam of death in his eyes, the Prince stared coldly down at his victim and growled, "Consider this to be both your first and last warning. Touch her again or mistreat any of the women of this castle and I will kill you just for the pleasure of seeing you die. Have I made myself clear?"

The dirty man nodded as best he could.

The Prince threw the half strangled, coughing man from him and looked to the man who again restrained Le'ell, adding, "That goes for all of you." He motioned to the fallen large man with his head and ordered, "Now collect your foolish colleague and leave before I lose my temper."

Le'ell did not know men could move so fast. Apparently, this prince was not someone to be trifled with in their eyes and half a moment later they were not to be seen in the compound. Slowly, she looked to the Prince, her eyes narrowing as he approached her. As he grasped her shoulders, she twisted away from him, backing away as she feebly ordered, "Let go."

The torture she had just endured had enacted a much heavier toll on her than she realized and her wits and strength suddenly abandoned her. Her next realization was him catching her short of hitting the ground. She could not even muster the strength to look up at him now and her head hung limply as he pulled her to him. She thought she heard her name spoken, but everything happening around her seemed more like a dream. She could barely think. The whelps left from her torture stung anew as he touched them, and in her disoriented, weary mind she was being whipped all over again. Sobbing, she pushed against him and whimpered, "No more."

Time swept by without notice. Le'ell was somewhat aware of being carried inside, bathed by gentle, caring hands, the compassionate voices of women encouraging her, letting her know that she was going to be all right.

When she finally regained her wits, she found herself lying in a huge bed with soft linens and a heavy blanket. Her back and legs where she had been whipped felt very sore, but no longer stung like they had. A cool breeze swept over her from somewhere. It felt good. Those gentle female voices could be heard, conversing with one another nearby.

She drew a breath, smelling flowers, fresh bread, some kind of soup or stew and faint perfume.

"She's awakening," a young woman's voice observed.

The bed shifted, feeling as if several people had just sat down on it and Le'ell felt her hair gently stroked by thin fingers.

Perhaps it had all just been a nightmare. Perhaps she was home in her own bed.

She opened her eyes, blinking to bring her world into focus, but what she saw was not her bedroom at Zondae, nor were the three women who surrounded her familiar. She glanced around her, a little fearful and still feeling light-headed, but she would not allow composure and dignity to escape her again.

She looked to the woman who sat beside her on the bed, the woman who tenderly stroked her hair. Her long black hair was streaked with silver and her gentle features were slightly wrinkled around her eyes and the corners of her mouth. Still, she was shapely and dressed as all of the other women seemed to be. Her top was white and clearly designed only to cover her chest.

The woman smiled and asked in a gentle, soothing voice, "How are you feeling, lass?"

"I have definitely had better days," she strained to respond, her voice feeling weak and taking much effort to make words.

"Just rest awhile," the woman ordered. "You've had quite the busy day and you'll be needin' to recover your strength." She spoke with an accent Le'ell had never heard before with slightly exaggerated 'r's and her word tense seemed a little backward.

"Are you a healer?" Le'ell slurred.

The woman nodded. "Aye, that I would be. My name is Teyli. I will be taking care of you. Just lie still and try to rest."

Stubbornly, Le'ell shifted, trying to sit up, but the whelps responded with shooting pain and she sucked a breath through her teeth and grimaced, and laid where she was.

"Are you in pain?" the woman asked.

"What do you think?" Le'ell snapped without realizing.

Teyli raised her brow and replied, "I think that sharp tongue and sour attitude is what got you whipped so badly."

Le'ell turned her eyes away.

"Good you think about that," the healer advised. "Last summer there was a lass much like you who crossed my care." She sighed. "So badly whipped was she that she died in the night. The moment you think that whip cannot take your life in the most horrible of ways is your first step into a funeral pyre. You'd best be remembering that."

Le'ell vented a deep breath, staring past the blond haired young woman who sat on her left, and looked out of the window. Pa'lesh had always been an incorrigible nag, always on her to stay clear of Enulam territory. How she hated that. How she longed to hear her voice telling her that same thing now.

Teyli blotted a cool, damp towel over Le'ell's face, assuring, "I know all too well it is hurting, lass, but I have some ointment that will make it all the better."

"You say that like you know for sure," Le'ell strained to say, feeling a little more alert.

"All too well I do," the healer informed coldly.

Le'ell's stomach churned uneasily as she stared out of the window. After a moment, she asked, "Why?"

Teyli was a long time in answering, but finally said, "It was my own fault and none the thing for you to be concerned over."

Le'ell looked to the healer, her eyes feeling tense as she insisted, "They cannot just beat you at their whim."

"You just put those thoughts from you right now," Teyli ordered. "They will only get you into more trouble. I do not care who you were or where you came from. You are a slave now and there is not to be changing that. Just do as you are told and accept your fate. You'll be livin' much longer that way."

Just from the tone of the healer's voice, Le'ell knew that she was not at all happy with her life as a slave, she had merely resigned herself to the fact. Le'ell did not plan to go even that far.

"Turn over, now," the healer ordered. "I'll be treating those lashes and keep them from scarring."

Le'ell had never felt modest at Zondae, but she did not know any of the women in her presence at this time, and kept herself covered as best she could as she turned onto her belly.

The cream that was gently massaged onto her back was cold at first, then began to burn the wounds left by the whip. Le'ell sucked a breath through her teeth and tightly hugged the pillow beneath her, her whole body tensing against the pain.

"I know it hurts," Teyli said sympathetically, "but it will pass and make you feel all the better, soon."

As promised, the burn went away and Le'ell relaxed, resting her head on the pillow as the healer massaged more into her back.

"Brace yourself, lass," Teyli warned. "I'll be treating the rest of your wounds, now."

Le'ell felt the sheet lifted from her, then felt the cream on her lower back.

The healer worked in silence for a time, then, after a few moments, she finally asked, "So, is it true?"

"Is what true?" was Le'ell's response.

"Oh," the healer sighed, "I was hearing that you were purchased for Prince Chail and that he is actually going to keep you. I also heard that he decided not to ride today just so that he could go to the stockyard and see you."

Le'ell's jaw clenched and she said through clenched teeth, "Did he, now?"

"Aye, that he did," Teyli answered. "Unusual for the Prince as he hasn't had trifle much interest in the other slave girls for the last several seasons."

"Much?" Le'ell snarled.

One of the other slave girls present laughed under her breath and said, "We were becoming concerned with his manhood. You know, like he prefers their company over women."

"Away with you," Teyli scoffed. "His highness is just a very selective lad who will not have just any lass in his bed."

"Not that I haven't tried," the other slave girl informed playfully, then giggled and added, "He had me once and I am certain that he will be back for more in time."

"Die," Le'ell growled.

"I think he would sooner have old Nessar," the healer laughed.

The younger woman, a petite, black haired girl who looked to be fifteen or sixteen, giggled and covered her mouth.

"Oh," the other slave girl barked, "like he would have a giddy little tramp like you!"

"Enough," Teyli sighed, then patted Le'ell's shoulder and said, "You should consider yourself a fortunate one. Prince Chail is a copious lot kinder to the slave girls than most of the other men here and he will be very good to you."

"As long as I am mindlessly obedient?" Le'ell asked dryly.

"I would not say that," the healer replied. "Just make certain you'll not do whatever it was that got you whipped so badly and you should be fine."

"Of course," Le'ell mumbled. As the healer worked more of the ointment over her legs, Le'ell pondered her situation again, wondering just how it came to pass that she should go from princess to common slave girl of her enemy in just a few hours, and how to remedy this problem. Perhaps the answer could be found in the healer. She needed allies here, and she needed to know about them.

Taking a deep breath, she snuggled into her pillow and asked, "So, how long have you been here?"

"Half my life," Teyli answered softly, wistfully.

"Haven't you ever tried to escape?" Le'ell asked.

The blond haired young woman gasped. Teyli's hands froze on Le'ell's legs and for a long few seconds a horrible tension gripped the room.

"Don't you even speak of such lot!" the healer finally said in a low, scolding voice. "Not if you don't want to end up under that whip again." She sighed and began working with the ointment again, her fingers more tense. "Many of the women who have tried to escape never have been seen again."

"So they made it?" Le'ell guessed.

Teyli shook her head. "No, they did not. Many were killed where they were found and left to rot where they fell. Most were brought back and made as examples for the rest of us. I am remembering one who was left hanging by her wrists in the stockyard for days. Marched past her, we were, for many days after, even after she was dead."

The blond haired young woman added, "One girl was caught only hours after she escaped. She was made to pull a plow and was chained in the stables with the horses at night for a month. They only fed her oats and water the whole time."

"Two others escaped last fall," Teyli said grimly, "a mother and daughter. They were caught less than a league away." She sighed a shaky sigh and continued, "When they were brought back, we all had to watch as they bound her in the stockyard and made her own daughter whip her. When the young lass could take no more of doing that to her own mother they made her watch as they whipped her mother to death. Horrible it was. Just put those thoughts of escape from you right now. The sooner you realize you are here to stay, the longer you will live."

"I would not mind such a long life with Prince Chail," the black haired girl said dreamily. "Of all the men who could own me, I would cut off an arm if it would make it be him."

Le'ell laughed softly, shaking her head as she murmured, "Oh, please."

Someone burst into the room and Le'ell looked to see a thin girl with long brown hair and wide, dark eyes rush to the bed and almost shout, "Did you hear what happened? Prince Chail killed one of the slave hunters!"

"No!" the blond haired young woman drawled.

"Yes!" the brown haired girl insisted as if barely believing herself. "The largest of them. They said he attacked the Prince and the Prince felled him with a single blow." She punched at the air. "They said he came to the rescue of a new girl that the slave hunters were torturing for no reason and he killed one and banished the others!" She looked down to Le'ell, pointed, and demanded, "It was you, wasn't it? You were the one he saved, the one he is actually going to keep!"

"It was me," Le'ell confirmed, laying her head back down.

"Isn't he wonderful?" the girl asked, almost bouncing where she stood.

Le'ell's lips tightened and she turned her eyes down, softly answering, "That remains to be seen."

"The Prince will not be killin' someone for just any reason," Teyli pointed out, "especially another man. He must consider you to be special."

"You are so fortunate," the brown haired girl squealed.

Le'ell nodded. "Fortunate me."

Teyli threw the sheet back over her and stood, turning to the brown haired girl. "Did you bring her clothing like I asked?"

The girl bit her lip and admitted, "I sort of forgot."

"Then why don't you sort of go and get them," the healer suggested, then turned to Le'ell and said, "You will need to be eating something to get your strength back. The Prince will be here soon and you'll need to be ready."

Le'ell's eyes narrowed and she assured, "Oh, I will be."

CHAPTER 5

Patience had always been one of Prince Chail's strong points. He knew the girl who had been purchased for him would need rest after her ordeal with the slave hunters. He had to busy himself.

First, he cancelled his ride, carefully telling the burly stable master that he was going to give the horses a rest for the day. Then it was off to one of the kitchens to order meals for him and this girl who awaited him. She would no doubt be very hungry, as the slave hunters did not have a reputation for taking very good care of their captives. That done, he was off to the linen and wash area, a small stone structure just behind the palace. Here, most of the castle's laundry was tended by the twenty or so slave women who worked there. This is where he would be able to find suitable attire for his girl. Teyli had probably already taken care of this, but it would be better to be sure. Besides, he needed activity.

All this done, and seemingly little time burned, he raced back into the castle and up the stairs, slowing as he reached his father's study.

The recently repaired door stood open and King Donwarr sat behind his desk with maps laid out before him. The black shirt he wore, one which was usually worn under the leather and steel armor he wore in the field, was not laced up and hung open as he leaned over one of the maps, his elbow resting on the table and his forehead in his palm.

Chail entered quietly, not wanting to break his father's concentration. He noticed a crystal bottle of wine on one side of the desk, nearly full. A half empty goblet of wine sat beside it.

Something was wrong.

Chail sat in one of the chairs across from his father and rested his elbows on the desk, folding his hands under his chin.

A moment later the King drew a long breath and turned strained eyes to his son.

"You look concerned about something," the Prince observed.

Donwarr nodded slightly.

The King's silence and the expression on his face told Chail that the situation was more serious than he had first thought, and he asked, "Thinking about more than my ride in the forest, today?"

"I'm afraid so," the King confirmed. "Loravar's patrol never returned this morning."

Chail nodded, finally feeling the full impact of his father's woes come to bear on him. "Well," he started, trying to sound as light-hearted as he could, "perhaps they are just enjoying themselves by the river. I mean, that particular patrol rout, so close to the border, can be stressful in more ways than one to a young commander like Loravar, and it is getting a bit hot today."

"Not even he has been five hours late before," the King pointed out, "and he knows better than to stay out so long."

Chail nodded again, then offered, "I could take a garrison out to try and find them. If they did fall under attack I don't see their attackers fairing well against a hundred of us."

King Donwarr shook his head. "Thanks for offering, but I have already sent three patrols out to find them." He looked to Chail and added, "You might put a garrison or two on alert, though."

The Prince nodded. "Consider it done. Oh, by the way. I guess I will go ahead and cancel my ride today."

Donwarr smiled. "You saw the new wench, did you?"

"I hate to admit it," the Prince conceded, "but you were right about her. Of course, the scars on her are not at all attractive, but—"

"Scars?" Donwarr interrupted. "She had no scars on her."

Chail shook his head. "The men you bought her from saw fit to give her some."

The King raised his chin. "Did they? Perhaps I should just see about that."

"I saw to them already," the Prince informed. "I don't think they will be back."

"I will see to that," Donwarr assured. "So. You do like what you see in her?"

"Very much so," Chail confirmed. "I am, after all, giving up my ride to spend some time with her."

The King nodded. "And that gives me such a feeling of relief that you could not imagine." He motioned to the door with a raise of his chin. "Go on and enjoy her."

The Prince glanced down at the maps.

Donwarr shook his head and ordered, "Just leave this headache to me, Son. I'll think better knowing that I have finally found a woman that interests you."

Chail smiled and stood. "I won't disappoint you, then." He turned and strode from the room, his thoughts shifting back to the young woman who awaited him.

He bounded back down the stairs, knowing he would have to allow her to rest a while longer. He exited the palace again and strode toward several smaller structures made of stone. They stood in a line, five of them about six paces apart. Many soldiers trained and sparred around them. Others sharpened weapons or cleaned armor or shields. Many horses were tied up in the shade, saddled and ready should they be needed in a hurry. Several of the younger soldiers tended them, brushing them down, walking them or seeing to the saddles and equipment they carried. The activity always seemed endless.

Chail strode through training and sparring soldiers toward the first structure, glancing around for the garrison commander, then heard his name from behind and turned.

The man who approached him was not quite his size, but close and dressed in leather and steel armor that looked as if it was designed to allow him to move freely. Long blond hair was restrained behind his head and carried on the wind. He walked with long, purposeful strides on black boots that propelled him quickly across the ground.

As he reached Chail, he extended his hand and greeted, "My Prince. A pleasure to have you visit my watch."

Chail seized the man's wrist and had his own grasped as he replied, "Captain Trehtar. Good to see you again."

"To what do I owe the honor, my Prince?" the garrison captain asked.

Chail folded his arms, feeling the tension in his own eyes as he informed, "Loravar's patrol never made it back."

Trehtar nodded. "I heard. Would you like me to send a search party for him?"

"King Donwarr has already taken care of that," the Prince sighed. "He seems to think a couple of patrols can hold their own against whatever or whoever might be responsible for Loravar's absence of person today."

"You do not?" Trehtar guessed, raising his eyebrows.

Chail pursed his lips and slowly shook his head. "Something in my gut tells me no."

"Far be it from us to question His Majesty's orders," the garrison captain said dryly, "and I've come to trust that gut of yours." He glanced back at some of the men training behind him. "I have a few lads who could use an exercise in the field. I could take a few squads of them out that direction, just for training, you understand."

"Of course," Chail agreed, almost smiling. "And with a full squad of more experienced warriors to help train them."

"Naturally," Trehtar confirmed. "I'll have some of the reserves and a few guards called up to fill in the gaps here. Very quietly, of course." His eyes slid to one side and he added, "We would not want someone to think we are going to war or on an unauthorized maneuver or anything of the like."

The Prince smiled and nodded. "I like the way you think ahead, Captain."

"Take a lesson, my Prince," the garrison captain laughed.

Chail also laughed, rolling his eyes, then he shook Trehtar's hand again, turned, and strode back toward the palace.

Once inside the palace, he slowed his pace, staring blankly ahead as he remembered he *had* to allow the girl to rest, just a while longer.

He wandered the corridor for a time, and as he turned down the hallway that would lead him to his room he saw three slave women ahead of him and instantly recognized one, calling, "Teyli!"

Carrying a basket that looked a little heavy, she looked toward him, then hurried to him and bowed, greeting, "My Lord."

The other two women, one appearing to be only in her middle teens, also approached and bowed, staying behind Teyli.

"Where are you off to?" he asked.

"Back to the care center, my Lord," she replied.

He took the basket from her and turned toward where she was going, striding slowly as he asked, "How is our girl?"

"She is a strong lass, my Lord," Teyli answered. "She was resting as I left and earlier I got her to eat and got her dressed for you. I think I got to her in time with the ointment, so she should not scar, but she will be powerfully sore for a time. It should pass by tomorrow or the next if we apply the ointment a few times a day."

Chail nodded and said almost to himself, "Good." He took a deep breath, trying not to sound too enthusiastic as he inquired, "So, how is she otherwise."

"None too happy to be here, I am afraid," Teyli answered apprehensively, staring ahead of her for a few strides before continuing. "I well understand what it is you see in her. Her face and shape are copiously handsome and she is a strong lass."

"You sound like you have reservations about her," Chail guessed.

Teyli sighed and turned her eyes down. "It is not my place to be questioning your judgment, my Lord."

"Everyone else does," the Prince pointed out, "why not you, too?"

Teyli laughed softly and glanced up at him, then turned more serious eyes to the floor, then ahead again as she said, "My Prince, she has a venomous personality and you would do good to keep her restrained, and not be turning your back to her."

Chail raised his brow. "You don't think I can handle her?"

"Of course you can," the healer said softly, turning her eyes down again, "but I do not trust a lass with such fire. She could very well kiss you one moment and put a dagger in your back the next." She drew a breath and added, "I went ahead and restrained her."

Chail felt a cold wave surge through him and he looked ahead and mumbled, "Oh, boy."

"Only her hands, my Lord," Teyli added quickly. "I only want you to be safe with her."

He patted the healers back and said, "Always thinking of me, aren't you, Teyli? Well, not to worry. I'll have her eating out of my hand before you know it."

"Be careful she doesn't bite it off," the healer warned.

They arrived at the door to the care center and Teyli took the basket from the Prince, looking very concerned as she turned her eyes up to his, advising, "Do be careful about her, my Lord."

Chail smiled and assured, "I won't hurt her."

Teyli rolled her eyes and pushed the door open, mumbling, "That is *not* what I meant."

"I'm just kidding," Chail defended as she and the other two young women entered the room, then he sighed as the door closed, staring at it for a moment before he shrugged and turned toward his own room, his thoughts shifting back to the beautiful young woman who awaited him, the beautiful young woman who *must* have rested enough by now.

He took the stairs to the second level two and three at a time, barely winding himself, and took long strides toward the door to his room. Never had the corridor to his room seemed so long. Anticipation lanced sharply throughout him seemingly as never before, his heart feeling like it was trying to hammer its way through his chest. It was not exactly his ride in the forest, yet somehow this was better.

Only a few paces away from the door, he stopped suddenly as it opened and a young slave girl emerged, one who looked to be about fourteen seasons old. She backed from the room and closed the door, staring at it for long seconds as if something within had frightened her.

Fearing the whelps left by the whip were worse than Teyli was letting on, Chail slowly approached and asked, "What is wrong?"

The slave girl spun around and curtsied, not daring to meet the Prince's eyes.

"Is she awake?" Chail asked.

The slave girl nodded, replying, "I am afraid so, my Lord."

That did not sound good.

The Prince folded his arms, looking dominantly down at the slave girl as he asked, "What happened?"

Hesitantly, the slave girl glanced up at her prince, then down again and shrugged as she reported, "I just told her she needed to be ready for your arrival. I know how you hate to be kept waiting." She drew a shaky breath, continuing, "She—" Her breath escaped without making any more words.

Chail nodded. "She has a temper, does she?"

"Like a dragon's" the girl confirmed, then looked up at the Prince and almost begged, "May I go, my Lord?"

Smiling, Chail ruffed the girl's hair and said, "Of course you can, but will you find me a bottle of wine before you flee too far?"

Nervously, the girl looked at the door.

"You can just knock and leave it outside if you like," the Prince assured. "I won't let her bite you."

The girl drew her shoulders up and turned her eyes down.

"Okay," the Prince conceded, "just have Nessar bring it up, later."

The girl curtsied to him and quickly said, "Thank you, my Lord," then she hurried past him, disappearing down the corridor.

Chail took the last step to the door and took the handle in his hand, drew a deep breath, then pushed the door open, freezing as he saw her standing at the window that was right across the room from the door.

Now dressed as the other slave women were, she complemented her new attire very well, more so than any Chail had ever seen before. Her back was to him and her shape was nothing short of incredible. The bright white fabric made her tawny skin appear even darker. Her long, auburn hair flowed gracefully and unrestrained almost to her lower back.

Slowly, she turned her head, then a little at the waist to see him, her dark green eyes, lancing right through his. Everything about her was sensuous, especially as her lips parted slightly when she saw him.

Chail found he could not breathe easily as he stared at this magnificent woman before him, one who was a normal man's height tall, but he maintained his bearing somehow and entered the room, closing the door quietly behind him. He approached her slowly, taking gentle, quiet steps across the room.

She turned fully to him, folding her arms defiantly as she stared up at him. The leather restraint, which was supposed to be around her wrists, dangled from her fingers, then fell to the floor.

He stopped about two paces from her, also folding his arms.

She looked away from him, appearing to be nervous herself, and a little uncomfortable, then finally looked back to him and, in three graceful strides, crossed the distant two paces between them, reached up and slid her hands around his neck.

He took her gently by the waist and pulled her to him, touching his lips to hers gently at first, then more and more passionately.

She pulled him closer, holding him tightly.

Chail slid his arms around her back and crushed her to him, almost lifting her from the floor. Just touching her in this way was amazingly arousing to him.

A moment later, perhaps two, she pulled back and gently pushed away from him, staring up into his eyes. She twisted slightly, freeing herself from his arms, then took a half step back and slapped him hard, snapping his head around.

Chail raised a hand to his stinging cheek and then looked down at her, his brow low over his eyes.

She set her hands on her hips, glaring up at him as she cried, "You took your sweet time finding me, didn't you?"

He rolled his eyes up and growled.

"And where were you when I was being whipped and manhandled by those animals?" she ranted. "I could have been *killed* for all you care!"

He loosed a not quite patient breath and defended, "Le'ell, I was trying to get things together to be there."

"Of course you were," she snarled. "That would explain why you are still here in your comfortable little palace while I am out there in the wilderness almost being trampled by Grardoxen, chased by dragons and my mother's soldiers and, oh, yes. Let's not forget about being captured by your people."

He shook his head. "You just wouldn't believe the day I've had."

Her eyes flared and she shouted, "The day *you've* had? After everything I went through to meet you, avoiding Grardoxen and dragons, getting captured by slave hunters and almost being whipped to death, you can stand there and tell me *you* had a bad day?"

"Well," he conceded. "I suppose it wasn't all that bad."

"You are damn right it wasn't!" she agreed loudly. "And I find it very convenient that I am captured by those men and brought here to find you haven't even left yet and I just happened to be sold to you as your little slave wench!"

A little surge of anger stiffened Chail's spine and he raised his chin and growled, "Just what are you saying?"

"What do you think?" she spat back.

He turned his head slightly, his teeth clenched as he asked, "Are you saying I sent them to capture you?"

"Did you?" she demanded.

The Prince stepped toward her and roared, "You know better than that! I have *never* broken a promise to you!"

"Then why are you still here?" she shouted.

"It doesn't matter what I say," he retorted. "You don't intend to believe me no matter what. As usual, you have made up your mind and that is that." He pushed past her and stormed to the window, leaning on the window sill and glaring out into the courtyard below. At times like this, he wondered why he had kept seeing her for the last few seasons, and if it was worth feeling about her the way he did.

A long, tense moment of silence passed between them.

"So, what happened?" she asked softly.

He did not answer, could not answer.

She slowly approached and stood beside him, also staring out the window for a moment before asking, "Does it have anything to do with those shirts on the floor?"

"In part," he replied sharply.

"They look like they put up quite a battle," she observed. "It's no wonder you were running late."

Slowly, he turned his head and looked at her.

She was looking up at him, her brow high over her eyes and the hint of a smile on her lips. She was clearly trying to get a smile out of him, knowing she had gone too far in accusing him the way she had.

Not getting the reaction that she wanted, Le'ell glanced out the window, then looked back to his eyes and said, "Very well. I forgive you for being late." She raised a shoulder, her lips pouting as she added, "But you still could have found me sooner."

Finally, Chail smiled as he countered, "I could also have allowed him to put that whip to you a few more times."

Le'ell smiled back, admitting, "Yes, you could have. But *I* think you would rather do that yourself, wouldn't you?"

He nodded. "Right now... Yes. Yes I would."

Her smile broadened and she leaned her head as she asked, "Even if I'm a good girl?"

Chail turned fully and took her by the waist, pulling her to him as he answered, "I don't expect you to be a good girl."

She slid her arms around him and raised her lips to his.

Of all the women Chail had been with in his life, only Le'ell made him feel the way he did. She was strong, sensuous and somewhat demanding, nothing at all like the women of Enulam and he had taken no other woman since meeting her. In her, he felt complete, and no other woman could even turn his eye, much less get him to take her in his bed.

Le'ell had not been touched in such a way for some time. All of the recent memories of the slave hunters and her torture seemed to blur away as she stared up into his eyes. All of the men at Zondae were weak and submissive, very much afraid to take any initiative. She had always considered this to be the way of things, that all men were so. Then she met Chail and from the first real touch of young lovers exploring each other she had found a different world. He was aggressive and went after exactly what he wanted, though he did not seem shy about her demands. From their first time together she knew he was strong and not at all timid, not at all submissive, and she had been with none of the men at Zondae since meeting him. He seemed to complete her.

He ran his hand gently over her hair, asking, "Do you have your strength back, yet?"

She raised her eyebrows and replied, "You be the judge," then kicked the back of his knee and pushed him hard toward the bed.

He stumbled and fell back first onto the bed.

Le'ell pounced on him before he could get his bearings and soon the two were engaged in a playful wrestling match, laughing and tickling each other.

Some time later, well into evening, Le'ell's scant clothing was piled beside the bed, right beside Chail's. The evening sun bathed much of the room in a bright orange glow, casting long shadows across the floor. Somewhere outside the window and close by, a bird made all aware of the coming of night. Already, cool air crept into the room through the window, not that the room's occupants minded at all.

Lying beneath the sheet and wool blanket on the bed, the Prince and Princess of enemy kingdoms still held each other, still tenderly kissed each other's lips, still gently caressed each other's skin. For some time neither spoke. Neither had to, nor wanted to, though there were things that needed to be said that Le'ell knew could not be put off forever. Chail also knew this, but for him, putting it off was much easier, considering the circumstances.

Le'ell drew a deep breath and turned to her back, nuzzling against him as closely as she could, then she stared at the ceiling blankly for a time as uncomfortable thoughts wandered about within her.

Chail gently ran his fingers down her neck, over her shoulder and down her arm, and finally broke the silence. "You seem distracted."

She glanced to his eyes, then looked back toward the ceiling and shook her head, replying, "Just thinking."

"What about?" he asked, although he already knew.

"Nothing important," she lied softly, never wanting her time with him to end. She looked out the window, then back toward the ceiling and said, "I would probably be on my way home by now."

"Or already there," Chail added. "That's it, isn't it? I understand, Le'ell."

"Do you?" she snapped before realizing.

"Just imagine if the situation was reversed," he advised, "if I was a prisoner in your kingdom. How would you feel about it? Glad to have me there with you and at the same time wishing I wasn't?"

She looked to him. "How would *you* feel if you were my prisoner?"

He smiled slightly and answered, "I can think of worse fates. Not many, but—"

"Bastard," she laughed, then, "So. How are we going to get me home?" His long silence made her uneasy and she added, "You do intend to return me home soon, don't you?"

"Of course I do," he assured quickly. "How, on the other hand, still eludes me."

She sighed. "You are just making it too complicated."

"How would you do it, then?" he asked.

Le'ell snuggled closer to him, considering her words for a moment before she answered, "Let's see. First, I would acquire a couple of horses, a blanket, a bottle of wine—"

"A picnic!" he exclaimed. "Why didn't I think of that?"

She rammed her elbow into his ribs and ordered, "Just let me finish! If your guards think that you are just taking me on an outing, then they will ask no questions, right?"

"Not necessarily," he replied. "Taking women outside the perimeter wall is not exactly common practice."

"But you are Prince here," she argued. "They have no right to question what you do."

"Even as Prince I am subject to the same laws and regulations as any other man here," he corrected, "even more so." He drew a deep breath and looked out the window. "Still, your idea does have some merit."

Le'ell turned toward him and slid her hand up his chest, agreeing, "Of course it does. Now let's get something figured out so we can get me home soon, tomorrow if we can." She vented a long breath. "I'll wager my mother is having kittens about now."

"Or basking in the peace and quiet of your absence," the Prince added.

She shot him a sharp look, then rolled her eyes and smiled.

"We will go for a walk tomorrow," he assured. "By then I should be able to come up with a plan to return you."

"Oh," she snarled, "that makes me feel better."

He turned his eyes down to her and asked, "Why do you say that?"

"Your plans never work, Chail."

"Your plan to be there early this morning worked out nicely," he reminded, "didn't it?"

"Don't chance the subject," she ordered.

When someone knocked on the door, Chail stroked his Princess' hair and asked, "Would you like some wine?"

She smiled and looked up to him. "Red or white?"

"Red, of course," he answered, then bade, "Come in."

The door opened slowly and a haggard, bent old woman in a long white robe and cape limped in, carrying a tray with a bottle of wine, two silver goblets, cheese and bread rolls, and a small, white jar. A hood covered her head, clearly there to conceal thinning white hair which dangled around her face like moss from an old tree.

She turned and closed the door with her foot, then turned toward the bed and looked to the Prince with deeply wrinkled brown eyes and slowly approached, saying in a voice as ancient as she looked, "You ordered wine, me Lord?"

"Yes, I did," he confirmed with a nod. "Just put it there on the night table."

She complied, then turned back to him, looking down at Le'ell as she nodded and mumbled, "The Prince's first."

"First what?" Le'ell asked hesitantly.

"First and last," the old woman said to her, then looked to the Prince and informed, "The time is at hand, Highness. You be putting your manhood, you word to the test." She glanced at Le'ell, then looked back to Chail and continued, "You leave soon for Zondae, then your odyssey begin. Hear the words of an old woman."

The Prince nodded and bade, "Very well. Tell me."

The old woman bent closer to him, her eyes widening. "Zondae and Enulam must not make war." She made a fist and held it up. "Only together can we as enemies and allies stand against them trolls and his mixed, bastard army. They come soon. Got to stop them before they leave the dark place."

Le'ell leaned her head and asked, "What makes you think we are going to war?"

The old woman looked down to her, her eyes widening further as she replied, "Can see it in the fire. Bodies hacked in pieces. Not Zondae and not Enulam. Them trolls. Them dark dwellers. Gotta pull us together. Dark times a commin' soon. You ride together and alone into the cold North, through the death of a forest and men. Follow a unicorn of snow."

Le'ell raised her brow and nodded. "Unicorn, huh?"

"Not be mockin' me, waif!" the old woman barked. "Only she holds death from you, keeps it in the belly of a dragon of night."

Le'ell's breath caught as she remembered the dragons she had seen that morning. Finally mustering a little courage, she asked, "What makes you think a dragon is going to come for us?"

"He not," the old woman corrected. "You go for him. The unicorn of snow take you to him. Pay heed to what she do, where she go. She and he, enemy and ally. She teach you the way of peace. He teach you the way of war. You learn from them both."

Chail nodded and assured, "We will, Nessar."

"Not mock me!" the old woman warned. "Your life and your death are in me words. You pay heed." She looked to Le'ell once more and said, "He take you. You give you to him. Only way." Then she turned and limped from the room.

Le'ell watched the door for a time after it closed, then said aloud to herself, "Strange."

The Prince reached over her for the wine, confirming, "She can be a scary old bat at times, that's for sure."

"She talks like a seer," Le'ell observed. "Have any of her words ever come to pass?"

He filled the goblets, took one and handed it to her, admitting, "Yes, she's actually been accurate sometimes. However, she has made many predictions that weren't." He took his own goblet and lay down beside her. "It's difficult to say when she is wrong or right, or if she just gets lucky."

Le'ell took a sip and said, "She mentioned a dragon of night."

The Prince shrugged. "So? She mentioned a lot of things."

Le'ell just stared down at her goblet for a time, then decided what she had seen that morning must have been a coincidence, and was much too frightening to think about for too long. So, she shook her head and softly replied, "I suppose it isn't important."

Chail took a drink from his goblet and looked to her, prodding, "What isn't?"

"My back is starting to hurt again," she said, still staring at her wine. "Can you rub some of that ointment on it?" A quick change of subject seemed to be the best way to avoid a discussion that she would rather not have.

"You're avoiding something," he accused, then ordered, "Roll over."

She complied, laying her chin on her hands and staring at the headboard before her. With the dragons haunting her thoughts again, she barely noticed as the ointment was slowly spread onto her back, then, as it began to burn as before, she sucked a quick breath through her teeth and raised her head, protesting, "Damn, but that stings."

"Don't be such a sissy," Chail scolded.

"You aren't the one having your skin burned from you," she snarled, "but if you wish I can show you what it feels like."

"I already know," he informed, applying more. "When I was much younger and just learning how to ride I had that stuff applied to me every few days."

She giggled. "Not a born rider, huh?"

"Well," he sighed, "it taught me to stay mounted."

Le'ell glanced back at him and smiled. "You do *that* well enough."

"It would amaze you what I can do, woman."

She laid her head back down and challenged, "Amaze me, then."

CHAPTER 6

The early morning sun was still behind the treetops but already illuminated the east side and training and work areas of the palace. Already, the whole kingdom bustled with activity with young warriors training and tending their equipment and horses. Women tended the gardens that were half way between the palace and the perimeter wall. Other women carried baskets of linens or vegetables from the gardens.

This was Prince Chail's destination. With Le'ell on his arm, he walked proudly from the palace, dressed in a black shirt that fit him tightly in the chest, shoulders and upper arms, much the way all of his shirts seemed to fit him. His trousers, also black, were loose around his legs, held in place by a dark brown belt on which hung his sword, dagger, and a half a dozen leather pouches about twice the size of his hand. Polished, dark brown boots reached not quite to his knees.

Le'ell was dressed as she had been when Chail found her in his bedroom, in the white attire worn by the other slave girls.

She stayed close to her prince, clinging to him like a nervous child in a new place as he led her into the heart of what had always been her enemy's stronghold. She could barely believe the level of activity so early. At Zondae, only the morning patrols, the guard changes and the servant men were up at this hour. Here, it seemed the whole kingdom was up and active before they could even see the sun. This made her a little nervous as she watched hundreds of soldiers train all around her.

Chail walked her around slowly, showing her the stables, the gardens and whatever else they happened to come across. He felt eager to teach her about his home, a certain sense of pride driving him.

"Mount!" a burly, armor clad man on the perimeter wall shouted.

Le'ell looked up at him, then to the half dozen stone structures that were lined up neatly near the perimeter wall. As she watched, men charged from between the buildings, leading saddled and equipped horses behind them. They lined up and mounted their horses, keeping their animals in two perfect lines about ten abreast.

Another man rode from the palace, stopping right in front of them. He said something to them that Le'ell could not make out and all of the riders in the formation responded with a single yell as if in one voice that was loud enough to make her flinch.

She looked up at Chail.

He glanced down at her and smiled, then motioned toward the timber gate in the perimeter wall.

She turned and looked as the gate swung open. Seconds later a score of riders charged through the gate and fell into their places in a formation that mirrored that of the riders who had just assembled.

The first rider to enter did not fall into place with the rest. Instead, he circled his men, then rode to the front of the formation and greeted the leader of the other group, drawing his sword. All of the men in his group followed suit. He yelled something that Le'ell could not understand and his men answered in one voice. The other group all drew their weapons and responded with a yell, then their leader turned and bolted toward the gate, his men whooping and yelling as they followed him out of the gate.

The thunder of hoof beats and the yelling the men did made Le'ell cringe and hold onto Chail's arm just a little tighter.

She drew a breath as the gate closed and observed, "They look like they are charging off to war."

The Prince patted her hand and assured, "They are off to one of the training holds in the forest."

Le'ell turned her eyes up to Chail, feeling a little surprised as she asked, "You mean you don't keep all of your army here?"

"Only about a quarter of it," he answered. "The rest of them are out in the field training and riding patrols."

"What if you are attacked?" she asked, almost sounding concerned. "With most of your force in the field, how can you defend the castle?"

He smiled. "We have more than enough to hold out here for many days or weeks against almost any onslaught."

"And after two or three days, then what?" she challenged. "Your enemy could reinforce and take your depleted defenders down in a few hours and take over your castle."

"Reinforcements would never arrive," the Prince informed. "That's where having troops already in the field comes in handy. Reinforcing troops usually don't expect to be attacked so they would be so thoroughly surprised that dealing with even a larger force would be fairly easy. If they are not all decimated or forced to surrender, they would no doubt be routed so that they would be useless to the main force. By then, *our* reinforcements from the other holdings would already be on the main force. Having dispatched the primary attack, any enemy reinforcements that did make it through would find themselves under attack by the bulk of the Enulam army."

Le'ell nodded, admitting, "You really have this thing thought through, don't you?"

"We've been attacked many times in the past," he informed, "mostly attacks from Aalekilk castle long before I was born. We learned what works and what doesn't."

"Aalekilk?" Le'ell questioned. "I read where Zondae would come under attack from them in our past. Our army routed one attack in the forest about five seasons before my mother was born and they never returned."

Chail turned his eyes down to her. "About forty-five seasons ago Enulam sent a large strike force against their castle. The returning soldiers reported that most of the Aalekilk force was not there when the attack began and they were in the process of sending more to the field. Their not being prepared led them to a quick and decisive defeat."

Le'ell looked up at him and said, "So, we defeated them together and did not even know it." She smiled. "How perversely romantic."

Chail smiled back, pulled her to him and kissed her.

They walked on for a while, passing the castle's north gate as the sun finally rose over the perimeter wall to shine on their backs.

As they rounded the corner of the palace, watching still more of the same activities taking place, Le'ell looked up at him and asked, "So why, exactly, did we get up so early today?"

He glanced down at her, informing, "I slept in today. I'm usually up before the sun this time of the season."

Shaking her head, she laughed under her breath and said, "You are either very dedicated to whatever it is you do or very foolish."

"I just don't want to waste my life sleeping it away," he replied. "You know. The way some people do."

She rolled her eyes.

As they circled around toward the west gate, Chail raised his chin as he saw a petite, blond haired slave girl standing about fifty paces from it, staring out of the open gate with her hands folded before her.

His eyes narrowed slightly as he mumbled, "I wonder what that is about."

Le'ell looked to her and shrugged, saying, "It's your kingdom."

"I wonder if she is planning to run," the Prince guessed.

Le'ell studied her a moment longer, then leaned her head and informed, "No, she appears to be waiting for something. Or someone."

They slowly strode to the girl, quietly approaching from behind and one side.

The girl did not notice them as she continued to stare down the road that led into the forest.

"Planning to storm the gate?" the Prince asked.

The girl wheeled around, surprise on her young features, then she smiled and curtsied to him, greeting, "Your Highness." She glanced out of the gateway, then turned back to the Prince and reported, "No, Highness. Of course not. I am waiting for my Lord Loravar to return."

Chail turned his eyes to the open gate, tensing up slightly as he asked, "He still has not returned?"

"No, my Lord," the girl answered softly, then straightened herself and assured, "He will be back any time, though. You will see. I have his bed prepared and a meal waiting for him."

"How nice for him," Le'ell mumbled.

"Quiet," the Prince growled, then looked down to the girl and asked, "Have you slept yet?"

She shook her head and replied, "No, Highness. I have been waiting for my Lord Loravar to return. He should be back any time and will expect me to be awake for him."

Chail nodded, then looked back out the gate and announced, "Here comes someone."

The girl turned and looked her eyes wide with hope.

Le'ell tugged on the Prince's sleeve and asked, "Who is this Loravar?"

Chail leaned to her, speaking softly. "His patrol did not return on schedule yesterday and he has apparently been missing ever since."

"Did you send someone to find him?" she asked, also speaking softly.

"Of course we did," the Prince confirmed. "I think this is one of the patrols that was sent yesterday." He raised his chin as he watched the riders file through the gate, but did not see any from Loravar's patrol with them.

Watching intently, the girl studied each rider, barely noticing how haggard and exhausted each of them looked. When the last of them entered and her Loravar was not among them, she ran to the squad leader and shouted, "Where is he?"

The leader just glanced at her and rode on. They all just rode right past her, none speaking.

The blond girl appeared to be near panic as she started after the last rider, glancing out the gateway as she cried, "But where is he? Didn't he come back with you?"

"Mind your place, woman," the last of the riders growled.

The girl looked out the gate once again, then ran to the last rider and pleaded with him to tell her that her lord was well.

Chail shook his head, mumbling, "This isn't good."

Clearly tired and frustrated, the rider stopped and turned his horse, kicking at the girl as he shouted, "I said mind your place!"

She backed away, crying as she whimpered, "Please tell me what happened to him. Please!"

The rider seemed enraged. He swung down from his horse and stormed to the girl, seizing her arms and shaking her brutally as he roared, "He's dead! They are all dead! Do you hear? Now mind your place and give me some room to breathe!"

Chail pulled his arm from Le'ell's grasp and strode to the man, pulled the girl from his grip and stepped right up to him, saying, "Perhaps you can tell *me* what happened, or should I mind my place?"

The soldier just stared up at the Prince for a moment with hollow eyes, then, "Dahkam has gone to report to King Donwarr." He glanced away, shaking his head. His face turned a little gray as he seemed to remember something.

"What did you find?" the Prince questioned.

"We found Loravar's patrol," the soldier answered. "They were on a road near the border, hacked to pieces." He turned away from the Prince and walked to his horse, taking its reins as he said, "I've never seen the like." As he slowly made his way toward the stable, he continued to mumble something to himself. Clearly, he was more shaken by what he had seen than he wanted anyone to know.

Le'ell slowly approached the Prince, staring after the departing soldier as she asked, "What did he say? Hacked to pieces?"

Chail nodded, also watching the soldier as he confirmed, "That is what he said."

"No!" the blond girl screamed as she ran toward the palace.

They watched her flee, then Le'ell said, "Just like the old woman told us."

The Prince looked down at her. "You don't actually believe that nonsense, do you?"

She just shrugged.

Chail took her hand and pulled her toward the palace, ordering, "Come on. Let's see what Dahkam has to say."

Nearly to the door of King Donwarr's study, the Prince stopped and took Le'ell's arm, turning her toward him and looking down on her with authoritative eyes. "Before we go in," he started.

"I won't embarrass you," she assured, raising a hand to his cheek. "I'll be your good little slave girl in there."

"I'm not worried about you embarrassing me," he said flatly. "If you don't behave in there the King will very likely send you back to the whip and there won't be anything I can do about it. Just mind your manners and don't say anything. Anything at all! Do you understand?"

She raised her brow. "I can be an obedient, attentive little slave girl, but quiet too? That's going to be hard."

"Shall I gag you?"

Le'ell looked away, then smiled and giggled under her breath.

Chail sighed and turned her toward the door, one hand firmly grasping the back of her neck as he pushed her toward the study. "Just do as I say, slave girl."

"I will, my Lord," she replied with just a hint of sarcasm.

Within, King Donwarr's study was a solemn place. Proud soldiers stared at the floor, not speaking as they seemed to try to forget something. An image would not leave their minds, an image of something quite horrible, as could be seen on their expressions. This was not what Le'ell had expected. Not even the man who was supposed to be giving his report to the King could talk, though, judging from the King's expression, he had given a report already.

Slowly stroking his beard, King Donwarr stared blankly at his desk, clearly deep in thought. A moment passed before he seemed to realize Chail had entered and he turned his eyes up to his son with a blink. His expression was cold and he just stared into Chail's eyes for long, tense seconds. When he finally spoke, it was not to his son, but to another. "Dahkam, can you repeat what you found out there to the Prince?"

Slowly, Dahkam turned and looked to Chail, his eyes blank and hollow as he reported, "We found Loravar's patrol on the road closest to the border. All dead. Their bodies had been hacked to pieces."

Le'ell winced, covering her mouth, more at the memory of the old woman's words than the news of the dismemberments.

Dahkam continued, "No weapons were taken that we could tell, no armor... It just didn't make sense. Even their horses were hacked up."

Chail considered, then, "Did any of their flesh seem to be consumed?"

Everyone within the room exchanged glances, and Dahkam was a long moment in answering. "I... We didn't observe anything of the like."

"No campfires?" the Prince questioned. "No signs of an encampment? Large numbers of hoof prints?"

Dahkam considered, looking away for a moment, then he shook his head. "No other hoof prints but the patrol's." He raised a hand to his mouth, rubbing his lips back and forth as he thought, then his eyes snapped back to the Prince and he added, "Arrows."

Chail raised his chin. "Longbow or crossbow?"

"Both," another man said. "There were many in the trees, some in the ground, some in the bodies and horses."

"That would explain how the patrol would be taken down so quickly," the King observed. "Do you think the attack was launched from Zondae?" His eyes turned to Le'ell.

She met his eyes, staring at him for long, fearful seconds, then looked up to Chail.

He would not look at her, but his eyes narrowed as he looked to his father, and he reported straightly, "I don't think so."

The King's expression remained as stone as he stared at his son, then, after half a moment, he asked, "Do you care to enlighten the rest of us?"

"The attack made no sense," Chail informed. "Why ambush a patrol of ten? Why volley arrows in such numbers? Why go to the trouble of chopping up the bodies *and* the horses?"

"Perhaps to send a message," another man guessed.

"What message?" Donwarr asked. "Dahkam, did you see any activity near the border?"

Dahkam shook his head. "None. Everything was very quiet."

Le'ell understood immediately that Chail could not strike down accusations against Zondae. He could do nothing that would make the King suspicious of her. To the King, she was a slave girl purchased yesterday to amuse his son. That's what he had to think.

As the discussion continued, Le'ell looked around the study, seeing a table at one side of King Donwarr's desk by the wall with almost a dozen clear flasks of various wine lined up and five goblets lying upside down in front of them. She liked the sweet taste of the Enulam red wines and quietly wandered over to the table, righted a goblet and filled it from the first flask to the right. Raising the goblet to her mouth, she inhaled deeply the aroma of the wine, then took a sip. Most of the wine at Zondae was dry, not appealing to a young woman of nineteen, and this sweet wine made by her enemy was a refreshing change. Taking another drink, she turned and froze, noticing that all of the men within were all quietly staring at her. Slowly, she lowered the goblet, her eyes darting to each of the men and locking for many tense seconds on King Donwarr's.

With much effort, she managed to swallow, then strode stiffly yet gracefully to Chail, offering the goblet to him. When he took it, she turned with purpose and approached the King's desk, took his goblet and turned to the wine table.

She was frightfully aware that the men were still silent and watching her, especially the King, and her gut squirmed within, but she was not so prone to panic or give herself away. Quite the contrary. She knew to play her part, for her and the Prince she loved.

Looking back to the King, she sheepishly said, "Forgive me, my Lord. I didn't mean to interrupt."

He nodded once to her.

"Red?" she asked.

He nodded again.

Le'ell's hands shook as she poured his wine, and as she turned to take it to him, he thankfully looked back to the Prince and asked, "Don't you think it would be even more dangerous for another kingdom to launch an attack so deep in our territory?"

He shrugged. "Depends on their motives."

Donwarr took the goblet from Le'ell and stared down into it for a time, then looked to Chail and informed, "I will need to see this personally."

"Are you sure that's wise?" Chail asked. "How do you know they aren't trying to draw you out of the castle?"

"I don't," he answered straightly.

Le'ell picked up another goblet and looked to Dahkam.

Shaking his head, Dahkam advised, "I won't question your judgment, my King, but I'm afraid I agree with Prince Chail."

Unexpectedly, Donwarr smiled. "You two are a couple of overprotective mother hens."

"Then hens we are," Chail informed.

Dahkam finally noticed Le'ell looking at him and nodded to her.

She filled the goblet and took it to him.

Chail noticed right away that she was offering her services to the men in order of rank after she had served her own master first, and a slight smile touched his lips. She was impetuous and headstrong, and yet he always marveled at how smart and adaptive she was.

Donwarr glanced at her, then rose from his chair and growled, "Well lets not all stand around and drink up all of my wine. Chail, assemble a heavy patrol and have them ready to take to the field within the hour. Dahkam, are you up to another outing?"

"I won't leave your side, my King," he answered.

"Nor will I," Chail added.

Donwarr looked to him with tense eyes. "We don't both need to be in the field."

"I'm going," Chail said straightly. "If we both don't need to be out there then you should remain here."

The King's jaw tensed. "I'm not a helpless old man, Son."

"Nor are you in your prime," the Prince pointed out.

Donwarr's eyes narrowed. "I'll show you what kind of prime I'm in when we get back, boy. Now get the patrol assembled." He smiled just a little. "Perhaps we can still link up with the garrison you sent out yesterday that I wasn't supposed to know about."

Chail's eyes widened and he looked away, then he turned toward the door and mumbled, "And you wonder why I'm always suspicious of you."

Le'ell followed him out the door, walking behind him as he made his way toward his errands to assemble the patrol, then back to the palace toward his room. She did not speak until they entered and she gently closed the door. "I hope you realize that you're right."

"About?" he asked as he rummaged through his wardrobe.

"It wasn't Zondae," she assured, watching him.

He hesitated, then resumed what he was doing and said, "I want to believe that, too."

"What if I have proof?" she asked.

He turned and looked to her. "What kind of proof?"

She drew a breath. "Yesterday morning the patrol I was on found Zondaen warriors who had been butchered the same way."

Staring at her, Chail folded his arms. His eyes were blank. "Le'ell, how am I supposed to tell my father about that? And how do I know for sure that's what you really saw?"

"Why would I make it up?" she barked, setting her hands on her hips.

"You really have to ask?"

"Chail, I wouldn't lie to you about this!"

"Then why didn't you tell me yesterday?"

She just stared back at him for a time, then looked away and folded her arms, admitting, "I don't know. Perhaps I had more on my mind than our kingdoms going to war."

"Like?"

Le'ell rolled her eyes. "Did you forget I had been tortured and chased by dragons yesterday?"

He raised his brow. "Chased by dragons?"

"I told you yesterday."

"You didn't elaborate."

Le'ell sighed. "Okay, I wasn't actually chased, but they were right there and could have eaten me at any time. And so could that drakenien."

"There was a drakenien too?"

"He came to get the Grawrdox that the dragon had killed that almost trampled me. They wouldn't share and I thought they were going to fight—"

"*And* a Grawrdox?"

"There was a herd of them. I found a calf and was getting some of the hair from it when the dragon swooped in and killed one of them."

"Just one dragon?"

She huffed a breath. "Weren't you listening? There were two! The big black one killed the old Grawrdox and called the little red one to come eat it."

Hesitantly, Chail nodded. "There was a black dragon, and he called a little red one to come dine with him. So, where does the drakenien come in?"

"I don't know. He just wandered into the clearing and the big black dragon stomped over to him and bit him on the face. He laid down and the dragons kept eating the Grawrdox. Why is that so difficult for you to understand?"

"And... What were you doing during this time."

"I was *trying* to not be noticed, but they kept looking at me anyway so I left as quietly as I could."

He nodded. "A black dragon, a red dragon, a Grawrdox and a drakenien. Was there a white unicorn in there anywhere?"

"No!" she spat. "Why would there be a unicorn out there?"

Chail rubbed his eyes. "Was this before or after your patrol found your butchered comrades?"

"It was after, Chail. I slipped away from my patrol and risked my life to come see you, remember?"

He nodded and admitted, "Yes, I remember. Let me ask you something. If I was late for our meeting and told you all of this, would you believe me?"

"*I* wasn't late," she reminded.

"Just answer honestly," he insisted.

Le'ell folded her arms and looked to the floor, softly admitting, "I don't know."

"So you understand that my suspicions have to be satisfied."

"You can't just believe me? You know I wouldn't lie to you about this."

"I know you wouldn't," he assured, "but I can't assume that you know for sure that your people aren't planning to attack us."

Le'ell turned furious eyes on him. "*You* would know for sure if you weren't so boar headed."

"Watch your tone with me," he growled.

She stormed to him and hissed back, "Perhaps you'd better watch yours!"

"You are way out of line, woman!"

Le'ell slapped him hard. "*Now* I'm out of line."

"That's it!" he shouted, grabbing her arms and pulling her down to the bed with him.

After a brief moment of wrestling, she found herself draped over his thighs as he sat on the edge of the bed. He was holding her arms behind her by the wrists and spanking her very hard. The sting of his hand on the whelps left by the slave hunter was almost unbearable and she screamed and struggled to free herself. Before she realized, she was laughing in her screams.

Chail stopped suddenly and looked to the door.

Le'ell also looked.

King Donwarr was leaning against the door jamb with his arms folded, staring back. He was dressed in a gray arming shirt now and wore a thick black leather belt that was laden with pouches and a sword hanging on his left.

"Are you ready to go?" Chail asked calmly.

"I'm ready," he assured. "Trouble with your woman?"

Le'ell laid her head down, staring back at the King with shamed eyes and pouty lips as she whimpered, "I was a bad girl."

Donwarr nodded. "I see that." He drew a breath and looked back to his son. "I'll be at the stable whenever you're ready." The smile that overpowered his face was conspicuous as he turned and left.

Le'ell released her tension in a long breath, then asked, "Are you through spanking me yet?"

He simply answered, "No."

Many hours later found them riding in the middle of a score of Enulam warriors led by King Donwarr himself deep into the forest. Chail could not be talked out of taking Le'ell with him, but for some reason was not pressured by his father to leave her, only the ranking members of the patrol. Just why Donwarr had no objections would not be known for some time. As a precautionary measure her hands were bound to her saddle horn and she was watched constantly.

She kept her eyes down for the most part, not liking the role she found herself in. At Zondae she had felt like a prisoner. Now, she really was one. The irony did not escape her as she had plenty of time to think about it.

Chail had ridden at her side for most of the journey, but now rode some distance ahead, talking with Dahkam about something that Le'ell could not hear, and this made her feel even more out of place, and very alone since she was the only woman in the group. Mistrust thickened the very air around her and she dared only fleeting glances at the men who watched her so closely. Riding was uncomfortable and she shifted in her saddle frequently.

One of the younger men, perhaps around seventeen or eighteen seasons, rode up beside her, a water bag in his hand. He took a drink, then looked to her and asked, "Are you thirsty?"

She glanced at him and just shook her head even though she really was.

"No need to be afraid," he assured. "Whatever took down Loravar's patrol won't stand a chance against twenty of us." He rode in silence for a time, then asked, "So, why did Prince Chail bring you and not leave you in the safety of the castle?"

Staring down at her bound hands, she grappled for an answer, finally replying, "It isn't my place to question his decisions."

"I suppose not," he sighed. "Don't you wonder, though?"

Le'ell found herself with precious little patience for such questions. A few paces later, she finally looked at him, answering, "I would assume to keep watch on me so that I don't find myself violated by some young bastard who has his brains in his pants."

He stared at her blankly for a moment, then smiled. "Prince Chail is a wise man, then. In his place, I wouldn't have left you, either."

Le'ell looked down to her hands, then back to the young soldier and asked, "Are you going to challenge him for the right to bed me?"

He glanced away, smiling broader. "You would be worth making such a challenge, vixen, but I would have a better chance against a mountain ogre or a dragon than Prince Chail."

Unable to help herself, Le'ell finally smiled. This young man sure was charming. "So, you're not going to make a challenge for me?"

"I'm young, vixen," was his answer, "not a fool."

She laughed, looking ahead, then turned her eyes back to him and asked, "Do you have a woman of your very own?"

"No," he sighed. "My father has one he lets me bed when I have the urge. She's almost his age, but still very beautiful and *very* experienced. I've used most of my earnings for my sword and armor and to purchase my horse from the stable so I have some saving to do before I go to the auction to find a woman."

"At least you have your priorities straight," she teased.

He nodded. "My life needs to be established and in order before I go about the task of keeping a woman. I've watched my father with his and it's a much bigger responsibility than many think."

Le'ell nodded. "So, does he still have your mother?"

"Of course he does," the lad answered in a matter-of-fact tone. "She's his alpha woman."

Le'ell's eyes widened. "How many does he have?"

"Three."

Turning her eyes ahead, she gave that a moment to sink in.

"They mostly tend the house and garden," he went on, "raise my father's younger sons and prepare meals and the like. I suppose such mundane duties are something you will never have to worry about."

She shrugged. "I'll do what Prince Chail needs me to do."

The lad smiled. "If you were mine you would never leave the bed."

Le'ell tried to fight back a smile but it was not to happen. "Isn't it a dangerous game to flatter the slave of a prince so?"

"Not if I don't touch her," he replied.

"Thaebin," one of the others called from behind.

The lad turned his horse, offering her one last smile. "Take good care of our Prince, Vixen."

She watched him ride toward the back of the patrol, then turned and looked toward Prince Chail, pushing herself up off of the saddle for a few seconds. She had never expected one of the warriors of her enemy to be so charming or friendly—or so open. In an instant she learned more about the Enulam men than she had in three seasons with Chail, and all of her schooling about them from Zondae suddenly seemed like fabricated stories told to frighten little girls.

Her thoughts shifted to the Prince himself, the first of the Enulam men who had dispelled the stories and myths about his people, and changed her life forever. There was a simple nobility about him, a calm and dignified charm she had never even imagined a man could have. In fact, most of the Enulam men she had encountered were so, but not like Prince Chail. His commanding presence could be felt by all around him and Le'ell seemed to feel it more with each passing moment with him.

She watched as he slowed his horse to come abreast of her. Other warriors subtly gave him room, and Le'ell could not help but feel his title of Prince had nothing to do with it. This was nothing short of respect. He never seemed to throw his weight around, and yet he commanded the respect of everyone around him.

Chail looked to her as his horse slowed to hers and said in a low voice, "We're coming upon the site of the attack. I want you to stay close to me and don't volunteer any information to anyone but me. If you see something I should know about, make sure only I know."

She nodded.

Looking ahead again, he continued, "If we're attacked out here I don't want you putting yourself at risk."

"We've been over this," she hissed through clenched teeth. "I'm trained at least as well as you are."

"Not many slave girls are," he pointed out. "I'm not questioning your abilities. I just don't want you giving yourself away."

"If it's a life and death struggle we may need everyone fighting," she countered. "If you're distracted trying to protect me then a battle could go poorly for us both."

"We will attend to that if it happens," he growled impatiently. "Just do as I say."

"I don't want anything happening to you, either," she informed softly.

He looked to her and smiled. "Then for your sake I'll see to it nothing does."

She smiled back and rolled her eyes, then shifted in her saddle yet again. "I'll sure be glad when we finally get there."

He glanced at her. "I thought you were accustomed to riding on long journeys."

"I am," she assured, "but my behind is still a little tender from all it has been through the last couple of days."

Chail snickered.

"I'm glad you're enjoying it," she snarled.

"I certainly am," he happily confirmed.

Rounding a turn in the road, the found a group of men already at the area of the attack, surrounding the area but not really invading the actual site where the bodies lay.

Donwarr, riding at the head of the column, raised his hand as he stopped his horse, bringing them all to a stop, then he dismounted and walked slowly toward the area, the men of his patrol following.

Chail swung down from his horse and handed the reigns to one of the squires who approached him, then he strode to Le'ell's horse and reached for her bound hands.

As he untied her, she scanned the road before her, her eyes a little wide.

"What do you see?" he asked in a low voice.

"Just like yesterday," she breathed. "All of the bodies should be on one side of the road and in many pieces, just like the old woman said." She dismounted, then took his arm and held on tightly as he escorted her toward the site of the massacre.

Chail's expression was as stone as he looked from one side of the road to the other, observing body parts and blood everywhere. All of the bodies had been chopped apart at the elbows, knees, ankles, shoulders, hips... All of them had been decapitated. Arrows were everywhere.

King Donwarr shook his head as he examined the grisly scene before him. "That's how they did it. They were ambushed by archers first and showered with arrows."

Le'ell looked around her, noticing many arrows in the nearby trees on both sides of the road, driven straight in by strong bows. A few arrows were in the torsos of some of the bodies, but none were sunk into the ground. She stopped walking and pulled away from the Prince, stepping back as she looked to the arrows in the trees.

Chail turned. "You see something, don't you?"

Hesitantly, she nodded, then pointed to the trees, one after another. "See that? All of those arrows were shot from right here."

"Are you sure? It was an ambush, after all. They probably had many archers hiding in the trees ready to shower the patrol as they rode by."

She shook her head. "No, you can't shower arrows like that in or from dense forest. You especially don't want to do that from both sides of the road since you could hit your own people. Even if they did then the arrows would be shot at an angle and would penetrate the trees downward." She squinted. "Look beyond the trees, Chail. There are no other arrows deeper in the forest."

He looked, his eyes narrowing. Glancing around, he concluded, "This was staged."

Le'ell nodded again. "Experienced archers wouldn't have missed this many times. If they had been ambushed by archers then there wouldn't be so many arrows shot. They also wouldn't have left this many arrows behind. They're time consuming to make so you want to use them as many times as you can." She approached a tree, reaching to the arrow that was in it, and slowly shook her head.

Chail followed, also looking to the arrow. "What is it?"

"It's Zondaen," she breathed.

"You're certain?"

Nodding, she confirmed, "Each archer paints her arrow differently and with her own mark and color pattern of feathers." Slowly, she turned her eyes to Chail. "This one was En'sheil's."

"And I'll bet she was a part of the patrol you found yesterday, wasn't she?"

She just stared up at him, then looked to the other trees, and down to the arrows in the bodies. "All of these arrows are from that patrol."

"How convenient," he growled.

Another soldier approached the Prince with one of the arrows, his brow low as he reported, "Zondaen arrows. I guess we know who attacked."

King Donwarr also approached, his eyes on Chail as he growled, "Are you suspicious of another party still?"

Chail folded his arms. "As a matter of fact I am, more so now."

The King nodded, staring at his son. "Okay, explain it to me."

"Zondaens are reputed to be some of the best archers in the land."

Donwarr nodded again. "And I see plenty of arrows around here."

"Too many," Chail explained. "Would expert archers miss this many times?"

The King glanced around.

"You also won't see any arrows beyond these first trees, and they are conveniently all about the same height in the trees."

Donwarr considered. "Perhaps it was a volley. They could have waited for Loravar's patrol to get close enough and then loosed their arrows in mass."

Chail shook his head. "At that range a few well placed arrows would make more sense. A dozen archers each shooting an entire quiver wouldn't be necessary, would it? And that still doesn't explain why the bodies were hacked to pieces like that and few armor or weapons were taken. For that matter, why would they kill and chop up the horses and not take them?"

Donwarr glanced at Le'ell, then turned to walk away. "Who knows what those barbarian women are thinking."

Chail followed. "So you are convinced that it was Zondae?"

"I'm convinced of nothing," the King answered. "Dahkam, have the garrison collect our brethren and take them back to Enulam, and collect all of the arrows you can find."

"Yes, my Lord," Dahkam complied, turning to carry out the order.

King Donwarr turned back to Chail and ordered, "We leave for Enulam in a half hour. There are preparations to be made." He raised his chin slightly. "Can I still count on your loyalty?"

Chail's jaw tensed. "You know you can."

Nodding, the King turned again, and was intercepted by another soldier.

"King Donwarr," the soldier reported. "There are no tracks leading away from the site, not on the road. There are a few signs of activity in the forest, a few footprints, but nothing that would lead back to Zondae or Enulam. Whoever did this traveled in the forest and covered their trail very well."

Donwarr considered, then looked to Chail, turned and continued on his way.

Le'ell took Chail's arm from behind, staring after the King as she softly asked, "What do we do now?"

The Prince stared after his father, and long seconds later finally answered. "It's his move."

CHAPTER 7

The first hour of the journey back to Enulam was a quiet one. No one spoke. That morning, Le'ell could not wait to leave that castle. Now, she could not wait to be back there. Even with Chail at her side she could not seem to relax.

The Prince himself seemed devoid of emotion. His eyes moved warily as he rode, but he moved his head very little. This was more than just a troubled man deep in thought. He seemed to feel something, as if the forest itself was trying to warn him of danger. Something was amiss, and he knew.

As they continued on, the men of the patrol seemed to become more and more tense, more restless. One rode about twenty paces in front of the others, his wary eyes scanning the trees on one side of the road, then the other.

Le'ell needed reassurance. Steering her horse closer to the Prince's, she reached out and took his arm.

Slowly, he turned his eyes to her, meeting hers with a gaze she had never seen before. Such intensity lanced from behind the pools of dark brown and black of his eyes that she barely recognized them as those she had gazed into on many an encounter.

The nervous parting of her lips and strain in her dark green eyes softened the Prince's features ever so slightly. The girl was already frightened and could make no secret of it. He reached to her hand and gently stroked her fingers, then her arm. Just his touch seemed to make her feel a little more secure. Turning away from her, he cleared his throat, then beckoned to a rider ahead.

Slowing his horse, the other rider brought his horse abreast of the Prince's, looking to him with the same strained gaze.

Chail looked to the other man's horse and asked in a low voice, "You found a souvenir?"

The soldier looked to the bow and quiver that were hooked on his saddle horn. "They were lying just inside the tree line. I filled it with as many arrows as I could fit within."

"Lucky for us," the Prince observed. "Mind if I take it off your hands for a while?"

"Not at all," the soldier replied, handing over the bow and quiver. "I didn't know you could shoot one of these."

"Not well," Chail admitted. "What is the news from ahead?"

"Fifteen," was the answer. "We're confident more will emerge down the road once we've passed."

The Prince nodded. "I see us going in outnumbered. We are tactically in a corner."

"We're pairing up. I'll be fighting at your side."

"No," Chail corrected. "I want you watching my father's back, and I'll watch yours."

"I have my orders," the soldier informed in a low voice.

"And now you have new orders," the Prince replied. "Just don't let him know you're watching his back."

The soldier looked to the King, then to the Prince and raised his brow.

Chail smiled at him. "I'll owe you one."

Nodding, the soldier rode on ahead of the Prince and he conspicuously rolled his eyes.

Keeping his hands low, Chail passed the bow and quiver to Le'ell, asking, "Do you know how to use this?"

"Oh, you're funny," she spat back. Hooking the quiver's strap on her saddle horn, she discreetly pulled an arrow from it and set it on the bow, half pulling the bowstring. With the horse's reigns held by her left index finger, she had a firm grip on the middle of the bow and had it perfectly ready to shoot without even looking down at it.

"I guess you've done that before," the Prince observed.

She nodded. "A time or two. So what are we supposed to do?"

"We're robbing them of the element of surprise. As soon as they attack they'll be facing down twenty swords held by twenty seasoned warriors."

"Chail, have you ever actually been in battle?"

"A couple of times," he assured. "Garrisons I was attached to were ambushed by nomadic barbarians called the Bludchon some time ago."

She nodded.

He turned his eyes to her. "I'm guessing this is your first time."

Her eyes only glanced at him, then a slight smile curled her mouth. "My first time was with you, remember?"

He also smiled slightly. "I remember. Just wait until the signal is given. If we stick to the plan then we all get home alive."

"Didn't you just change the plan?" she asked. Without warning she raised the bow and loosed her first arrow. Seconds later an armored form fell from a tree near the middle of the patrol. Before the Prince could even get his sword or his first scolding words out, a second arrow whizzed through the air and found its mark on the other side of the road, and another raider fell from his perch in a tree near the front of the patrol.

Forced to launch their attack early, raiders wearing armor, fur and leather charged from the trees, all of them raising a battle call as if in one voice.

The Enulam warriors drew their weapons and raised their own battle call, meeting their attackers with speed and ferocity to match their enemies, and an arrow claimed another attacker before swords could meet in battle.

The soldiers of Enulam paired up, half of them swinging down from their horses to meet their enemies on the ground. The Prince also abandoned his horse, charging three of the invaders before they ever made it out of the trees. Le'ell aimed and shot with a true aim, reducing that number to two.

From her horse, Le'ell had a good view of the chaotic battle, but found herself unable to affectively get a clear shot, and her agitated horse was further disrupting her aim. One just emerging from the forest caught her eye and she aimed and shot, then swore under her breath as the arrow glanced off of his armor. When he stopped and turned toward her, she reloaded and shot again, this one lancing through his throat right below the chinstrap of his helmet and through his spine, and he fell quickly.

As the battle raged, Le'ell finally swung down from her horse and readied another arrow, quickly realizing she was down to two. Enulam men fought all around her. Yelling and the clank and ringing of armor and weapons stung her ears, but she was too excited and near panic to even realize. Swinging around, she saw two young Enulam soldiers engaging four raiders and barely holding their own. Their backs were to her and they swung their weapons wildly to fend off their enemies, and were slowly backing toward Le'ell.

As the two raiders on the ends tried to flank around the Enulam men, Le'ell raised her bow and slammed an arrow through the unprotected ribs of one as he raised his weapon. As he went down, she took her last arrow and aimed at the fourth as he turned and charged her.

One of the Enulam soldiers yelled wildly and wheeled around, his sword striking the attacker low across the abdomen. Sharp steel overwhelmed the leather armor and as the soldier drew his sword across its victim's belly and turned back to engage another, blood spewed forth and the invader doubled over and fell. No longer outnumbered, the young Enulam soldiers went on the attack.

Le'ell turned back to the main fray, her eyes finding King Donwarr locked in battle with two of the attackers. Much to her surprise he seemed to be enjoying himself, and was fighting at very close quarters. His sword rammed through the breastplate of one and his free hand seized the sword-arm of the second. He drove them both backward, his superior strength becoming apparent as others tried to break away from their scuffles with other Enulam men to assist.

Then she saw movement behind the king, a large raider in leather and fur who was stalking toward him. Le'ell's eyes widened as the raider poised his weapon, and she slowly raised her bow. With the King dead, Chail would be in charge, Chail would be King.

She took careful aim. With the King dead, no one would question Chail's order to release her, no one would question his order not to invade Zondae. Her people would be safe from attack for a while. She would be free to go home.

The second of the King's opponents found himself impaled on the King's sword.

The raider behind the King grabbed him around the neck and drew his arm back to thrust his weapon into his enemy's back.

The arrow flew—and found its mark.

King Donwarr turned his eyes to Le'ell, his mouth falling open as he staggered to keep his feet.

Le'ell met his eyes, fearful of what she had just done.

Donwarr wheeled around and let the stricken raider fall from him, then turned to engage two others.

Running toward him, Le'ell raised the bow as if it was a sword and slammed it into the head of one of them. Before he could turn, she hit him again, then backed away.

Snarling behind the face plate of his helmet, he charged toward her, then hesitated.

Le'ell was pushed aside and stumbled a few steps as the charming young Enulam soldier engaged the raider with a mighty yell. Swords met many times before Thaebin half turned and kicked his enemy, knocking him off balance just enough to swing his blade past the raider's and open the side of his neck. As his enemy fell, the young warrior turned and smiled at Le'ell, then charged back into battle to defend his king.

A smile touched her lips, then she looked for Chail, finding him ten paces away and locked in battle with three raiders. She knew the Prince was immensely strong, something which his enemy was just finding out, but she would still not leave him outnumbered and fighting for his life. Charging toward the skirmish herself, she used her bow as before, slamming it into the side of one of the raiders whose back was to her.

He groaned and backed away from Chail, angling away from Le'ell as he turned toward her.

Now down to only two opponents, the Prince struck one's sword hard with his own, then lowered his shoulder and charged into them like an angry bull, sending them stumbling over each other to the ground. As he spun to regain his footing, he tossed his sword toward Le'ell and swooped toward the ground, snatching up a battle axe one of the others had dropped.

His attention still on Le'ell, the raider facing her did not know of the axe coming at him until it crashed through his armor and ribs and he fell quickly.

Le'ell took the time to pick the Prince's sword up from the ground and held it firmly in both her hands.

They looked at each other, their weapons ready, then they looked at the two raiders who had gotten to their feet and charged them.

As weapons battered each other with loud metallic rings, Le'ell complained, "This thing's heavy!"

Chail parried with his axe, then kicked his opponent hard in the belly, spinning as he did and slamming his weapon hard right between the shoulders of the raider Le'ell was fighting. In one motion, he wrenched the axe from his vanquished enemy and spun back, sinking it into the armored chest of the other as he charged. Wrenching it from the second raider, the Prince turned to Le'ell and informed, "That's my lighter combat sword. I use the heavy one for training."

She smiled. "No wonder your arms are so big."

Looking around them, they realized the fight was over.

King Donwarr approached, bleeding from a deep gash in his left arm near his shoulder and holding some injured right ribs with that hand. Although clearly in pain, he had a smile for his son as he informed, "I killed five of the bastards, just like I was in my prime."

Chail nodded. "I killed eight and I don't have a scratch on me."

The King raised an eyebrow and nodded. "I'm surprised you only killed eight." He turned his eyes to Le'ell, glancing at the sword she still held. "I would have killed six, but your woman dispatched one for me." He approached Le'ell, towering over her as he nearly met Chail's height and just stared down at her for a time, then looked back to his son and asked, "So what inspired you to arm your woman?"

The Prince took his sword from her and returned it to its sheath, then casually slid the handle of the axe into his belt as he answered, "We were outnumbered as it was, and she took quite a toll on them with that bow."

"I noticed," Donwarr agreed with a nod. "I don't think a seasoned Zondaen archer could have done better."

She nervously turned her eyes away from him, looking to Chail.

"We dispatched most of them, I think," the Prince observed. "How did we fare?"

The King glanced at him, then sheathed his weapon and turned toward his regrouping men.

Chail finally met her eyes. She was afraid all over again. He gently stroked her cheek, then walked past her, following his father.

Le'ell followed him, remaining behind him until she saw the man being attended to on the roadside. Gasping, she darted around the Prince and knelt by the young soldier's side.

Thaebin looked back at her with strained eyes. A sword had found its mark in his side and he bled badly from it.

One of the men attending him held his hand over the wound and ordered, "I need bandages."

Le'ell turned and tore away some of her already short skirt. She quickly rolled the fabric and said, "I know what to do."

The soldier moved his hand and watched her press the bandage to his wound.

Thaebin groaned in pain, then unexpectedly smiled at her. "It will have to be tied in place. Perhaps you should use that top piece you're wearing."

She turned her eyes to his. "I could just use your belt."

"But then I would be deprived of seeing you undress for me," he retorted.

"Perhaps when you recover," she offered, then looked to the solder who still knelt beside him.

Staring back at her, he nodded, then looked to an approaching soldier and took a saddle bag from him. As he opened the flap and began pulling out bandages and healing powders, he said to Le'ell, "Keep the pressure on until I can get a clean bandage in place."

She nodded. "I will."

King Donwarr nudged Chail as he turned, facing Dahkam who had just approached.

Dahkam looked up to the King and reported, "Two more injured but not badly. The raiders drug off their wounded and disappeared into the forest. Shall I dispatch a squad to pursue them?"

Donwarr shook his head. "Not into their element. Let's collect what we can here and return to the castle." He turned to Chail. "See to it we bring the bodies of the raiders with us and everything they brought with them. Scout twenty paces into the forest in both directions and see what you can find."

Chail nodded. "You are taking the wounded back to the castle?"

"I think Thaebin needs more attention than we can give him out here," was Donwarr's answer. "I'll leave you with the bulk of the patrol, just in case they decide to attack again. Make sure you stay on you guard."

The Prince glanced behind his father and asked, "And should you be ambushed on the way back?"

"We're only an hour or so out, Son. I don't think a sizeable force will venture that close to the castle. Besides, we're sure to meet one of the other patrols on the way."

Le'ell backed toward Chail, watching as Thaebin was helped to his feet. She glanced up at the Prince and asked, "Chail, should he be standing like that? He's wounded pretty badly."

"He'll be fine," the Prince answered. "He's not the kind of lad to just lay down on a litter. He would probably try to march home if he'd lost a leg."

"He can't ride like that," she complained. "He's sure to pass out on the way and fall off of his horse."

Donwarr glanced at his son, then looked to Le'ell and assured, "Not with you holding him up."

She looked to him, her eyes wide and her lips parting nervously.

The King looked back to Chail and informed, "I am borrowing your woman for a while. I'd hate for you to have to look after her out here while you are seeing to this recovery task."

Chail turned his eyes to her, clearly straining to maintain his bearing as he said, "I wouldn't want you to be burdened looking out for her, either."

"I'll put her to good use until you get back," Donwarr informed. "I want you no more than an hour behind me."

The King's tone told Chail that he would win no arguments with him. Tactfully, he looked to Le'ell, then reached to her, took her chin in his hand and ordered, "I want you on your best behavior for the King, woman."

When he winked at her she almost gave away a smile, but she was able to regain her composure enough to just nod and assure, "I will, my Lord."

He patted her cheek, then walked past her to go about his tasks.

Le'ell's eyes followed him, then turned back to the King. Hesitantly, she asked, "What would his Majesty wish of me?"

The journey back to Enulam seemed to be a frightening test of patience without the company of Prince Chail.

Le'ell held Thaebin tightly to her, making certain he would not fall. The first half of the ride he was fully awake and alert, but consciousness tried to elude him more and more as they continued on. Along with the King, six others accompanied them, including the two other injured soldiers. Everyone was on their guard, just in case the raiders should return for them.

A little over half way, another heavy patrol—a full score of Enulam warriors—met them. Half continued on their way while the other half surrounded the King and his party and escorted them back to the castle.

Once there, Le'ell dismounted and tried to help the other Enulam soldiers take Thaebin from the horse, but she was pushed away by one who ordered her back. Although still concerned for him and a little insulted, she knew she dare not protest. They laid him onto a litter that was rushed from the castle and he was taken inside. Le'ell tried to follow all the way to the care center, but this was not to be.

King Donwarr seized her arm and ordered, "Stay with me."

She glanced at him, then looked back to the injured soldier as he was carried away.

The King slipped his arm around her shoulders and assured, "He'll be fine, vixen. You needn't fuss over him."

Le'ell glanced up at him again and nodded. Then an unusual realization hit her. He did not seem to be treating her like a slave. He was acting almost fatherly toward her. While she despised being treated like a child, his treatment of her did not seem even to annoy her.

For at least a half hour she accompanied the King on his various errands around the castle. This seemed easy for the most part. All she had to do was quietly remain at the King's side. Many of the men they encountered, especially the large soldiers, looked her way with eyes that frightened her, but in the presence of the King she felt safe from them.

Finally returning to his study, King Donwarr entered the room rubbing his eyes and releasing a deep breath.

Lingering near the door, Le'ell just watched him, nervously holding her hands to her.

As he sat down, Donwarr reached for some papers and his inkwell and ordered, "Close the door and come over here."

She complied, still feeling a little fearful of being alone with him.

He scribbled on a paper for a time, then glanced at her and suggested, "That wine isn't going to pour itself."

Her breath caught and she darted to the wine table, carefully pouring a goblet for the King and taking it to him.

He took a couple of gulps, then scribbled some more. A moment later he turned his eyes to the door and ordered "Enter."

The door slowly opened and Dahkam peered in. "I hadn't even knocked."

Donwarr smiled. "You should approach more quietly if you want to knock."

Nodding, the soldier entered, followed by three others.

They stood behind the chairs that sat in front of the desk, looking down at the King as they awaited his word.

He stared back at Dahkam, then demanded, "Your report."

Dahkam glanced at Le'ell, then looked to the King and complied, "We examined the dead brought back from the field. They are definitely not Zondaen."

King Donwarr nodded. "But they all had Zondaen weapons on them."

"Some," Dahkam confirmed. "It seemed that most of the armament they used came from a different forge. It looked like their weapons came from a castle's forge, as if they were making many weapons for many soldiers. They also seemed to be reasonably well trained but I'm not convinced that these were the best soldiers they could offer up."

The King considered, then looked to one of the others and asked, "And just who would you say we were dealing with?"

He took a deep breath and answered, "They weren't all human." He hesitated for a moment, glancing around at the other men, then continued, "From what I could tell there were—"

Another soldier interrupted, "So our enemies are recruiting forest trolls and gnomes. They haven't the courage to face us themselves."

"I want less speculation and more facts," the King barked. "What do we know of their tactics? If they come from a kingdom with an organized army then why were they dressed and equipped as wandering barbarians? Where did they get Zondaen weapons? Where did they get their other weapons and armor? Do we have these answers yet?"

The other men were quiet.

"We should all know something about their tactics," Donwarr continued. Someone knocked on the door and the King summoned, "Enter."

Teyli entered, carrying a basket that was laden with bandages and flasks of powders. Ignoring everyone's eyes on her, she went directly to the King and knelt down beside his chair, looking to his wounded arm.

Donwarr turned his eyes back to his men and said, "There have been no reports of unusual movements near the Zondaen border, but there has been some activity noticed by several patrols near the Northern border."

Dahkam raised his chin. "Could the Zondaens be flanking around the northern border?"

Another soldier answered, "It wouldn't make sense to travel fifty leagues out of their way and exhaust their armies on a long march like that."

Still another added, "And I don't see Zondae recruiting outsiders. From what we know they keep to themselves."

"My Lord," Teyli summoned gently. "Could you be removing that shirt?"

He shot her an irritated look.

She simply raised her brow.

With a deep sigh, the King stood and removed his shirt, throwing it to Le'ell, then he sat back down and looked back to Dahkam. "We might have to consider that we have a new enemy." He winced as Teyli dabbed a damp bandage against his wound and he looked to her again and barked, "Woman! Must you do that right now?"

She turned her eyes to him and informed, "I'll not have my Lord and King with a festering wound. If I'll be treating it now then it won't grow septic and my Lord will be spared a copious lot of pain."

Le'ell could not fight back a slight smile.

He just stared at her as she continued to work, then he loosed another deep breath and looked to his men. "Explain something to me. Forest trolls are known to be solitary. Gnomes do not like the company of men. They especially have no use for trolls. Why would they all be fighting together?"

Everyone in the room considered.

Le'ell did as well. Now would be an excellent time to enlighten everyone present as to what had happened to that Zondaen patrol, yet she knew that would be impossible given the current circumstances.

Teyli finished bandaging the King's wound and smoothed out the bandage with both hands, then leaned toward his arm and tenderly kissed it. She turned her eyes to the King's and offered him a warm smile. "My Lord's arm will be feelin' all the better now."

He nodded and stroked her cheek. "Go on and let us attend to this matter."

She stood and took her basket, striding around the desk toward the door, then she looked back to him and asked, "Shall I have the Prince's woman along with me?"

"No," he answered, looking toward Le'ell. "I'll keep her here until he returns."

Teyli nodded to him and turned to the door. "Aye, my Lord."

As the door closed behind her, Donwarr looked back to his men and ordered, "Find me answers, not more questions." He watched them hurry from the room, then turned to Le'ell and said, "Refill my wine, and have some yourself."

Hesitantly, she complied, filling his wine first, then filling a goblet for herself.

He extended his hand to one of the chairs.

Obeying the silent command, she gingerly sat down, never taking her eyes from him.

"My son is quite taken with you," the King informed. "It's a relief that he's finally found a woman that interests him." He held his goblet toward her. "To Chail's manhood."

She held her goblet toward him, then they both drank.

"Ah," the King drawled. "Refreshing as hell. I hate dry wine after a long patrol. It just doesn't quench one's thirst."

Le'ell nodded.

"You like it?" he asked.

She nodded again and took another sip, then a gulp, then another.

"Chail seems to go for some of those drier wines at times," King Donwarr observed. "I never quite acquired a taste for them. I suppose that's his grandfather's influence. So tell me. Are you as taken with him?"

Le'ell nodded, answering, "Very much so, your Majesty."

He nodded back smiling slightly. "That's good to hear. I noticed a sharp turn in your behavior after that first night with him. You were something of a wild forest cat when you were brought here. I was afraid he would have to put you to the whip himself to tame you."

She glanced away, taking a moment to answer. "Chail is very good to me. He's a strong man who knows just how to use his strength."

"He's made quite an impression on you, has he?"

"From the first moment I saw him," she answered truthfully, then took another gulp of her wine.

The King considered, then gulped down the rest of his wine and set his goblet down. Slowly, and with his fingertips, he pushed it across the desk to her, his eyes locked on hers. "You know what is even better than that sweet red?"

Hesitantly, she shook her head.

He glanced at the wine table. "Get that bottle of gold."

Le'ell looked, then stood and stepped to the table, gingerly picking up the full bottle. She turned her eyes back to him, finding herself seeking approval, which she got in a nod. Taking it to the desk, she sat it down near the King's goblet and worked the stopper out, then she poured his goblet nearly full and sat back down.

"Join me," he offered.

She finished the wine in her goblet and poured some of the gold into it. Glancing at him again, she took a sip, finding it sweeter than the red and tasting something of apples. This surprised her and her brow shot up as she took another sip.

King Donwarr smiled. "I thought you might like it."

"I didn't know wine could be made from apples," she confessed, taking another drink.

The King sipped from his goblet. "This one's a blend, white grapes, apples... Something else I'm sure, peach or something. It's a trite stronger than the red. Kills the pain from the day's wounds." He winked at her.

She smiled just a little and took another drink.

Donwarr looked into his goblet for long seconds, then turned his eyes back to her and asked, "So, do you like this better than the red?"

Le'ell nodded almost eagerly. "I do, thank you, your Majesty."

"Better than that blush my son has no doubt made you try?"

She nodded again. "Yes, my Lord. I like the blush but this is much sweeter."

"Better than that Zondaen red?"

"Oh, much," she confirmed. "I've always loved sweet wines and there aren't many made at Zondae. It's like horrible dry wine is a right of passage or we just...." Her eyes widened and the breath froze within her.

The King's expression did not change.

Le'ell's free hand grasped the edge of the desk and she braced to spring up and run.

"Where would you go?" King Donwarr asked. "There are two guards outside the door waiting for you. There are more down the corridor, also waiting for you."

She glanced around the room, out the window. Feeling like a caged animal, her breath returned in short gasps. There was no way out. She had been discovered and was in the middle of her enemy's castle, their largest fortress. Despair finally swallowed her and she grasped her goblet tightly with both hands, staring down into it.

"Did you really think I wouldn't figure out that you're from Zondae?" he asked.

She just stared into her goblet for long seconds, and simply shrugged.

A horrible silence filled the room.

"Well this is awkward," he observed. "You were finally starting to talk to me a moment ago."

Le'ell slowly raised her eyes to him.

He raised his brow.

Her mouth trembling, she managed to ask, "What would you have me do now?"

Donwarr pursed his lips. "I would have you finish your wine. Then we can talk."

She gulped it down, then set her goblet on the desk.

Another long silence slowly passed, one which was finally broken by the King. "So what should I do with you now?"

She could only shrug again.

"You already know what I want from you," he informed.

Her eyes hardened and she spat back, "I won't betray my people."

"I wouldn't ask it," he replied. "Tell me what you know of the attacks."

"It wasn't Zondae," she answered.

The King nodded. "I'm listening."

Le'ell took a deep breath, releasing it through pursed lips before she spoke again. "Yesterday, the patrol I was on found a Zondaen patrol from the evening before, butchered in the same way." She turned her eyes down. "I knew well two of the women on that patrol. None of us could believe what it was we found." When she looked back to the King, she found him staring at her, slowly stroking his beard. She continued, "The arrows we found where your men had been slaughtered were from that patrol, and some of the weapons that had been conveniently dropped."

"Two bows were found," the King informed. "I can see arrows as disposable, but not bows."

She nodded. "No archer would have left her bow behind."

"Unless it was part of a ruse," he countered.

"I promise it was not!" she insisted. "All of our warriors are trained to defend our castle, not attack yours."

Donwarr stared at her a moment longer with features of stone, then finally turned his eyes from her, considering his words before he spoke again. "How can you expect me to believe you? Convince me you aren't a spy."

"I got whipped in that little torture hut out there," she pointed out. "I got sold at auction and was used to pleasure your son all night. What spy would willingly go through all of that?"

His eyes snapped back to her. "One who wanted to end up where you are right now, sleeping at the side of the Prince of Enulam. Perhaps I could get more answers out of you back in that little torture hut."

Le'ell's lips parted and she slowly shook her head. "You don't need to do that."

He just stared at her.

"Please," she begged, the whipping she had received now fresh in her mind again. "Don't send me back there! I can tell you nothing that you don't already know!"

"Answer me truthfully three times and convince me and I won't." He leaned forward, folding his hands on his desk. "Why did that arrow find the raider and not me? Why did you not just let the raider kill me?"

She turned her eyes down. "I couldn't. You're Chail's father."

"And there it is again," he observed.

Looking back to him, she noticed his predatory glare and swallowed hard, finally managing, "There what is?"

"You referred to him by name," the King informed. "Not Prince, not your Lord, not Highness, but by his name."

Her lips tightening, Le'ell realized the King had seen through her further.

"Just how long have you and my son known each other?"

She was hesitant to answer, but finally confessed, "Three seasons." She stared back for long seconds, then watched as he buried his forehead in his hands. He seemed to be weeping at first, then she realized he was laughing.

When he finally looked back to her, he had to wipe tears from his eyes. "You'll never know what a feeling of relief that is!"

Le'ell raised her brow. "Your Majesty?"

He laughed again, shaking his head. "That's about how long ago he lost interest in the women around the castle. That's when he insisted on these lone rides near the border. That's when I started to worry for his manhood!" He stood and walked around the desk, picked her up by the arms and hugged her so tightly she could barely breathe.

With her arms pinned to her sides, she hung there in his embrace, suspended from the floor as he swung her back and forth. She felt like a rag doll in his grasp. The King felt like he was stronger than a bear and the origin of Chail's strength was clear. When he finally put her down, she stumbled back into her chair.

King Donwarr finally returned to his chair, smiling at her as he said, "You've finally brought some peace to my troubled thoughts." He looked down to his desk. "Now, just one more matter to attend to."

"The attacks," she said.

The King nodded, then looked to her and asked, "Where are your loyalties?"

She hesitated to answer again, finally saying, "With Zondae."

"And yet you ran away from your kingdom to meet my son for an afternoon's pleasure," Donwarr pointed out. "I think your loyalties are stronger with him. You love him, don't you?"

Her eyes were locked on his, then she tore them away, looking down to her hands as she nodded.

"I see," the King said softly. "Well, then I can assume he feels the same. Do you feel you know him well?"

She nodded again, looking up to the King.

Donwarr raised his brow. "Then we both know he's going to do something foolish, like try to return you to Zondae and tell me you ran away or were eaten by a dragon or something of the like."

Le'ell shrugged.

"He's probably formulating a plan as we speak," Donwarr continued. "He'll take you out of the castle somehow and you will ride toward Zondae. You will spend much of your time trying to figure out something about the attacks, who and why, and he'll concoct some other plan to bring them into the open and defeat them."

"How do you know all of this?" Le'ell asked.

King Donwarr smiled slightly. "Because he's me at twenty. Tell me. How can you assure me that Zondae won't send troops into Enulam territory to stop the attacks they no doubt think we launched?"

"I can't," she confessed, "but I can make certain we don't start a war with you."

"How will you do that?" he questioned.

She turned her eyes away. "I don't know. We'll think of something."

"You and Chail."

Le'ell looked back to him, confirming, "Yes, me and Chail."

He stared at her for long seconds more, then nodded. "I believe you. Give your queen a message. I'll be on the main road at the Spagnah River at high sun in four days with one hundred men."

Concern and fear seized Le'ell's features.

"If she will meet me there in person," he continued, "then perhaps we can avoid any further complications. Will you do this?"

Not sure what to do, Le'ell finally assured, "I will tell her."

"Outstanding," the King said, then he motioned to the door and ordered, "Go on to the west gate and wait for him, and try to stay out of trouble."

She nodded to him and stood, and as she reached the door she turned back to him and asked, "Is there anything I should tell him for you?"

Donwarr shook his head.

"What about the guards?" she questioned.

He smiled. "They'll keep an eye on you, but they won't bother you otherwise." When she turned to leave, the King stopped her with, "One more thing."

She looked back at him.

He raised his chin, authoritative eyes locked on her as he ordered, "I will still expect you to pleasure my son tonight, just so he won't suspect our little talk."

Le'ell smiled. "The pleasure will be mine, my Lord."

The new dilemma was this: Should she tell Prince Chail that the King knew about them?

Le'ell wandered toward the gate, halfway oblivious to what was going on around her. Her thoughts were whirled and she was unable to focus. The King of Enulam had found her out and now conspired to send her home. All of the stories she had been told since childhood pointed in a different direction. She knew she should be on the receiving end of that whip again, right in the middle of an interrogation. More and more the men of Enulam did not appear to be the brutal heathens she had always been told they were. The men who had beaten her were not even from Enulam. Nothing made sense anymore, but for one thing: Someone wanted Zondae and Enulam at war!

A commotion near the gate drew her attention and she looked to see Loravar's slave girl in the grasp of two castle guards, being drug by the arms toward the cottage she had been tortured in. The girl screamed and fought them, begging them to let her go. As they neared, Le'ell noticed that one of the guards had a leather satchel over his shoulder, and she could hear what the girl was saying.

"You have to let me go find him!" the slave girl insisted, crying as she pulled hopelessly against their grasps. "My Lord Loravar needs me! Please, let me go to him!"

"You know the penalty for trying to escape, wench," one of the guards growled to her. "Take it proper and just get it over with."

Not thinking about the consequences, Le'ell approached and sternly said, "She wasn't trying to escape."

They stopped, and the guards turned toward her.

Le'ell looked to them in turn and continued, "She just wants to find her master."

Looking to each other, the guards shook their heads and one observed, "This one seems to have forgotten her place." He looked back to Le'ell and informed, "We'll be takin' care of you shortly."

When he turned away and continued on, Le'ell pursued and grasped his shoulder, insisting, "She doesn't deserve to be tortured for—"

He spun around, the back of his hand slamming into her jaw with enough force to spin her around.

Le'ell's next realization was her wits returning to her as she lay face down on the ground. Someone seized her arms and jerked her up and she heard the guard say, "I guess this one will be havin' her turn first."

He turned her around and she was slammed into the belly of another man, a very big man who had just exited the cottage.

Slowly, she turned her eyes up.

The man was wearing a leather apron and no shirt. He stood over a head height taller than Chail and was double his girth! Everything about him was huge! He stared down at her for several terrifying seconds, then looked to the guard holding her and asked in a gruff voice, "What do you think you're doing?"

"This isn't you're concern, Gartner," the guard answered. "This one just needs to be taught her place."

Gartner wrapped his hand around the back of Le'ell's neck, his fingers meeting at her throat, and he pulled her away from the guard and moved her over. "I saw what happened. Why are you taking that little one to the cottage?"

"She tried to escape," the other guard, still holding the girl answered.

The huge man took the satchel from the first guard and opened it, rummaging through it for a time before he mumbled, "Food, water bladder, bandages, clean shirt...." His eyes returned to the first guard and he motioned toward Le'ell with his head, informing, "This wench is right. She is on her way to find Loravar."

"Look, Stablemaster," the second guard started. "We caught her trying to leave the compound. You know as well as anyone...." He backpedaled away as the huge man approached him, and he left the girl in the Stablemaster's path.

Gartner stopped right in front of her, looking over her for a time.

She just stared hopefully up at him.

He gently cupped her jaw in his massive hand, bending her head back as he said, "Listen to me. Loravar's dead."

Her mouth began to quiver and tears streamed from her eyes. "He can't be."

"He's gone," the Stablemaster assured. "You need to be strong for him and accept it. He was a warrior who died a warrior's death. Be proud he was such a brave man."

The girl broke down and backed away. She sank to her knees and covered her face with her hands as she cried.

Le'ell felt for her. She approached and knelt down beside the girl, slipping her arms around her.

"Well, then," the second guard started. "I suppose since Loravar's gone I'll be layin' claim to this woman." He approached and grasped her arm, pulling her away from Le'ell and to her feet. "Come on, Vixen."

Le'ell turned pleading eyes up to the Stablemaster.

He gave her but a glance, then growled to the second guard, "You have no claim to this woman. She's coming with me." He took her other arm and pulled her back to him. "I'll not be trusting such a sweet, loyal little vixen to the likes of you."

"Look, Gartner," the first guard spat, his hand on his sword. "You know the law, and you have no claim to this woman." He seemed much braver with his hand on his weapon.

Until the Stablemaster's hand found his throat and wrapped around his neck.

"Draw that weapon!" Gartner snarled, moving the girl aside. "Draw it and see what I do."

The guard released his sword and grasped his huge opponent's arm.

The second guard approached, ordering, "Gartner, release him. Now!"

Much quicker than he looked, the Stablemaster seized the second guard's throat and neck, drawing both men toward him as if he was some huge predator. He growled, then seemed to pick both men up and slammed them back-first onto the ground with bone chilling force.

Le'ell winced, watching as both men just lay there moaning.

"Gartner!" came Prince Chail's voice.

The big Stablemaster slowly turned, folding his arms as the Prince swung down from his horse and approached.

Chail looked down to the not quite conscious guards, then up at the Stablemaster and scolded, "How many times have I told you to take it easy on the help?"

Gartner just stared back.

"You're going to end up really hurting someone," the Prince continued. "If you like I can get you a Grawrdox bull to play with, but go easy on the guards!"

"How about a big, smart-mouthed prince?" the Stablemaster suggested, glaring down at Chail.

The Prince's eyes narrowed. "Always remember something, Gartner. I can run faster frightened than you can angry, and I can keep going long after you've dropped from exhaustion."

The Stablemaster smiled just a little. "Care to put that to the test, boy?"

Chail raised his chin, then conceded, "Not today. I've more important things to attend to." He glanced at the guards as they slowly got their wits about them. "So... What roused your ire this time?"

"You know how I feel about men who mistreat women," was Gartner's reply.

The Prince nodded. "And I see two more have felt your wrath." He looked to the slave girl and beckoned to her with his finger.

Still sobbing, she sheepishly walked to the Prince, her eyes on the ground before her and her arms to her sides.

"So you're the cause of all of this," Prince Chail said.

Hesitantly, the girl nodded.

Unable to hold her tongue any longer, Le'ell stepped forward and declared, "She was not trying to escape!"

Gartner half turned his head and ordered, "Hold your place, woman."

"She's my woman," the Prince informed.

The Stablemaster looked to him and nodded, then half turned his head again and ordered, "Hold your place, Prince's woman."

Chail rolled his eyes. "Okay, who is going to tell me what happened?" He looked to Le'ell and observed, "You seem eager to tell me something. Go ahead. What do you have to say?"

She looked up at the big Stablemaster, almost feeling she needed his approval to speak.

He just nodded at her and looked back to the Prince.

Le'ell turned her eyes back to Chail and reported, "She was desperate to find Lord Loravar. She was taking him food and a change and bandages should he need them and she does not need to be beaten for it."

Chail looked to the slave girl and asked, "You tried to leave the compound?"

The girl would not look at him and nodded again, then finally asked, "Is it true, Prince Chail? Is my Lord Loravar dead?"

The Prince drew a breath, then softly admitted, "It's true."

She cried again, sinking to her knees as if she had just heard this for the first time.

Slowly, one of the guards rolled to his side, his mind clearing enough for him to defend, "We caught her trying to escape. What were we to do but what we did?"

Chail turned his eyes down to the man and answered, "You could have taken her before the King or myself, or someone more competent than you."

The guard looked up to the Prince and said, "Trouble you with so trivial a matter?"

"I do not regard beating a young woman as a trivial matter. Consider yourself lucky you did not whip *my* woman or I would leave you in that cottage with Gartner for a couple of hours."

The Stablemaster grunted at him.

Out of the corner of her eye, Le'ell saw the King approaching with a rather tall woman who had graying black hair following him, and she turned as he reached them.

"What the Hell is the commotion down here?" the King shouted. When he looked down and saw the guards still lying on the ground, he turned his head and growled, "For the love of God, Gartner."

Finally, the Stablemaster seemed to show some remorse, turning his eyes down and away.

"They were trying to implement some unauthorized discipline," Chail reported. "Gartner was just letting them know that he disagrees with their decision to do so."

The tall woman approached the Stablemaster, staring up at his eyes as she did. She had very long hair, most of it restrained in a pony tail behind her back. This was a woman in her forties, noticeably taller than Le'ell and thicker build, very attractive and statuesque, though quite plain to the eye, and dressed much as the other slaves around the castle were but for a longer skirt, one which went all the way to her knees.

Finally noticing her, the big Stablemaster looked down at her and ordered, "Take this girl to our home and give her something to eat. Make sure she rests."

The woman looked to the slave girl and said, "Loravar's. We will be taking her in?"

"We will," Gartner confirmed.

Complying with the order, the woman took the slave girl under her arm and led her away, giving her gentle, reassuring words as she did.

Watching them leave, the Prince asked, "What will you do with her?"

"She needs to be cared for," the Stablemaster replied. "I'll find her another man when she's ready."

"You won't keep her yourself?" Le'ell asked before realizing.

Gartner turned his eyes to Le'ell. "I already have two and all of the kingdom's horses to care for." He glanced at the departing girl. "And she's far too small." He glanced at King Donwarr, then turned and followed the slave girl and his own woman.

The King shook his head as he watched the Stablemaster depart. "There is no bigger man in the land, nor any bigger heart." He looked down at the guards who finally dared to get to their feet and ordered, "You two stay out of his way from now on, and leave deciding the discipline of the women to me."

They nodded to him and stiffly returned to their posts.

Donwarr looked to Le'ell and shook his head again, then glanced at his son as he turned back to the palace, saying, "See if you can keep her out of trouble."

Chail looked down to her. "What was that about?"

Le'ell was watching the King as he walked away, then she just shrugged.

They took their evening meal in Chail's room again, this time sitting across from each other at a small table. There was no conversation for a time and Le'ell ate very little, too distracted by her thoughts to have much appetite. The Prince, on the other hand consumed his usual gargantuan portions, his eyes resting most of the time on his distracted girl.

Near the end of their meal, he finally broke the silence. "What did you and my father have to talk about?"

Startled, she turned her eyes to him, then back to her neglected meal and shook her head, replying, "Nothing important." A glance at the Prince found him just staring at her. He knew more than he was admitting. "He is a sweet man," she continued. "He reminds me of you. We talked about wine and if I'm happy with you and you with me."

"And that incident in the forest?" he questioned.

"What incident?" she asked back, not looking at him.

Chail rested his chin in his palm. "You're telling me that everyone on the patrol knows that you saved my father's life out there but you don't?"

She nervously turned her eyes away. "I… We—We were all fighting for our lives out there. Of course I shot as many of the raiders as I had arrows."

"My father's death would have meant your freedom," he pointed out.

"But not yours," she replied softly.

He nodded. "Fair enough. So, I suppose I have one last night with you as my slave girl."

She looked up to him. "You know how to get me back?"

"Of course," he answered. "First, I shall don my best attire."

Le'ell nodded. "You're a real man of action."

"Well," he started with a sigh, "I should look my best when I meet with your queen."

Her mouth fell open and she managed, "Oh, you can't be serious."

"I am."

"Chail, my people will take you as… You can't do this! Just get me out of here and let me go back to Zondae on my own!"

"There's more at stake here, Le'ell, and we both know it."

She looked away. "I can't believe I'm hearing this. You're going to end up on the receiving end of what I did."

"Not as *your* man," he pointed out.

Her eyes darted back to him.

"You see," he continued, "if I go into your castle as your property, no one will question you taking me there, will they?"

Her disbelieving look spoke for her, but still she said, "Chail most of the men at Zondae were born there. Others had months of conditioning before they were purchased. They are also not the stature of *any* man I've seen here at Enulam. How am I supposed to explain *you?*"

He wiped his mouth with his napkin and assured, "You'll figure it out. Let's get to bed. We have a long day ahead of us and we'll need to rest up for it."

Le'ell watched him as he stood and she folded her arms, countering, "The sun's not down yet and you aren't going to just let me go to sleep tonight, anyway."

"That's why we have to go to bed now so we'll have plenty of time to rest," he informed as he took her arm and pulled from her chair and her toward the bed.

CHAPTER 8

The Abtont Forest would prove to be a sultry place the next morning and the early morning sun was not quite so comfortable in such humid air. Still, activity at Enulam Castle would not be thwarted and humans and horses would go to and fro on their daily tasks. As the sun rose fully, a heavy patrol of forty charged out of the West gate, thundering hooves still kicking up a cloud of dust despite the damp air.

Two more riders paced their animals steadily toward this gate, riding in silence. Saddlebags were heavy with supplies, but the horses seemed not to notice. Prince Chail, attired in a new, white swordsman's shirt and black riding trousers, looked like a man who had not a care on the world. He loosely held the reins in one hand as he stared out of the open gate, seeming to ignore the four guards who stepped into his path. Riding at his side and wearing one of the Prince's light mantles over her slave girl's attire, Le'ell was not so care free. She shifted nervous eyes from the advancing guards to the Prince, then back as she tightly held the reins of her horse.

Chail pulled on his reins, stopping his horse as he turned his eyes down to the senior guard, Le'ell stopping beside him.

The guard shifted his gaze from the Prince to Le'ell and back, asking, "Good morning, Prince Chail."

"Morning," the Prince responded. "Promises to be a hot one."

"That it does," the guard confirmed, glancing at Le'ell again. "Going for an outing, I see."

Chail nodded. "Going to visit a swimming hole I know of on a creek that feeds the Spagnah River. I figure I have a day to myself before the King assigns me a lifetime of duties."

The guard nodded. "So, I see you are taking your woman on this swim with you."

"You would have me swim alone?" the Prince countered.

With a laugh, the guard conceded, "No, I wouldn't. Wouldn't think of it. Still, my orders are that only heavy patrols leave the castle until further notice. I concur, especially considering the attack."

"Hence I'm staying close to the castle," the Prince informed. "Just far enough away for a little privacy, just close enough for security."

The guard glanced at Le'ell again. "May I ask where this swimming hole is?"

Le'ell turned and jerked one of the saddle bags open, then the other, then looked ahead and declared, "Oh, dear."

Chail and the guards looked to her.

Le'ell looked to the Prince with the eyes of someone who expected a good scolding. "I forgot to pack the goblets. My Lord I'm sorry. I'm so sorry. Shall I go back for them?"

The Prince's lips tightened and he drew a hard breath as he just stared at her.

Looking down at her hands, Le'ell whimpered, "Forgive me, my Lord. I know you wanted to be there early. I can go back for them. I won't be long, I promise."

Chail looked down to the guard and shook his head, then asked, "Did you at least remember the blanket?"

"I did, my Lord. I wrapped the wine bottles in it."

The guard looked to Le'ell, then back to the Prince. "Seems like two less things to carry. I always drink right from the bottle, myself."

The Prince seemed to reluctantly nod, then glanced at Le'ell once more, still looking a little irritated. "I suppose."

Another guard said, "I don't see you making much time for a swim and wine, anyway, my Prince. I wouldn't."

All of the guards laughed softly.

Finally, Chail smiled. "Very true." He looked to Le'ell and ordered, "Let's not waste any more of my time." As he kicked his horse forward, he nodded to the senior guard and informed, "See you in a few hours."

They were some distance down the road toward the river when Chail finally said, "You're good."

Le'ell just smiled.

Nearing the river, Le'ell realized they had not spoken much during the three hour journey, not at all almost the last hour. She looked to him frequently, noticing he was deep in thought. Releasing a sigh, she finally informed, "You still have time to turn back."

He turned his eyes to her and nodded, confirming, "I know."

"We aren't quite at the river," she went on. "There's been plenty of time for something to happen to me. You could always tell them I was drug under and drown."

"And the attacks on both sides would continue," he informed, "until your kingdom and mine finally go to war."

"What are you hoping to accomplish?" she questioned. "You are going to be taken prisoner by my people and they'll do Goddess knows what to you."

He glanced at her. "Even in your company?"

She sighed again. "It isn't going to be that easy. They aren't going to assume that you belong to me just because you arrive with me. Most of the guards and soldiers know almost all of the men around the castle so they'll know you as an outsider on sight, especially since there are no men at Zondae anywhere near as big as you."

"How is that a disadvantage?" he asked, smiling.

Le'ell rolled her eyes, shaking her head as she mumbled, "You are such a man."

"I know," he sighed. A few paces later he stopped his horse, staring ahead.

Le'ell glanced at him, then looked where he looked and also stopped.

They were near the river flood plain where the forest opened up into a huge grassy field. The river was just beyond and they could already hear the water running along with the hiss of the wind in the tall grass. The sun shown brightly on the field and waves rippled through the grass. Right in front of them was a mountainous form lying in the tall grass of the field. Spikes were folded to its body and its eyes were closed tightly against the sunlight.

Her eyes locked on the beast before them, Le'ell asked in a low voice, "Do you believe me now?"

Hesitantly, the Prince nodded.

They stared at the drakenien for long moments.

"We should probably not wake him," she suggested.

"Then quit talking," he ordered. "Let's see if we can get behind him."

"Shouldn't we just find another trail?"

"Le'ell, we need to try and make it to Zondae before nightfall. Another route could put us hours behind."

"I'd rather be late than eaten by that thing."

"Just relax. If we keep our distance and stay quiet then we should be able to get by him without waking him." He kicked his horse forward, veering away from the drakenien's head.

Le'ell reluctantly followed, keeping her eyes intently on the gigantic beast.

The grass and hoof-steps were alarmingly loud to the two riders, who were more on edge than their horses. The horses, sensing no danger from the sleeping drakenien, were much more relaxed than their human riders. The beast did not even stir as they circled wide around him.

Nearly to the water's edge, they seemed clear, but yet another threat awaited them, one they could not see until they were almost on top of it.

The serpent was over a man's height long and while not venomous, wanted the horse to think it was. Assuming a strike posture that vipers would, it hissed and struck at the horse's leg, trying to appear as threatening as possible.

Chail's horse reared up and whinnied loudly, backing into Le'ell's and sending it toward panic as well.

"Whoa!" Le'ell shouted as she was almost bucked off. She barely stayed in the saddle, trying not to pull too hard on the reigns. When her horse came back down she was slammed forward against its neck and almost fell off again, but managed to remain mounted.

Chail was having similar woes with his horse, which was still panicked after seeing the snake so close. "Easy," the Prince commanded as his agitated horse danced backward. "Easy. It's gone."

As their horses calmed, Chail and Le'ell looked back at the drakenien.

The commotion had awakened him and he slowly lifted his head and looked behind him, sluggishly looking toward them.

"This isn't good," Le'ell observed.

"Up river," Chail ordered.

They turned their horses and fled.

Seeing them run, the drakenien lumbered to his feet and turned in pursuit.

"This was a *wonderful* idea, Chail," Le'ell spat. "What now?"

He glanced behind him. "He's gaining. Drakenien's are faster than horses in the open. We'll have to find a path in the forest where we can lose him."

"And hope he doesn't overtake us when we do," she retorted.

With the drakenien only about fifty paces behind, the horses abruptly stopped.

Chail and Le'ell exchanged terrified looks. Despite their efforts, the horses would not move and were unusually calm.

The Prince swung down from his horse and pulled Le'ell from hers, hoping to make it to the trees before the drakenien overtook them.

Seeing them running toward the trees, the drakenien roared and veered toward them, then he stopped, his spikes flaring out as he stared beyond them.

Le'ell pulled back against the Prince, ordering, "Chail, stop running! Stop!"

He turned toward her, shouting, "Are you insane? He...." Seeing the drakenien not moving, he pulled Le'ell to him and tightly held onto her.

Still glaring beyond them, the drakenien bared his teeth and growled.

Chail finally heard the footsteps and looked over his shoulder, freezing where he stood as his wide eyes found the approaching unicorn.

Holding her head low and her ears flat against her head, the snow white unicorn had her eyes intensely locked on the drakenien and was slowly stalking toward him. Her horn was enveloped in an emerald glow which was bright even against the light of the sun. A similar glow could be seen around her brown eyes.

Chail seized the back of Le'ell's hair and forcibly turned her head.

Protesting at first, Le'ell gasped as she saw the little unicorn, finding herself unable to move. Never had she been so awestruck, even at the sight of the dragons days before.

Fearlessly approaching the huge predator, the unicorn's eyes bored into him.

Before two unbelieving human witnesses, the drakenien began to back away. He barked a quick roar, then the spikes on his body folded against him and he turned and loped back down river.

As Chail looked back to the unicorn, he briefly got the image of a huge black dragon in his mind. Blinking, he shook his head to clear his wits.

Le'ell turned in Chail's arms, her eyes on the unicorn. She could not speak or take her gaze from the beautiful creature before her. She could barely breathe. Tears began to blur her vision and she leaned her head into the Prince's chest.

When the drakenien was safely down river and out of sight, the unicorn turned her attention to Chail and Le'ell, the emerald glow around her horn and eyes fading until it was gone. Her white and ivory horn had ribbons of gold within the spirals, and her brown eyes looked fearlessly upon the humans whose lives she had just saved. Turning fully, she casually approached, looking them over as if to be sure they were unharmed.

Finally managing to breathe, Le'ell whispered, "She is so beautiful."

The unicorn leaned her head and blinked. She seemed to understand, but also seemed puzzled. Distracted by something near the river, she turned her head and whickered, making a higher pitched sound than a horse would.

Chail looked, his breath catching as he saw the horses approaching, following another unicorn! This one was much bigger than the first, as big as the horses and a shiny red-brown color with a glossy black mane and tail and beard. Copper colored ribbons gleamed from within his black and dark red horn, his eyes locked on the white unicorn almost possessively.

The white unicorn whinnied something at or to the bay, then looked back to Le'ell and barked a quick whinny to her.

"She's trying to talk to me," Le'ell breathed.

The bay reached them and looked them over, then looked to the white unicorn and snorted.

She turned and whickered back, then watched the bigger unicorn pace toward the trees. Looking back to Chail and Le'ell in turn, she whickered again, then reared up and whinnied loudly before launching herself into a fast gallop around them to take the big bay's side.

Chail and Le'ell watched them disappear into the forest, just staring at the place where they had disappeared for some time.

Slipping her arms around Chail, Le'ell rested her head on his shoulder, unable to keep the tears from streaming from her eyes, unwilling to.

Gently, he stroked her hair and held her more tightly to him. "You've always wanted to see that, haven't you," he asked softly.

She nodded, admitting, "Since I was a little girl."

"White unicorn," he said absently. "Your black dragon. Bodies in pieces."

Le'ell looked up to him. "The words of that old woman."

They both felt a chill.

"Come on," he prodded, turning with her toward the horses. "If she's right, we have a war to stop."

Hours later found them approaching the field where Le'ell had found the Grawrdoxen, witnessed the dragon's hunt and the one-sided battle with the dragon and the drakenien. The carcass of the old

Grawrdox, the half that had not been eaten, was still lying in the field. Vultures, wild dogs and long tailed tree cats shared the scavenger's bounty, clearly not bothered by the already putrid odor it was giving off.

"So this is the fellow that was killed by that black dragon," the Prince guessed.

Le'ell nodded, still preoccupied with her encounter with the unicorns.

"Smells pleasant," he observed. "I'm guessing it probably smelled a little better a couple of days ago."

She nodded again.

"I really didn't doubt what you were telling me yesterday," he assured, "but seeing this puts your story in a whole new light."

Once again, she nodded, still staring blankly ahead.

He looked to her, then admitted, "I've been with every woman at Enulam at least twice since we met. Some of the men, too."

Le'ell nodded yet again, then turned a disgusted look on him and barked, "What?"

He smiled. "I just wanted to see if you were paying attention."

She sighed and shook her head, looking forward again. "Sick bastard."

"How close are we to your castle?" he asked.

"About three more hours," she answered. "If we quicken our pace we can make it in two, assuming we don't run into any patrols along the way."

"And if we do?"

She glanced down. "I'd rather not think about it."

"I don't think it will be as bad as all that."

Le'ell was silent for many paces, then said, "I so wish you would turn around and go back to Enulam."

He stared at her for a few paces more, then replied, "And yet you are glad to have me at your side."

She would not look his way, instead turning away from him as she complained, "Why can't we just be together? What is so important that our kingdoms can't put their differences aside?"

"Many generations of mistrust," was his answer. "I've heard many horrible stories about Zondae and you have no doubt heard similar stories about Enulam."

"The stories I heard about your people simply aren't true," Le'ell informed straightly. "I've been brought up to believe you are all mindless barbarians bent on the rape and murder of every Zondaen you see. It just isn't true. I don't think I was mistreated at your castle."

"You were whipped in the cottage," he reminded. "Then there was the run in with those guards yesterday."

"All of those men paid for their deeds, some by your hands and some by that big blacksmith." She finally turned to Chail. "Where did you find him, anyway? Is he part ogre or something of the like?"

The Prince smiled. "He may just be part ogre. He's a good man, though."

Le'ell nodded. "He doesn't look like one who would be very compassionate, and yet he is." A hint of tenderness touched her eyes. "Just like you."

Chail had to look away from her.

"That was my experience with many of the men I met there," she went on. "Do you think we were told those stories to make certain our generation carried on this foolish standoff?"

The Prince just shrugged. "I don't know. I think there are those who really believe the stories. I'm sure there are many Zondaens who believe we *are* just mindless barbarians."

Le'ell turned her eyes forward, staring down the road. "Some of what I heard you do to women who try to escape would lead me to believe so."

He gave her a sidelong glance. "What did you hear?"

She glanced back. "Hanging a woman by the wrists until she was dead, having a daughter whip her mother to death, leaving one in the stables for a month with nothing but straw to eat and making her pull a plow..." She finally looked to him. "Shall I continue?" She raised her brow as she saw him snickering. "You think such mistreatment is funny?"

"No," he laughed. "What's funny is how you swallowed Teyli's stories so easily."

Le'ell's eyes narrowed. "What are you saying?"

Shaking his head, he answered, "She tells all of the new girls those stories. It keeps them from thinking about escape so soon."

"Stories?" Le'ell barked.

"Think about it. If you had made such an investment in a woman and she tried to run, why would you torture her to death? Why would you abuse her to the point where she would be useless to you?"

"As punishment," Le'ell informed.

The Prince shook his head. "There are far more effective means of punishment."

"Like your guards whipping a woman who tries to escape?"

"The guards usually don't," he corrected. "If a woman is caught then she is handed over to someone of rank, myself, my father, a garrison captain… Someone like that. Punishment is usually carried out by a higher ranking woman of the castle."

Le'ell blinked. "So, the woman who tries to escape is whipped by another woman?"

Chail glanced at her again. "Not quite. She's assigned a heavy regiment of duties for a given number of days and watched more closely. Keep her too busy to plan and she doesn't have time to plot another escape. At the end of the day she collapses from exhaustion. To be perfectly honest about the cottage, its main purpose is to work with leather and armor. Gartner and his helpers spend many an hour in there every day."

"And the two guards who meant to beat that girl and me yesterday?"

"Will answer to the King," he informed straightly. "It isn't allowed. They're lucky my father didn't turn Gartner loose on them right there. It seems to me they were just trying to assert themselves for one reason or another."

She nodded. "Compensating for something."

"Exactly," he confirmed.

"You come from an odd place," she observed.

He turned his eyes to her. "Am I heading for an odder one?"

She smiled ever so slightly. "You just might be."

He smiled back, then his attention darted forward, his eyes narrowing as he saw three riders emerge from the trees on the other side of the clearing.

They were Zondaen and appeared to be fleeing as two of them kept looking behind them. One on the left flank appeared to be wounded but also appeared to be too frightened by something to notice.

Not waiting to see the threat, Chail pulled the axe he had won in battle the day before from its place behind him and gripped it near the end of its handle, then he drew his sword and tossed it to Le'ell, hilt first.

She caught the heavy sword perfectly, then turned bewildered eyes to him and demanded, "What are you doing?"

He kicked his horse's flanks and yelled, "Yah!" as it sprang forward. He was charging right for the fleeing Zondaens!

Le'ell pursued, ordering, "Chail, stop! What are you doing?"

Seeing him rapidly approach, the Zondaen soldiers veered away and right behind them appeared five raiders clad the same as they had faced the day before.

The Prince closed too fast for the first of them to affectively react and he swung the big axe with killing force, striking the armored breastplate of the raider and sinking the blade deep into his chest. As the raider rolled backward from his horse, Chail lost his grip on the axe and he allowed it to tumble to the ground with his enemy. Pulling on the reins, he slowed his horse and jumped off as the other four raiders charged by.

Still pursuing him, Le'ell watched him wrench the axe from the raider's body and turn to engage two others as they turned on him. Looking up, she noticed the other Zondaens had stopped their horses and were turning to attack! With her own battle cry, Le'ell charged to the defense of her Prince. One of the raiders turned to engage her, leaving the other to fend for himself.

This would prove to be costly.

Feeling safe on his horse, the raider facing Chail charged toward him, greatly underestimating how clever his enemy was.

Waiting for his opponent to near him, the Prince instead swung his axe at the horse's face, causing it to shy away and hesitate, then he spun his whole body around with the swing of the axe, bringing it full circle and down into the raider's thigh. When the raider yelled and reached for the axe, Chail pulled him from his horse, slamming him onto the ground to finish him off.

Still not used to the Prince's heavier sword, Le'ell found herself having a bull of a time fending off her enemy. Her swings at him were sluggish, and while her parries were skilful, the weight of the sword and constant corrections to her horse were quickly wearing her down. One good swing knocked his weapon away, then he arched his back and groaned, throwing his head back, and he fell from his horse, the Prince's axe still firmly imbedded in his back.

Chail looked to the Zondaen soldiers as the last of the raiders fell to one's blade, then turned his eyes to Le'ell and nodded to her. "Nice bit of swordplay."

Still breathing heavy, she turned the sword over and handed it back to him. "I'll be so glad to have my own blade back in my hand. That thing is going to tear my shoulder off!"

He smiled at her as he sheathed his weapon, then wrenched the axe from the body of his last vanquished foe. "I remember how well you can use that blade. I can't say I would want to be on the receiving end of it when you wield it in anger."

She leaned down on her saddle horn, smiling as she informed, "Then you'd best stay on my good side."

"Not to worry," he assured. Looking behind her, he noticed the other Zondaen riders approaching, their weapons still in their hands and their eyes locked on him. "We have company."

Without looking at them, Le'ell ordered in a low voice, "Say nothing and do exactly as I tell you."

He nodded, feeling absolute trust and faith in her.

Le'ell turned to them and raised her chin, greeting, "Good morning."

They all stopped their horses only a few paces away, astonishment on all their faces and one declaring, "Princess Le'ell!"

"We heard you had been captured," another reported. This one had long black hair restrained behind her. Her armor was polished and decorated with brass and white fur.

Le'ell smiled. "I'm sure you heard a great many things." She glanced down at one of the fallen raiders. "I'm also sure you've seen the truth by now."

The black haired warrior looked down at the raider and nodded. "Yes we have. Enulam scouts."

Shaking her head, Le'ell released an obvious sigh of impatience and asked, "Do they really look like men from Enulam?"

"They do," the soldier confirmed.

Le'ell looked to Chail and ordered, "Remove his helmet. Show her."

He threw the axe down and did as she said, then turned the body over. The face was bearded—and human. Slowly, he raised his brow and turned his eyes to her.

"Check the others," she commanded. "See if we find what we did last time."

Chail nodded to her and went about the task.

"What are you looking for," the brown haired Zondaen warrior asked.

"What you found last time?" the commander questioned. "What are you talking about? Found when?"

Coolly turning her eyes to the elaborately armored black haired woman, Le'ell reported, "We engaged part of a garrison of these raiders yesterday. They aren't all human."

All of the warriors exchanged glances, then two turned their eyes to Chail as he strode past to check the two they had killed.

Le'ell watched him check the last of the raiders, then turned her eyes back to the commander as he started back toward them. "Most of the raiders we killed yesterday were forest trolls or gnomes. Only a few were men."

"Then you know about the patrols we found," the brown haired warrior guessed.

"My last patrol found one of them," she informed.

The commander shook her head. "I don't understand. You were reported missing two days ago. Now we find you with an Enulam soldier and you bring tails of a battle you fought against some raiders who are not from Enulam—"

"I will tell you what you need to know," Le'ell interrupted, "*when* you need to know it. Is that clear?"

Raising her chin, the commander glanced at the brown haired warrior, then turned her eyes back to Le'ell and complied, "I understand, Highness."

Le'ell looked behind her as Chail approached and harshly barked, "Report."

He shook his head. "Human. Same armor and weapons the trolls had, but they're human."

Le'ell's eyes narrowed. "That doesn't make sense."

"Unless," Chail added, "they were meant to be found on this side of the border."

Glancing at the perplexed commander, Le'ell guessed, "So Zondae would think they are from Enulam."

He nodded. "Convince at least one side and you have your war."

She considered, then ordered, "Get on your horse. We have to get to Zondae."

Nodding to her again, he strode to his horse and took the reins.

The commander shook her head and said straightly, "Your Highness, forgive my forwardness but this just—"

"Don't call her that out here," Chail ordered, swinging up onto his horse.

The black haired warrior shot a glare at him. "Did you just speak to me without permission?"

He looked calmly to her. "If there is an archer hidden in the forest, you just have made her a target. If more attack, she'll be the first to die."

Le'ell's lips parted slightly and she just stared at him.

"You need to watch that mouth of yours," the commander spat. "You do not give orders here, yob, do you understand me?"

"I do give orders here," Le'ell informed through bared teeth, "and you may consider that order from me. Where is the rest of your patrol?

The commander stiffened, then replied, "I sent them toward the castle to split the enemy forces."

Nodding, Le'ell said, "Very well. You will take the lead and escort us home."

Chail did not expect to be welcomed to Zondae with open arms, and he wasn't.

As they rode through the gates of the fortress city, activity all around seemed to just stop and people dropped what they were doing to stare at the huge man who rode in at the Princess' side.

Looking around him, Chail realized that this kingdom was not so unlike his own, but for the reversal of the roles of men and women. Most of the women he saw were tall and well muscled, clearly warriors. All of the men he saw were much smaller than most any man he had ever seen at Enulam. On average they were a head height shorter than the women and all appeared to have very lean, slender builds. Their hair was kept short or restrained behind their heads if long and they were dressed in simple clothing that looked functional and comfortable. Men in different areas seemed to be wearing slightly different colors, some with green shirts, some yellow, some red. Many just wore white.

"I didn't realize there was going to be a dress code," he murmured.

Le'ell smiled slightly. "Feeling a little out of place?"

"A bit," he confirmed.

"Then perhaps you should have turned around at the river."

"And miss seeing your home? I wouldn't think of it. Do you have a plan or am I going to have to fight my way out of here?"

"Just stay close to me," she ordered. "I won't let anyone hurt you, my little yob."

"What's a yob, anyway?" he asked.

"You," was her answer.

"Someone from Enulam?" he guessed.

She shook her head. "A male. Men here are called yobs, much the way your people call women vixens or wenches."

He raised his brow. "I'm insulted."

"Who cares?" she snarled. "Get used to it while you're here, and make it a point not to call me vixen or wench or whatever else you call women where you're from."

"Done," he confirmed. "What should I call you?"

She shot him a sidelong glance and a slight smile. "That depends on how much time you intend to spend in the dungeon."

"What if I want to spend none there?"

"Then you address me as Lady Le'ell or Mistress Le'ell."

"Is there a difference?"

"You will refer to me as Lady Le'ell if I don't own you, Mistress Le'ell if I do."

He glanced at her. "Do you own me?"

"I can. We wouldn't want anyone else laying claim to you."

"They already know I'm from Enulam," he pointed out.

"Yeah," she sighed. "I'm working on that. It would have been much easier if you had just turned back at the river."

"We could just be honest with them, tell them I'm from Enulam on a diplomatic mission. What's the worst that could happen?"

"Considering the feelings toward your people and the circumstances, you could be hanged."

He nodded. "I'm sure we don't want that."

A number of Zondaen warriors approached from all sides, three of them with bows
trained on Chail.

Le'ell looked to them and ordered, "Put those down. He's here with me."

They glanced at each other and complied.

Swinging down from her horse, Le'ell looked to Chail and ordered, "Give your reins to that yob and come with me."

He dismounted and saw a small man with a yellow shirt standing two paces away, staring up at him with wide eyes. This man was not quite as tall as Le'ell was at the chin and he was as thin built as most of the others. This was amazing to Chail as the smallest man he knew was Ralk, one of his father's advisors, and even Ralk would tower over this small fellow. Still, he did not stare at the little man long and threw his reins to him, then turned to follow Le'ell the rest of the way to the palace.

She seemed to ignore him as she strode toward a thick timber door that seemed to be the only way into the palace on this side.

Chail was careful to follow her closely *and* remain behind her. Out of the corners of his eyes he saw many of the Zondae woman and an equal number of men gathering to have a look at him. Even as tall and well muscled as the Zondaen women were, he felt like something of a giant in this place. The gathering crowd was also looking at Le'ell, and he finally noticed the cloak he had given her was opening at the front as she moved, revealing her Enulam slave's attire beneath. He momentarily thought about alerting her, but decided that would be a bit too obvious.

As Le'ell grasped the brass handle that would open the door, a woman's voice from behind taunted, "I see you're home, little sister." Hearing the voice, her grip on the handle hardened until her knuckles were white. She just stared ahead for a time, her lips tightening and pulling away from her teeth ever so slightly.

Chail turned to see a tall, black haired woman approaching. She looked to be a few seasons older than Le'ell, more experience in her blue eyes and a slight smile curling her mouth. More slinking than striding, her eyes were locked on Le'ell in a vengeful stare. As she neared, Chail noticed that she was very well muscled for a woman, heavier built than Le'ell and perhaps half a hand width taller. This was a formidable looking woman and a very attractive one as well. Dressed in tight fitting black leather that was low cut at the front and sleeveless, her curves caught his eye and would not let go for a time. Her black riding boots stopped near her knees and ended in white fur. Her thighs were bare from her knees almost to her hips, well muscled and a little pale from winter, though they clearly had been dark once.

This tall woman gave Chail but a glance as she strode past him, then she stopped behind Le'ell with her arms folded and leaned her head. "We've been worried sick about you. You missed your bedtime story and Ama and I couldn't even tuck you in last night."

Slowly, Le'ell turned her head and snarled, "Not now, Le'sesh."

The black haired woman's lips pouted. "You didn't miss me, little sister?"

Turning fully, Le'ell strode the last two steps toward her and glared into her eyes, warning, "I am in no mood for you, so if you don't want to be gutted and left for the vultures you will leave me alone!"

"Such a temper," Le'sesh said as if talking to a child. "Do we need a nap?"

Le'ell's hands clenched into tight fists. "I'll give you a nap."

Le'sesh laughed at her. "Oh, you and your girlish little threats. How I missed you around the castle the last couple of days."

"I didn't miss you," Le'ell growled, turning and yanking the door open. "Come on, Chail. I don't like the smell here suddenly."

"I told Ama that you're home," Le'sesh informed.

Le'ell froze.

"She's waiting for you in her study," the black haired woman continued. "You'd better go on up and try to explain yourself." She turned and looked Chail over. "I trust you have an interesting tale to tell."

Le'ell huffed a breath and stormed into the castle.

Chail followed, glancing behind him at the tall Zondaen who walked away and he continued to watch her until the door closed. He raised his brow and turned back to Le'ell as they reached a huge set of stone stairs, saying, "You never told me you had a sister."

Le'ell spun around and slammed her finger into his chest, shouting, "She is *not* my sister! She's my mother's other daughter!"

Raising his hands before him, he offered, "Sorry."

She wheeled back and stormed up the steps.

Following as closely as he dared, Chail asked, "Have you figured out what you are going to say?"

"Just shut up," she snarled. "You don't need to be caught talking to me so casually."

He nodded and followed in silence until they reached the top, where a huge open oval opened up with five corridors at about equal intervals radiated out like spokes on a wagon wheel.

Le'ell turned abruptly to the left stormed down one, then looked ahead and froze.

Pa'lesh stood five paces down the corridor with her arms folded, glaring at Le'ell. She still wore her field armor and looked like she had not bathed or rested for some time. Looking up from Le'ell to Chail, her eyes narrowed and she clearly tensed up, almost expecting something to happen.

Chail remained calm and as unthreatening as he could. Not wanting to even hint at a challenging stance, he turned his eyes away from Pa'lesh.

Swallowing hard, Le'ell slowly started forward again. She was more nervous now than all of her time at Enulam and could not help that her face betrayed this. As she neared, Pa'lesh seemed to grow angrier and when the Field Captain unfolded her arms Le'ell stopped.

Closing the remaining distance with only three strides, Pa'lesh seized Le'ell's arms and pulled her face to face appearing to pick her up to eye level as she shouted, "What were you thinking? Are you completely out of your mind?"

Unable to respond, Le'ell looked away from her, her mouth quivering horribly.

Pa'lesh shook her violently. "I told you to stay with the patrol! You could have been killed out there!"

"But I wasn't," Le'ell retorted. She was clearly trying not to cry.

Chail's lips tightened and he felt his patience quickly draining away.

Pushing Le'ell away, Pa'lesh glared at her for long seconds, then grabbed the cloak and hissed, "I've been sent to make sure you get to Queen Le'errin's study without getting lost again. You will not give me any more trouble or I *will* put you over my knee."

"Quit treating me like a child," Le'ell cried.

Pa'lesh grabbed her arm, digging her fingers into her flesh as she jerked her along and growled, "Just consider yourself lucky the Queen wants you in one piece."

"Ow!" Le'ell protested. "Stop! That hurts!"

Patience was gone.

Chail strode forward and seized Pa'lesh's arm, spinning her around and bending down so that their noses nearly touched.

Losing her grip on Le'ell, Pa'lesh stared up into the Prince's eyes with a mix of terror and rage, finding herself unable to respond as quickly as she would have liked.

Glaring down at the Captain, Chail snarled, "If you touch her again I'll tear this arm right off of you." When she tried to pull away, he jerked her back, just glaring at her for long seconds.

Her second attempt to free herself was successful and she backed away, still staring up at him with wide eyes. When he stood fully erect, towering over her, Pa'lesh's hand found the hilt of her sword and her retreat stopped.

Chail strode forward, closing the short distance and he growled, "Pull it! Let that blade taste air and see what happens!"

Pa'lesh's neck grew taut and she backed away further. He was half a pace away and looming over her, his size and power giving her such pause that she had never experienced. Finally mustering her wits, she called, "Guards!"

Le'ell took his arm from behind and pulled him away, then spun him around and slapped him as hard as she could and snapped his head around as she shouted, "Who told you to touch her? You were not ordered to intervene, now back away!"

Chail rubbed his stinging cheek and glared down at her, then turned his predator's eyes on Pa'lesh once again. Seeing quickly through the cloud of anger, he realized that Le'ell had done what she had done more for his benefit than hers. He looked back down at her, then away and softly offered, "Forgive me. I thought she might cause you harm."

Raising a hand to gently stroke his cheek, Le'ell comforted, "It is all right. Just remember that when I need your help I will tell you."

He nodded, not looking at her.

Turning back to Pa'lesh as the guards rushed forward, Le'ell folded her arms and informed, "He's very protective. Consider yourself fortunate you didn't really hurt me or I may not have called him off."

The Captain's eyes shifted from Chail to Le'ell, then to the four approaching guards and she ordered, "Escort Princess Le'ell to the

Queen's study and three of you stay with me so that this yob can be dealt with."

"No need, Pa'lesh," came an older version of Le'ell's voice. "I saw everything."

They turned, and Chail raised his chin as his gaze fell upon the woman who approached.

This was Le'ell in her mid forties, long auburn hair streaked with silver, almost the same face, even how she walked was the same. Her body was heavier, clearly from bearing children, her hips a little wider, but she still was a formidable woman. As she neared, her eyes, almost identical in shape and color to Le'ell's, were locked on Chail, staring up at him with the glare of a protective mother. She wore no armor, rather she was still in a bathrobe that was tightly tied at her waist. Gray riding trousers covered her legs and black boots that were topped with white fur spotted with the gray and black marks of its former owner clopped loudly on the floor as she strode forward.

She just stared up at him for many tense seconds, then she looked to Le'ell and seemed near tears as she reached to her and pulled her into her arms, embracing her as tightly as she could.

Le'ell hugged her back, her face buried in the Queen's neck.

Stroking her daughter's hair, Queen Le'errin whispered, "I was so worried about you my Little Dragon."

"I'm sorry, Ama," Le'ell whimpered back. In her mother's embrace, Le'ell seemed more like a little girl than the formidable and quick tempered warrior Chail had come to know.

Many moments passed, and as the Queen's hand stroked down Le'ell's back, the Princess winced from the whelps that were still tender. Responding instantly to her daughter's pain, Queen Le'errin pushed her away, concern in her eyes as she looked into Le'ell's face, then she tore the cloak open, slowly shaking her head as she saw the slaves attire she wore. Le'errin took Le'ell's arm and forcibly turned her, pulling the cloak from her back and wincing as she saw the whelps left from the whip.

Looking back at the Queen, Le'ell quickly informed, "Ama, you don't understand."

"I understand plenty," Le'errin hissed, then turned to Pa'lesh and ordered, "Bring him."

"Ama, wait," the Princess begged. "This isn't what it appears."

"We'll talk in a moment," Queen Le'errin comforted, taking Le'ell under her arm and leading her toward her study.

Chail watched them walk away, feeling a certain warmth within him at the Zondaen Queen's tenderness toward her daughter. When

Pa'lesh approached and reached toward him he did not look at her, he simply warned, "Mistress Le'ell is not here to call me off you."

Pa'lesh froze, staring up at him.

Slowly, he turned his eyes down to the Field Captain.

She backed away a step, then extended her hand toward the study.

One of Chail's eyebrows cocked up and he finally strode down the corridor. Glancing around, he noticed that the inside of Zondae Castle was not so unlike Enulam Castle. One not intimately familiar with either could barely have told them apart.

Chail entered the study to find Le'ell in her mother's embrace once again, and he almost smiled.

Pa'lesh and the guards filed in behind him, taking their positions around him and keeping a vigilant watch on him.

Queen Le'errin pulled away and framed Le'ell's face with her hands, ordering, "Sit down, Little Dragon."

Le'ell shook her head, protesting, "Ama, you don't—"

"Sit!" Le'errin commanded in a louder voice.

Her eyes told Chail that she had nearly lost hope when she looked to him. Her brow was arched high and her lips were parted ever so slightly. Finally, she sat in one of the two chairs that waited in front of the Queen's desk.

Le'errin turned and strode the short distance to him, folding her arms as she glared up at him.

Though she was the same size as Le'ell, an average man's height, she seemed much more intimidating and Chail glanced away from her.

Many long, tense seconds slowly crept by.

The Queen drew a breath, then finally spoke. "Le'ell will no doubt tell me some fanciful tale of what happened out there, how those marks got on her, how she ended up in the attire of a slave girl of Enulam and how she managed to bring you to Zondae, so I will hear it from you first, without coaching from her."

He looked to Princess Le'ell, who was half turned in her chair looking back. Apparently, she had not the time to formulate any kind of plan to deal with this situation and he could think of no way out himself.

"I'm waiting," the Queen impatiently said.

Chail looked down at her, then pointed to Le'ell and informed, "She told me not to talk."

"Chail!" Le'ell hissed through clenched teeth.

He looked to her and protested, "But you told me—"

"Now is not the time!" the Princess scolded.

Queen Le'errin half turned her head and ordered, "Quiet!" then she looked back to Chail and raised her brow.

He turned his eyes away again, loosing a deep breath, then finally asked, "May I speak with you privately?"

"No," was the Queen's answer.

He set his jaw, then looked back down at the Queen. "I know of the attacks against your patrols the last couple of days."

Le'errin nodded. "I'll bet you do."

Chail continued, "And Le'ell knows of similar attacks against Enulam patrols."

The Queen raised her chin, her eyes narrowing slightly.

"We were riding back from investigating one," the Prince went on, "and our patrol fell under attack. With Le'ell's sharp eye and steady bow we were able to thwart them and killed most of the raiders."

Le'errin nodded. "That doesn't tell me how she got those marks on her back."

Chail looked to the floor. "When she was first brought to Enulam... I just didn't get to her in time."

"So I am to believe that you went running to her rescue?" The Queen's tone was of complete disbelief.

"You'll believe what you will," he replied.

"He's telling you the truth," Le'ell interrupted.

Half turning her head again, Le'errin barked, "I told you to hush!"

"But it's true," she argued. "Ama, he even killed one of the men who beat me."

Chail's eyes snapped to her. He was hearing this for the first time.

Queen Le'errin looked back up at him, prodding, "Is that true?"

"I wasn't aware that I'd killed him," the Prince admitted, "but I suppose he got what he deserved." He turned his gaze back to the Queen and finished, "Such treatment of women at Enulam is expressly forbidden."

She nodded. "I'm sure it is. That would explain the marks on my daughter. Is there anything else you wish to tell me?"

He glanced at Le'ell. "What would you like to know?"

"A great many things," she answered. "In the meantime, why don't I have the guards take you to where you can rest? I'm sure you are weary from that long journey. Oh, and your sword."

He nodded, then slowly removed the sword from its sheath with his left hand and offered it to her, then he raised his brow and asked, "Dagger and sword breaker too?"

"If you don't mind," she said, taking the sword from him. It was clearly heavier than she expected it to be and she looked to Pa'lesh, asking, "Captain, would you take possession of these and see to his room?"

Pa'lesh took the weapons, then looked up at Chail and motioned to the door with her head.

Before turning to the door, Chail bowed to Queen Le'errin and offered, "Your Majesty," then strode out behind one of the guards.

As the door closed behind them, the Queen turned to Le'ell and leaned her head as she looked down at her once again. She no longer had the look of a distraught and relieved mother, rather a scolding parent.

Staring back, Le'ell drew her shoulders up and asked, "Are you going to let me explain?"

Queen Le'errin's lips tightened and she just shook her head. "You've lied to me so many times... I just don't know when to believe you anymore."

"I had my reasons for lying to you," Le'ell defended.

Le'errin shouted, "There is *never* a reason to lie to me!"

Le'ell stood and shouted back, "I wouldn't if you would quit treating me like a child all of the time!"

"And you wonder why I treat you so," the Queen drawled. "Tell me what happened, why you left the castle, how you got those marks on you, and how you returned with a warrior from Enulam following you! The truth this time!"

Turning her eyes down, the Princess found she could not answer.

"There was a time I could trust you," Le'errin said more softly. "What happened to that girl? Where has she gone?"

"She grew up," Le'ell answered. "Why can't you see that?"

The Queen walked around her desk. "You are no more grown up than you were when you were ten. Now tell me what secret are you guarding so closely?"

"You wouldn't understand."

"Wouldn't I? You act like I was your mother my whole life. Would it surprise you to learn I was nineteen once, myself?"

Le'ell just sat back down, staring at the floor.

"What happened to you out there?"

The Princess did not answer.

Le'errin loosed a sigh, then almost smiled as she informed, "You know, I once kept secrets from *my* mother."

Le'ell's eyes snapped to her.

"I did," she insisted. "Some she found out, some she didn't. But no matter what I kept from her she was always my mother and was always there for me, as I am for you." When Le'ell looked away from her,

Le'errin sat back in her chair, just staring at her for some time before asking, "Why won't you talk to me anymore?"

"What is there to talk about?" Le'ell asked back. "You're the Queen first and my mother second."

"Is this about the choice of succession again? We've been over that more times than I can remember."

"And still you don't listen to me. You never have."

"Ell, your sister is older and first born."

"So that makes her better?"

Le'errin released another hard breath. "She's also more mature than you—and much more responsible. When she goes on patrol she doesn't wander off and get herself captured by Enulam."

"She doesn't go on patrols at all," Le'ell pointed out. "She's too good to do anything with anyone beneath her—and she considers *everyone* beneath her. She uses that big yob of hers to intimidate people and blatantly breaks the law with him every day and you've done nothing about it."

This time it was the Queen who turned her eyes down as she softly admitted, "I know. He shouldn't be allowed to touch any woman without her consent. I'll speak to her about that."

Le'ell nodded. "I expect that to do about as much good as it did the last time. You let her get away with everything and you strangle me with restrictions, then you wonder why I want to get away from here." She turned her eyes to her mother, clearly angered by this situation. "In the short time I was at Enulam I never saw King Donwarr treat Chail that way. He always respected his word and listened to him. If someone broke the law they were punished no matter who they were."

Slowly, the Queen raised her eyes to Le'ell. "So, you're saying Chail's father listens to him better than I listen to you?"

"Yes he does," Le'ell spat. "He involves Chail in everything and gives him the freedom...." Her eyes widened and her mouth fell open as she realized she had been outmaneuvered yet again.

"So," the Queen started, folding her hands on her desk. "We have *Prince* Chail of Enulam in our company, do we? How interesting."

Le'ell covered her mouth, turning her eyes down.

Queen Le'errin raised her brow. "I can think of no one better to answer for what happened to you."

Infuriated, Le'ell stood and shouted, "He didn't do anything! He stopped the men who hurt me and killed one of them! Why won't you listen to me?"

"Don't raise your voice at me again," the Queen warned, her eyes narrow. "Now sit back down! Now!"

Le'ell complied, glaring back at her mother.

"Why is he here?" Queen Le'errin asked straightly.

"He tried to tell you," was Le'ell's answer. "You didn't listen to him any more than you ever listen to me."

"The attacks," the Queen answered for her. "I listened, but the Prince of Enulam did not come here himself to tell me they had been attacked too. Why did he come?"

"I don't know," Le'ell admitted softly. "I told him to turn back many times and he insisted on seeing me all the way here."

"Perhaps he wanted to protect you," Le'errin guessed.

Le'ell shrugged.

"Not many people are willing to challenge Pa'lesh," the Queen pointed out, "and I think that's the first time I've ever seen her actually back down from anyone."

"She didn't have her garrison behind her," Le'ell pointed out.

Queen Le'errin laughed under her breath. "I don't think that would have made a difference. Your Prince Chail is an army by himself."

Le'ell glanced at her, then turned her eyes back to the floor.

Le'errin stood and walked around the desk, moved the chair beside Le'ell's to face her and sat down, then took the Princess' hands and held them tightly. "Talk to me, Ell. Pretend I'm not your queen or mother and just talk to me."

Slowly, Le'ell turned her eyes to her mother's.

"I promise I will listen," the Queen insisted.

Tears rolling from her eyes, Le'ell slowly shook her head and whimpered, "That's all I ever wanted."

❦

Chail could not be sure how long he had been sitting in that dungeon cell. It felt like hours. The only thing he was certain of was that he was bored.

A wooden bed covered with hay and a blanket were the only remarkable features of the cell he was in. Two by three paces, it was small, cramped, damp, dark and just not where he wanted to be. Sitting on the wooden bed, he just leaned back against the wall with his arms folded and drifted in and out of sleep. Every time a cell door was opened or closed or a group of guards passed he would awake, then settle himself to fall asleep again. The smell was the worst part. He just could not get used to it. He had spent some time in the dungeons of Enulam, mostly for training and conditioning, but twice on his father's orders to be taught a lesson in his youth. The dungeons at

Zondae castle were very much like those, as was the boredom of the confinement there.

As he dozed off again, a gentle voice asked, "How are you doing in there?"

He looked to the barred window in the door, smiling as he saw Le'ell looking back at him. "I'm just gathering some much needed rest. How are things on the outside?"

"It's getting dark," she informed, then just stared at him for a long moment after.

He stood and walked to her, ducking down to see her in the door's window. "You have something on your mind, don't you?"

She slowly nodded.

"Like?" he prodded.

Le'ell turned her eyes down. "They... You're supposed to be questioned tomorrow."

"I see."

She turned her eyes back to his and he could see how she despaired inside.

"It will be okay," he assured.

"They mean to force answers from you," she informed, then shook her head. "I cannot bear the thought of what they intend to do."

"I'm a big boy," he said. "Besides, if they mean to whip me to get their answers, it's only fair, right? You got whipped at my castle."

Her lips tightened and she shook her head. "All the more reason I don't want you to endure that. Will you promise to cooperate as much as you can?"

Smiling slightly, he agreed, "For you I will. We don't want my torture to distress you any more than necessary."

She leaned toward him and hissed, "You're a bastard."

He leaned toward her and hissed back, "I know."

Le'ell finally smiled, then looked past him and asked, "Are you comfortable in there?"

"It's like paradise," he answered. "Care to join me?"

"I don't think so," she replied. There was a click near the latch and she declared, "Oops. I think the door came unlocked."

"You're going to get into more trouble," he pointed out.

She shrugged and pulled the door open. "At this point I don't think it matters."

CHAPTER 9

The morning sun would find Princess Le'ell still fast asleep, lying on her side with only a soft sheet to cover her. Her canopied bed had always been something of a sanctuary. The wood had been painted white many seasons ago and was chipped in places. Lacy covers draped to the floor and the white, pink and red satin and silk was in disarray as the room slowly illuminated. Larger than Prince Chail's room, Le'ell's had three wardrobes against one wall, a cluttered desk against the opposite wall, tapestries showing unicorns flanking the two windows. A big stuffed dragon occupied a plush white and red chair on the other side of the room from the bed. Thick rugs were on the floor on all sides of the bed. Sitting in the windows were carved and glass figurines, one window with dragons and the other with unicorns. This was a girl who liked her things.

As the sun crept into the room, she turned away from it, snuggling up against the huge form that was lying beside her.

Chail gently caressed her shoulder and she moaned a weary moan and stirred more, then finally opened her eyes and looked up at him.

He turned toward her, slipping his arm around her back to pull her closer to him.

She smiled and closed her eyes again, asking, "Do you know how many times I have wanted to awaken like this?"

"I'm hoping every day for about three seasons," was his reply.

She laughed under her breath and confirmed, "Something like that." Drawing a deep breath, she looked back to him and said, "I'm hungry. Are you hungry?"

He nodded. "I could use a meal, especially after last night."

She smiled. "Do you think we're in trouble?"

"You are," he assured.

She giggled. "I think you're in worse trouble than I am."

"I don't know about that. You seem to be in pretty deep with Queen Mother."

"We talked yesterday and some last night, so right now I don't think it's all that bad." She sighed. "I guess today you get to have your talk with her."

Chail considered, then, "Shouldn't they have come for me before now?"

Le'ell shrugged. "They usually like to start those things promptly at dawn. You should have been awakened before sunup." Her eyes widened and she declared, "Oh, Goddess! They'll look for you in the dungeon!" She pushed on him and ordered, "Get dressed! We've got to get you back!"

They were up and more or less dressed in a couple of moments, and as Chail sat on the edge of the bed pulling his boots on and Le'ell sat on the floor doing the same, someone knocked on the door. They looked to each other, then Le'ell stood and straightened her white swordswoman's shirt, smoothing it over her white trousers as she bade, "Come in."

A palace guard opened the door and stepped in, reporting, "Princess Le'ell, I've been sent to..." She trailed off as she looked up at Chail.

Le'ell nodded. "I found him. I just wanted to find out if he is willing to talk before the interrogation begins."

Hesitantly, the guard nodded. "I see. I should inform Her Majesty." She turned to leave.

"No!" Le'ell barked, feeling a little relieved when the guard stopped and turned. "I'll let her know. I'm supposed to go to her study this morning so that we can continue our discussion from last night, so I'll just bring him with me."

The guard nodded again. "I understand. Shall I escort the prisoner to—"

"Don't bother," the Princess interrupted. "I can handle him."

Her brow tensing, the guard looked to Chail and asked, "Are you sure I shouldn't leave some guards with you?"

Le'ell glanced at him and shook her head. "I'll be fine. I have him under control. Just tell the Guard Captain she does not have to search for him any longer."

The guard seemed confused and hesitantly informed, "Princess, we weren't searching for him. I was just sent to make certain you knew to go to the Queen's study this morning and get him something to eat."

Le'ell's brow arched. "She knows he's here?"

The guard nodded yet again. "Everyone knows he's here." Then she turned and left, shaking her head as she slowly closed the door.

Raising a hand to her eyes, the Princess shook her head and mumbled, "This is it. She's going to kill me. While you watch she's going to have me whipped to death and fed to the dogs."

Chail finally stood from the bed and approached her, wrapping his huge arms around her as he comforted, "If you ask me, last night was worth it."

"Shut up, Chail."

The heavy timber door to Queen Le'errin's office was closed. Experience had taught Le'ell that this was not a good sign. With Chail at her side, she slowly approached, then stopped in front of the door and drew a soothing breath. Glancing up at the Prince for a look of reassurance, which of course he gave her, she finally knocked on the door.

"Enter," came the order from within.

Hesitantly, she reached for the handle and turned it, pushing the door open and striding in.

The Queen was also dressed in a red swordswoman's shirt and sat at her desk looking over some parchments. Pa'lesh stood near the door wearing her field armor and sword. Her eyes were on the Prince and her arms were folded.

Le'ell stood in front of the Queen's desk for a moment, knowing she was being ignored. The Queen herself was clearly irritated and was making no secret of it. Still her daughter hesitantly greeted, "Good morning, Ama. You wanted to see me?"

"No," Queen Le'errin corrected. "Pa'lesh does. Go with her and leave him here. You are dismissed." She never looked up from her parchment.

Glancing up at Chail, Le'ell suggested, "I wouldn't want him to be in your way. Are you sure—"

"I said you are dismissed," the Queen repeated more loudly.

Le'ell nodded and looked up at the Prince, ordering, "You behave for her Majesty."

"I will," he confirmed.

She stroked his hand with the back of hers as she followed Pa'lesh out the door.

Le'errin looked to the door as her daughter left with her Field Captain and waited for it to close before she finally put the parchment down, then she turned her eyes to the Prince, just staring at him for a time.

Unsure what to do, he smiled at her.

Unexpectedly, she smiled back. "Did you enjoy your evening, Prince Chail?"

For the first time since arriving at Zondae, a surge of panic coursed through him. He suppressed it and nodded, answering, "Actually, I did. Thank you for asking."

In an instant her smile was gone and her eyes narrowed.

"It was Le'ell's idea," he defended.

"Sit down," she ordered.

He complied, the chair creaking under his weight.

She stared at him a moment longer, then asked, "What should we do with you now?"

He drew a deep breath, then replied, "I'm sure you have many questions."

"Very perceptive," she said with a nod. "I suppose you already know the first."

"You want to know what I do about the attacks against your patrols."

She nodded again, prodding, "Go on."

"It would help me to know what Le'ell has already told you," he suggested.

"I know it would," she confirmed sweetly, "but it would help me if you didn't already know that. Now just start from the beginning."

He turned his eyes down, collecting his thoughts, then noticed something on her desk. His eyes fixated on it. It had clearly been put where he would see it easily, but he did not realize this. He reached to the desk and picked the dagger up, looking to the markings on the hilt, then he turned his eyes to the Queen and said, "This came from one of the patrols you found, didn't it?"

"Continue," she commanded.

He looked back down at the dagger, turning it over in his hands as he informed, "It belonged to a young officer named Loravar. His patrol was discovered two leagues from the border where they had fallen under attack." His eyes turned to the Queen's. "Zondaen arrows were found in the bodies and some of the trees, and two bows were found where they had been dropped."

"So, naturally, you think Zondae attacked this patrol?" the Queen guessed.

He glanced at the dagger. "You think Enulam attacked yours?"

She, too, glanced at the dagger, then asked, "Would you have left it behind?"

"The dagger? No, I wouldn't."

"And yet someone did. How do you know it is this Loravar's?"

He set the dagger on the desk and slid it to her hilt first. "His name and rank are on it. It was presented to him by King Donwarr when he was promoted."

Le'errin picked the dagger up and looked it over, reading the words scribed on it, then she asked, "How is King Donwarr?"

"He's well," Chail replied. "A little on edge about these raids and how you will respond, but otherwise in good spirits."

She nodded, still staring at the dagger. "Any idea why he would want to meet me at the border?"

"I wasn't aware he did," was Chail's response.

Le'errin turned her eyes to him. "Apparently he had quite a talk with my daughter before you left. She thinks very highly of him. Says he reminds her of you."

Chail smiled slightly. "Perhaps me in another twenty seasons."

The Queen also smiled. "You're a charming man, Prince of Enulam. That's what has me afraid for Ell's safety around you. And yet, I've seen you put yourself at risk to defend her. Answer me truthfully. Would you lay down your life for her?"

The Prince looked her in the eye and answered straightly, "I would kill or die for her."

"You *have* killed for her from what I understand. How long have you known one another?"

He turned his eyes down. "We are supposed to keep this secret, but about three seasons."

"She was sixteen," the Queen informed, "and already a headstrong little girl."

"I've heard you call her your Little Dragon."

Queen Le'errin smiled. "It's my pet name for her. She earned that when she was just a baby and was more than a handful even then."

"I can't imagine," he laughed.

"Even so," the Queen continued, "she seems to trust you. She also seems very fond of you, more than any man she has ever been in the company of. Can you tell me why that is?"

Chail shrugged. "I suppose because I've never betrayed her. I've never given her cause to mistrust me." He glanced at the corner of her desk where a wine flask sat and asked, "May I?"

She also glanced at it, then shook her head and scolded, "The sun has barely been up an hour!"

"Just a taste," he assured. "My father has this strange thirst for sweet wine and after what Le'ell has told me about some of the Zondaen wines I've been dying to try it."

Queen Le'errin sighed and shook her head, then conceded, "Very well, go on."

He took the flask and an empty goblet from the desk and poured just a little, set the flask down and swirled the wine, taking a good sniff of the aroma before tasting it.

"To your liking?" she asked.

He smiled and nodded. "If you are kind enough to release me then I *must* take some of this with me."

"Your father likes sweet wine," the Queen observed, "my daughter likes sweet wine, you and I abhor it and prefer a dry." She shook her head.

"Strange, I know," he observed, then took another sip. "Here we've been on the brink of war, mistrusting each other and preparing for hostilities any moment for ten generations, and yet we are so similar."

She nodded. "I'm still concerned about that war we've been on the brink of."

"As am I," he assured. "My father wants to get to the heart of the matter without going to war." He looked to her and added, "May I offer a suggestion?"

"You may," she confirmed.

"Keep your patrols about two leagues away from the border. Don't appear threatening. I might also suggest you shore up your defenses to the North."

She raised her head. "We've observed some activity to the North."

"As have we. That is where the raiders are coming from, I think."

Queen Le'errin was silent for a moment, then informed, "You know, I do have to consider that this is a trick to have us let our guard down."

He nodded and set the goblet back onto the desk. "In that case shore up your defenses here at the castle as well. Make it look like a routine day, but be vigilant and ready for an attack. You might also station troops in the forest to blindside an attacking army and set traps off of the road in the tree line to take a toll on those trying to approach unnoticed."

Her eyes narrowed. "Why are you so eager to help us?"

He raised his chin slightly. "Like it or not, I believe we have a common enemy, and our best bet is to thwart their efforts to drive us to war."

"And King Donwarr's thoughts?"

"I feel he thinks as I do. He just won't admit it."

She nodded, considering, then, "He told Ell he would be at the border with one hundred soldiers in three days. How would you respond?"

"With one hundred soldiers," Chail replied straightly. "No more, no less."

Queen Le'errin had little time to consider before a knock on the door distracted her and she ordered, "You may enter."

Pa'lesh and Le'ell stormed in and Pa'lesh informed, "We have a problem. I interviewed the warriors from yesterday's Eastern patrol. The men who attacked them were not from Enulam."

The Queen looked to Chail and asked, "And how do you know this, Captain Pa'lesh?"

"First off," she reported, motioning to Chail with her head, "this man savagely killed three of them. He and Le'ell were under the impression they were forest trolls or gnomes for some reason and he was surprised to discover that they were human. They didn't seem to use Enulam tactics, either. It was a simple ambush that appears to have been meant to fail. Nothing about this makes sense."

"Or everything about it does," Queen Le'errin suggested, still staring at the Prince. "Captain Pa'lesh, assemble a strike force of exactly one hundred soldiers, no more, no less. We will march to the border in two days. I will lead them myself. Le'ell, find De'lar and tell her to double our defenses on the battlements and call up all of the reserves she can muster." She looked up at them and barked, "Now!"

They glanced at each other, then fled the room.

"I'm a little surprised to see that you trust me so," Chail admitted.

"I don't," she corrected. "You may have told me to take those precautions as a diversion. If I mistrusted you I would have an alternate plan, wouldn't I, an alternate plan that you would anticipate if you were trying to deceive me."

He stared blankly at her for a time, then shook his head and said, "Your logic is as dizzying as my father's."

She smiled slightly. "Then it's one more thing we have in common. Have you had anything to eat today?"

He shook his head.

"Find a guard outside," Le'errin ordered. "Tell her I have ordered that you be escorted to the yob meal hall. They will take care of you."

He nodded to her and stood. "Thank you, your Majesty."

"We will speak again later," she added.

"I understand," he confirmed, then turned to the door.

The yob dining hall was a very plain looking place. Ten long tables that were each about four paces long were in rows of five in the middle of the room. On the opposite end of the room was a row of tables that had various foods laid out and was tended by four small men, all wearing white shirts.

As he scanned the room, the guard escorting him patted his arm and said, "Go on, and try to leave something for the smaller yobs here."

Only about thirty or so men were still eating and they all stopped and stared at him as he entered. He largely ignored them on his way to the buffet. The men who stood behind the buffet tables all stared up at him as if they were seeing a monster in their company. Looking over what was offered, he nodded and asked, "What do you recommend?"

They all glanced at each other, one finally saying, "It should all be to your liking."

He nodded again. "Okay, if you insist I'll sample everything."

They glanced at each other, then went about the task of filling plates.

None of the other men cared to share a table with the huge visitor, so Chail found himself dining alone. With five of the tin plates empty, he was half way through his sixth and still going strong. He drank cool water directly from the pitcher and had it nearly empty as well. Finding much of the food bland, he discovered it all had good flavor to it and several of the dishes were downright spicy.

Pa'lesh sat down across from him, resting her elbow on the table and her chin in her palm as she watched him.

Noticing her, he stopped chewing and looked at her, then offered her a half empty basket of biscuits.

She politely shook her head.

He set the basket down and resumed his feeding frenzy.

"Hungry?" she finally asked.

Taking the time to chew and swallow, he took a gulp from the pitcher and replied, "Not so much anymore."

Her brow arched. "How can your kingdom afford to feed you?"

He took another bite and answered, "Large treasury."

Pa'lesh rolled her eyes and almost smiled. She watched him a moment longer, then said, "You didn't have to come to the aid of that patrol yesterday."

He nodded and said with a half full mouth of food, "They were outnumbered. I figured they could use a hand."

"You could have let those raiders kill them," Pa'lesh pointed out.

Chail nodded again as he tossed the sixth plate aside and reached for the seventh. "I could have, but your people have done me no harm. Those men on that Enulam patrol they killed were more than my soldiers and comrades. They were my friends, and it was payback time."

She glanced away, then looked back and asked, "What will you do if we are here and they attack the castle?"

He looked right into her eyes and answered, "I'll kill as many of them as I can."

"You would defend Zondae?"

Chail just stared back at her and chewed for long seconds, then nodded.

"And what if your people attack?" she asked in a hard tone.

"I don't expect them to," he answered straightly. "If they do, I will put a stop to it and send them home."

"Even if they're led by King Donwarr himself?"

He nodded again and took another bite.

Pa'lesh shook her head. "Le'ell must mean an awful lot to you."

"She does," he confirmed. A moment later he threw aside the seventh and final plate, then leaned back and patted his belly. "Do your slave men always eat this well?"

The Captain looked down at the empty plates and replied, "Not as much as you. I'm hoping there is enough left for the rest of them."

"Not to worry," he assured. "I'm not going back for seconds." He wiped his mouth on his sleeve and leaned his forearms on the table, asking, "Are you here to escort me somewhere?"

"Just to keep an eye on you until her Majesty wants you," was the Captain's reply. She eyed him for a moment, then said, "I think it would only be fair to be frank with you, Chail of Enulam. I don't trust you. If it was up to me you would still be in that dungeon under heavy guard, not running about the castle like you live here. Make no mistake. You are still our enemy until you can prove to me otherwise, no matter what Queen Le'errin thinks."

He stared back at her, then nodded. "I respect that. I trust you will be keeping a close watch on me yourself to make sure I don't batter your walls down?"

"That's right," she confirmed. "One step out of line and I'll carve you like a winter goose."

Chail smiled slightly. "You know, I would look forward to sparring with you."

She raised her brow.

"You seem to be a warrior of considerable skill," he continued. "I think I could learn a great deal from you."

Pa'lesh turned her eyes down, then back to his and said, "I wouldn't mind such a challenge. It's been a while since I had any formidable competition."

"We should plan to do that," he suggested.

She stood and bade, "Come with me."

Chail really did not expect to be taken to the drill field on the castle's north side, but that is where they ended up. Sectioned off in six ten by ten pace squares by knee high stone walls, it had the appearance of a place that was frequently used. No grass grew in the dirt within the squares, but well manicured grass grew around them. A small hut was on one side, a three height timber wall on the other. Women climbed the wall, pulling themselves up with thick ropes that dangled on both sides. They were in lines of four, eagerly awaiting their turn. Senior warriors yelled to them, prodding them on. Within the squares, pairs of warrior women sparred with wooden swords, carefully watched by seasoned warriors who were clearly trainers. Still more women ran in groups around the perimeter of the training area. On the other side of the hut there were two dozen archers shooting arrows at targets hung on the castle's perimeter wall, and shooting very accurately.

Chail scanned the area, his eyes darting from training activity to training activity. Beyond the timber wall other women trained in unarmed combat. While not as large as the Enulam warriors, they were quick and tenacious, and would clearly be a formidable army in open combat.

"Where should we begin?" Pa'lesh asked.

He motioned toward the hand to hand training area and suggested, "How about with that?"

Pa'lesh nodded. "Sword box it is." She turned and walked toward the hut.

Chail shrugged and followed. "Lead on."

The Field Captain approached a woman with graying hair who had her back to them and took her shoulder.

The woman turned and greeted, "Good morning, Captain." Then she looked behind her and declared, "Oh, my!"

Smiling slightly, Pa'lesh motioned toward him and said, "He wants to spar."

The trainer raised her brow. "He wants to spar *you?* He must be a very brave yob."

"Actually, I wanted to wrestle," he corrected.

"Do you have a box and some training swords open?" Pa'lesh asked, clearly ignoring the Prince.

The trainer looked him up and down again, also smiling slightly as she nodded and confirmed, "I think I can open one up." She turned and started barking orders at the women in the closest training box, Pa'lesh following.

Glancing around him, Chail noticed a crowd begin to gather. Still, he followed Pa'lesh into the training box and took the wooden sword from the trainer. It was clearly weighted, but still only a fraction the weight of his own blade.

Taking her own sword, the Field Captain cut it through the air many times in very quick strokes, giving him a hint at her speed. She took her battle stance and circled around him, her eyes on his as she asked, "Tell me, Chail of Enulam. What is the first law of combat?" She swung the sword quickly from the side.

Meeting it with his own, Chail demonstrated his own speed in meeting it and had a firm grip on her wrist and his blade at her throat before she could realize, and he answered, "Don't underestimate your opponent."

She glanced down at the sword held to her throat, then glared up at him.

He knew right away he had embarrassed her, but he had also made his point. She had considered him to be a huge, lumbering beast, and now she knew he was a formidable opponent.

When he backed away, she nodded, then took her battle stance again and complimented, "Very good. You may be worth my time after all." She swung her sword again, this time withdrawing quickly as he parried to block. Pa'lesh had clearly learned that strength was not his only asset as he proved to be much quicker than she had anticipated. Still, she attacked relentlessly and soon had him half-stepping backward.

Chail found himself guessing which direction she would attack from next. This woman had considerable skill and was able to strike with surprising force with a fore-strike or a back-strike. He also found himself on the defensive—not a place he liked to be. It was time to slow her momentum.

When he easily blocked a low strike, she spun around completely and brought the sword high. Anticipating this, he dodged out of range, the tip of the sword barely missing his face. His sword was free to strike back! Bringing it up in a low thrust, he turned into the move, but underestimated her speed as she recovered and parried and she spun and slammed her sword into his back. He yelled and arched his back, stumbling away from her.

Shaking her head, she was smiling and informed, "In combat, you would already be dead."

He turned his eyes to her, smiling back as he retorted, "I'm not so easily killed," then he swung his sword hard and with brutal force. When she went to block her defense collapsed under the force of his blow and she stumbled away, barely keeping her grip on her weapon.

By the time she recovered he was upon her again and she barely got her sword raised in time, meeting his less than confidently and barely stopping it, the blow almost sending her weapon into her own head. She spun away, raising her weapon to meet an attack that was almost assuredly coming.

Chail just stood there, staring back, his weapon at ease but ready. His expression was almost blank, but for stone-like eyes and the subtle hint of a smile at the edges of his mouth.

Everything else around them seemed to disappear. The nearly hundred warriors and slave men who had gathered around seemed to fade from notice. All they saw was each other. Simultaneously, they raised their weapons and charged. A fierce exchange followed, each warrior calling on all their skill and experience, their strength and speed. The surrounding warrior women cheered them, most for Pa'lesh but there were those who actually cheered for the warrior from Enulam. Her blade found him once more, stinging his side. His blade found her as well, right across the belly. She doubled over, but thrust at him, slowing him just long enough for her to recover and resume the battle at full speed. No one would know how long they continued, but each clearly enjoyed the match.

One good parry knocked the Field Captain's sword safely out of the way and the Prince lowered his head and charged, slamming his shoulder into her midriff and driving her backward until the stone wall stopped her and she flipped over it, the breath exploding from her as she slammed onto the grass outside back-first, and the spectators scrambled out of the way.

Pa'lesh took many long seconds to get her wits back about her as she lay on the grass with her calves still on the wall, then she looked up at him and barked, "What the hell was that?"

He smiled and answered, "That is called knocking my opponent on her back." He strode forward and offered her his hand, and when she took it he pulled her back over the wall and to her feet.

"Is that the kind of tactic we can expect if we ever meet you in battle?" she asked sharply.

He nodded. "That and more. Are we to expect such ferocity out of you should we meet in battle?"

She half smiled back at him. "That and more."

The spectators around them cheered and applauded.

Chail tossed his sword to one of the trainers as he turned and headed out of the training box.

Pa'lesh swung hard, slamming the broad side of her practice sword hard into his buttocks.

He jumped forward and swung around, rubbing his stinging backside as he stared at her with wide eyes.

Laughing, she tossed her practice sword to the trainer and beckoned him to follow, chiding, "Come along, Chail of Enulam."

They had not quite arrived at the palace when a small man in a yellow shirt ran up to them and bowed to Pa'lesh, reporting, "Captain Pa'lesh. I bring word form her Majesty."

"Go on," she ordered, setting her hands on her hips.

He stood and glanced up at Chail, then looked to Pa'lesh and continued, "Her Majesty wishes your company and the man from Enulam immediately."

The Field Captain turned her eyes up to Chail, then hit his arm hard with the back of her hand and said, "Come on."

He followed her as she hurried into and through the castle. They bounded up the steps and strode quickly down the corridor toward the Queen's study. Arriving, they found four guards standing at the door—and Chail knew that was not a good sign.

They entered the Queen's study to two more guards within, a young Enulam warrior standing between them! Chail's eyes found him immediately and he froze where he was. This soldier was young, and attractive and well made man who had been assigned to a fast scouting patrol. This time, he was clearly not fast enough. He wore no armor, just a green swordsman's shirt and black trousers with brown riding boots. His belt and weapons had been taken. His shoulder length brown hair was matted and tangled, clearly from a scuffle with the Zondaens. A small cut at his hairline had stopped bleeding, but dried blood was caked on part of his face and darkened his shirt. His hands were bound behind him and a guard still held each arm.

Seeing the Prince, the soldier's eyes widened, but he wisely said nothing.

Sitting behind her desk, Queen Le'errin's eyes shifted from the scout to the Prince and she said flatly, "We have a new problem."

Chail nodded and agreed, "I see that." He looked to the Queen and asked, "May I ask that he be shown the same hospitality I was? Perhaps treat his injuries and give him something to eat?"

The Queen's eyes turned back to the young soldier. "He was caught in Zondaen territory, part of a patrol of five. He does not seem to want to explain to me what he was doing there. Perhaps you can."

"Easy," the Prince informed. "He was under orders to watch for movements along the border."

"He and his patrol were in Zondaen territory," the Queen reminded. "That is what I want explained."

Chail turned his eyes to the lad, staring at him for long seconds, then asked, "I only ask that you treat him well. Cut him lose, feed him and tend his injuries and I'm sure I can convince him to tell you what you need to know."

His eyes flaring, the young soldier declared, "You can't!"

One of the guards raised her hand to strike him.

Chail caught her wrist half way to the lad and he advised, "You may want to reconsider how you treat your prisoners."

The guard looked to the Queen.

Le'errin glared at her and snarled, "You are dismissed." As the guard hurried from the room, the Queen looked to the other guards and ordered, "Free his hands, tend his wounds and give him something to eat." She looked to the Prince and raised her brow.

He nodded to her, then approached as the other guard untied his hands and ordered, "Don't give them any trouble and talk to no one but Queen Le'errin or myself."

Hesitantly, he nodded.

Chail looked to the guard behind him with narrow eyes and informed, "I will expect him to be treated well."

"As will I," the Queen added sternly.

Once he was escorted from the room and the door was closed, Chail rubbed his eyes and sat across from the Queen, then looked to her and said, "We have a problem."

She nodded. "I know we do."

He looked out the window, shaking his head. "Why send scouts? The raiders would cut a patrol that small to pieces in short order."

"You sound like you're trying to guess your father's next move," Le'errin said, reaching for the flask of wine and goblets. As she poured the wine, she glanced at the door and asked, "Would you like some?"

"No, thank you, Majesty," Pa'lesh answered.

Chail had forgotten she was in the room and he looked to the Queen.

"I trust no one more," Le'errin told him straightly. "Tell me something. Why should I trust that Enulam is not going to attack? Surely they know that we have one of their scouts by now."

"And the King knows I'm here by now," the Prince added, stroking his chin.

"Will they send a rescue party for you?"

He shook his head.

Pa'lesh approached. "That makes no sense! Of course they're going to come for you! That's what the scouting party was for."

Chail shook his head again. "I have a feeling my father knew what I was going to do before I did. He'll let me play this out on my own." He turned and looked to Pa'lesh. "What were the soldiers who captured him doing at the time?"

"I was sparring with you," she said dryly. "How would I know what they were doing?"

"Were they looking for the raiders?" he pressed.

The Queen raised her head and confirmed, "That's exactly what they were doing!"

Chail turned back to Queen Le'errin. "If they were tracking the raiders, and that scouting patrol was tracking the raiders…"

The Field Captain looked to the Queen. "That makes sense. A small, elusive band of raiders could easily have led that scouting party across the border."

The Prince nodded. "And when we ask Ardrek, I would be willing to stake my horse that we'll get the same story from him."

"Ardrek?" Pa'lesh questioned.

"Your prisoner," was the Prince's answer. He picked up his wine goblet and sat back in the chair, which creaked again under his weight. "What if I told you I have a plan?" He raised the goblet to his mouth.

Pa'lesh grabbed it from his hand before it arrived there and she took a couple of gulps, then snapped, "Why should we trust your plan?"

Chail looked down at his hand, then back to her.

"I'm listening," the Queen informed, reaching for the flask and another goblet.

"Release him," the Prince advised. He gave a moment for that to sink in before continuing. "Treat his wounds, feed him, question him, then put him on his horse and send him on his way."

The Field Captain took another gulp of wine, then asked, "We would do this, why?"

He leaned forward and took his second goblet of wine from the Queen, then looked back to Pa'lesh and smiled. "Because they won't expect it. You're thought of as mindless barbarian women by my people. Such a demonstration of good will may just sway that feeling and give King Donwarr pause about going to war."

"He'll tell them everything he's learned about us," she argued.

"Exactly," the Prince agreed.

Pa'lesh just stared back at him for long seconds, then looked to the Queen and set her goblet down on the desk. "I think I should go and question him privately, just to see what he is willing to say." She turned and strode toward the door.

"I don't want him mistreated," the Queen barked.

The Field Captain looked back at her and smiled. "Then I'll do the opposite."

As she left, Queen Le'errin shook her head and finished off her wine, then poured another goblet full.

Chail's brow arched and he asked, "Is she going to do what I think she's going to do?"

Staring into her goblet, Le'errin nodded, then looked to him and informed, "Not to worry. She won't force him."

The Prince smiled. "Knowing Ardrek, she won't have to."

A knock at the door drew their attention and the Queen bade, "Enter."

The door opened and Le'ell peered in, her eyes finding Chail first.

"Come in, Little Dragon," the Queen ordered.

Clearly hesitant, Le'ell entered the room and gently closed the door, then stood beside the Prince's chair with her eyes on her mother as she reported, "I've sent your orders to the Guard Captains and they are shoring up all of our defenses and calling up reserves. Your strike force is also being assembled and will be prepared to depart when ordered." She glanced down at Chail, then continued, "I understand a soldier from Enulam was captured near the border."

"On our side of the border," the Queen confirmed. "He's being attended to."

The Princess' brow arched. "May I ask how?"

"You seem worried about him," Le'errin observed.

Le'ell glanced at the Prince again. "Well... Considering the circumstances, if he is mistreated we—"

"I've already considered all of that," the Queen interrupted. "He is being questioned now, then we will feed him and send him back to Enulam." She turned her eyes to the Prince and finished, "As a show of good will."

Nodding, Le'ell looked back to the Prince of Enulam, knowing his negotiations had enabled this. "What shall we do now?"

Queen Le'errin leaned back in her chair, her eyes on her daughter as she informed, "As soon as the last patrol returns from yesterday's attack then I will know more. Until then you just need to be sure everything here is at the ready."

Chail raised his chin, asking, "Last patrol? How big a patrol?"

The Queen's eyes shifted back to him. "It's a patrol of fifteen. They are recovering the bodies and weapons from the last attack."

Looking to Le'ell as she looked at him, he said, "If the raiders follow their pattern...."

The Princess' mouth fell open and she looked back to her mother, declaring, "We need to send a strike party out there now!"

Le'errin's eyes showed a mix of suspicion and concern as she asked, "Why?"

Chail answered for her, "Le'ell and I went on such a recovery patrol with King Donwarr the other day. We fell under attack on our way back to the castle. If the raiders are following the same pattern then your patrol may already be under attack." He stood and looked to Le'ell. "We've got to get to them first."

The Queen raised her brow. "*We?* What makes you think—"

"There isn't time to argue about it, Mother!" Le'ell snapped. "Our sisters are in peril and they need help now! For Goddess sake will you listen to me for once?"

Queen Le'errin stared at her for long seconds, then asked, "Shall I send for Pa'lesh?"

"I can lead this force, myself" Le'ell answered directly. "I've seen how these raiders work and I know what to expect."

Her lips parting slightly, the Queen nodded, a long absent look of pride in her eyes as she ordered, "Bring them all home, Little Dragon."

Le'ell's lips tightened and she complied, "I will, your Majesty."

Looking to the Prince of Enulam, Le'errin ordered, "Take him with you. His sword is in the cabinet behind you." Her eyes narrowed. "My daughter had better return to me unharmed, or you will be the first casualty of the war they want to start."

He smiled at her. "I'll be thinking of you when I cut the first one down, your Majesty."

Le'ell turned and slapped his chest, ordering, "Come on, yob. Get your sword and let's go."

Chail paused at the cabinet to get his sword, dagger and sword breaker, tucking them under his arm as he trotted to catch up to Le'ell, who was already half way down the corridor. "Where are you going to round up enough volunteers to launch this attack?"

She did not even glance at him as she replied, "I have that garrison assembled for my Mother's meeting with your Father. I think they will do."

"One hundred riders?" he asked.

"Just whoever is ready to ride," she answered. "I need to swing by my room and get my sword and belt then we will go to the stable and get our horses and army."

"What about your armor?" he asked.

"There isn't time," she snarled back. "If I'm to bring that patrol home I have to get there now."

He nodded. "I'm not usually one to be so cautious, but—"

She stopped and swung around; glaring up at him as she snapped, "Listen carefully! You are in *my* kingdom, this mission is *mine* to command and you will *not* question me further about it! Do you understand?"

He half smiled at her. "Don't worry. I'll be a good yob."

"See that you are," she snarled, then turned and strode on her way.

Her sword retrieved and hanging on her side and Chail's on his, they raced outside and toward the stables where the Queen's garrison was still assembling horses and equipment. As she approached, she pointed at one of the small men in a brown shirt near the stables and ordered, "My horse and this man's horse."

He bowed to her and hurried into the stable.

Le'ell approached a well decorated soldier and informed, "I need as many warriors as are ready to ride to assemble at the East Gate now."

The soldier, a red haired woman who appeared to be near forty, looked back at Le'ell with a mix of confusion and disbelief, then hesitantly nodded and turned to the garrison, ordering, "All prepared to ride, mount your horses and assemble at the East Gate!" As they scrambled to get on their horses, the officer turned back to the Princess and asked, "May I ask what this is about?"

Le'ell folded her arms. "I have reason to believe our last patrol has fallen or will fall under attack before they arrive at the castle. We are going to reinforce them."

"I see," the officer confirmed. "Does the Queen know about this?"

"I am leading this force by order of the Queen," Le'ell informed impatiently. "If you are not up to joining us, then tell me now and I will leave you behind!"

Raising her chin, the officer assured, "I'm up to it, Highness. I'm just a little surprised to see you leading any strike force."

Chail growled, "If she questions you again I may have to injure her."

Le'ell's eyes narrowed as she stared at the officer. "I may have to let you. Follow my orders and do not question me again, Field Captain, or the Queen may have to hear of your inability as an effective leader."

The officer glanced up at Chail, then nodded to the Princess and complied, "Yes, your Highness." Then she turned and hurried to her own horse.

"Well done," the Prince complimented.

"And to you," she said back as she strode toward the stable, a slight smile on her lips.

"Did we ever find my axe?" he asked as he followed.

Le'ell glanced back at him. "You have your sword, Chail."

"I know," he sighed, "but I've grown quite fond of using that axe. It has hitting power my sword doesn't."

Rolling her eyes, the Princess informed, "I don't know what they've done with it. If it isn't still with your horse then we can look for it when we get back."

"The fight will be over by then," he argued.

She stopped, staring at the ground before her. As he stopped behind her, she wheeled around and barked, "Are you being difficult on purpose?"

Chail nodded. "I am."

She loosed an impatient breath, then punched his stomach and turned back to the stable.

With a coy smile, he rubbed his belly and followed. "By the by, you aren't bringing your bow with you?"

"I'm commanding the strike force," she informed, sounding irritated. "I can do that better if I'm not out there nit-picking for someone to shoot at."

"Oh," was his reply. "I had so counted on seeing you in action once again."

"You will," she informed. As they entered the stable, she pointed to a wall and snarled, "There's your stupid axe! Now quit complaining about it."

He walked to the wall where it was hung and took it down, looking it over before he followed the Princess and complained, "Someone's been splitting wood with this. It's half dull."

"So just hit harder with it," she sighed, then raised her chin as she saw the two horses being led to them. She took the reins to her mare and turned, heading toward the exit with strained eyes. "We need to hurry. I shudder to think what my sisters are going through out there."

Chail took his horse and followed. "That's assuming the raiders actually attack them."

Le'ell hesitated. "What if they don't? What if this is all for nothing? I'll look like a fool and my mother will never trust me again."

163

"Or," the Prince added, "she will see you taking more responsibility for others and will trust you even more."

"I doubt it," Le'ell mumbled.

Only one thing could have been worse for Le'ell than finding a battle in progress or a massacre: Nothing.

Weary horses charged for nearly three leagues before the returning patrol was found. Fifteen Zondaen warriors were surprised by nearly seventy of their comrades coming to their aid. Stopping only about five paces apart, Le'ell found herself confronting the leader of the returning patrol who had nothing to report. They had collected their fallen comrades, bundled them on field-made litters and were taking them home. Nothing else to report.

The ride home was a long one and Le'ell did not speak as she led the eighty plus women and the Enulam Prince back toward her home.

With the turrets of the castle in sight, the patrol leader finally rode up to her side, her eyes on the Princess as she asked, "Permission to speak?"

Le'ell drew a breath and nodded.

Looking ahead, the patrol leader informed, "Several of the women saw signs of activity in the forest and two reported seeing someone shadowing us. I personally saw what looked like a man ducking into a thicket in the same area."

Feeling a slight chill, the Princess glanced at Chail, who had ridden up to her other side, then looked forward again. "Did you see anything else?"

The leader shook her head. "No, Highness. Only glimpses."

The Prince nodded. "I think they weren't up to dealing with the larger force."

"Or they weren't there at all," Le'ell said grimly.

"I'm still glad you happened along," the patrol leader informed. "We feared attack any second and I wasn't sure we would live to make it back to Zondae. I will include that in my report to her Majesty."

Le'ell nodded again and offered, "Thank you."

The arrival at Zondae was not met by the accolades she had first hoped when she left. It was a routine event like any other.

Leaving their horses at the stable, Le'ell and Chail strode back to the castle, down the corridor, up the stairs…

Nearly to her room, they heard a voice tease, "I'm so relieved you fought off the imminent attack from Enulam."

Le'ell froze, her hands clenching into tight fists.

Her sister strode toward them from a crossing hallway, a smile on her lips and a malicious look in her eyes. Her white swordswoman's shirt and loosely fitting black trousers were clearly meant for comfort. She had no sword hanging from her side but she did have a large, blond haired man behind her, one with a heavy, muscular build which was shown off by the black jerkin he wore open. His tightly fitting white trousers showed off muscular legs. He was a hand width taller than Le'sesh and from his proximity to her and his body language was completely loyal to her.

Le'ell turned and glared at her sister, snarling, "Just turn around and go back the way you came."

Her mouth falling open, Le'sesh gingerly placed a hand on her chest and chided, "Why little sister. Why would you be so hostile? Oh, are we upset about that little charge you led into the forest to save a patrol that didn't really need you?"

Le'ell looked away from her, clenching her teeth.

"There are other things you can do for Ama's attention," Le'sesh went on. "You don't need to waste the time of fifty soldiers just to amuse yourself." She folded her arms. "In fact, when I'm Queen, you won't be wasting anyone's time. You'll be doing what you do best: Nothing."

Looking up into her half sister's eyes, Le'ell growled, "I do more before sunup than you will do in your lifetime."

Le'sesh glanced at Chail. "I'll bet you do. I'll bet you and your little dolls and trinkets have all sorts of fun at night. You should really grow up and try a man. I'll bet the one behind you wishes he had a woman who could satisfy him, not some spoiled little girl with no place in life and no such talents." Le'ell slapped her hard and she staggered backward, reaching for her face. With the shock on her face turning to anger, she snarled and ordered to the man behind her, "Ardrose!"

The man advanced, reaching for Le'ell.

She retreated, saying, "Chail!"

Chail stepped forward, pulling the Princess behind him and stopping Ardrose with a hand to the chest. His eyes that were more angry dragon than human.

The yob of Princess Le'sesh was indeed a large, powerful man, but was clearly no match for the Prince of Enulam, and both men knew it.

He took a step back, his slightly fearful eyes on Chail's.

The standoff did not last more than a few seconds and Ardrose backed away and looked to his mistress.

Knowing her slave man had been simply outclassed, Le'sesh turned her wicked eyes on Le'ell and hissed, "You can be sure Ama is going to hear about this!" She turned and stormed away.

When Ardrose tried to follow, Chail grabbed his jerkin and pulled him back, spinning him around to glare into his eyes once more. "That was just a warning," he growled. "Even think about touching her again and I'll utterly destroy you. I won't even leave enough of you for the vultures." He pushed the slave man from him, watching as he stumbled to keep his footing and catch up to his mistress.

Le'ell slowly approached the Prince, sliding her arms up to his shoulders as she purred, "You have earned something special tonight."

He turned and took her waist in his hands, pulling her to him. "I have something special every night you're with me."

She smiled and grasped his neck, pulling him down to her for a kiss.

Pa'lesh cleared her throat. When they looked, she was standing a few paces away with her arms folded, shaking her head. "I don't know if you two are more cute or sickening."

Le'ell turned and stepped toward her. "I know what you are going to say—"

"No you don't," the Field Captain corrected. She glanced up at Chail, then looked back to the Princess with authoritative eyes and continued, "You led seventy troops into the field because you felt that a recovery patrol would fall under attack. Why you thought that I don't know. Queen Le'errin tells me that you and Chail of Enulam here suspected it based on what happened to you two days ago."

Nodding, Le'ell confirmed, "That's right. I was wrong and I admit it."

"You weren't wrong until just now," Pa'lesh informed. "Had I suspected an attack like that I would have done much the same. Perhaps not with seventy soldiers, but I surely would have responded." She nodded. "Just about the time I was thinking you could not be taught I see you're finally learning."

Le'ell's lips parted slightly. "You aren't angry?"

Pa'lesh shook her head. "You did what you did because you knew in your heart you were acting for the good of Zondae and the women in the field. You completely disregarded your own safety and status to leave the safety and comfort of the castle and charge to the aid of others. I'm proud of you. Now report to the Queen's study." She turned and walked away.

The Princess was stunned and simply did not know what to say as she stared after the Field Captain. "She's trained me since I was nine," she remembered. "That's the first time she's ever said she was proud of me."

"Initiative has a way of swaying people so," the Prince informed. "We'd better get to Queen Mother's study if she's waiting for us."

Le'ell nodded and led the way, and when they arrived at the door, she stopped and stared down at the handle for long seconds before saying, "I've never been able to really stand up to Sesh, especially since she got that big yob."

Chail grasped her shoulder. "You're yob is bigger."

She smiled. "That he is. He also has a talent for bringing out the best in me."

"So, you're not going to sell me tomorrow?"

Le'ell laughed under her breath and shook her head. "No, not tomorrow."

"I'll be at your side as long as you can stomach me," he assured.

She finally looked up at him. "That's going to be a long time, so I hope you're up for it." She grasped the handle and opened the door, striding into the Queen's study to find the patrol leader already there. Showing no fear, she walked abreast of her and faced the Queen with confident eyes.

Queen Le'errin looked to the patrol leader and ordered, "You are dismissed." As she left, the Queen turned her eyes back to Le'ell and raised her brow. "No attack?"

The Princess shook her head. "They either weren't there or our numbers frightened them away.

Le'errin nodded. "Lan'fwar would seem to agree with the latter." She looked to Chail. "I don't suppose you saw anything."

He shook his head. "My orders were to keep Princess Le'ell safe. That's where my eyes were."

"Very good," the Queen complimented. "So, how shall we remember this? Learning experience? Training? Waste of time? I have seventy warriors who are wondering why they were in such a hurry to escort a patrol home. I have fifteen more who were happy to see you charge to them. A few swear they saw bandits or some enemy soldiers hiding in the trees. Le'ell, do you feel your presence may have prevented an attack on our patrol?"

The Princess glanced down, then answered, "I think so."

The Queen's eyes shifted to Chail. "And what do you think, Prince Chail of Enulam?"

He raised his brow. "Honestly? I don't think the raiders are willing to attack our armies. They seem to be whittling away at patrols, ambushing small numbers with larger numbers."

"Hence, they need Zondae and Enulam to go to war," the Queen guessed. "One side destroys the other, but is weakened by the conflict."

Chail nodded. "That sounds like their plan."

Le'errin sighed, looking down at her desk. "They'll feed on generations of mistrust. Donwarr and I can talk peace, but thousands of soldiers may not see it that way." She turned her eyes back up to Chail. "Worse, if this third party is a very formidable force, we may have to find a way to cooperate to defeat them. I'm not sure that's possible until we actually see a common enemy."

"They'll have to be lured into the open," Le'ell said flatly. "We need prisoners. We need someone who can be made to talk about their plan."

"We just need to find them," the Queen added. "Most of the activity has been to the North. We could start searching there."

"King Donwarr probably already is," Chail advised. "The raiders seem to hide from large forces and attack smaller ones. That makes finding anything problematic at best."

Nodding, the Queen agreed, "That it does. Perhaps my meeting with King Donwarr will be productive." She stared down at her desk again, appearing to daydream.

A moment later, Le'ell summoned, "Ama?"

Queen Le'errin turned her eyes to the Princess and said, "We will figure it out later, Little Dragon. Go on, now. I'll see you in the morning."

Le'ell nodded to her, agreeing, "Okay, Ama. Good night." She then turned and left, her thoughts distant as she wandered back toward her room.

Even after they arrived, Le'ell was lost in her thoughts and Chail did not disturb her. He removed his belt and weapons, his boots, then he sat on the bed and watched her pace, which she did for some time.

Finally stopping, she turned to him and informed, "She's hiding something. She doesn't want us to know what she's really doing."

He raised his brow. "You're mother, you mean?"

Le'ell nodded, looking to the floor. "I think she still considers your kingdom a threat and just doesn't want you to know. In her eyes everything you told her is a lie and you are manipulating me to deceive her more."

"Why did she trust me on the patrol with you?"

"If you think she trusts you then she will more easily see your true intentions. All this time she's been using you as a tool against your own people and neither of us saw it until now."

He considered. "Will she still release Aldrek?"

Nodding, Le'ell confirmed, "I'm sure of it. He'll be a more useful pawn to her if she does. He'll tell your king exactly what she wants him to and won't even realize it."

"Any way we can get through to her?" Chail asked grimly.

Le'ell loosed a breath, then shook her head. "Like it or not, she's preparing for war with Enulam." She considered, then, "She won't be swayed from that unless we find proof that there is another enemy out there."

His eyes narrowed. "How are you proposing we do this?"

"I'm not sure," she admitted, "but we have to do something and do it quickly."

"Something like lure the raiders into the open?" he asked.

She turned her eyes to him, just staring for a moment. "You're concocting some kind of plan to do that, aren't you?"

He nodded.

Le'ell's lips tightened as she looked away. The King of Enulam had been right about that, too. Shaking her head, she observed, "You and I have become as predictable as the coming night and day."

"Then perhaps it's time to do what they won't expect," he said flatly. "They can't clearly see the truth, so we'll have to put it in front of them."

She considered, then sat down on the bed beside him and laid her head on his shoulder. "When did my life get so complicated?"

"About three seasons ago," was Chail's answer.

CHAPTER 10

A new morning would not wash away the same old problems from the day before.

Le'ell woke before the sun, her mind in too much turmoil to allow her to rest further. Lying in the dark beside her big prince, she stared at the ceiling, turned and stared out the window at the setting moon which was no longer full but very bright nonetheless. Some time later she carefully, quietly slid from the bed, trying not to wake Chail, found her bathrobe lying over a chair and crept out of the room, wandering down the dimly lit corridor for a short time. Looking ahead, she saw the door to the Queen's chamber slightly ajar, light lancing out into the corridor. She leaned her head and quietly approached, hearing voices within. As she got to the door she heard the Queen in what sounded like a heated argument, and she stood by the door to listen.

"I don't know what I was thinking, either," Le'errin grumbled. "And I'm not talking about letting the Enulam man run about in the castle; I'm talking about my choice for succession!"

"What's that supposed to mean?" Le'sesh barked.

"I had to choose between a rebellious, quick tempered and immature girl who showed some hope of motivation and you, a self-centered, lazy brat who thinks she's above the law simply because she's my daughter."

"I'm older and more responsible!" the Princess snapped back. "That's why you chose me! I don't go running away from patrols and meeting a soldier of our enemy for little rendezvous. There's no telling what she might have told him about us."

"Your sister may be a head-strong brat and prone to little bouts of utter defiance but do *not* accuse her of treason again! She is far more loyal to Zondae than you are!"

"How dare you!" Le'sesh cried.

"And another thing!" the Queen continued. "If that big yob of yours touches another woman of this kingdom on your command or otherwise I will put him to death myself! Is that clear?"

"What about Le'ell's Enulam yob?" the Princess countered. "He could have killed me yesterday!"

"No more of your whining! You remember what I said. And if you send him after Le'ell again I may just let her Enulam yob take care of you both! Now get out of my sight!"

Le'ell gulped a breath and moved to the other side of the door, pressing herself against the wall to avoid being seen as the door opened and her sister stormed out of the room and stomped down the hallway toward her own room. Remaining motionless, Le'ell watched her sister disappear behind her door, then she heard her mother approach and gingerly close the door. Before it closed completely, she could hear the sound of her mother weeping within.

Closing her eyes, the Princess gingerly placed a hand on her mother's door. Not just for her people, but for her family she would have to risk everything. With a deep sigh, she strode down the hallway to her room, gently closed the door, and just as gently roused Chail.

They dressed, ate, and before they left the castle to get their horses ready, Le'ell stopped by her mother's study to leave her stuffed dragon on the Queen's desk. Looking up at Chail, she gently stroked his cheek, then they left the castle together, hoping an opportunity would present itself. They knew time was growing short. Something would have to be done, something drastic.

Saddlebags were laden heavily on each horse. Neither wore armor, just the attire from the day before. Communication consisted of glances that said more than words could.

As they emerged from the stable, they led their horses to the two score of waiting soldiers that was assembled and standing beside their horses near the East gate. There, Lan'fwar walked the line, inspecting weapons and saddle packs, armor and horses. She looked to the Princess and strode to her, greeting, "Good morning, highness."

"Good morning," Le'ell responded. Looking over the waiting soldiers, she nodded and observed, "Looks like you are ready for patrol."

"We're ready for anything," Lan'fwar confirmed. "We're ordered not to engage Enulam troops should we encounter any near the border, just get our guest there and get back."

Le'ell's eyes snapped back to her. "Our guest?"

"The Enulam Soldier," the patrol leader explained.

Nodding, the Princess confirmed, "Oh, yes. I didn't know it was your garrison that was returning him."

"Are you and the other Enulam man coming with us?" Lan'fwar asked.

Hesitantly, Le'ell nodded. "Yes. Should we encounter any Enulam hostiles near the border then Chail here would come in handy, I think." She glanced back at him, then looked back to the patrol. "And the prisoner is where?"

"He's being escorted here by Captain Pa'lesh," was the patrol leader's answer. "I'm told she is personally seeing him here to make sure he doesn't try anything, but I also heard she had him in her room all night." She smiled and raised her brow. "You know, *making* him talk."

Le'ell laughed under her breath and nodded. "I'd heard that as well."

Almost as if summoned by the conversation, Pa'lesh approached with her prisoner. They simply walked side by side, and when they reached the patrol, the Field Captain looked to the patrol leader and informed, "He's all yours, Lan'fwar. I've done all with him that I can."

Andrek's eyes panned to her.

Pa'lesh nodded to Lan'fwar and Le'ell in turn, then turned her eyes up to Chail's, asking "A word?"

He glanced at Le'ell, then followed the Field Captain a few paces away.

She turned back to him and folded her arms, her eyes locked on his as she informed, "I feel that Le'ell is planning to do something very foolish. The Queen shares this feeling. I won't ask you if it is true or not. I don't want you to have to lie for her."

He nodded, then guessed, "You want to ask me something."

Glancing away, Pa'lesh continued, "I would only have you look after her. I think she truly believes that you don't want to go to war with us. I believe it as well, and yet I also believe that you don't want this war. I'm honestly not sure what to think. While I don't trust you, I know in my heart you would die to defend Princess Le'ell."

"I would," he confirmed.

She just stared back for long seconds, then ordered, "Don't let me down, Chail of Enulam. I'm hard on her, more than any other I've had to train, but I love her as if she was my own. I don't want to see you return without her."

"If she doesn't return," he informed, "I will be lying dead beside her. You have my word on that."

Pa'lesh placed a hand on her chest and softly said, "To my heart."

When she turned to walk back to the patrol, he grasped her shoulder and asked, "What did Aldrek have to say last night?"

Looking back up to him, she smiled just a little. "He didn't say much." Then she turned and strode back to the patrol, pausing at the Enulam solder and leaning toward him to whisper something in his ear.

Aldrek turned and watched her as she walked back to the palace, then looked to the approaching Prince.

Chail stopped in front of him and folded his arms. "Are you ready to return home?"

Glancing back at the departing Field Captain, the Enulam Soldier shrugged and replied, "I suppose, if I have to."

With a patrol of forty with them, the journey to the border with Enulam was uneventful, though the air seemed unseasonably cool in the forest. Once at the river, Chail bade farewell to Aldrek, giving him instructions as to what to tell King Donwarr about his experience at Zondae as well as his own disposition, knowing that the news that arrived at Enulam could very well decide if the two kingdoms went to war.

Less than a league into the ride back to Zondae, Le'ell took her leave of Lan'fwar and her troops, telling the patrol leader to give her love to the queen and not to search for her, and not to go to war without hearing from her first. Riding north, they made their way back to the river, then continued on until way after high sun when they found what appeared to be white smoke rising above the treetops some distance away.

Chail stopped his horse and looked up at the smoke, his eyes narrowing.

Stopping beside him, Le'ell looked to it, then turned her eyes to him and asked, "What is it."

"It may be an encampment," he guessed.

She looked back to it, then to him and corrected, "It's steam. The hot springs are over there."

"Hot springs?" he asked.

"You know," she explained, "it's a spring of water, but the water comes out hot. That's why they call it a hot spring."

He turned his eyes to her, a sting of sarcasm to his voice as he replied, "Thanks for clearing that up."

"I've visited them once or twice a season since I came of age," she went on. "It's a nice place to be when the air is cool, really nice in the snow."

"The air's a trite chilly this morning," he pointed out.

Her eyes slid to him. "Aren't we on a mission to stop a war?"

"I don't think a delay of a couple of hours will make a huge difference," he said.

She nodded, a slight smile on her lips. "I suppose we do need to stop for a bite. I'm a little hungry." She glanced back at her saddle bag. "By the way. Why did we have to bring so much gold with us?"

"I thought it might come in handy to buy information or favors," he answered. "It often speaks much louder than brute force or diplomacy. That and there's this inn a few leagues north of the Enulam border. Good food, quiet rooms, warm soft beds...." He looked at her and raised his eyebrows.

She raised hers back, then looked back to the saddle bag, pulling the flap up. Movement behind caught her attention and a glance back became a hard look. Closing the saddle bag, she looked straight ahead again and asked, "Have you figured out what to do if we meet any of those raiders out here?"

"Depends on how many there are," was the Prince's answer. "I figure we can take out four or five without much trouble. More than that and we might have a problem."

"Chail, we have a problem."

He looked to her, then behind, seeing over a dozen raiders following. Even though they were almost a hundred paces away, Chail knew that outrunning them might still be difficult. He turned his attention forward again, drew a deep breath and blew it out through pursed lips.

"What do we do?" Le'ell asked nervously.

He considered. "They're not trying to catch up to us."

"That's good, right?" Le'ell sounded more and more frightened.

"No," he corrected. "That means they may have more ahead, waiting to ambush us."

"How is that plan coming?"

"Working on it."

"Work on it faster, Chail."

His eyes panned back and forth. Ahead, he saw a trail that led to the right off of the main road and he raised his chin toward it, asking, "Do you know where that goes?"

"The hot springs," she answered. "It's a shortcut, but still half a league away."

"That's where we're going," he informed straightly. "On my signal, cut your horse hard down that path and go as fast as you can."

"Chail, the hot springs come out of a cliff and into a pool! There's no place to go once we get there!"

"We aren't going to the springs, merely toward them. Are you ready?"

"No."

"We're almost there, just another twenty paces or so. Try not to look anxious. We'll need to take them by surprise."

"How do you know that they... Chail, look!" she suddenly declared, pointing toward the path they were to take where a white unicorn was just emerging.

For a moment they forgot about the imminent danger behind them, forgot that they needed to flee. This second sighting of a unicorn was unheard of! Few people ever saw one of these magical creatures in their lives, and now they had seen one twice!

The small unicorn paced into the road before them, and as their horses grew agitated she calmed them with a whicker, then looked behind them to the raiders that followed. Laying her ears back, she lowered her head, her eyes narrow as she stalked toward the raiders.

The Prince and Princess watched her pass by them, astonished that this little unicorn, only pony sized and built more like a deer than a horse, was advancing on a dozen armed raiders, and seemed to be fearless of them. Only about five paces behind them, she stopped and looked back at them. She barked a high pitched whinny followed by a whicker. When they did not respond right away, she snorted and repeated her whinny and whicker, then stared at them for many long seconds, finally turning her eyes up and huffing a hard breath. Looking back at the raiders, she reared up and whinnied loudly.

Responding to her, all of the raider's horses also reared up and whinnied, most throwing their riders.

As chaos ensued behind them, the little unicorn turned and bolted back around them, whinnying again, and the horses carrying the Prince and Princess responded to her, launching into full gallops and following her down the path toward the springs.

Taken by surprise by his horse's sudden flight, Chail found himself struggling to remain in his saddle, and when he was finally settled there, he glanced at Le'ell and informed, "I guess we're following the unicorn."

"We *need* to follow her!" Le'ell declared. "She's trying to help us!"

"What makes you think she's trying to help us?"

"Chail, this is the second time she's come to our aid."

Feeling their horses come back under their control, Chail and Le'ell kicked them faster, following the unicorn as she sped down the narrow path through the trees. Frequently, she would glance back at them, slowing her pace many times as they began to fall behind.

Ahead, the trees grew smaller. A short distance later they gave way to thick brush.

Even over the thundering hooves, they could make out the sound of a waterfall and the faint smell of sulfur, and headed to it. As they burst into the open around the steaming pool, they suddenly stopped their horses, looking up at the brown and black stone concave cliff that stood fifty paces in front of them and at least eight heights high. A small waterfall cascaded from the top of the dark cliff in a thin sheet on one end, crashing into an oval pool that was almost ninety paces long and sixty wide. The other end of the pool fed what appeared to be a creek that meandered into the forest. Ripples from the waterfall skimmed across the surface and the steam rising from the surface mingled with the mist created by the cascading water.

The forest on the left, near the waterfall was thick and no trails penetrated it. The cliff wrapped around the right, following the creek. As the creek turned out of sight, the forest thickened there as well. They were cornered!

Halfway to the water, the unicorn stopped and wheeled around, sprinting back to them and whinnying, then she turned and headed back toward the water, only to stop yet again and turn back to them.

"She wants us to follow her," Le'ell observed.

"Follow her where?" Chail growled. "There's nowhere to go here!"

Le'ell kicked her horse forward, and when she did the unicorn backed toward the water, her eyes on Chail.

Shaking his head, he followed Le'ell.

Turning to the pond, the unicorn bolted toward it, whinnying a long whinny.

When they were less than twenty paces from the pond, the surface was disturbed, and a dragon's dark red horns emerged from it!

They stopped their horses.

The unicorn also stopped, turning her eyes up as the scarlet dragon rose from the water and waded toward the shore, her eyes on the unicorn.

"Oh, Goddess, no," Le'ell whimpered.

Chail pulled the axe from its saddle strap and kicked his horse forward. Turning as he heard hoof beats, he looked behind them and shouted, "Le'ell!" as the raiders emerged from the forest.

She looked, then kicked her horse forward, directing it toward the waterfall and praying she would find a path into the forest.

Chail followed, glancing back at the pursuing raiders.

The retreat ended in thick, thorny brush with green and red leaves, boulders beyond, and steam rising from the ground somewhere behind. They turned their horses, Le'ell drawing her sword as they prepared for their final stand.

The dragon looked to them, to the raiders, to the unicorn, then back to the raiders.

The little unicorn turned and reared up, whinnying at the raiders, then she came down and held her head low and her front hooves planted out in front of her with a wide stance and her ears laid back as she snorted.

Bearing her teeth, the dragon trumpeted a warning at them.

Stopping when they heard her, eight of the raiders drew axes, swords, spears and crossbows, facing the sleek predator and fanning out to bring their weapons against the three height tall dragon.

Dragon and unicorn exchanged glances, and the dragon looked to the raiders and slowly shook her head. She trumpeted once more, this time higher pitched.

The four raiders still advancing on Chail and Le'ell stopped and turned.

Looking toward the water, the Prince and Princess tried to back their horses away as something else disturbed the water.

A huge volume of air had been released beneath the water and the surface boiled for only a second before something huge exploded through it. Roaring like something of the worst nightmares, the black dragon appeared to be part of the water itself as it cascaded from him, then he separated from it fully as he strode from the pond, turning red glowing eyes on the raiders that threatened the scarlet.

While they were willing to fight the smaller red dragon, this black brute was far too big, clearly too powerful, and their courage failed them.

No matter.

As they retreated back toward the road, the dragon charged, another horrible roar thundering from between his murderous teeth.

Le'ell's horse responded in a panic, rearing up and throwing her.

Chail swung down from his horse, running to her and pulling her up by the arm as she groped for her sword His eyes were still locked wide on the dragon who mauled and slashed his way through the dozen raiders.

The fight was brutally short. None of the raiders escaped his wrath and in a moment they all lay broken and dead with their horses.

Slowly, the black dragon turned, blood dripping from his jaws.

As the dragon advanced on them, Chail drew his sword and pulled Le'ell behind him, poising the blade to defend his princess.

Le'ell tore her eyes from the dragon, looking to the Prince's axe, then she backed away and set her hands on her hips, crying, "That's just terrific, Chail! Brilliant! He can use that to pick your bones out of his teeth after he's eaten you!"

He growled back, "If we're going to die then we're going to die fighting!"

"Did you stop to think that one of us might not *want* to die today?"

Turning his gaze from the dragon, the Prince looked back at her and ordered, "Just get that sword ready!"

Instead, she threw her sword down and shouted, "What good is that going to do? There isn't a sword in the world that's going to kill that thing!"

He turned fully, lowering his axe. "Even now you just have to be difficult, don't you? Did it occur to you that dragons have soft underbellies? One of us could get a lucky shot in!"

"Or he could just burn us both alive! Or he could just stomp on us? What makes you think we even have a chance against him?"

"Le'ell, this is *not* the time to try my patience!"

"I think it's the perfect time. *You* got us cornered here!"

"How can you say that?"

She folded her arms, glaring up at him as he advanced a step toward her. "Whose idea was it to follow that unicorn here, huh?"

"Yours!" he spat back.

As the argument raged, the dragon looked down to the unicorn and the unicorn looked up at the dragon. The unicorn shrugged and slowly they looked back to the fighting humans.

Her mouth trembling in anger, Le'ell just stared at him for long seconds, then she snarled, "Quit trying to backtrack this all on me. I didn't even want to come this way."

The Prince growled and advanced another step, bringing their faces a finger length apart. "Might I remind you—"

"Excuse me," a loud, deep voice thundered from behind.

Chail wheeled around, poising his axe as Le'ell grasped his shoulders and hid behind him. They both stared up at the dragon with horror filled, wide eyes.

Staring back at them, the dragon seated himself and continued, "I hate to interrupt, but you seem to have forgotten about the dragon menace you were arguing about."

"It talks," Chail breathed.

The dragon glanced at the little unicorn, then looked back to him and nodded. "Yes, it talks, fluently in thirteen languages."

His axe shaking, the Prince glared back as best he could, trying his hardest to look intimidating as he informed, "We have no quarrel with you."

"And yet you come with a weapon in your hand," the dragon countered.

"I hold it to defend us," Chail informed.

The dragon nodded again. "I see. And I'll bet you think you will actually do some good with it, seeing as how we dragons have soft underbellies."

"Do you want me to test that?" the Prince asked defiantly.

"Let me save you the trouble," the dragon offered. "It's a myth. My belly is no softer than the stone you are courageously trembling on. Many weapons have been broken against it. But, if you are just determined to fight, then let's fight."

"We'd rather not," Le'ell offered timidly.

"I figured not," the black dragon sighed. He glanced back at the mangled corpses of the raiders and their horses, finishing, "I had hoped to avoid any combat today, but it often seems to find me, much the way you did." His eyes narrowed and he growled, "Strange."

"What do you see?" the Prince asked, also looking to the vanquished raiders.

"Forest trolls," the dragon answered. "Gnomes. There are some higher humans with them. That's an unusual mix, especially considering they usually tend to avoid each other and they are all wearing armor and garb from the same place. That's why you came here, isn't it? You wanted me to attend to them for you."

Le'ell peered around Chail, informing, "We didn't even know you were here. We followed that little unicorn hoping to escape them. We weren't looking to anger you."

"You haven't," he assured, then looked back at them with less than pleased eyes. "You have, however, disturbed an otherwise peaceful day, and that does annoy me."

"Then we will be on our way," Chail said flatly.

The dragon asked in a half interested tone, "On your way to what?"

Le'ell answered, "We have a war to stop. Someone has been attacking patrols on both sides of the border and wishes to make each side think the other is responsible."

Raising his brow, the dragon said, "I see. How are you looking to stop this war?"

Le'ell stepped around the Prince, feeling a little less afraid of the dragon as she answered, "We need to find whoever is responsible and bring them into the open."

"And then what? Once you find them they are not likely going to be willing to just expose themselves to your kingdoms and foil their own plans."

Chail finally lowered his weapon. "What should we do, then?"

"Contrary to myth," the dragon informed, "advice is not always free."

They just stared up at him for a moment, then Le'ell asked, "What do you want?"

He looked at her horse. "How about the gold in your saddlebag?" He raised his hand and the saddlebag lifted up and flew to him, slamming into his palm. "Hmm…" rolled from the dragon's throat as he rummaged through the contents with the claw of one finger.

"How did you know," Le'ell asked in amazement.

"I'm a dragon," was his answer, then he turned his eyes to her. "Half of this is silver."

Chail looked down to her. "Silver?"

She shrugged. "I brought what I could find."

The dragon tossed the saddlebag to Chail. "No thanks. I could stop your war, but not for such trifles." He stood and strode back toward the pool.

The Prince pursued, shouting, "You can stop the war? How?"

Stopping, the dragon half turned and looked down at him. "*How* comes at a high price, and you aren't willing to pay."

"Name your price," Chail insisted.

"A life," the dragon answered, then he glanced at Le'ell and finished, "Hers."

The unicorn sprinted forward, snorting.

The dragon growled to the unicorn, "Quiet, you. I'm negotiating."

The Prince took a step back, pulling Le'ell behind him and raising his sword as he snarled, "No! You're price is too damn high!"

"One life for both your kingdoms and the thousands who you could spare," the dragon chided, then he huffed and turned back to the pond, finishing, "I knew you wouldn't pay. Enjoy your war."

"That isn't fair!" the Prince yelled at the dragon, who ignored him and strode on.

"Wait!" Le'ell cried, rushing around the Prince.

The dragon stopped and half turned, looking down at her.

"Le'ell, no!" Chail ordered as he dropped the saddle bag and grasped for her.

She pulled away and walked gingerly toward the dragon. "If I give my life to you, will you promise to stop the war?"

He shrugged and turned fully. "I'll do what I can, assuming it doesn't involve too much effort on my part." He laid down to his belly, propping himself up on his elbows. "Of course, my bargain must be with him, not you."

Chail took her arm and turned her toward him, ordering, "You aren't doing this!"

Raising her hands to frame his face, Le'ell countered, "I have to. We have to. Chail, there is no other way. If he can save thousands of our people then we must."

"It isn't fair," he growled through clenched teeth, tears in his eyes.

"You have to let me," she insisted, tears in her eyes as well. "Please, Chail. You would do it for me. I know you would." She pulled him to her, kissing him as hard and passionately as she could, one last time. Finally pulling away, she backed from him, holding onto his hand until she was out of arm's reach, then she turned and approached the dragon, who had his attention focused beyond her and was tapping the ground with one claw. Her eyes were low and her hands folded before her as she softly said, "I'm ready for you."

His eyes shifted to her and he mumbled, "What?"

"Please, just kill me quickly," she asked. "I won't resist."

He looked away again, just tapping his finger as he countered, "I'm sure you won't, but I have no appetite for humans today."

She backed away a step. "You aren't going to eat me?"

He snarled and looked back to her. "You were just sucking on his mouth. That doesn't exactly inspire one's hunger. Besides, you're worth more alive to me than dead."

Le'ell blinked. "What would you have of me?"

"In time," the dragon replied. "How important is stopping this war to you?"

"Important enough for me to give my life to you," she reminded.

"So it would seem," he confirmed. "You have quite a journey ahead of you."

Chail approached and informed, "We were heading north, toward this village on the other side of the border. I thought we might find a few answers there."

"You can stop there at your own peril," the dragon corrected, "but your answers are elsewhere. Do you know where the Dead Forest is?"

"I've heard of it," the Prince replied. "From the scripts I've read, nothing lives in there. The trees are dead but don't rot. The rain doesn't fall there and many who have ventured there have never been heard from again."

"And you will have to be one of the few who will be," the dragon said. "North of the Dead Forest is where you will find your answers. Follow the road that takes you through the heart of that forest and be on your guard from the time you leave here to the time you find your answers, and take care of my property." He looked down at the little unicorn, grunted to her, then he stood and turned back toward the pond.

"Dragon," Le'ell called, striding quickly toward him a few steps.

He stopped and looked over his shoulder.

She looked almost hopefully up at him and timidly asked, "Do you remember me?"

Raising a brow, the dragon answered, "The girl who likes to run in Grawrdox herds. Of course I remember you." He turned back to the pond and dropped to all fours, sliding back into the water. The scarlet dragon followed him.

Le'ell suddenly felt a certain sense of importance as she watched the water calm. She had been acknowledged by the most feared, most awesome creature in the world. He actually remembered her, remembered that day he had first seen her.

Chail approached from behind the Princess and took her shoulders, offering, "We'll figure something out. When this is over, I'll find a way to get you back."

"I trust you," she whispered back, staring into the pond. She finally realized that the unicorn was standing in front of her, just staring at her, a certain curiosity in her eyes.

Le'ell dared to reach to her and gingerly scratched her between the ears, and she smiled as the unicorn lowered her head and stepped closer to her. "This seems to make everything worth the sacrifice," she said softly. "She's so soft. She feels like she's made of magic and dreams."

Chail reached to the unicorn and gently scratched under her jaw, smiling slightly as she closed her eyes and raised her nose, then he glanced at the pond, asking, "Is that the dragon you saw the day you were captured?"

She nodded, her eyes on the unicorn as she gently stroked her mane.

"Unicorn of snow," the Prince recalled. "Dragon of night."

Le'ell looked back to him.

He stared down at the unicorn and continued, "She teach you the way of peace; he teach you the way of war. Listen to them both." His eyes shifted to Le'ell's.

"Pay heed to what she does and where she goes," Le'ell also remembered aloud. "She said the unicorn would lead us to the dragon of night, that I would give myself to him. Chail, we've done everything the old woman said!"

The unicorn looked up to her and softly whickered.

He turned his eyes to the unicorn, then nodded and agreed, "We need to do the rest, then. She mentioned the death of a forest. The dragon mentioned the Dead Forest."

"Dark place," Le'ell recalled. "Do you think she meant the Dark Mountains?"

He considered, then met her gaze. "The Dark Mountains are just north of the Dead Forest." His eyes widened. "Aalekilk Castle is in the Dark Mountains."

The Princess' lips parted slightly as she stared back at him. "They— They tried to bring our kingdoms down before. I thought we had destroyed them forty seasons ago."

"Apparently not," he corrected. "We may need to pay Aalekilk a visit."

"And if we find it deserted?" she asked. "That's a long journey to take for an assumption. Of course, that's where the dragon seems to want us to go."

He nodded. "We may just find it rebuilt, rearmed and re-manned. She mentioned trolls and a mixed bastard army *before* we brought the raider bodies back to Enulam."

"*His* mixed bastard army," she corrected. "Who could hold such power over forest trolls and gnomes?"

"And a number of other men," the Prince added. He turned and strode to his waiting horse and as he secured his axe behind his saddle, he looked to the unicorn and asked, "Are you coming?"

She whinnied back at him, dancing restlessly.

He looked to Le'ell and observed, "Well, at least we have one ally."

No one spoke much as they journeyed north. The unicorn stayed a few paces in front of them, glancing back occasionally. Chail and Le'ell trusted that she knew where she was going and simply followed.

This trust in her was absolute, as if the prophecy of the old woman at Enulam was certain to come to pass.

Unexpectedly, the unicorn stopped, looking ahead and to the right side of the road.

Chail stopped his horse, Le'ell stopping beside him. As they watched her stalk toward a thick clump of brush, their hands slowly, discreetly found their weapons.

The little unicorn's eyes were locked on something, her head low. She sniffed something in the bush, her eyes locked on it.

Le'ell whispered to the Prince, "She sees something."

With one more step, the unicorn sniffed the bush again, then began to nibble off some of the blue and purple berries that grew on it.

"Or," Chail guessed, "she's hungry."

They exchanged looks, then they turned their eyes back to the unicorn.

She nibbled away, seemingly oblivious to their presence for some time.

The confidence the Prince and Princess had felt earlier seemed to slowly slip away.

Chail pursed his lips, wondering aloud, "Does she really know where she's going?"

Le'ell glanced at him. "It was your idea to follow her, right?"

He shook his head.

"That's what I thought," she murmured. When the unicorn raised her head and looked at her, she just smiled and bade, "Don't let us disturb you. You just go right on and eat your fill."

The unicorn blinked, then went back to the berries.

Loosing a deep breath, Chail said, "Well, I suppose the horses could use some rest, perhaps some grain." His eyes locked on the unicorn as she half turned her head, her ears twitching. For a moment she stood perfectly still and seemed to be listening for something behind her, in the trees on the other side of the road. His horse grew slightly agitated, then quickly calmed. "Le'ell," he ordered in a low voice, looking to the trees there. "Your bow."

She reached for it, looking where he did. When she finally heard something take a step just out of sight, she froze, her eyes widening.

The brush moved.

Chail tightened his grip on his sword.

Branches pushed forward and separated and the big bay unicorn emerged from the brush on the other side of the road, his eyes on the little white unicorn.

She turned fully and paced to him, nuzzling him. He did not seem to return her affection and, in fact, appeared to be a little annoyed. When he looked up to the humans in his presence, a snort confirmed this. He was annoyed.

As Le'ell and Chail watched, he nudged the white unicorn and whickered. She backed away and barked a quick whinny, and as his eyes narrowed and he whickered again, she laid her ears back and lowered her head, looking up at him like someone who had taken a good scolding. He bayed, apparently *at* her and nudged her with his nose again, turning her toward a path, following and nudging her again. She looked back and whickered at them, then turned and bolted into the forest, the bay following. In a few seconds they were gone, not even to be heard in the distance.

"He seems a little overprotective," Le'ell observed.

Chail nodded. "He definitely doesn't approve of the white one so close to us, that's for certain. I'm wondering if that is her father, her mate, or just what he is to her."

Le'ell shrugged, then slid her eyes to him. "Would you approve of me in the presence of others?"

"Absolutely not!" he scoffed. "The very idea." He kicked his horse forward. "The next man who even glances at you will have his entrails torn from him."

Smiling, Le'ell followed.

"That's unless he angers me," he went on. "If I get angry I might just do something nasty to him."

She giggled as she caught up to him and asked, "Like what?"

He glanced at her. "Things too horrible to even mention, things so horrible I don't even know what they are."

Le'ell laughed, and laughed more as he continued on, clearly to amuse her. This was the attention she always craved from him, and he would not disappoint her.

The town was simply called Border. Nestled between the territories of Aalekilk, Zondae, Enulam, and Red Stone, this small settlement had grown over the seasons to a bustling center of trade. Since it was recognized to be either in neutral or disputed land, it became a hub of commerce and diplomatic talks. With no monarch to lead the people within, the only law seemed to be whatever was right at the moment. Law was most governed by those doing business there, those who sought business, those who sought trade and commerce... Oh, I could go on.

Needless to say, there was no recognized central government. Visitors would come from all over the land to attend their affairs or, for those of good fortune, to just take holiday. Rooms, food, and the pleasures of both men and women were traded as freely as gold and silver.

This is the place sought by two people who should never have met. Rivals would ride abreast down the central road of the sprawling township, attracting many an eye as they absently looked around them, marveling at the many grand structures of wood and stone that were all around them. Many on horseback or horse-drawn carriage passed by, many more afoot to visit the seemingly endless shops and taverns that abounded here. Goods were traded from sunup to sundown, goods which included covert information, the very kind sought by the travelers who came to this place of money and sin from rival kingdoms.

Each knew that no others could know their identities. A prince or princess would bring a hefty price in ransom for their kingdom or a rival, or they could just be sold into the expanding slave trade of the region. They simply had to appear to be a pair of travelers looking to trade in this busy place.

Prince Chail raised his chin to a huge, three level stone structure on his left. "There it is. The *Lucky Merchant Inn*. Dahkam visited there once or twice and told me of the lavish attractions within. He said the food is also pretty good."

"That's the word I'm looking for!" Princess Le'ell announced, turning her horse toward it. "Can we sample everything?"

"We don't have that much time," he reminded. "I figure we can stay the night, perhaps get some information and supplies and head out in the morning or afternoon tomorrow. I hear they also have maps there. That could come in handy."

She sighed. "All I want right now is a hot meal, a hot bath and a warm bed."

He glanced at her and smiled. "You shouldn't tease me like that."

Le'ell glanced back at him, a slight smile on her lips. "Or you'll what? Ravish me like a barbarian all night?"

"I may."

She smiled broader. "Then I should go on teasing you, shouldn't I?"

He pursed his lips, then turned his eyes to her and smiled back. "We need to get you fed and into that bath."

Within, the Lucky Merchant Inn was everything they expected. The ground floor alone was forty paces deep and almost as wide. The stone floor was polished gray marble. The fifty or so tables all around a central lobby, clearly a place where all forms of comforts were demanded, were all oil lamp lit and made of dark wood. Most were small and round with two or three chairs around them, but a few, distributed among the smaller ones, were long ovals surrounded by up to ten chairs. Most of the larger ones half of the small ones were occupied by a variety of people, many there for the entertainment offered by the place and many others simply doing business. There was such a mix of patrons that one wondered how they all coexisted together without total mayhem ensuing. Hundreds of people were in there; barbarians to court advisors to palace stewards, warriors from many kingdoms, diplomats, common traders… They were all present and more. The sounds of the many conversations, laughter and heated negotiations melted together in a single low roar.

Looking to their left as they entered, there was an elaborately decorated wall with many doorways leading to the other side. The sounds of a bustling kitchen would pierce the roar of the patrons from time to time. To their right was a staircase that spiraled up to the next level. Beyond it was a long desk or bar where many transactions appeared to be taking place.

Two score of wenches, each dressed in a long red skirt and low cut, sleeveless white top carried trays of food and drink to the tables from the kitchen and empty dishes and goblets from the tables. Most of them smiled and seemed to enjoy the flirtatious banter of the patrons. Many flirted back. Rendezvous were planned by some after the end of their shift. Others scoffed and went about their duties. The chaos would remind one of an ant mound, and yet there was a certain order to it.

Chail noticed right away the strategically placed large men who kept watch over the activity. They were armed with clubs as opposed to swords and many wore helmets. Their dress was simple: White jerkins and red trousers. He reasoned that these twenty or so large men must be the guards, those who maintained order.

Le'ell found herself captivated by the ornate and colorful decorations that were scattered about the large hall and hanging from the exposed timbers of the high ceiling. Her eyes found the central lobby where deep, red cushioned chairs were distributed on animal skin rugs. An open fire pit in the center burned brightly and scantly clad male and female servants tended the people who did their business there. Many of the seats were empty and she secretly hoped that Prince Chail would take her there, knowing that he would not.

Finding an empty table, he thoughtfully pulled out a chair and invited her to sit. She flashed him a flirty smile and daintily settled herself into it, allowing him to push her up to the table. She watched him as he walked around the table and seated himself, and her smile never faltered. This would prove to be contagious as his eyes met hers. For some time they just stared into each other's eyes. Such communication between them said more than words ever could.

Le'ell finally tore her eyes away, first looking down, then to the long desk behind the stairs.

One of the wenches, a red haired woman with a generous bust-line approached and asked in a strong accent of the area, "Would the strapping gentleman like a cold drink?"

He glanced at her, then turned his gaze back to Le'ell and replied, "How about a pitcher of stout ale."

"Two tankards?" the wench asked.

He shook his head. "Just one."

"And the lovely lady?" she continued, looking to Le'ell.

The Princess glanced at her, then looked to her Prince and raised her brow.

He smiled just a little more, answering, "The lovely lady will have your sweetest wine, although you'll be hard pressed to find one that truly compliments her."

Looking away, Le'ell raised a hand to her mouth, trying not to giggle.

The wench also smiled. "I see the gentleman has good taste. Anything to eat?"

He turned his eyes to her. "Whatever you recommend."

She nodded and turned toward the kitchen. "I'll be right out with that ale and wine, Love, snap snap."

As the wench hurried off, Le'ell panned her eyes back to the Prince, a slightly seductive smile curling her lips as she said, "I could gladly grow old listening to you speak to me so."

"I could gladly grow old speaking to you so," he answered. A distraction tore his gaze from her and he turned his head slightly, his eyes narrowing as they locked on something.

Le'ell turned and looked, clearly not seeing what he did and she asked, "What is it?"

"Perhaps nothing," he replied, then he pushed away from the table and bade, "Pardon me one moment. I'll be right back."

"Hurry back," she ordered. "I'll get lonely."

He nodded, then turned and strode to a table some paces away, a table with four tough looking soldiers or barbarians seated there.

This was clearly what he had referred to a couple of times as a man thing so she would not approach herself, nor was she interested in watching his interactions with them. His walk and posture did not hint at anything challenging, so she took the time to look the room over, her eyes shifting from table to table, person to person.

The wench returned with the wine and ale and put them on the table in turn, asking, "Where would the lady's strapping young gentleman be?"

"He's making some friends," Le'ell replied.

Nodding, the wench turned back toward the kitchen, informing, "I'll be back in a short with your meal."

Le'ell gave her but a glance as she waded back through the tables. Of interest to her was how many of the men and women interacted as equals. This was a foreign concept for her, one that intrigued her. If only the warriors of Zondae and Enulam could be so. She could finally have a life with her prince.

Lost in her thoughts, she did not notice the three men who approached her with greedy, lustful eyes. When the largest of them seized her chair and brutally turned her, she finally took notice, meeting his gaze with surprise and a little fear. He was a large man with dirty swordsman's trousers and scuffed boots, a broad leather belt laden with a broadsword, pouches, and two daggers. His shirt had the sleeves torn off, revealing thick arms. Long, greasy dark hair did not appear to have been groomed for months and his face bore about a week's beard. His two companions were of similar dress and grooming, though smaller. They had the look of those who might hover around a larger man almost for protection, clearly feeling safer in his presence.

A glance at the Prince, whose back was to her, drained fear from her and she raised her brow as she stared up at the man before her.

He was an arrogant sort and propped a booted foot on her chair right between her legs.

She glanced down at his leg, then back to his face.

Looking her over, he finally nodded and said to his comrades, "Aye, this one looks like one good to bed tonight."

"I'll have her second," one of his companions laughed. "Don't wear her out like the last, mate!" He slapped the larger man's shoulder and they all shared a good laugh.

Le'ell smiled and folded her arms, asking, "What makes you boys think you are worthy to even compete for me?"

The larger of them sneered at her. "I'll change your mind when I have you on your back, wench."

She huffed a laugh. "Or I'll lie there and laugh." She pushed his boot from her chair and waved them away, ordering as she turned her chair back toward the table, "Go on and play with each other. It's the closest you'll get to a woman today."

He turned her chair again, leaning down toward her as he snarled, "Sounds like this one could use a lesson in respect. Maybe give her one right here."

Le'ell half turned her head, meeting his eyes without even contempt in hers as she informed, "You must have nothing else to live for." She sighed, shaking her head. "If you want me, you'll have to win me in a fair fight, and I really don't think you're up to it."

He laughed and pushed off of her chair, backing up a couple of steps as he leered down at her. "It's a fight you'll be wantin? Let's get it done, then. I'll try not to be hurtin' ya, not until you're in me bed."

She glanced at one of his companions, then shook her head and corrected, "You don't fight me, moron. You fight the man I'm with, and I *really* don't think you're up to the task."

He folded his thick arms, snarling, "I'll tell you what I'm up to, wench."

"All three of you?" she asked.

He huffed a laugh. "I've bested better than you think. Why would I need help for the likes of him?"

She motioned behind him with her eyes.

He looked over his shoulder, then up.

Prince Chail stood less than a pace behind him with his massive arms folded, staring down at the big man with narrow eyes.

Slowly, the big man turned back to Le'ell, looking much less than confident. As his companions backed away, he met her gaze and found himself unable to speak.

Smiling ever so slightly, she raised her brow and informed, "He knows a thousand ways to kill you—and a thousand ways more to make you wish he had."

He turned his eyes down and nodded. "I'll be taking your word for it."

Chail's eyes remained on him as he and his companions hurried toward the door, then he took his seat across from Le'ell and raised a brow at her. "Can't I leave you alone for a single moment?"

Le'ell picked up her goblet of wine and raised her brow back at him, countering, "I told you to hurry back. So did you find anything out?"

He poured a full tankard of ale, his eyes on it as he replied, "That dragon wasn't entirely right. Those men I talked to are mercenaries hired by a castle in the Dark Mountains. They were approached by a number of soldiers who were all heading to the Southwest from here about four days ago."

"Into Zondaen territory," she finished for him.

He nodded and picked up his tankard, turning steely eyes on her. "Quite possibly some of the very raiders we killed on our way to your castle." Drawing the goblet to his mouth, he took several deep, loud gulps from it before putting it back down.

"That could be the good news," she guessed. "If they're hiring mercenaries and they need our kingdoms to go to war, then they could very likely not have much of a standing army to attack us with."

Chail took another couple of gulps, then added, "Or, they could just be unwilling to commit their main army so soon into a conflict. They could be using mercenaries and the forest trolls as pawns to feel us out before their main assault."

She looked to her own goblet and nodded. "Whittle our forces down, bring us to war with each other, then when we're depleted they strike in force." She turned her eyes to him and asked, "Do you have a plan to stop them?"

"Without relying on the help of that dragon?" he countered.

She shrugged.

He vented a long breath and took another couple of loud swallows from his goblet before he answered. "Those men over there have invited me to go with them, you as well if I wish to bring you. That could be our way in."

"They don't know you're from Enulam?"

Chail shook his head. "I told them we came across the hard lands from the Territhan Valley seeking our fortune. They seemed to believe me."

"You do have a way with words," she complimented.

"Paling to yours," he countered. "A thousand ways to kill you? Simply brilliant."

He got a flirty smile in response.

CHAPTER 11

Le'ell awoke the next morning right where she wanted to be and where her Prince wanted her, wrapped in Chail's massive arms. However, their morning would not remain so appealing. Barely up and dressed, they found themselves engaged in yet another heated argument.

Dressed in a red swordswoman's shirt and black riding trousers, Le'ell threw her white shirt from the day before at him and shouted, "No, I shouldn't understand! You act like I would be in your way!"

Standing on the other side of the bed, he caught her shirt with one hand and threw it back, countering, "That isn't remotely what I said. These matters are usually attended to between *men!* That doesn't mean one brings his woman to such meetings."

She threw the shirt back at him. "So now I'm not even an equal? Do you think we're back at Enulam where I would be considered your property?"

Catching the shirt with the same hand, he corrected, "That's not what I'm saying, either."

"Then what *are* you saying?"

He loosed an impatient breath and hurled her shirt back. "I'm saying the world outside of the Zondaen border is not what you think it is. Such men as I'm meeting with will see you as a distraction."

She set her hands on her hips and glared at him, snarling, "So now I'm nothing more than a distraction. Don't you think my presence would at least—"

"No I don't!" he shouted. "Would you pull your thumbs out of your ears and listen for once? These men don't care that you want to be considered equal to them."

"Well, they should!"

"They don't!" he said slowly. "Le'ell, all of the warrior prowess in the world will not change the fact that you're a woman and that's all they will see!"

"Is that all *you* see?" she spat back.

He growled and turned his eyes up. A second later the shirt hit him in the face.

Laughing, Le'ell covered her mouth, pointing at him as she tried to say something but simply could not talk.

Chail plucked the shirt from the air before it could hit the floor and slowly he turned his narrow eyes to her. Much quicker than he appeared, he launched himself over the bed, one stride finding the middle of it as Le'ell barked a scream and turned to retreat. There was really nowhere to go and he was upon her quickly, enveloping her in his arms from behind and picking her up off of the floor.

Half screaming and half laughing, she struggled to free herself, kicking her still bare feet wildly as she was carried backward toward the bed. Her next realization was being hurled through the air and landing on the bed face down. Laughing anew, she turned over and raised her hands to defend herself as the Prince pounced upon her, and she managed to get in one good kick before he seized her wrists and pinned her down. She groaned loudly as his bulk crushed the air from her, then a strained giggle escaped her as she looked up at him.

He could not help but smile, but managed not to laugh as he lowered his face to hers and ordered, "Give it up now, woman."

Her giggling stopped and she just stared up at him for long seconds, then she raised her face and seized his lips with hers.

Their kiss lasted for some time, Le'ell's head sinking back to the bed.

When he finally pulled away, he raised an eyebrow and asked, "Do you give up yet?"

"No," was her answer as she kissed him again. She pulled back a moment later, demanding, "*You* surrender."

"Don't think so," he replied.

She kissed him forcibly again before asking, "Do you give up now?"

He looked away and considered, then met her gaze and conceded, "Sure, I give up, but you still aren't going."

"Chail!" she complained.

"Like it or not," he said over her, "I have a promise to keep to your mother and I am going to look out for you as long as there is breath in my body."

"I don't need to be looked after," she informed harshly.

"I know you don't, Le'ell, but you have to understand how things here work. The men I need to talk to would see you as something of barter and I'll not have them leering at you so while I am negotiating with them."

A slight smile curled her lips. "Oh, so I would be more a distraction to *you* than them. I see." She drew a breath and nodded. "Very well, go on and play with your yob friends. I'll just wait here like a good girl."

He raised a brow again. "Do you expect me to believe that?"

"No," she answered. "I may just go and have a look around."

Chail sighed. "And you wonder why I worry so much."

"I'll stay out of trouble," she assured. "You just do the same."

"Where are you going?" he questioned.

"We passed a market on the way to the inn," she replied. "I just want to have a look around, see what I can find that appeals to me."

"And spend all of our money," he added.

"Hey," she protested. "It came from *my* kingdom."

He kissed her and got up, offering his hand to her as he ordered, "Just remember that we're trying to stop a war and try to remain somewhat focused."

She grabbed his hand and he pulled her to her feet, and she assured, "I remember." Then she cocked an eyebrow up and ordered, "Just don't let your eyes stray."

Chail smiled slightly. "Le'ell, no woman has yet been born who could possibly appeal to me more than you."

The Princess watched him as he walked to the door, taking his sword and belt from the bed as he walked by, then she watched the door for long seconds after it closed. Her head leaned toward her shoulder as a sigh escaped her, and she whispered, "Don't be long, my Prince."

❧

The market was everything she had hoped and more. Many colors and smells tantalized her from every direction. Many foods and an endless variety of goods were all around her, as was quite a crowd of people for this early hour. Coming this far north, especially outside of the Zondaen border was forbidden and she doubted if anyone at her kingdom had ever seen this place or anything like it before.

She stopped at many of the shops and tents she found along the way, purchasing something small to eat at a few of them, trinkets at a few more. For the most part, she enjoyed looking at all of the things around her. The jewelry caught her eye, but did not really appeal to her. She stopped to sniff fresh flowers, looked at some impressive sculptures, then froze as she came upon one tent. Within, there were hand weapons of many kinds, at least fifty different swords, a hundred daggers, bows, crossbows, arrows and bolts, axes, halberds, shields, maces… This place was an armory for sale!

Hesitantly, she went in, her eyes darting about from piece to piece. Though the tent was a little drab on the outside, it was well lit within and decorated with a few tapestries, busts guarding the entrance, suits of armor on three sides and even a vase of flowers. A table on the far side had many elaborately decorated daggers and swords lay out on red velvet. She approached the table, her eyes locked on the silver and brass metal, the etching and the gold ribbon in some of them. There were even elaborately decorated arrows lined up neatly on one side.

So involved in the display was she that she did not even notice the very dark skinned man who approached from the corner of the tent.

"Do you see anything you like?" he asked in a pleasant voice.

Le'ell spun around, her hand on her sword as she faced the tall man.

His skin was very dark brown, his long hair shiny black. He wore a brown leather jerkin over a very well developed chest, and also wore high boots, tan trousers and a bronze gauntlet around his left forearm. A gold medallion hung by a chain from his neck, a medallion in the shape of a long, sharp tooth.

Sporting a friendly smile, he raised his hands before him and assured, "My apologies. I didn't mean to startle you." He had a strange accent she had never heard before.

She raised her chin but kept her hand on her sword. Looking him up and down, she realized he was unarmed and relaxed just slightly. She met his eyes with a cold, challenging stare.

He glanced around through the long seconds of tense silence and finally broke it with a simple question. "So, what appeals to you? Believe me; I am far more interested in selling you a blade than testing one in your hand."

Something about his tone and posture made her believe him and she slowly moved her hand from her sword. She looked him up and down again, then looked to one side of the tent and informed, "I just came in to see what you have."

"I understand," he responded, then added, "If you care to hold anything, please feel free to do so. I have many pieces in here that would fit your grip nicely."

"Oh, really," she chided, looking behind him to a sword in the middle of a stand with six others. Her eyes narrowed and she raised her chin toward it, saying, "I've never seen a sword like that before."

He turned and nodded, then strode to it and picked it up, turning back to present it to her. "It's called a scimitar, the preferred weapon of many warriors to the south of here."

Le'ell took the hilt, expecting a weapon with such a broad blade to be much heavier than it was and raising her brow when she discovered it was not.

"It cuts through your enemies as easily as it cuts through the air," he continued. "It is balanced to handle and parry easily and yet with enough weight near the end to deliver a killing blow, even through leather armor."

"What about steel armor?" she asked, her eyes on the weapon.

"That all depends on the quality of the armor," was his answer. "A single chop from that blade will not do the damage a battle axe will, but it will do more than a sword will. Anyone who would challenge you with that in your hand would have to be a brave one."

She finally turned her eyes to him. "So you're telling me this weapon has an advantage over my sword?"

He shrugged and folded his arms. "I suppose that depends on how comfortable you are with your sword. While you might know how to maneuver your sword easily, with just a little training you could handle the scimitar just as easily." He looked down at her sword and asked, "May I?"

Le'ell drew her sword from its sheath with her left hand and handed it over to him, never taking her eyes from the shiny weapon she held.

He looked it over, turning it over in his hand several times and closely examining the hilt, finally pursing his full lips and nodding. "Zondaen."

Her eyes snapped to him.

Looking back at her, he continued, "I've seen the work before and managed to acquire a few of these recently. I've also always marveled at how such a light, supple blade can do so much damage in battle."

She raised her chin slightly. "You seem to know quite a bit about Zondaen weapons."

"Knowing about weapons is my business," he informed.

Le'ell glanced at her sword and asked, "So, have any crossed your path of late?"

He motioned with his head across the tent and informed, "Those two over there were brought to me yesterday."

She turned and looked, seeing two cleaned and polished Zondaen swords leaning on a wooden rack that was clearly meant for eight swords, though it was just the two. She absently handed the scimitar back to him and approached them. The marks on the hilt of one showed it to be carried by a soldier of low rank, but the other was more ornate, more customized, and clearly showed the marks of its former owner. Le'ell knew the woman who last carried it, and her lips tightened as she asked, "How did you come by these?"

"They were brought to me by travelers," was his answer. "They were not marred and did not appear to have been used in battle and they were not asking that much for them. In fact, I think I got quite a bargain on them, considering their quality."

Nodding, she turned and looked to him, trying not to seem suspicious. "Did these travelers say how they came by these swords?"

He shook his head. "I don't make others' business mine. They simply came to me to trade, and trade we did."

She looked at her own sword, still in his hand, then turned her eyes to his. "Perhaps I will trade with you, if you have what I need."

Raising his inquisitive, bushy eyebrows, he nodded and said, "I never turn down a beautiful woman, not one that wishes to do business with me."

Le'ell smiled slightly. "Since you put it that way, perhaps we can."

"Interested in that scimitar?" he asked hopefully.

"I may just be," she answered. "I'm more interested in something else."

He became uneasy and took a half step back, a nervous smile on his lips as he informed, "You are the most seductive temptress I've been approached by for many seasons, but I have a wife and family and my loyalty is completely with them."

She just stared at him for a moment, then covered her mouth and giggled slightly, trying not to be impolite. Straining to regain her composure, she shook her head and explained, "No, you don't understand. That isn't what I want."

He folded his arms. "Well. I'm both relieved and insulted."

She laughed again. "I'm sorry. That's not what I meant, either."

Turning his face away from her, he raised his chin in a display of overacting and spat, "You think I am not worth your effort. I understand plenty. You have wounded me."

Le'ell shook her head, smiling as she just played along. "Okay, I'm sorry. Of course I would bed you. But we both have—"

"So those *are* your intentions," he accused. "I knew you had foul thoughts."

"Okay, so how do I ease your mind?"

He glanced at her. "That depends on what you intend to trade."

"And if I buy that scimitar?" she asked.

Raising a brow, he turned his eyes to her. "By chance, that might win my trust."

She giggled and took it from his hand, looked it over, and turned narrow eyes on him, a smile still on her lips as she insisted, "I want to try it first."

He smiled back. "A demonstration would be my pleasure." He carefully put her sword on the table and took another one on his way out of the tent.

Le'ell followed, parrying the scimitar many times to get a feel for it. She clearly did not expect him to wheel around and attack so suddenly, but she found that many seasons of training had honed her reflexes and the weapon in her hand responded to her command before she realized. Her opponent was a strong man, very quick for his size, and his blade slid off of hers and cut toward her again. She met it smartly a second time, and met his third with a parry that sent him off balance and before he recovered he found the scimitar at his throat and froze. Le'ell was not even winded, but shook her head and smiled slightly as she said, "You made that almost too easy."

Turning his eyes to her, he smiled back and admitted, "I never claimed to be an expert swordsman, but as a procurer of fine weapons, I can easily tell that the blade simply likes you."

She withdrew her weapon, staring back at him. "Or do you just want me to think it likes me?"

"I'm sure it does," he assured. "Did the blade itself not convince you?"

"It's trying," she answered. "I might be convinced to buy two others, for the right price."

He smiled broadly and informed, "I have the best prices on steel in Border. Feel free to ask anyone."

"I would rather get my answers from you," she countered.

Nodding, he extended his hand to the tent and offered, "Then perhaps we should negotiate. I'm sure I have more for you than just blades after all."

For such a long conversation, Le'ell learned very little about where the Zondaen swords had come from. While the merchant did his best to accommodate her, he simply did not have the knowledge she sought. Still, as she listened to what he did know, she felt she had something of an ally in him and that she could trust his words. While she learned little about her mission to stop the coming war, he gladly shared many exploits of his young sons and would occasionally go on about his lovely wife.

Glancing outside the tent, Le'ell wondered if Chail was through with his negotiations. She stood and stretched, smiling down at him as she said, "Well thank you for your hospitality and for pricing the swords like you did."

He also stood, extending his hand to her and offered with a smile, "Thank you for the visit and for your business. I'll be sure to have the swords as you requested. Perhaps your Chail will visit me as well soon."

She nodded. "I'll bring him by. You have many pieces in here that are sure to catch his eye, and you do have a charming way of selling."

He laughed softly and admitted, "I'm not sure such charm would work on any but a beautiful woman, but I'm willing to try if I must. Come and visit me again if you have time, if for no other reason than just for the company you offer."

Le'ell nodded to him and assured, "I'll do that. Good day." She turned to leave, then stopped and turned back to him. "You know, I never did catch your name."

He raised his chin slightly and announced, "I am called Noorain."

"I'll remember," she assured. "I'm Le'ell." She turned and walked casually away from the tent, her eyes still panning back and forth as she looked for anything interesting as she made her way back to the inn.

Near the edge of the marketplace she found another tent that looked very busy and veered toward it. Inside she found many fine pieces of leather, belts, sheathes, jerkins and the like. Further in were more pieces, these appearing to be more for restraining slaves. Seeing them gave her a chill, and as she turned she saw an assortment of whips hanging on a display board and she froze. Memories of days before assaulted her and she found herself trembling, finally tearing her eyes away and making for the exit. Le'ell stopped again, her eyes finding the slave girl who had been used as bait on the day she was captured.

Dressed as she had been, the slave girl sat on a stool and casually glanced around her. She was sporting many of the restraints that were being sold within, including a collar that seemed to have her loosely tethered to the stool. Ankle and wrist restraints made of fine leather and bronze were tightly in place but seemed not to bother her.

Her eyes narrowing, Le'ell slowly approached, folding her arms when she was about a pace away. "Well well," she snarled, "what a small world this is."

Looking up at her, the slave girl's eyes widened and her mouth fell open.

"Still helping them trap innocent women?" she spat. "I think you like what you do for them. I think it's good sport for you."

Slowly sliding from the stool, the slave girl tried to back away.

Le'ell pursued a step, her lip curling as she growled, "I've been hoping I would run into you again."

The slave girl shook her head, pleading, "I just do like I'm told. I'll be punished if I don't obey."

"No, you like what you do," Le'ell guessed, "almost as much as I'm going to like giving you back some of the frustration I went through— and some of the pain!"

"I'm sure you would," a man agreed from behind.

Le'ell spun around, finding herself face to face with one of the slave hunters from days before. He was her height, clearly not much of a warrior, but the look in his eye told her he was not alone. When she turned to leave she encountered another, who struck her hard across the jaw with the back of his hand, nearly rendering her unconscious. Before she had her wits about her she was drug from the tent and into an alley between two of the buildings near the inn. Her hands where bound behind her. Her belt was removed from her and a thick leather collar was secured around her neck, a tether securing it to her wrists.

Before she realized, she was slammed back-first into a stone wall and found herself confronted by the dirty man who had whipped her.

He smiled, his breath stinking worse than she remembered as he said, "Well now. Look what we've found."

She glanced around. Most of the men who had been there when she was captured were there with him, along with two new ones.

"Looks like we've found us a runaway," the dirty man continued. "How much'll that king pay to have 'er back?"

Another said, "I'll be wagerin' we'll get a better price just sellin' 'er."

Le'ell swallowed hard, recognizing the taste of blood in her mouth and feeling it trickle from the corner of her lips. She knew she would have to find Chail as soon as possible, knowing that he could easily take all of these men at once. She just prayed she would get to see it.

The dirty man raised his chin, his eyes narrowing as he sneered, "We'll be takin' ya to the stable with the rest of the slave wenches. Don't give me no trouble or I'll be takin' you to another hut where I can have at ya with me whip again. Ya hearin' me?"

Hesitantly, she nodded.

"Ain't gonna give me no problems?" he asked, half turning his head.

"I won't," she assured. "Please just don't hurt me again." She had to make him believe she had been broken, at least until she saw Chail.

With a man taking each arm, she was led from the alley, her mind racing as she pondered a way out before they arrived at this corral. Her eyes darting around, she prayed she would find her Prince and he would once again come to her rescue.

It was not to be.

Nearly to the stable, the dirty man was confronted by someone who stopped the whole group. This was a huge man whose size rivaled the Stablemaster at Enulam. His skin was deep brown, almost black. He had full lips and piercing dark blue eyes. Wearing nothing on his head, not even hair, his scalp shined in the bright sunlight. He wore loosely fitting black trousers and high black boots. A thick black belt had many pouches hanging from it and was fastened by an elaborate gold buckle. A red jerkin fit tightly around his trunk, his chest bulging through it. His back and broad, thick shoulders were covered by a heavy cape that appeared to be made of brown Grawrdox hair. Dangling from his neck was an amulet, a perfect emerald sphere in a web of gold suspended by a heavy gold chain. Judging from how elaborately decorated his jerkin and cape were, he seemed to be a man of some wealth and importance, a wizard who knew how to live comfortably.

Behind him was a tall woman, at or a little over Pa'lesh's height, with dark amber eyes and fiery red hair. She wore a long cloak with the hood down and appeared to be scantly clad if at all beneath it. She also wore an amulet that was just like the large black man's, but smaller.

He approached Le'ell with purpose, staring down at her with eyes that looked upon her with some familiarity, yet scrutinized her as if she was something for sale in the market. He waved his hand to the two men who led the small entourage that escorted Le'ell toward the stables and they moved out of his way as he strode up to her and looked her over for some time.

She stared back nervously.

After a moment of study, he looked over his shoulder to the red haired woman, asking in a thunderous voice, "What do you think?"

She stepped up to his side and raised her brow, looking Le'ell up and down, and simply shrugged.

The huge black man nodded and he looked to the dirty man, informing, "Very well. I shall have this one."

The dirty man looked to one of his comrades and said, "I'm not sure we'll be sellin' this one so quick, wizard. She'll bring quite a price at auction."

"Of course you will," the black wizard assured, reaching to a pouch on his belt. He withdrew his huge hand with many large gold coins, looking down at them for long seconds as he pondered how much to offer.

The dirty man wiped his mouth as he saw the gold and glanced around at his colleagues. "You, uh, sure you'll be payin' our price?"

The wizard turned his eyes to the dirty man, then to Le'ell and reached for her face, grasping her jaw where she had been struck. "She appears to have been abused and is clearly quite a bit of trouble for you. I'll take her off your hands and give you a handsome profit, but I'll not give you my fortune for her."

As he ran his hand over her face, Le'ell felt her swollen jaw grow warm, then almost hot. The pain went away, as did the taste of blood in her mouth. When he finally withdrew his hand even the blood on her mouth was gone.

He looked to the dirty man and extended his hand, seven large gold coins in his palm. "You will take this for her. Seven of you here and it's a nice profit for you each."

Staring at the gold, the dirty man licked his lips and finally turned his eyes up to the wizard's, countering, "If I don't and sell her at the auction?"

"This offer stands until my arm tires," the wizard informed. "After, I will pay less for her at the auction and you may all get very sick with some skin eating disease shortly after. Choose quickly but wisely."

The slave hunters just glanced at each other, then the dirty man took the coins and extended his hand to seal the deal. "You're offer's a good one, wizard."

"You'll forgive me if I don't wish to touch you," the wizard said flatly. "Move aside now. Hallaf, take the girl and let's be on our way."

The red haired woman reached to Le'ell, took her arm and pulled her along. She looked like a strong woman, but was actually stronger than she appeared and pulled Le'ell along with little effort.

As they walked down the street past the inn, Le'ell's eyes were locked on it the whole time as she hoped beyond hope that her prince would emerge and take her to safety.

Once again, it was not to be.

As they passed the inn, the wizard stopped again and looked to a middle aged woman who carried a large basket of breads. "You there. Tell me where I can find something to eat that is worthy of my pallet."

As the woman looked him up and down, Le'ell prayed she would direct him to the inn.

Instead, the woman motioned behind with her head and answered, "A place about sixty paces down that way, Love, one called the Dragon's Talon. You can get yer fill of ale and food there."

"What about wine?" the wizard demanded.

"They've got a copious bit as well, barrels in the back I think."

He reached into a pouch and withdrew a silver coin, tossing it into her basket of bread. "My thanks to you."

They continued on without stopping again. Le'ell felt more than ever as someone's property, almost like a prize horse or hunting dog. She did not think she could pull away from the red haired woman's grip nor did she really want to try, especially bound as she was. As people passed them with looks and gawks, she felt more embarrassed and humiliated than ever. Three days ago she had gone from Princess to slave girl. The day before she had gone from slave girl back to Princess. Now, back to slave girl.

Finally reaching the elaborately decorated Dragon's Talon, she was escorted in behind the wizard, who stopped just inside to scan the room. It did not look much different than the Lucky Merchant Inn, though it was decorated with more brass and copper. A collection of bones assembled on the far wall were clearly the remains of a young dragon. All of the servant wenches were dressed in long white skirts and wore low cut blue tops and black jerkins. Each carried a wooden sword, clearly an ornament to amuse the patrons. Along the wall to the right were many deep cushioned booths where important looking men sat to eat their meals and negotiate with other men, drink wine and ale, and many had the company of women with them. This is where the wizard turned and headed, for a booth occupied by two men.

All of the booths were occupied, but he approached one anyway, seized one of the men sitting there by the shirt and hurled him out, informing, "You're done." As the man hit the floor some distance away, the wizard took Le'ell's arm and pulled her toward the plush red leather bench seat. Pushing her into it, she barely had time to maneuver out of his way as he sat down beside her. He met the eyes of the other man and raised a brow. "If you're not buying my meal then you need to be on your way and let my woman sit there."

He nodded and fled, collecting the first man as he reached him.

The red haired woman sat down across from the wizard, eyeing him with a slight smile as she shook her head.

He winked at her, then beat his palm on the table many times and shouted, "Wench! You have a wizard over hear with an empty belly and heavy pockets!"

One of the women turned and rushed to him, her dark brown hair flowing behind her. As she reached his table, she offered a friendly smile and asked, "What would this nice wizard with heavy pockets like?"

He looked to the red haired woman and asked, "Wine?"

She just shook her head.

Turning his eyes back to the servant, he ordered, "Water for her and a carafe of your best wine for me. And bring me your best beef and lamb. I haven't eaten for hours."

"Anything with it?" the servant asked.

"Just the meat," he demanded. "And keep bringing it until I tell you to stop."

"That I will," she assured, then turned and hurried away.

The red haired woman raised her brow as he met her eyes.

"I would think you would want wine," he told her. "I know it's been a time since you had any."

She just smiled and shook her head.

Feeling her hands going numb, Le'ell timidly asked, "Excuse me, may I be untied?"

The wizard's eyes panned to her, his head not really moving.

She just stared back hopefully.

His eyes narrowed.

"Please," she begged. "It hurts. I won't be any trouble, I promise."

He gestured casually and looked back to the red haired woman. "I will arrange a place to stay here for the night. I want to wander that marketplace and see what else I can find."

To her amazement, Le'ell felt the rope around her wrists was gone, as was the collar they were tethered to. Slowly, she pulled her arms in front of her and rubbed where she had been bound, her eyes still on the wizard.

"I predict," the wizard continued, "if we stay long enough we may just fill my stable by the end of tomorrow." Looking back to Le'ell, he finished, "This one will make a fine addition, don't you think? I don't want her worn by a long journey, so I'll purchase another horse and perhaps a wagon to carry her and any others I buy."

Le'ell's thoughts shifted quickly to Chail, to the war they had to stop, to Zondae. She *had* to try and reason with this wizard, had to make him understand that she must be freed. He did not seem receptive to the needs and wishes of others, but she knew she had to do something. Mustering all of her courage, she asked, "May I speak?"

Once again his eyes panned to her. His disapproval was evident.

Knowing she should not allow herself to be deterred, she prodded, "May I?"

"Do you have something important to say?" he questioned.

Hesitantly, she nodded.

"Then say it," he demanded.

With a glance at the red haired woman, she arched her brow and offered, "I want to thank you for taking me away from those men." He was silent for long seconds, just staring at her, and she dared to continue. "They kidnapped me and beat me. They meant to sell me as a slave to someone."

"They meant to and they did," the wizard pointed out. "Get to the important part."

Her mouth fell open. Apparently, her plight fell on unfeeling ears. "They kidnapped me! I'm no slave girl."

He finally turned his head and looked down at her, informing, "You are now. I paid a large price for you."

"I'm worth far more than you paid," she spat.

"I know," he confirmed. "Did you really expect me to pay full price to such weak minded riff-raff?"

"But I'm not a slave!" Le'ell insisted, half turning to face him. "Please, I have to get back to my family. I have a husband who is looking for me as we speak."

The wizard nodded. "Perhaps he should have kept better watch on you."

When he turned his attention back to the red haired woman, Le'ell declared, "He will reward you handsomely for returning me to him!"

One of the wizard's brows cocked up and he looked back down at her. "Will he, now? How much of a reward?"

She raised her chin. "He is a prince. The reward will be a great one."

"So, you are a princess? That would mean that a higher reward would be in order. Or, you would be more valuable if I negotiate with your father for land and trading rights, horses and wenches, your weight in gold, perhaps." He looked back to the red haired woman and declared, "I've stumbled upon riches I hadn't expected!"

"Please," Le'ell begged. "You have to let me go. Many lives depend upon a quest the Prince and I have embarked on."

"And now you're on a quest with this prince," the wizard said with a tone of disbelief.

"I can prove what I say!" she insisted. "Please just give me a chance!"

He raised his brow. "Even if you can prove it, prove to me that I'll profit from it."

She glanced away, her mind racing for an answer.

Folding his thick arms, the wizard loosed a long breath, then said, "Do you have proof, or are you just telling me all of this so that I'll release you?"

Le'ell sighed and turned her eyes down. "The proof is with Prince Chail."

"Of Enulam?" the wizard questioned. "I didn't know they took wives at Enulam. I thought they just collected slave girls as I do."

Quickly realizing she was stumbling over her own words yet again, Le'ell looked to the red haired woman for some sign of reassurance, simply getting an interrogating look instead. Shaking her head, she looked back up to the wizard and pled, "How can I convince you of the importance of this quest we're on?"

"By telling me how I can profit from it," was his answer.

Frustration mounted as she stared at him, and she finally answered, "I don't know."

"So I'm to just release you without compensation," he guessed, then smiled and shook his head. "If nothing else, you will be entertaining for me."

"What can I do to convince you?" she asked desperately.

"Not for me to say," he replied. "Like everyone else here, I'm looking for property and profit, and so far you haven't told me how freeing you gets me either."

She looked away from him. After loosing an impatient breath, she offered, "There is a castle in the Dark Mountains that wishes to start a war between Zondae and Enulam. Help us stop this war, help us bring down that castle and all of their riches will be yours. I promise!"

He glanced at the red haired woman, who just shrugged, then he looked back to Le'ell and asked, "How can you promise that? Do you speak for these kingdoms?"

She raised her chin, straightly answering, "I speak for Zondae."

The wizard nodded. "Just like you're the wife of the Prince of Enulam and not just his escaped slave girl."

Le'ell rolled her eyes from him. "He's better at these negotiations than I am and he has most of our money with him. Can we please go find him?"

He turned back to the red haired woman and folded his hands on the table, answering, "My food's not here yet and I'm hungry. We will continue after I eat." He looked back to her. "Are you hungry, wife of Prince Chail of Enulam?"

What she had eaten in the marketplace was gone and her stomach wanted more now. Still she felt shamed to admit that she was and just turned her eyes away.

"A good meal always helps put things into perspective," the wizard informed. "We will find your prince, but I will eat first, and so will you." He nudged her with his elbow. "Come, now. Enjoy yourself! I'm paying for the food and wine!"

CHAPTER 12

Enulam and Zondae had gone to war twice in their history. Both times were bloody, futile events that simply left thousands dead and tensions between them unresolved. At a meeting in the town of Border twenty-two seasons past from now, King Roegrell of Enulam and Queen Le'Tesyr of Zondae were able to come to an agreement to establish their borders and bring an end to the hostilities that plagued them. They each brought with them fifty soldiers and each brought their only child, Prince Donwarr of Enulam and Princess Le'errin of Zondae. The repercussions of the decision to bring the Prince and Princess along would quietly follow both kingdoms for two decades.

No other meetings would take place between their ruling bodies until this fateful day.

King Donwarr, good to his word, led one hundred of his soldiers down the wide road that led to the shallows of the Spagnah River. The road was wide enough at this point to allow the armored and heavily armed soldiers to ride five abreast behind their King. As the road emptied into the wide flood plain, the groups of five joined into groups of ten, then they spread out further and expanded into lines of twenty. The King himself was not interested in the maneuvers taking place behind him. His eyes were locked on the auburn haired woman who sat atop a white horse across the river in front of one hundred armored soldiers of her own.

He stopped his horse ten paces from the water's edge, staring with blank features at the woman across the river who stared back. His next move would determine how their negotiations would go—and the fates of both their kingdoms.

Glancing at the men behind him, he swung down from his horse and beckoned to one of the soldiers, who dismounted and led his horse to the King. Donwarr handed the soldier his reins, then removed his sword belt and hooked it on his saddle horn.

Dahkam rode up to him, his eyes on the discarded weapons as he asked, "May I ask what you're doing?"

The King looked up to him with steely eyes and replied, "It's a demonstration of trust."

The Field Captain shook his head, reminding, "We *don't* trust them, though."

Donwarr smiled. "They don't have to know that." He turned and strode with purpose to the river and into the current. Careful of his footing in the knee and then thigh deep, icy cold water near the middle, he strode on, his eyes on the auburn haired woman's. Hearing water disturbed behind him, he stopped and turned, seeing young Aldrek following him.

As he met his King's eyes, the young soldier stopped and just stared back.

"And you're going where?" King Donwarr asked.

Aldrek glanced at the opposite bank. "I've given my word to Prince Chail that I should stay close to you."

Donwarr nodded. "And if they all attack me you will fend them off by yourself?"

"If I have to," was the soldier's answer.

King Donwarr motioned to his waiting men and ordered, "Go back to the garrison."

"I can't do that, my King," Aldrek insisted. "You may have me punished later, but Prince Chail will rip me limb from limb if I don't stay at your side."

With a deep sigh, Donwarr nodded. "That he will. Very well, just stay behind me, keep your hand away from your sword and don't do anything foolish. We're on a mission of peace."

"My next move will be at your command," Aldrek insisted.

The King turned and continued on, striding out of the water on the other side a moment later. He approached the auburn haired woman, looking up at her with features of stone as he greeted, "Queen Le'errin."

The plate armor she wore was polished almost to a mirror finish. The leather headband she wore restrained her hair somewhat and also had the crest of the Zondaen royal family on an arrowhead shaped silver medallion in the middle of it: a crescent moon with a star on one side and a sword on the other. She regarded him coldly from atop her horse and simply answered with, "King Donwarr."

Long, tense seconds of silence followed.

Captain Pa'lesh guided her horse up beside the Queen's, her eyes shifting from the King to his soldier escort, and remaining there.

"You have something you want to discuss?" Queen Le'errin asked.

Confirming this, Donwarr nodded, replying, "I do, and I think you already know what."

"Then say your peace," she demanded. "I don't intend to spend all day out here."

King Donwarr glanced at Pa'lesh, then folded his arms. "And I don't intend to fight with you."

"Then why the show of force?" the Queen asked. "You didn't bring a hundred soldiers here for me to just look at."

He smiled. "Actually, that's exactly why I brought them."

She glanced across the river at his garrison. "I'm tiring of this already."

"We need to talk," he insisted, "but not like this. We can argue of mistrust, attacks across the border and our sorted past until the ground swallows us both, but we both know that will get us nowhere. I stand before you in your realm and my sword is still in mine."

Pa'lesh raised her chin to Aldrek. "His is still at his side."

"As is yours," the King pointed out. "Queen Le'errin, may we take a walk?"

"Why would I want to?" she asked dryly.

His lips curled up ever so slightly as he replied, "Does the rose ask the wind why it blows or does it just enjoy the caress?"

Le'errin looked away, her cheeks flushing as something tugged at her memory. Still she remained as dignified and hard as a stone as she responded, "How do I know you aren't going to lead me into an ambush?"

"Because you are going to lead the way," he replied.

She considered, then looked down at him and insisted, "One escort apiece."

He nodded and agreed, "Done. I already have mine."

Le'errin glanced back at Pa'lesh and they both dismounted.

Taking the Enulam King's side as he turned, she folded her hands behind her, staring ahead as she walked slowly up river with him. Perhaps twenty or so paces along, she finally glanced up at him and scoffed, "Or does it just enjoy the caress."

He returned her glance. "You thought they were sweet words twenty-two seasons ago."

"I was young and naïve," she informed, "and I think you used those words to take advantage of me."

He nodded. "You know, thinking back I'm not sure who took advantage of whom."

Le'errin raised her brow and finally looked up at him.

His eyes slid to her. "You can't tell me you weren't just as intrigued with the idea as I was nor any less aggressive."

She rolled her eyes away. "I was curious." A few steps more and she confessed, "Okay, I was intrigued. You were charming, handsome, well made and I wanted to try you out. Don't make anything more of it than that."

He laughed under his breath. "You did more than try."

"Did we come all this way to reminisce?" she asked harshly.

"We came to find common ground," he answered, "and we already have some. It seems like a good place to start."

Le'errin stopped and turned toward him folding her arms. "I think you just want to bed me again."

He also stopped but did not face her right away as he admitted, "Errin, the thought has been on my mind for twenty-two seasons. You never left my mind after the conference and you won't leave my mind after we part ways today, or my heart."

She just stared up at him for long seconds, then insisted, "Things are different now."

Donwarr nodded, confirming, "Yes, things are different. Our parents are dead and we rule our respective kingdoms." He finally turned and looked down at her. "We also carry on this ridiculous stand-off that started almost three hundred seasons ago."

"The conference at Border kept us from going to war again," she pointed out.

"And did nothing else," he countered. "Do you remember the long nights we talked? Do you remember how we were going to unite our kingdoms and live at each others side instead of at each others throat?"

"That was a long time ago," she insisted. "Things have changed. We have changed. Now that we are actually on our respective thrones…" She looked away. "We were going to save the world and bring peace to our kingdoms. Now we know the bitter reality. It just can't be done."

"Don't you see what's happened?" he asked. "The legacy we started is just being carried on by our children."

Her eyes snapped to him. "You knew you had my daughter?"

Raising his brow, he informed, "Your family name in her name was a good hint, that and she's you twenty-two seasons ago."

"And you just released her," Le'errin finished.

He shook his head. "No, I had to let Chail think he was doing that himself."

Le'errin finally smiled. "You know, he's you twenty-two seasons ago, but more charming. Gets that from his mother?"

Donwarr laughed. "You know I'm just as charming as he is."

She stared into his eyes for a time, a flirty smile on her lips.

The King glanced at their escorts, who stood five paces away watching with wide eyes and gaping mouths.

Queen Le'errin looked to Pa'lesh and ordered, "Stay here. We're going to walk a little further."

The Field Captain nodded to her and assured, "I'll keep this Enulam man occupied so that he doesn't disturb you."

Glancing at each other, Donwarr and Le'errin turned up river, walking in silence for several moments.

The Queen finally shook her head and grimly said, "I knew letting you into my bed would come back to haunt me."

"Or has it haunted you most of your life?" he asked.

"Hadn't thought about it," she sighed, then she glanced up at him.

He raised a brow, his eyes trained on her.

Le'errin stopped again, loosing a deep breath before she spoke. "Donwarr, you know things are different now. We have to think about what's best for our kingdoms."

"Like not going to war with each other," he suggested.

She stared up at him for long seconds, then finally agreed, "Exactly."

"I could have sent my proposal to you by courier," he informed.

"Then why didn't you?"

"Perhaps I wanted to see you again. Perhaps I've dreamed of seeing you again for twenty-two seasons."

"You're showing vulnerability," she observed. "It's not a wise thing to do when one is negotiating with a current enemy."

He took a step toward her, his body almost touching hers. "I could never think of you as an enemy."

"Just stop," she ordered. "Circumstances are what they are."

"Circumstances are what we make them, Errin."

She stared silently up at him for a time, then, "You sired a child with me."

His lips silently parted, his eyes widening slightly.

"My mother was furious," Le'errin continued. "She said if the child was born male she would put it to the blade as soon as it breathed air." She lowered her eyes and turned away from King Donwarr. "I was so relieved to find a little girl in my arms that you cannot imagine. I lavished all of the love and affection I had on her. I gave her everything I could, even my succession to the throne."

"What is her name," he asked softly.

Le'errin drew a breath, answering, "Sesh."

"Unity in the old language," he said. "You had hoped she would bring us together."

"Ell came three seasons later," the Queen went on. "By the time she was ten it was clear that her older sister had been horribly spoiled and ruined by the love of her own mother. I was never hard on Sesh. I was always too afraid to be, and yet I was so strict with Ell. My hope became a curse, and my youngest child must pay for that."

"Your youngest child has the same dream that you did," he pointed out. "The dream still lives, Errin." He took her arm and turned her. "But now *we* have the power to make it happen. We aren't living under someone else's rule anymore."

Slowly, she shook her head, saying almost in a whisper, "And yet we are." She raised a hand to his face, gently stroking his bearded cheek. "We both know the ongoing destinies of our kingdoms. We don't dare trust one another. We can't. Ell trusts your Chail with such certainty that she has embarked with him to find who is at the heart of these attacks and stop the war."

"Where did they go?" he asked softly.

She shrugged, admitting, "I don't know, north, I think. Your Chail is a bright, determined lad, like his father. I want to trust him with Ell, and yet the thought frightens the very life from me."

"So we are to remain in this foolish standoff?" he asked, anger in his voice.

"We must," was her answer. "You know it as well as I."

Shaking his head, he growled, "I know no such thing." He took her shoulders and pulled her to him. "Know this, Errin. If you see me leading Enulam soldiers into Zondaen territory it will be to come to your defense, my word on that."

She stared back up at him and ran her hands gingerly up his thick arms, finally looking down at them. "That's what attracted me to you first, those big arms of yours. I didn't know enough to fear them. I do a little, now."

"You shouldn't, Errin."

"I don't want to, but I must. I have to think of my people before myself. I'm sorry." She pulled away from his grasp and took his hand, her eyes on the ground before her as she strode with him at her side back toward her waiting soldiers.

A few moments later they arrived at the place where their escorts were supposed to be waiting. What they found was not what they expected: Aldrek and Pa'lesh locked in a tight embrace and joined at the mouth. They exchanged almost concerned looks, then they turned their eyes back to their escorts and Donwarr loudly cleared his throat.

The two jumped back from each other and faced the King and Queen.

Pa'lesh quickly rubbed her lips and reported with quick words, "I, uh, kept him from disturbing you as promised, Majesty."

Le'errin nodded, then ordered, "Return to the garrison and have them ready for the ride back to Zondae."

The Field Captain nodded to her, then glanced at Aldrek and hurried on her way.

King Donwarr looked to Aldrek and raised his brow.

The young soldier nodded and said, "I'll see that the garrison is ready to ride by the time you return." He turned and hurried on his way.

Le'errin looked to Donwarr with a cocked up brow and asked, "You still don't think such unity between us would be dangerous?"

He shrugged and strode on, answering, "They don't seem to think so. Why would I?"

Rolling her eyes, the Queen walked at his side. Before they were in sight of her troops, she pulled her hand from his grip and hardened her features, and as they approached her garrison, she looked over her riders with commanding eyes.

King Donwarr's expression remained almost blank as he followed her to her horse.

Turning toward her rival kingdom's leader, Queen Le'errin raised her chin and ordered loud enough for her troops to hear, "King of Enulam, return to your realm. I will consider your words and send my answer within the next couple of days. Until you hear from me I would ask you not to cross the border again."

He stared down at her, then nodded. "I will have a detachment here to receive your answer. My word to you will stand until I hear from you." He glanced at her waiting troops, then turned and waded across the river to his own soldiers.

As he strode from the water, Dahkam met him at the bank and took his side as he walked to his horse, asking, "How did it go?"

"Just as I expected," he sighed. "Word from our strike force?"

"Three thousand troops are a league behind us. Three thousand more have assembled from our northern keeps at our north border about half a league from Zondaen territory and are awaiting your orders. A regiment from the southern keep is marching north to reinforce Castle Enulam should they be needed."

King Donwarr nodded. "What did the scouts see?"

Dahkam simply answered, "We were watched."

Reaching his horse, the King turned to Dahkam and said, "Send a runner to the northern regiment with orders to cross. They will find a well traveled road that goes straight to Border City. They are to turn south toward Zondae Castle for two leagues where they will stop and prepare an ambush."

His lips tightening, Dahkam informed, "This will be risky."

Donwarr nodded, then replied, "If my information is correct, it will be risky not to."

"And Prince Chail?"

"I expect him to have things well under control where he is."

CHAPTER 13

"Le'ell!" Prince Chail shouted, his eyes panning back and fourth over the crowd in the central street. His instincts told him something was horribly wrong. She was not to be found anywhere in the market. Panic and rage were a whirlwind inside of him. He stormed through the marketplace, looking over the hoards of people who came to and fro on their many errands. Entering the first of the many tents he would invade on his search, his eyes were intense and desperate as he glanced around for a glimpse of the auburn hair and red shirt he knew would reveal her. Not finding her, he left and went to the next, then the next.... He called her name again in the street, then went into a building of wood and stone, exiting even more frustrated.

He could not know how long he searched before happening into a tent full of swords, bows, daggers and other weapons. He stopped in the center, noticing only three people there. Two looked much like the mercenaries he had been negotiating with. The third stood behind them, his long, shiny black hair glistening in the lamplight within the tent.

When this third man turned and smiled at the Prince, his white teeth sharply contrasted the very dark skin around them and he asked in a pleasant but foreign voice, "May I interest you in something?"

The two mercenaries looked up from the daggers on the table, and upon seeing the massive man who had just entered they took their leave of the shopkeeper and slipped out.

"Come back again," the dark skinned man bade. "I'll have some new blades out tomorrow that might interest you."

Chail's eyes followed them out, then locked on the dark skinned man as he approached.

Looking up at the Prince, the shopkeeper offered him that warm smile and invited, "Please feel free to have anything you see in your hand. But be warned, you might find that one that will convince you to take it with you."

Meeting his gaze almost coldly, Chail as politely as he could countered, "Another time, perhaps. I'm looking for a girl."

The shopkeeper nodded. "I see." He pointed out of the tent and up the street toward the inn. "There's a place eight buildings up called the—"

"I'm not looking to buy one," the Prince interrupted. "The girl I'm with is missing and I need to find her. She's about this tall with long red-brown hair, red swordsman's shirt, dark green eyes—"

"Ah!" the shopkeeper barked, holding a finger up. "I've seen this young lady. Well made, very tall and built like a Zondaen. She was here about an hour ago shopping my blades. She even bought three."

Chail nodded. "Did you see where she might have… Three?"

"Yes. She bought a scimitar that almost sang to her and had quite an interest in some Zondaen steel I acquired only yesterday. I am having them delivered to where she wanted them to go, and she even paid me extra to do so."

The Prince's eyes narrowed. The scimitar had been an impulse that he knew she was prone to. The Zondaen blades she bought for another purpose.

"Would you be the lucky man she shares this room with?" the dark skinned man asked, then his brow dropped as he only now seemed to realize what the Prince had said before. "Did you say she's missing?"

Raising his chin as he stared down at the dark skinned man, Chail confirmed, "I was expecting to find her back at our room when I returned or at least somewhere here in the market. Where did she go when she left here?"

He pointed out of his tent again and answered, "She was heading for the leather works across the street. In fact, I'm certain she entered there." He held up a finger again as he backed toward the rear of his tent and said, "One moment." Turning, he summoned, "Quaz! Get out here!"

A moment later another dark skinned man dressed much as this one was slowly emerged from a hidden flap at the back of the tent. Judging from his droopy eyelids, he had been sleeping.

The merchant regarded him sharply and ordered, "Keep watch on the shop. I've an errand to run. And no more discounts for the promise of a night's pleasure!" He reached under the table and withdrew a double-wrap swordsman's belt, putting it on very quickly, and as he hurried to the tent's exit, he snatched a sword from its stand and shoved it into the sheath. With a glance at the Prince, he beckoned, "This way."

Chail hesitantly followed.

Halfway across the street, the dark skinned man half turned and extended his hand. "I am Noorain, and I'm guessing you must be Chail."

The Prince took his hand and nodded once.

"She spoke fondly of you," the merchant informed, walking at the Prince's side. "Despite her being lost, you are a lucky man to have her heart."

"I'll feel luckier when we find her," Chail growled. "I don't mean to be rude, but may I ask why you are so eager to help?"

Noorain turned steely eyes up to the Prince's. "I have a beautiful wife, my friend. I can only imagine what my heart would go through if she was missing."

Chail nodded and replied, "Fair enough."

Raising a hand to the Prince's chest, the merchant stopped and squinted at a man twenty paces ahead, then reported when he had the Prince's attention, "I recognize that hilt. Wait here. You will know when to approach." He strode to the man and offered a friendly greeting to draw his attention.

Chail watched for a moment, his eyes narrowing as the shopkeeper coaxed the man's sword from him and looked it over. When he held the tip straight up and looked the blade up and down, he snuck in a glance to the Prince and a subtle nod, and Chail strode toward them, his hands clenching into tight fists.

"Where did you get this one?" Noorain asked. "It's a fine blade that I simply must trade you out of."

The unkempt man huffed a laugh and informed, "I might trade for gold, but you'd better be makin' it worth me while."

Smiling broadly at him, the merchant offered, "I could trade you something even better than gold, something you'll appreciate even more."

The man raised his chin, eyeing the merchant suspiciously as he demanded, "Something like what?"

Chail grabbed the man from behind and spun him around, his other hand finding the man's throat as he growled, "Another day to live. Where did you get the sword?"

Despite being half drunk, the man knew fear of the Prince on sight and showed it with bulging eyes and a gaping mouth.

"I won't ask twice," Chail snarled, pulling the man closer to him.

"You might want to answer soon," Noorain advised. "He doesn't seem to be very patient today and I'm sure he can pop your head right off of you."

The man's mouth trembled as he finally answered, "We got it off a slave girl!"

Chail's hand squeezed a little tighter. "What slave girl? What did she look like?"

"Auburn hair," he choked, "Red shirt. Really tall."

"Where is she," the Prince demanded, squeezing slightly more.

"I don't know," he strained to say. "Sold her as soon as we got her."

Noorain shook his head and observed, "If you don't tell him what he wants to know your head's going to come off of there."

"Trohick," another man shouted as he emerged from the tent. "What is it gives out here?" His eyes widened as the Prince turned toward him.

Chail recognized the dirty man right away and his hand lanced forth, seizing the dirty man's shirt and drawing him in. As he released the other man, who fell to the ground, he grasped the dirty man with both hands and hoisted him from the ground and to eye level as he demanded, "Where is she?"

With wide eyes, the dirty man found he could not speak.

Coughing, the other man grasped his throat as he stood, then pulled his dagger and froze before he could take a step.

With Le'ell's sword held firmly to the man's back, Noorain took his shoulder with his free hand and asked, "We don't want to be choked *and* skewered today, do we?"

Shaking his head, the dirty man tried to explain, "I—I—I don't know. We don't have 'er!"

"You're little friend here had her sword," the Prince growled, "and you've got until the last grain of my patience runs out to live unless you tell me where she is!"

"He'll reach into your chest and tear your heart right out of you," Noorain warned. "It's messy and really painful, I hear."

"But we don't have 'er!" the dirty man tried to explain. "A wizard bought 'er. He hexed us and made us sell 'er to him. I was gonna bring 'er back to ya, I swear!"

"What wizard?" Chail snarled.

"Never seen 'im before," the dirty man answered shakily. "He bought 'er and went that way toward the inns there, maybe lookin' for somethin' to eat. That's all I know!"

The Prince stared at him for long seconds, then, in a fit of rage, yelled and hurled him many paces away where he slammed into the support post of a nearby building and crumpled to the ground. Turning on the other man, Chail saw the dagger still in his hand and slammed his fist into the man's gut, and when the man doubled over, he brought his fist down into his back with such force that it planted him face-first into the dirt road.

Watching the man go down, the merchant turned his eyes up to Chail and pointed a finger at him, informing, "I was going to do that, then I realized you probably would like to yourself and I didn't."

"Now where do we look?" the Prince questioned, the ring of despair in his voice.

Noorain considered, then, "What wizard would buy a woman from dogs like these? Unless he's a man of some importance and she's more of an ornament for him." His eyes narrowed. "Two possibilities. I'll explain as we walk." He paused to pick the man's dagger up and examined it as they made their way down the street. "What cheap goat dung is this? The steel is poor and the workmanship is among the worst I've ever seen. I would be lucky to give this away."

"Keep it with you," the Prince ordered. "It might come in handy later."

Shaking his head, Noorain slid it into his sword's sheath and grimly murmured, "Not for trade, I think."

They ended up searching two inns, including where Chail and Le'ell were staying, and finally ended up at the Dragon's Talon where they stood near the doorway and scanned the large dining hall first.

"There are many rooms in this place," Noorain observed. "I don't see us having much luck searching them all, but I know many of the servants here and the man who collects money for the rooms owes me a favor."

Chail scanned the cavernous room once more. "Where would a man who considers himself important sit to eat?"

"Somewhere comfortable," the merchant answered, then pointed to the right and declared, "There. The seats have deep cushions."

Looking that way, the Prince turned and strode toward the lesser lit section of comfortable, red cushioned booths, his dark skinned friend following. Chail searched intently, noting hair color first. Le'ell's long hair seemed to be unique to her and he knew that he would recognize it on sight. Keeping his distance from the patrons themselves, his eyes paused on every woman who had long, dark hair.

Ahead, a large, bald, darkly skinned man stood from one of the booths and the Prince froze. A red haired woman sitting across from him also stood. The large man, who appeared to be nearly Gartner's size, turned toward the booth and laughed as he offered his hand to an auburn haired woman who was just sliding out.

"I don't want to have to carry you out of here," he joked. "Your shape belies your appetite. I think you ate more than I did."

"Okay," Le'ell conceded, taking his hand. "I was hungry." She finally stood on less than steady legs and the bald man and red haired woman laughed as she fell into him.

"You were also thirsty," the bald man observed.

She pushed off of him and giggled, then looked toward the Prince, her eyes widening as she cried, "Chail!" When she tried to go to him, the wizard seized her arm, not so much to restrain her as to keep her from falling.

The Prince did not see it that way as he strode toward them, his eyes narrowing.

Clearly holding onto the big wizard for balance, Le'ell reached for her Prince as he neared and slurred, "Chail, I'm so glad to see you!"

He looked down at her and folded his huge arms, countering, "Both of me?"

A wobbly nod was her answer.

His eyes shifted to the wizard's. Here was a man who appeared to be a little taller, a little thicker, and supposedly trained in the black arts. Chail could not feel intimidated. He wanted Le'ell back and made no secret of it.

The wizard looked him up and down and nodded. "Is this the Enulam Prince husband you spoke so fondly about?"

"This is him," she confirmed. "I told you he would find me, and here he is." She looked to the Prince and ordered, "Tell him, Chail. Tell him you're my Enulam Prince husband." She covered her mouth and laughed, then shook her head and offered, "I'm so sorry. That's the best I could come up with."

Chail looked down and met the merchant's eyes.

Noorain shrugged and observed, "I'd say she's had a cup or two."

"A barrel or two," the Prince corrected, looking back at the wizard. "I suppose you know by now she was abducted and sold to you illegally."

The wizard shrugged. "That's none of my concern. I came here looking to fill my stable and make a profit. Are you saying I should just give her to you on your word?"

"She's already my woman," the Prince insisted.

Raising his chin, the wizard regarded Chail coldly through narrow eyes. "Your woman, is she? How can you convince me?"

Le'ell looked up to him and reminded, "I already told you that I'm his. You have to believe both of us because there's two of us and only one of you."

The wizard glanced at her, then looked back to Chail and informed, "Money has changed hands for her already, so legally she is mine."

"Money at a legal auction?" the Prince asked.

Cocking a brow up, the wizard had no answer for him.

"I have no wish to fight you for her," Chail assured, "but—"

"That's good," the wizard interrupted. "I can kill you both with a thought."

Noorain stepped forward and suggested, "Perhaps there is somewhere we can go to continue negotiating. I don't feel this is a very healthy setting for that."

He got a glance from the wizard, who nodded and agreed, "Fair enough. I have purchased lodging here for a few days. I think that should make us comfortable, and then we can talk clearly, Chail, Prince of Enulam."

Truly, the wizard's accommodations seemed to be the best the inn had to offer. Plush, deep cushioned chairs covered with soft blue material were arranged in a circle in the center of the room that was closed by a loveseat of the same construction. Tapestries adorned the stone and timber walls. A large table between the two open windows was laden with several flasks of wine and a few silver goblets. Seated in the deep chairs were the wizard, merchant, and the red haired woman. Chail sat on the loveseat with Le'ell passed out beside him, her head leaning on his arm.

Staring blankly at the Prince, the wizard finally admitted, "You have an odd honesty about you, and you weave an interesting tale similar to what she told me." He glanced at the sleeping girl at the Prince's side. "If this is true, then the balance of the land as a whole could be cast into turmoil. Border itself could be jeopardized. That would be almost tragic."

Noorain took a gulp from his goblet and added, "Especially for those of us who do business here."

Slowly, the wizard nodded. "Aalekilk, huh? I had thought that place long abandoned. No farmland yields much food around it, the hunting is dismal, much of the water is toxic in that area and there is nothing to be gained by living here." He took a sip from his goblet and finished, "Except for the gold in the dark mountains. I have heard that gnomes inhabit many of the caves in that area and mine the gold. They also have no use for humans but for trade. I can't see anyone conscribing them into an army, either. Forest trolls, yes. They are strong and aggressive, about man sized and could be easily trained for combat if you can teach them to work together. Gnomes would seem to be too small for a fighting army. Have you proof of all of this?"

"At Enulam," the Prince reported. "We took some of the bodies back with us after a failed attack of theirs and found what we found: Forest trolls and gnomes."

The wizard responded with a slow nod again. "I see." He considered. "I also see possibilities here."

Chail exchanged glances with Noorain and asked, "Possibilities?"

"The gold in the Dark Mountains," the wizard replied. "If they have conscribed gnomes, then there must be a plethora of gold at the castle." His eyes narrowed. "To get such a motley bunch to actually work together takes more than just someone with a convincing tongue. You would need to control their minds to some point."

"Black magic?" the merchant guessed.

"You may call it that," the wizard offered, "but I feel there is more happening than just someone wanting to go to war with you. Have you considered why?"

Chail took a sip from his goblet. "I've been pondering it, but I haven't concluded anything. We defeated them four decades ago, but I wasn't aware of anyone still around who would be holding a grudge."

"I remember that war," the wizard informed. "I don't know of anyone who was left, myself. The castle was in ruins and nothing remained but its walls."

Noorain raised his chin and said, "Castle walls can be a good place to start. Well made walls and a dry roof can attract those who sleep in the cold."

"And those who sleep in the cold can be the start of an army," Chail added.

"One grim reality hangs over all of this," the Wizard said flatly. "Where there is war, there is profit. Chail of Enulam, you wish to stop a war between your people and hers, and, perhaps, join to fight off these invaders you speak of. What will happen to the riches of Aalekilk?"

"The spoils go to the victors," the Prince answered, "and to those who are the victor's allies."

A smile cracked the wizard's hard expression. "I like the sound of that. Perhaps it was the same fates that keep me rich that brought your woman to me. However, she is still mine until I am compensated." He reached into a pouch on his belt and removed a small glass vile, not quite the size of a finger, then he handed it and his dagger to the red haired woman, who took them and approached Le'ell, kneeling beside her."

Chail maintained his composure, but his eyes widened as the Hallaf took Le'ell's hand and pricked one of her fingers, then filled the vial with her blood. Turning his eyes to the wizard as the Princess' finger was bandaged, he asked, "What is that about?"

"That is my assurance," the wizard explained. "Absolute trust is too risky in my business, so part of her remains with me. I don't expect treachery, but this will assure that there is no temptation." He looked to the red haired woman as she approached and took the vial from her, slipping it back into its pouch. "So long as I have the girl's blood, I have the girl. With a gesture and a few words I can strike her down with illness, madness, or I can just kill her outright no matter where she is."

Staring at him for a long moment, the Prince finally asked, "How do I get that vial back?"

The wizard met him with steely eyes and replied, "You are going to Aalekilk anyway, so when you find out what you need to know, simply tell me what you know and how much gold is involved."

"And their army?" the Prince asked.

"That's really your problem," he wizard informed, "but I may be persuaded to lend a hand if there's plenty of gold to be found." He looked to the merchant. "And what is your part in all of this?"

Noorain shrugged and answered, "I'm a businessman dealing in swords and other fine weapons, which I notice you don't have."

"No need for one," the wizard informed, then he held his goblet up and ordered, "Hallaf! More wine so that we can seal our bargain properly."

When Le'ell's eyes slowly opened, she found herself in the room that they had paid for the night before, and still dressed as she had been. As her wits slowly returned to her, two things became abundantly clear: She felt a little sick and her head was throbbing with pain. She was slow to sit up and covered her eyes against the dim lamplight as she did. A pathetic moan alerted the Prince that she was finally awake.

He approached unnoticed and folded his arms as he stood beside the bed and stared down at her. As she drew another breath and rubbed her eyes, he softly asked, "How did you sleep, Princess?"

Covering her ears, she whined, "Don't yell at me!"

Having been through this himself when he was younger and just discovering his limits at wine drinking, he smiled and shook his head, giving her a moment before he spoke again. "So, would you like something to eat?"

She grasped her stomach and shook her head.

"Not hungry?" he asked, trying his best not to laugh at her.

"No," Le'ell whimpered.

"You might feel better if you eat something," he advised.

"No I won't," she argued.

He finally chuckled. "Either way, you need to get up."

"I don't want to."

Chail reached down and took her hands, gently pulling her to her feet. Once standing, she fell forward and wrapped her arms around him, burying her face in his chest, and nuzzling into his shirt.

"Come on," he prodded, pushing her off of him. "We've got things to do and a long ride ahead of us today."

She fell back into him and whined, "I don't want to go. Let's go tomorrow."

"It *is* tomorrow, Le'ell."

Slowly, she turned her eyes up to his. "Huh?"

"You've been asleep since yesterday afternoon."

"So all of that was just a dream?" she asked hopefully.

"No," he corrected, "it sadly wasn't. I'll fill you in as we ride."

"I want to stay one more night," she complained. "I didn't get to see much."

"After we stop the war," he assured. "Come on, now. Let's get you going."

Once their horses were packed and Chail got Le'ell stably on hers, they rode north out of Border and into the thick forest of pines and the thin brush that struggled beneath them. A couple of hours later they crossed a river, probably a northern part of a smaller river that fed into the Spagnah River. Already, as they rode into a large prairie in the thick of the forest, they could see the snow-capped peaks of the Dark Mountains in the distance. As they trekked on, the trees grew less and less healthy, many of them small and struggling to keep their green leaves or needles. Even the larger ones were thin of new or healthy growth. All the signs were there. They were entering the Dead Forest.

An ominous feeling overtook Le'ell as she glanced around her, hearing less and less wildlife as they rode deeper. She looked to Chail and informed, "You know, Border isn't that far behind us. We could always go and get our room back and spend the night in comfort." She raised her brow. "I might even let you seduce me."

His eyes slid to her. "That's no great task, and we're not going back."

Tight lipped, she looked forward again. "I don't look forward to sleeping on the ground."

"Even with me at your side?"

"If you think I'm going to be easily seduced tonight you're quite wrong."

He smiled slightly. "We'll see."

She shot him an irritated look. "Did you at least bring something to eat?"

"In your saddlebag."

"So that wizard who bought me isn't going to help but he expects to share in the spoils? I thought you were a better negotiator than that."

"I thought you were going to stay out of trouble yesterday."

"I wasn't looking for that to happen to me, Chail."

"And yet it seems to *keep* happening to you, *Le'ell.*"

"You say that like nothing ever happens to you."

"Never been sold into slavery. You've been now, what, twice?"

"Shut up, Chail."

"And now I find myself trying to pay off a huge debt to free you yet again."

"You say that like it's my fault this keeps happening to me."

He slowly turned his eyes to her. "Might I remind you that all you had to do was stay in the room for an hour yesterday and it wouldn't have happened?"

"Oh, so I sit there all day, bored to tears while you are doing Goddess knows what out there."

"I was negotiating with mercenaries."

"It must not have gone well since I don't see any around here."

"The negotiations were to get us into the castle, not get us escorted *to* the castle."

"An escort might be a good idea, considering where we're going."

"I think you are making a mountain out of a pile of pebbles."

"Dead Forest, Chail. Do you have any idea why they call it that?"

"Because it's dead?" he guessed.

She sighed. "Why did I agree to come here with you? Why didn't I just stay home?"

He shrugged. "I think it had something to do with preventing our kingdoms from going to war. Something like that, I can't be sure."

"Quit being a sarcastic bastard!"

He smiled. "I wasn't sure that wouldn't go over your head."

"How about I send something *into* your head?" she countered.

"Perhaps you should keep your eyes open instead," he suggested. "We're in unfamiliar territory and this place could be crawling with bandits or those raiders."

She glanced around. "If they're smart they will not be in this part of the forest." Shuddering, Le'ell's eyes darted quickly to the seemingly depthless shadows all around, and she finally realized they had trekked deep into the Dead Forest. "Couldn't we have gone around this forest?"

"We could have," he admitted, "but that would probably have cost us two or three more days."

"And?"

He shot her an irritated glance. "We have a war to stop, remember? They won't wait for us to take a more scenic road."

"It won't matter if we never get out of this place," she pointed out. "I've heard stories about packs of Dreads, blood sucking tree leapers and giant leaches that suck the lifeblood from you and you don't even know it." She shuddered again. "I feel like we're being watched."

"I'm sure it's just your imagination," he comforted. "I could use a bite. Can you get some of that jerky out of your saddlebag?"

"And your thoughts go right to food," she grumbled, turning to open the saddlebag. Movement behind drew her attention and she looked, then closed the saddlebag and faced forward again. "Chail, we're being followed."

His eyes slid to her and he murmured, "Again?"

Le'ell looked to him and smiled. "Yes. We have company again."

They both looked behind them.

Ten paces back, the little white unicorn followed, staring back curiously.

"I don't believe it," Chail said, a smile overpowering his lips.

"I told you she's here to help us," Le'ell insisted. "Unicorn of snow, remember?"

"Dragon of night," he reminded. "That part didn't go so well."

The unicorn caught up to them and they steered their horses apart.

Meeting their pace between them, the little unicorn looked up to them in turn, then whickered at Chail. When he did not seem to understand, she whickered again, then laid her ears back and snorted.

"She's trying to talk to you," Le'ell informed.

"I don't speak unicorn," he grimly said. "I wonder what she's trying to tell us."

The sun began to grow dim from the West, darkened more by the ominous clouds that relentlessly rolled in from the Northwest. The road actually looked a little better traveled, better maintained, which was a relief to them as darkness loomed. Ahead, where the road straightened out, they saw the turrets of a castle rise above the trees. Although they quickened their pace, the clouds opened before they could reach the castle and began to drench them with cold, driving rain. There was no time to pull out mantles or capes, so they drove their horses faster toward the castle with the unicorn following closely behind, occasionally protesting in a short whinny.

The ancient front gate was open and they rode up to the very old and dilapidated double doors that led into the palace. Thankfully they were sunk well into an arch within the dark stone that made up the palace wall, which was covered by many seasons of vine growth that had clearly stopped growing and died some time ago.

With the rain driving from the other side of the castle, the entryway, perhaps nine paces deep and seven wide, was still dry and just big enough for the horses. Dismounting, they hurriedly walked their horses under cover.

Le'ell shot Chail a furious look and snarled, "Never rains in the Dead Forest, huh?"

He shot her an irritated look back, then grasped the large, iron handles of the doors and pushed them open.

As they entered, they found the long hallway before them lit by torches on both sides. They stopped only a few steps in, the burning torches sending sharp chills up both their spines. They stared into the castle, eyes panning back and forth in search of any movement, any threat.

Le'ell tugged on Chail's sleeve and whispered, "Burning torches. Do you think someone is here?"

Chail shook his head. "No, they've probably been burning for three hundred seasons or more."

Curling her lip up, she elbowed him hard in the ribs.

He rubbed his ribs and glared down at her, then looked behind him and observed, "The unicorn's gone."

Le'ell spun around and looked for her, then shook her head. "Do you suppose the castle frightened her away? Or the storm?"

"Hard to say," he responded. "Not much is known about unicorns."

"I was hoping she would stay with us."

Chail nodded, admitting, "So was I."

Le'ell clung to the Prince as they slowly made their way down the long hallway. As it opened into a cavernous and elaborately furnished and decorated central room, Chail looked to the staircases on each side and shouted, "Hello!"

Cringing, Le'ell hissed, "Shh! What are you doing?"

"We're in someone else's home," he pointed out. "We should be here as guests, not intruders." He looked back to the stairs and shouted, "It's storming out. May we have shelter here?"

They waited for several long moments for a reply which did not come.

"Sun's almost down," the Prince observed. He motioned with his chin to a large fireplace in the center of the room. "I'm going to build a fire. There was some wood outside in a dry pocket near the door I can get. I'll be right back."

When he turned to walk back to the door, Le'ell spun around and barked, "You're leaving me alone here?"

He glanced over his shoulder and ordered, "Just relax. If anyone comes down just tell them the storm drove us in and politely ask if we can stay the night."

Le'ell watched him as he turned back down the long hallway and called after him, "Just don't be gone long." Turning back toward the fireplace, she glanced nervously around her, feeling a chill of fear over the chill in the air on her wet skin. She watched the balconies as she slowly walked toward the fireplace, almost expecting to see someone appear any moment. When she reached the open fireplace, more of a fire pit made of stone, half a height tall and over a height in diameter, she looked down into it, seeing it cold and unused for some time, perhaps many seasons. Spider webs were within, and Le'ell knew that they would not be there if there had been a fire there recently. This really did not make sense, since winter had just ended.

Wet clothes were just not good and she glanced around once more as she sat down on the edge of the fire pit to pull her boots off. With them set aside, her eyes shifted nervously as she slowly untied the lace at the top of her shirt. There was a dry one in her saddlebag and she hoped Chail would think to bring the bags in with or before the firewood. She pulled her shirt off and laid it out on the stone that surrounded the fire pit. The air inside the castle was indeed very cold and she crossed her arms over her chest against it. While she did not enjoy being in the open in such a strange place half naked, she knew that Prince Chail would very much enjoy finding her so.

He had been gone for some time.

She looked around again.

On the other end of the room, directly across from the hallway, a doorway closed by two timber doors rattled against the wind outside. The tall windows on that wall lit up as lightning outside flashed and she cringed as thunder cracked outside. On another side of the room that was not as well lit was yet another huge fireplace, this one in the stone wall. As the lightning flashed again she glimpsed the tall painting above it. It was of a thin, well dressed man who appeared to be the local nobility, perhaps the master of the castle and land at one time. Another long lightning flash gave her a better glimpse of the painting. He appeared to be a tall, confident fellow with long black hair and piercing eyes. His chin was held high and his white shirt and gold braided black overcoat gave one the impression that he was indeed a man of importance.

His stare was something that Le'ell knew would be with her for a while. Those eyes seemed to lance out at her every time the lightning flashed, and the following thunder sent her closer to terror and panic. She felt like the painting itself was staring at her and she could not help but stare back, her eyes on the eyes of the man in the painting.

Lightning flashed again, illuminating the large room, the painting, and the man who stood unnoticed two paces away from Le'ell's left.

She could feel eyes on her—and not the eyes of the painting. Her attention darted around the room, and when the lightning flashed yet again she finally saw the man in the long black and yellow cape standing a pace away from her!

Le'ell sprang up and faced him, snatching her shirt from the rim of the fire pit to cover herself as she backed away a step.

He smiled as he stepped toward her, into the brighter light of the torches. "Forgive me," he said in a deep, soft and very gentle voice. "I did not mean to frighten you."

She swallowed hard and assured, "It's okay. I just didn't hear you come up on me."

"My apologies for that as well," he said with a nod. "The castle is dark tonight and the noise of the storm can deceive the ears. Perhaps I should have announced myself when I came down. I am Duke Nevarr, the master of this castle."

"I—I—I'm, uh, Le'ell. We're traveling north toward the Dark Mountains and the storm broke and we came looking for shelter."

"You are of course welcome here," he assured. "I don't have many visitors of late and your company is a welcome distraction. Where is your companion?"

Le'ell found her eyes locked on his and she could not look away. "He's collecting some wood for a fire and getting our saddlebags."

"You look as if you could use a change of clothing," the Duke observed. "Perhaps I have something that will fit you." He raised his chin, looking her up and down. "You look cold. Where are my manners?" Reaching to his throat, he unfastened the chain that held his cape in place and pulled it from his shoulders, then he approached the last two steps and flung it around Le'ell, fastening it around her neck. "This should keep you warm until your companion arrives with your dry clothes."

"Thank you," she breathed, pulling the cape closer to her. She wanted to retreat from him, but found herself unable to. Something about him was powerful, something about those eyes. She could not look away.

"I have plenty of rooms," he informed, "so if you and your companion wish to stay the night I can easily arrange lodging for you." He extended his hand toward the furnishings and fireplace across the room and invited, "Please, make yourself comfortable."

As he stepped that way, so did Le'ell, but she did not feel that she did so of her own choosing. More than ever, she felt she needed Chail present.

Duke Nevarr looked to the fireplace and raised his hand. Instantly, flames erupted to consume the dry logs within. Candles and lamps on the mantle, the walls and the tables that accompanied the chairs also lit up, illuminating the room in a warm glow.

Le'ell hesitated, looking around her as all of the fire suddenly appeared, and she heard herself ask, "Are you a wizard?"

He laughed softly and shook his head. "I dabble, but I'm no wizard, just someone with a few tricks to show off. Sit, please. Make yourself comfortable."

Looking to her right, she chose a loveseat and settled herself into the middle of it, praying he would not sit there with her.

He did not, instead sitting in a plush chair that faced the loveseat. "So where do you come from?"

She glanced away, not wanting to reveal herself as Zondaen. "We came from the Territhan Valley."

"Quite a long journey across the desert," the Duke observed.

Le'ell nodded, staring at a lamp on the table beside him.

"I don't want you to be afraid here," he told her. "Please think of this as your home during your stay."

She nodded again, feeling herself unable to look at him, and feeling more of her own will as long as she did not. Turning her eyes toward the fireplace, she found the painting again, her eyes widening as she realized the man in this ancient painting was sitting beside her!

He also looked. "That was done long ago. I'm almost surprised to see it in the fine condition it is in after two centuries."

Something inside of her felt very cold and she hopefully asked, "Is that your grandfather? He looks just like you."

Duke Nevarr laughed softly again. "No, that's not my Grandfather." He looked to her, meeting her eyes. "That's me."

Le'ell's spine went rigid. Despite her wide eyes, she managed to suppress panic and simply joked, "You sure have aged well."

"I haven't aged at all for two hundred seasons," he corrected. "You don't have to age anymore, either."

She felt herself trembling and even closer to panic, but knew that could be a horrible mistake. Showing fear at all was something she had been taught from childhood never to do, so she leaned her head and asked, "Really?"

He responded with a slow nod. "Do you want to remain young and beautiful forever?"

Le'ell shrugged. "It sounds appealing."

Smiling slightly, he gazed deeply into her eyes and seemed to bore into her very essence. "It should. Sickness, age, injury, death... That can all end. It has for me. Your wanderings can end, too. You can finally be home."

She nodded, trying to sound more interested than frightened as she asked, "So, what do I have to do for this?"

He smiled broader, showing her his teeth, and she took notice of the long, pointed canines he had, her eyes locked on them as he stood. "You won't have to do anything," he assured, slowly approaching her.

Panic finally won.

"Chail!" she screamed, trying to leap to her feet. As she moved, the cape closed itself tightly around her, cocooning her within so tightly she could barely breathe. Her arms were pinned to her sides, her legs wrapped together too tightly for her to even move them. As the Duke moved closer, Le'ell screamed again for her Prince, shrinking away from him as the cape conformed tightly to her, almost like a second skin.

He held her gaze with his as he loomed over her, and he shook his head. "I thought you wanted my gift. No matter. You can choose in a moment, when I have your lifeblood drained to bring you to the edge of death." He lowered himself to her, propping a knee on the loveseat beside her as he reached for her neck.

"Please don't," Le'ell whimpered, feeling the cape grow even tighter around her.

"Now," he assured as he grasped her neck and turned her head to the right. "It will hardly hurt at all. At the worst you will feel sleepy."

"Don't do this to me," she begged as his thumb hooked under her jaw and forcibly turned her head. She tried to fight back but he was just too strong. Her horror filled eyes were turned to him to their limit and hurt to be so, yet she could not take them from the fangs that drew closer to her. "Please, I don't want the gift. Let me go, I beg you!"

He hesitated, then drew back and looked down at her with an ominous smile. "You don't understand. You'll either join me, or you'll be just another meal. Which do you prefer? Beauty forever or rotting corpse?"

She could not answer. She could only stare into his hungry eyes.

"You'll choose to stay with me in a moment," he informed.

When he opened his mouth and bent to her again, she tried with everything she had to struggle away one last time, and screamed with all of the terror in her heart. Part of the cape tore away from her shoulder and wrapped itself around her mouth and head many times, silencing her.

His breath on her throat was cold.

As his fangs grazed her skin, he was torn away from her, pulled backward, and the surprise in his eyes was almost a relief.

Chail turned him and slammed his fist into the vampires face with crushing force.

Stunned, Nevarr staggered backward toward Le'ell.

The Prince grabbed him again and punched harder, snapping his head around, then slammed his fist into the Duke's chest. The sharp crack told Le'ell that something had broken, and she prayed it wasn't Chail!

The vampire stumbled backward and over the table beside the loveseat, falling back-first to the stone floor.

Chail only glanced at Le'ell, then turned his predatory eyes back to his foe as he ordered, "Get up! I'm not through with you."

Slow to get to his feet, Duke Nevarr stood and faced Chail, smiling as he rubbed his jaw. "You are very strong for a mortal."

"That's what I'm told," the Prince confirmed.

Glancing around, Le'ell realized that other vampires had appeared from the shadows and were slowly advancing. There were four of them, all women, all lightly dressed, and all staring at the Prince. One among them looked very young, perhaps fifteen. This one still seemed to cling to some of her innocence, and yet she was a hungry predator bent on making a meal out of Chail.

Nevarr shook his head. "You are young and very foolish. The gift will not be yours tonight, only hers."

"She doesn't want it," the Prince growled, "and you're not giving it to her."

The vampire laughed softly, glancing around at the other vampires who were only three paces away from their next victim. "You don't seem to understand, mortal. Don't you know what you are to me?"

Chail smiled slightly and answered, "A diversion."

Nevarr's smile slowly curled down and his fellow vampires stopped where they were. He stared into the Prince's eyes, showing just a hint of fear in his.

The clop of hooves approached from behind the loveseat Le'ell was trapped on and an emerald glow pierced the darkness. With her eyes locked on the Duke, the little white unicorn paced out of the shadows.

The vampires did not move as the unicorn approached. They all just stared, not reacting otherwise to her except the youngest of them, whose brow arched and lips fell open as she saw her.

Chail backed away, his gaze locked on the vampire. "I'd say your control here is not quite as absolute as you thought."

His eyes shifting back to the Prince, Nevarr smiled slightly and corrected, "Quite the contrary. You've brought me a wonderful gift."

The unicorn stopped advancing, her eyes still on the vampire, but no longer appearing so confident.

Duke Nevarr looked back to the unicorn, continuing, "She is young from the look of her, quite inexperienced, but still she will give me just what I need to walk in the daylight. She is indeed a wonderful gift. Perhaps I will spare you after all."

Unicorn and Prince exchanged glances.

Two of the vampire women appeared behind the unicorn.

"You didn't know did you?" the Duke chided, slowly approaching the unicorn. "Unicorn blood can make me the most powerful being in the world."

Chail continued to back away, moving a little quicker as he asked, "Isn't their essence deadly to you?"

Stopping a pace away from her, the vampire smiled and leaned his head, eying her possessively as he answered, "Yes, if she only knew how to use it. She is innocent, even for her kind, and I doubt she could bring herself to kill even me. Her blood will endow me with power you cannot even imagine."

The unicorn raised her head and backed away a step, glancing at the Prince.

Reaching the wall across the room, the Prince slid toward the door and reached his hand toward the bolt. "What makes you think she can't kill you right now?"

His gaze on the unicorn's Duke Nevarr smiled a little broader and answered, "I can see the inexperience in her eyes. She is willing to sacrifice herself to save you and your companion." He raised his hand and a sword lifted from its resting place on the wall near the fireplace and flew to him. As he grabbed the hilt from the air, the vampire turned toward Chail and offered, "Your life I give you back for now. Go."

"And the girl and unicorn?" the Prince asked in a challenging tone, his hand tightly grasping the bolt of the door.

The vampire's eyes narrowed. "I have returned your life to you. Don't throw it away trying to be a hero."

Chail raised his chin. "Then let me at least take the girl."

"No," was the Duke's response. "Unless you mean to take her by force, which we both know you cannot, you will go now, or I can simply kill you."

"Why don't I just take them both and leave you dead here?"

Huffing a laugh, the vampire turned fully and strode toward the Prince. "I was an excellent swordsman in my life, and more so after. Draw your weapon so this girl's last living memory will be your death. Now come and die."

Chail pulled the bolt back and opened the door, countering, "You first."

Wind and rain, leaves and the sounds of the storm blew in and the big bay unicorn entered with them, rain water running off of him as he paced inside with lethal intent. His horn glowed a bright crimson, as did his eyes that were locked on the vampire.

Duke Nevarr stopped where he was, his own dark eyes widening and his mouth falling open. This unicorn was clearly experienced and very powerful, and the vampire seemed to feel it.

Turning and lowering his head, the bay unicorn loosed two blinding bursts of ruby light from his horn, each striking home on the chests of the two vampire women behind the white unicorn.

They screamed as the light exploded on them and they seemed to burn from within. The red flames consumed them in seconds and they fell together, hitting the floor and scattering in a cloud of dust.

Turning his eyes back to the Duke, the big unicorn snorted and stalked forward, the deep clop of his hooves echoing about the room.

Nevarr backed away, his gaze trapped by the unicorn's. Raising his sword, the vampire bared his teeth and hissed.

The bay unicorn responded with a deep whicker and pressed his attack.

Leaping over the loveseat Le'ell was still cocooned on, the white unicorn charged forward, lowering her head and her emerald glowing horn plunged into the chest of the last vampire woman who had quietly removed a spear from the wall and was positioning it to hurl at the bay.

Falling away from the unicorn, the vampire woman screamed and dropped the spear, emerald light spraying from the hole in her chest. Green flames erupted from the wound and rapidly consumed her and she fell and scattered into dust as the first had.

Two vampires remained.

Having watched the demise of his last vampire woman, the Duke turned his eyes back to the bay unicorn, raising his sword as he hissed, "Finish me then, damn you!"

Crimson light lanced from the bay unicorn's horn and struck the vampire, consuming him in red flames immediately.

Screaming in agony, the vampire dropped his sword and sank to his knees. A moment later the flames thinned and burned out, leaving the Duke intact.

Raising his head, Nevarr laughed a victorious laugh and reached for his sword. "I am far too powerful, mortal." He stood and locked his gaze on the Prince. "His power cannot harm me again and he knows it, nor will he even try."

Chail met the eyes of the big unicorn, who seemed to raise his brow in response.

Slowly striding toward the Prince, the Duke laughed again and cut his sword through the air many times. "That's right, mortal, he cannot harm me now."

Looking back to the unicorn through narrow eyes, the Prince drew his sword and announced, "He can't, but I sure can."

Swords rang loudly as they met, then again. Chail expected to be met with a vampire's strength, but no longer felt such strength from his enemy. He was, however, met by an opponent of considerable skill and quickness, one who smiled as he parried and attacked, one who did not expect to lose this night.

Le'ell noticed the cloak that had her trapped was loosening and she struggled to free herself, and as she struggled, its grip on her weakened more.

A parry from the Duke and a step back separated them and the smaller man smiled, poising his sword as he taunted, "You can't win, mortal, but I am enjoying our game."

"I hope you did," Chail responded. "It ends now." He swung his sword hard, knowing it would be met by the Duke's, then he spun around and kicked his opponent hard right in the chest, a sharp crack sounding as he struck.

Nevarr landed hard on his back some distance away and slid a short distance more on the stone floor. His sword danced across the floor further, stopped by a chair. He was slow to stir and sat up with a hand over his chest. This was pain he had not experienced for two centuries and his breath did not return easily. Cradling his broken ribs, he turned fearful eyes to his enemy for the first time.

Approaching slowly with his weapon held low, Chail regarded him coldly and growled, "Do you get it yet? The unicorn won't finish you because you're mortal now, but I have no such reservations."

Duke Nevarr clumsily scrambled away, groping for his sword.

The Prince watched him, then pursued as his enemy found his weapon and struggled to stand. When the Duke poised his sword, Chail simply knocked it away then rammed his own blade into his enemy's chest.

Nevarr just stared into the Prince's eyes for long seconds, and as his foe wrenched the sword from his chest, he dropped to his knees and finally slumped over dead.

Chail turned to find his Princess, then there would be one more thing to attend to.

One vampire remained.

The vampire girl stood where she had been, her eyes locked wide on the white unicorn, her mouth trembling, and a tear rolling down one cheek.

Seeing this, the little unicorn approached her.

The big bay unicorn's eyes narrowed slightly and he turned and followed.

With the white unicorn only a pace away, the vampire girl slowly sank to her knees, looking up to the unicorn with eyes that wept for the first time in many seasons. Her girlish innocence still lingered deep within a heart that had died so long ago. Her body quaked as she silently wept and reached to the unicorn with outstretched arms.

Hesitating that pace away, the unicorn stared down at her and the human onlookers knew she felt pity for the monster before her. With one more step, she lowered her glowing horn to the girl's forehead, touching her ever so gently.

A smile broke through the vampire girl's features and she closed her eyes as she was enveloped in an emerald glow, and as the glow faded she darkened and crumbled to dust, her dress collapsing in on itself as it fell around all that remained of the girl.

Le'ell pulled the remains of the now brittle cape from her and dropped it to the floor as she approached the Prince, her eyes locked on the dress that was crumpled over the small pile of ash that lay before the unicorn. Gently, she took his arm and pressed herself to him, leaning her head on his shoulder as he slid his arm around her back.

The unicorns looked to them, the white one approaching. She whickered, then leaned her head as she stared up at the Prince.

He smiled and nodded, confirming, "I understood enough. You have my thanks." He looked to the big bay and added, "You both do."

The big unicorn whickered softly and nodded back to him. Without warning, he stepped forward and nipped the white unicorn's haunch, and when she whinnied in surprise he turned and fled out of the open door with her only a few paces behind him.

"What was that about?" the Prince asked, a little surprise in his eyes.

Le'ell smiled. "I suppose it's their way of playing tag." She looked up to the Prince, asking almost fearfully, "Do you suppose it's safe to stay here?"

Another whinny outside in the rain confirmed that the unicorns were still there and Chail nodded and turned her back toward the loveseat. "Something tells me they are going to stay the night close to us."

"How did you know to open the door for the big one?" she asked.

He shrugged, sitting on the loveseat with her. "I'm not sure. They met me at the door when I went for the firewood and I got images of the vampires here in the castle in my mind. I'm not sure how the plan fell together like that. I just knew what I had to do."

Le'ell nodded, moving in closer to him.

Chail looked down at her, stroking her still wet hair. "Are you okay?"

She nodded again, softly confirming, "Yeah." With a deep breath, she asked, "Chail, do you remember earlier when I said I didn't want to come this way?"

He rolled his eyes from her. "Don't start, Le'ell."

"Oh, no," she continued. "You keep saying that I get myself into trouble all the time, but I don't think tonight was my fault, it was yours!"

"How was it *my* fault?"

"I wanted to stay in Border, remember?"

"We didn't have time to stay another night. I've already told you that."

"Do you know for sure when this war is going to start? How do you know we have to rush up to Aalekilk?"

"I don't, okay? It just seems to make sense that the sooner we put a stop to this the sooner we can get back to our peaceful lives."

She sighed. "And the sooner we can get back to sneaking out of our castles just to see each other."

He turned his eyes down to her, then pulled her tightly to him and wrapped his other arm around her as well. "I may just kidnap you and take you back to Enulam to live."

She smiled and snuggled into him, closing her eyes. "I would like that."

They held each other for a time, just enjoying the moment as recent memories of the vampires drifted from thought and the playful whinnies and running of the unicorns outside offered a pleasant distraction.

Chail finally looked down to her again and asked, "By the way. Where is your shirt?"

She turned narrow eyes up to his, and offered him a flirty smile.

CHAPTER 14

All appearances pointed to one grim conclusion: The battle had not gone well for Zondae.

Well polished and cleaned armor was now dirty and spattered with dried blood. Many Zondaen warriors found themselves packed into wagons that had once been used to haul supplies to and fro. Some still sat atop their horses. Others marched down the center of the road. None spoke. No weapons could be seen on any of them. Other wagons hauled the spoils of battle, food, weapons, clothing. Thousands of Zondaens found themselves on a journey they thought they would never undertake, one that would lead them to their enemy's castle. Surrounding them were battle hardened Enulam soldiers who still outnumbered them at least two to one.

The smell of fire and battle was still fresh for Queen Le'errin. Atop her horse and leading her people into the hands of her enemy, her one thought was on the future. She glanced around her at the quiet procession, praying this decision had been a wise one. Thousands of her warriors had been spared the blade, now their futures were in question. What had they been spared for?

Looking over the treetops ahead, she saw the six turrets of Enulam Castle, a sight she thought she would never see. Her eyes were blank as she just stared ahead at the stone fortress she and her people grew closer to. A long breath escaped her. Perhaps her daughter had been right after all.

Less than a league later was the defensive wall and huge timber gate of Castle Enulam and inside the procession went.

A huge encampment was established, tents erected, and the logistics put in place for her people's needs and comfort. All of the horses were taken to the Enulam stable but hers. After stretching her legs, she mounted her saddle to patrol between tents, circling the camp that had once been a training field for Enulam soldiers. This place was simply not big enough for three thousand and more soldiers, but it would have to do. Her eyes frequently shot to the hundreds of Enulam men who warily observed.

On one lap she was met by three men: two guards and a man in a leather apron who appeared to be more the size of an ogre than a man! She stopped her horse and looked down at one of the guards, her eyes narrowing.

The guard glared up at her, gruffly ordering, "Okay, off the horse, wench."

The huge man slapped the back of the guard's head hard enough to knock him down. "That would be the Queen of Zondae and you'll show some respect!" He turned his eyes to her as the guard slowly got to his feet, looking more across to her than up. This betrayed his size, and Le'errin finally realized that her daughter had not been exaggerating about him. "I'll need to be taking that horse from you."

She defiantly raised her chin, not daring to show the fear she felt for him. "I may just choose to keep my horse."

He sighed and glanced away. "Can't we just do this easily?"

"Why should I give him to you?" she questioned. "Perhaps I wish to use him to help my people get settled in."

The big man nodded. "Okay, first of all, King Donwarr wants to see you. Second, the animal needs to be tended to. I doubt he's eaten for a while. Third, if you want to ride around the camp then I'll get you another horse. Now can you please dismount so that I can take care of him?"

She eyed him for a long moment, then slowly swung down from her saddle and handed the huge man the reins. Le'errin realized she had to crane her neck to look up at him, and as he took the reins from her, she ordered, "I want him well cared for."

"I'll tend him myself," he replied. "Follow these guards and they'll take you to see the king."

Looking at the guards, she saw nothing but contempt for her, so she looked back up to the Stablemaster and straightly said, "I would prefer that you escort me yourself. Your guards may take my horse to be cared for."

He rolled his eyes. "I have many horses to attend to and not much day left."

Her lips tightened. She was used to men following her commands without question. She was clearly not at Zondae and the men here would not simply comply. Still, this gigantic man before her had been nothing short of polite and had even corrected a rude guard, yet he would clearly not respond to a strong woman. "Will you please escort me yourself?" she asked.

He growled and turned toward the palace, beckoning as he sighed, "This way."

This man had long strides and Le'errin found that keeping up with him was something of a challenge. He took the stone steps up to the palace door two and three at a time, easily lumbering his bulk up to the top. Once inside, he veered toward another flight of stairs and climbed them the same way.

Once on the second level, Le'errin took his arm to get his attention. "May I ask a favor of you?"

He growled again. "I'll tend your horses as if they were my own."

"No," she corrected. "I want you to help with my people. I don't entirely trust your guards with them."

"Why would you trust me?" he asked.

She shrugged. "I'm not sure. I just know that I do. If you go to the camp and ask for Sem'rika she can rally enough of my own people to help with your burden."

He glanced down at her.

"Sem'rika attended the horses at Zondae," she explained. "I believe she could be of great help to you. It might also help to keep as many of them busy as we can."

Nodding, he agreed, "I'll find her and put them to task. There's plenty to be done."

"What do they call you?" the Queen asked.

"Gartner," was his direct answer.

She smiled. "Somehow that name suits you. Why do you tend to the horses and not lead a legion of soldiers?"

"I like horses better," he replied.

"And if you're castle is attacked?" she pressed.

He glanced down at her again. "I'm in the reserve garrison. Anyone attacks here will pay for it."

She shook her head. "Gartner, I wouldn't attack you without at least a hundred soldiers and two catapults."

He nodded. A moment later he turned toward a door and banged his huge fist into it.

"Come in, Gartner," King Donwarr bellowed from the other side.

Opening the door, the Stablemaster ducked into the doorway and announced, "I've brought Queen Le'errin to see you."

She entered behind him, finding the King out of his armor and changed into a clean swordsman's shirt.

Seated behind his desk, he casually stood as she entered, his eyes locked on hers. "Why didn't you have the guards bring her up?"

Gartner turned to the door, grumbling as he left, "She insisted."

As the door closed, Le'errin turned back to King Donwarr and folded her arms.

He extended a hand to one of the chairs across from his desk and invited, "Make yourself comfortable."

She glanced down at it, then took her time seating herself. "These aren't just real comfortable."

Sitting himself, the King folded his hands on his desk and countered, "It's more comfortable than standing. How are your people faring out there?"

"As well as can be expected."

"I've cleared a wing of the palace for as many of your officers and soldiers as can be housed there," he informed. "Spring rains can come without warning and I want as many of your people as comfortable as I can make them."

She nodded. "That's very generous of you. And my wounded?"

"Teyli should be on her way to attend to them. She'll take those who are in need to the care center."

Le'errin nodded again, turning her eyes down. "I find myself questioning the wisdom of this decision. I'm not one prone to surrender so easily."

"I know," he assured.

She looked across the room. "Why did you offer to do this?"

"We both know why," he replied.

The tension on her face seemed to rupture and she smiled slightly. "I think it's just a ploy to get me back into your bed."

He leaned back in his chair. "Do you really think I would commit my entire army to get you here just for that?"

Her eyes slid to him. "Am I not worth it?"

"That and more," he confirmed.

"And if I refuse?" she asked.

Donwarr smiled slightly. "Then you can sleep in a tent outside."

"That's where I belong, with my people."

"But where would you rather be?"

She just stared at him with flirty eyes and that slight smile on her lips.

A knock on the door broke the new tension in the room and the King beckoned, "Enter."

The door opened and a guard entered, glancing at the Queen as he reported, "There is a man here to see you, says he's a merchant from Border."

Donwarr raised his brow and ordered, "Bring him in."

A very dark skinned man with long hair entered, carrying a long bundle wrapped in oiled burlap. He had a smile for the King and Queen and nodded to them in turn before turning his full attention to King Donwarr. "Your Majesty, thank you for seeing me on such short notice. My name is Noorain. I sell fine and exotic blades from around the land. Someone told me that you might be interested."

The King regarded him blankly for a moment, then informed, "We make most of our weapons here at the castle."

Noorain nodded. "I see, but can your blacksmiths match the craftsmanship of my fine blades?"

Le'errin folded her hands in her lap and countered, "A pretty sword won't help you in battle. Our weapons must be made for the wielder."

"As they should be," the merchant agreed. "Still, I think I have some you would like." He stepped forward and set the bundled swords on the desk, untying them as he informed, "In fact, a fine young gentleman named Chail thought these might be of interest to you."

Donwarr's eyes found the Queen's, then he reached forward and removed the first sword from the bundle.

Le'errin gasped aloud as she saw it, then she took the second, recognizing it instantly. She looked to the merchant with wide eyes and gaping lips and demanded, "Where did you get these?"

"He said you would ask," Noorain said straightly. "I purchased these from travelers a couple of days ago. A young lady called Le'ell took a liking to them and purchased them from me. She even paid me a little extra to deliver them here." He looked to Le'errin and insisted with a broad smile, "You must be her sister. She looks just like you."

"I'm her mother," the Queen corrected.

"No," Noorain drawled. "You're her sister. You can't make me believe you are old enough to have a grown daughter. She said your mother would be very interested in them and that King Donwarr should deliver them to her. Can you save him the trouble?"

She rolled her eyes, fighting back a smile as she looked back to the swords. "You already have. Do you know where she went?"

"The young lady who purchased the swords, you mean? I believe she and Chail were heading north, through the Dead Forest and toward a castle in the Dark Mountains. I didn't want to pry into their business, but that's what I overheard."

Le'errin looked to King Donwarr and raised her chin. "As we suspected."

He nodded, then looked back to the merchant and asked, "You happened to come here for the first time, how exactly?"

"Chail was very insistent that I could do business here," Noorain replied, then he motioned to the nearly empty burlap and continued, "That sword that's left in there is one meant for her mother."

Glancing at the King, Le'errin put the sword she had gingerly on the desk and hesitantly removed the one still in the burlap, her lips slowly parting as she recognized the hilt and the markings on the sheath. Turning her eyes to the merchant, she stood, gripping the sword tightly by the hilt as she demanded, "Where did you get this?"

Backing away a step, Noorain answered, "From Le'ell herself. She's decided to carry the scimitar I sold her and insisted that I bring this one to her mother. She paid me a little extra to deliver it."

"What did she say?" the Queen questioned.

He shrugged. "She told me to deliver the bundle here and accompany that sword to her mother. She and Chail thought that his father and your mother would meet somewhere and his father would give you the sword and her words."

Donwarr's eyes narrowed. "What words?"

Considering for a moment, the merchant finally recalled, "Don't worry about your little dragon. Unify at the northern borders and our enemy will be stopped."

The King's eyes turned to Le'errin. "And did Chail also send a message?"

"Only that he is sure you would know what to do, and something about Zondae first, something like that. We had been drinking and I cannot recall exactly."

"You recall enough," King Donwarr informed. "How did you get here?"

"My horse and wagon," Noorain replied. "I have quite a collection of wares to sell." He looked to the Queen. "Le'ell told me your mother would be buying all of my arrows and really insisted that I bring them all, and I have hundreds!"

Le'errin shot a fearful look to the King. "Donwarr...."

He raised a hand, silencing her, then looked to the merchant and suggested, "I'm sure if you set up shop between the palace and the west gate you will sell everything you have in there. Just tell the guards that I have endorsed you."

Noorain smiled and nodded to him. "Your majesty, I will do just that. I promise that your people won't be disappointed in what I have." He glanced at Le'errin. "I can see you like pretty young women, but this one seems a bit young for you."

The Queen smiled. "I get it. You're very charming. Get out."

Smiling back, he nodded to them in turn and quickly fled the room.

As Le'errin sat back down, her eyes on the sword in her hands, King Donwarr asked straightly, "The purchase of all of those arrows is a message to you, isn't it?"

Slowly, she nodded. "She expects us to engage a very large army soon, one with many archers." She looked to him with intense eyes. "This is her sword. She expects me to return it to her on the battlefield."

He just stared back at her for long seconds, then, "It's almost a shame you and your army have surrendered."

She regarded him coldly, then, "Tell me again why you set fire to the stables and upper levels of my palace."

Donwarr smiled slightly. "A message."

"If our children are correct, it will draw the raiders to the castle to finish off any loyals who remain, and then you will be next. If I were them, I would hit your northern keeps first. Take them and you can't rely on reinforcements from them. In fact, they would call to be reinforced from Enulam Castle."

He nodded. "A pity so many of my men here would be committed to guarding prisoners taken from Zondae, and more guarding those taken to the southern keep."

"A pity," she agreed. "So, how do you respond to such a threat?"

Donwarr shrugged. "I don't know of any such threat."

Le'errin's eyes narrowed slightly. "You have more up your sleeves than your big arms, I think." She sighed and put the sword on the desk. "Okay, King of Enulam. I suppose we should go about the ugly task of terms. I want my people cared for, treated well and not humiliated by their captors. Will you give your word on this?"

The King folded his hands in his lap, just staring at her.

She raised her brow. "I need your word on this."

He turned his eyes to the ceiling.

Le'errin loosed an impatient breath and conceded, "Fine. We'll negotiate in your bed chamber. But I'll want things in return."

Donwarr finally looked to her—and smiled.

CHAPTER 15

S uch a storm was not one to blow out quietly, but finally it would lose strength near high sun and move on. The dark castle near the middle of the Dead Forest was not a restful place. With the castle's master dead and his minions dust, life around his castle seemed to slowly return, and as the sun shined brightly in the wake of the retreating clouds the sounds of living things returned to this part of the forest for the first time in two centuries.

Sleep would come late to the four living things in the castle and awakening would come later. The four of them, two humans and two unicorns, emerged into the sunlight, their eyes skyward as they saw a clear sky for the first time in what seemed like a very long while. They heard birds returning, pursuing the flying insects and other small things that had been long absent from this forest. Green things also returned, blooming all over the forest like wildfire.

Le'ell breathed in deeply, smiling as the nectars of new blossoms filled the air.

His eyes sweeping the awakening forest, Chail said absently, "It seems that with the death of Duke Nevarr the forest can live again."

The big bay unicorn glanced at him and whickered, seeming to agree.

"We shouldn't tarry long," the Prince advised. "There's still a long journey ahead."

Le'ell nodded. "I know I would like to have some distance between me and this castle, the more the better."

In short order they were on their way and before long they had two leagues behind them before they realized. For reasons the humans could not know, the unicorns kept their company. Their presence was more than the company of mystic creatures few people ever saw, they were a great comfort. The Princess was content to talk freely, often directing her conversation to the little white unicorn who seemed to listen, intently at times and absently at times. Her chatter seemed more than idle, rather she seemed to be trying to put the events of the night as far from her mind as she could. By contrast, Prince Chail was very quiet, most of his attention committed to the big bay unicorn. The two exchanged looks quite often, communicating with glances that the young woman and mare with them did not realize. With the bay unicorn alert and sensitive to what was around him, he had the attention of the Prince who was on guard for many hours and felt only scant relaxation on this journey.

Many hours into their journey, as the sun was low in the western sky and the Dead Forest not quite a league behind, the bay unicorn's ears perked and he raised his head, staring ahead of him with wide eyes.

Alerted to this, Chail's hand moved toward his sword.

Le'ell absently continued with some story she was telling the white unicorn. "I really don't understand what the fuss was about. I mean, Sesh was always so cruel to me, I didn't think one little prank on her would be such an issue to someone. The snake I put in her bath wasn't even poisonous."

The white unicorn whickered a laugh, then, as the bay snorted, she became alert to him, perking her ears forward.

The bay slowed his pace.

Riding abreast of him, Chail stared forward, his eyes locked on the trees there. He looked down to the road, seeing that it had clearly not been traveled for some time, perhaps many seasons. Leaves and pine needles covered it, and grass grew up through the thick litter.

"No one's come this way for a while," the Prince observed.

The big unicorn glanced back at him, then motioned to the trees.

Le'ell came to the Prince's other side, nervously asking, "What is it?"

"Not sure," he replied. "Get your bow ready."

The bay looked back at him and snorted, then looked to Le'ell and shook his head.

"I don't think he wants me to," she informed.

The four rode abreast on the narrow road for many paces. With Le'ell on the outside of the line, to Chail's left, she nervously glanced around her, trying to tell herself that the movement in the trees was the wind blowing in the branches.

One ancient looking oak a few paces ahead caught her eye, then her full attention. A glisten in two knotholes that were side by side and almost two heights up seemed to follow her. The trunk flexed and the tree seemed to turn toward her. As she passed by, the saw that the shiny knotholes were eyes—trained on her!

Tearing her gaze away, she looked forward, managed to swallow and reported in a low voice, "Chail, the trees are watching us."

He nodded.

"What do we do?" she whimpered.

"Shh," he ordered.

Looking behind her, she noticed the road only ten paces behind had been swallowed by the forest, as if the trees had moved into it. She gasped as another tree with its glistening eyes turned its attention to her, and she turned back around.

The bay whickered and the white unicorn whickered back, then slowed her pace and gave Le'ell a short whinny.

Glancing back at her, Le'ell slowed to join her.

Scanning the forest ahead, the big bay whinnied loudly, then whickered at Chail and threw his head toward the rear.

Chail understood and slowed his horse, allowing the big unicorn to take the lead. His eyes widened as he watched the bay approach a large tree that was slowly moving into the road twenty paces ahead of them.

With a shriek, Le'ell stopped her horse, staring up at the ominous form that slowly moved closer to them.

Stopping at its base, the bay unicorn looked up at the tree and whinnied. The tree bowed slightly to him and responded in a very low note that seemed to shake the very ground. This exchange continued for a moment. The unicorn was actually talking to it!

Kicking her horse forward, Le'ell rode up between the Prince and the white unicorn, who were standing only ten paces behind the bay unicorn, and she stopped between them, nervously saying, "Chail, he's talking to a tree."

"It's an imp," the Prince informed. "They're the guardians of the forest."

"They're walking trees, Chail," she countered. "I thought imps were just creatures from fairy tails."

He nodded. "Just like unicorns are."

The white unicorn shot him a sour look and snorted.

"Sorry," he offered. "Le'ell, just don't move or do anything threatening."

"What can I do to threaten *that.*" she said straightly. "Besides, you're the one with the axe. Maybe you should try to hide it."

"We want to hide nothing, Le'ell. Just don't move."

The unicorn turned and paced back to them. The big imp followed. Other imps moved in from the forest, closing the road in front and behind.

Chail knew fear at this moment that he had never experienced. This was more fear of uncertainty, and not knowing how he could protect his princess should he need to.

Whickering to the Prince, the bay unicorn walked around behind him, taking the white unicorn's side and looking up at the imp himself.

Looking first down at the little white unicorn, the imp bowed to her, then it looked to Le'ell and finally to Chail. Unexpectedly, a very deep, thunderous chuckle escaped the tree guardian and it said in just as deep a voice, "He says you cannot understand him. Can you understand me?"

Hesitantly, the Prince nodded once.

"Then we can talk," the imp slowly informed. "You've come this way seeking those from the north. Their travel does not pass through here."

"We don't mean to trespass," the Prince said straightly.

"And you aren't," the imp assured. "The unicorns brought you this way for a reason. It seems that those you seek fear this part of the forest. They fear us. They will not come this way again."

"You've seen them?" Chail asked.

"We've seen them," was the deep reply. "It is feared that they will return despite our warnings. They seek to conquer those outside of their borders. This we know."

The Prince's jaw tensed. "So our suspicions are true. They wish to bring Enulam and Zondae to war and eventually conquer us."

"They have moved many men into Zondae already," the imp informed "many men of different kinds. We all fear that their ambitions go beyond the conquest of your kind. All others everywhere who do not join their vision of conquest could be imperiled."

Chail's eyes narrowed. "So this goes well beyond the conquest of Zondae and Enulam."

"It is thought you are just the start," the imp replied. "If you seek to stop them, be warned that you will not find the head of the beast where you seek it."

"Will unifying our people make us strong enough against them?"

The imp glanced at Le'ell. "That is an undertaking in itself. We have watched battles between your people for centuries. But if you do come together, you could perhaps stop their first thrusts into the forest."

Le'ell nodded. "If we stop their first thrusts then they may think twice about invading in force."

"Perhaps," the imp agreed. "You are free to pass here. The unicorn has told me that your intentions are just and good." As the imp moved aside, the others cleared the road and it finished, "Be well, Prince of Enulam, Princess of Zondae. May you succeed, and may we see you both again some day, united as you wish to be."

"You have our thanks," the Prince offered, kicking his horse forward.

Le'ell nervously followed, offering a timid, "Thank you," to the big imp as she passed. Catching up to Chail, she commented, "He seems very nice."

He raised his brow and panned his eyes to her.

Not quite a league later, darkness was falling and it was time to make camp. They veered into the forest and found a clearing with flat ground and soft leaves and pine needles to roll out their bedding. Not wanting to build a fire so close to the imps, the forest guardians, their camp would be dark this night and they would have no fire for warmth or safety. The unicorns wandered off into the forest, leaving them alone.

After a bland meal and a bottle of wine, they settled under their blankets, cuddling close together against the quickly cooling evening air and finding safety in each other's arms as they drifted off to sleep, the half moon overhead bathing them in a light blue glow.

⚜

Awaking first as usual, Chail slowly raised his head, looking first down to the Princess who slumbered peacefully in his arms, cuddled up against him on her side against the chill of the air. He gently combed the hair from her face, a smile touching his lips as she did not even stir at his touch. With the sun just barely casting its glow on the horizon, she was illuminated in the orange flicker of the campfire. At these times the deep seated feelings within him, feelings he could never speak of openly, began to nudge their way to the surface. The Prince found himself content to just watch her sleep for a time, almost wishing she would open her eyes just so that he could see that glint of firelight there in the depthless pools of deep brown.

He stared down at her for some time, lost in his thoughts about her until one striking realization hit him: They had not built a campfire!

Slowly, he turned his eyes to the fire.

A man with long black hair sat on a log about five paces away with his back to them. He wore a woodsman's shirt of buckskin and a white and gray leather jerkin over it. He also wore dark buckskin trousers and heavy leather boots all the way up his calves. As the Prince watched him, he casually poked at the fire with a stick. Hanging from a makeshift A-frame near the fire were some skinned small animals, slowly cooking.

Chail glanced around, seeing a third horse tied up near his and Le'ell's. Their swords were still leaning against the saddles, too far away to quietly reach, but the axe lay beside him and his hand was quick to find it. He slowly moved his side of the blanket over Le'ell and wrapped his hand tightly around the handle of his axe. As noiselessly as he could, he stood and turned toward the black haired stranger, his eyes narrow and locked on him. With the chill of the air stinging his bare chest, he straightened his back and lowered his chin.

The black haired man raised his head slightly, still staring into the fire as he said in a low voice, "Please tell me you have your pants on."

"I do," Chail confirmed.

Nodding, the black haired man poked at the fire again.

A long silence followed.

Chail cautiously approached.

The black haired man pointed his stick at another log a pace away from his own. "Join me if you like. The rabbits should be done by sunup."

The Prince hesitantly complied, his eyes on the black haired man as he turned the head of the axe to the ground and set it between his feet as he sat down.

The black haired man's face was free of beard and his deeply chiseled features were dark bronze, even in the firelight. As he turned his intense, almost black eyes to Chail, his face was expressionless as he informed, "I have a flask of mead. You're welcome to join me if you like."

"Perhaps later," Chail politely but straightly answered.

"You're wondering why I'm here," the black haired man told him.

Chail nodded.

"A mutual friend told me where to find you," he continued. "She said something about a quest to the Northlands and thought I might be of some help."

"Mutual friend?" the Prince asked.

"Someone who has been along with you for some days. You often did not even know of her presence."

His brow slowly lifting, Chail breathed, "The unicorn."

The black haired man nodded. "She was not sure what else she could do for you. She and the stallion fear the land north of this forest."

"Why do they fear it?" the Prince asked.

The black haired man looked back to the fire, poking at it with his stick. "They have good reason. The men there have no regard for them beyond how they can profit from them. They simply haven't opened their eyes to the damage they do."

"How do you know all of this?"

Shamefully, the black haired man lowered his eyes and admitted, "I was once among them."

Chail looked to the fire himself. "I see. And now those unicorns are mutual friends."

"It took a huge presence to open my eyes," the black haired man told him. "I'm hoping I can open yours. There is more awaiting you than you realize."

"So Aalekilk has been rebuilt," the Prince guessed.

"In a sense," the black haired man answered. "Why are you going there?"

"I think they're trying to bring our kingdoms to war."

The black haired man nodded. "And you and this woman are going to stop them?"

"We only need to expose them," the Prince answered.

"And hope that Zondae and Enulam will make peace to stand together against them," the black haired man said flatly. "A common enemy will sometimes do that, but a common enemy can also deceive them into going to war." He turned his eyes to the Prince. "How do you plan to expose them to your people?"

"We'll go inside," Chail answered. "Once there we pose as a couple of the mercenaries they've been hiring, collect the information we need and then slip out."

The black haired man just stared at him for long seconds, then, "Suppose you are discovered."

Chail shrugged. "I'll figure that out if the time comes."

Looking back to the fire, the black haired man poked it with his stick again and informed, "They have allies. You think that bringing your kingdoms to war is the body of their plan, but it is only a small part of a larger plan known only to them."

The Prince's eyes narrowed. "You seem almost eager for me to know this."

"Perhaps I am," the black haired man replied. "As I told you, my eyes have been opened to a great many things. Alone I can do nothing." He looked to the Prince. "Perhaps helping you helps me. Perhaps helping you helps the land."

Chail stared back at him for a time and finally admitted, "For some reason I feel compelled to trust you."

"You trust your instincts," the black haired man told him. "When the time comes you will lead your people well."

"You seem to have me at a disadvantage," the Prince informed.

"I am called Traman," the black haired man said.

The Prince extended his hand and replied, "Chail."

The two men shook hands, then turned back to the fire, and Traman reached for the flask of mead and pulled the stopper from it, offering it to Chail first. As they stared into the fire and sipped from the flask, the black haired man observed, "Dry early spring."

Chail nodded. "That usually means a wet summer."

"The spring melt should keep the rivers flowing until then. The game shouldn't migrate too deeply into the forest."

"I'm wondering why that drakenien happened this way," Chail said curiously.

"A drakenien? I've never heard of them coming so far south."

"We encountered one near the Spagnah River some days ago."

"That's unusual. I haven't had a run-in with one of those for many seasons. That one was North of the Dark Mountains. This area seems to be far too warm for them."

"Perhaps he'll make his way back north this summer."

"He would be wise to do so. Many dragons hunt the Abtont Forest."

They sat and talked of many things even after the sun finally illuminated the sky and the few heavy clouds that cruised overhead. They took turns with the flask of mead and grazed on some flat, salty biscuits that Traman had with him.

With the brighter light, Le'ell finally awakened and rubbed her eyes, sitting up as she heard voices. She watched the two men at the fire for a time, not really interested in what they were saying. Finally rising, she pulled her shirt on and picked up the blanket, then approached the fire and laid it around Chail's shoulders.

He half turned and smiled at her, then moved over just a little to allow her to sit beside him, and as she hesitantly sat down, her eyes on the black haired stranger, he introduced, "This is Traman. We seem to have a mutual friend.

She nodded to him, still feeling leery despite his presence with Chail. Glancing at the fire, she asked, "Is it wise to build a fire so close to an imp protected forest?"

"They don't mind," the black haired man assured, "that is, if you're careful and don't cut wood from living trees."

Le'ell nodded again.

Chail offered her the mead, and when she took it he asked Traman, "Will you be continuing on with us? We could use another sword."

He turned his eyes to the Prince's. "I'll ride with you for a while, but I'm known by the kingdoms of the Northlands. That could be more of a danger to you than a help." He looked to Le'ell and nodded. "I saw the Queen of Zondae once. You are very much her bloodlines."

The Princess raised her chin slightly.

"Yes," he confirmed, "I know who you are. I was sent to find you."

"Who sent you?" Le'ell asked suspiciously.

Chail answered for him, "Would you believe a white unicorn did?"

Her lips parted slowly and she raised her brow. "You can talk to unicorns?"

Traman nodded. "Anyone can. Just listen more with your heart and your instincts than your ears." He glanced at the cooked rabbits and suggested, "We should eat. I have much to tell you before we depart."

As the black haired man stood to baste the meat once more, Le'ell turned concerned eyes up to Chail's, clearly looking for reassurance. She found that trust was not so easy to come by, especially for those she knew nothing about.

Laying his arm and the blanket around her shoulders, he pulled her to him and kissed her gently on the forehead.

The black haired man seemed to know every trail through the forest. He led them off of the main trail many times onto smaller, narrower and clearly less traveled trails, only to lead them back to the main road again. What the Prince and Princess did not know at the time is that they avoided several Aalekilk patrols that happened along. He did not look it, but this man was listening to everything the forest could tell him.

Most of the day passed before he finally stopped his horse where the trees abruptly stopped growing and stared ahead at the gently climbing slopes at the base of a mountain range of dark gray and black stone."

Chail and Le'ell stopped at his sides, also staring at the mountains ahead of them. Silence lingered in the air for long moments.

"We part ways here," Traman informed. "Let me have the gold you have in those saddlebags and keep your weapons in sight."

Le'ell turned challenging eyes on him and demanded, "Why do you want our gold?"

"Mercenaries would not be carrying so much gold," he answered straightly. "Most are looking for employment after spending most of their money on drink and women. You must have this mentality. If they think you are not seasoned warriors and murderous barbarians then you won't be accepted. They may even kill you as intruders. Simply act as they do and show off none of your highborn mannerisms."

Le'ell turned and unfastened her saddlebags, mumbling, "That won't be much of a stretch for Chail."

He turned an insulted look on her and countered, "I'll have you know I can be a perfect gentleman."

She smiled and handed the saddlebags to Traman. "I prefer the barbarian in you."

"I'm sure you do."

Traman cleared his throat. "You should also not act so casually toward each other. You shouldn't bicker." He looked to Le'ell with narrow eyes. "Accept him as the dominant half of your pair. Fail to do so will doom you both."

She sighed loudly, complaining, "Why can't *I* be the dominant half for once?"

"Le'ell," the Prince growled, "don't start."

"It isn't fair!" she continued. "I'm just as capable as—"

"Princess!" the black haired man barked. "That is exactly what will get you killed. Chail is clearly the stronger of you. It will be clear to everyone you will encounter and it is all they will believe. You must decide now if you wish to stop this war or if you wish to feed your own ego."

Le'ell would never have tolerated any man speaking to her so. She never even let Chail get away with it. Only Queen Le'errin and Captain Pa'lesh had ever scolded her so and not faced a fiery retaliation—until today.

There was just something about this Traman, the way he spoke, the way he carried himself. He was such a strong presence that she felt herself humbled. Staring back into those stone-like eyes for long seconds, she finally turned her eyes down and nodded, knowing full well he was right, and she felt her ego quickly drain away.

He did not pursue the matter further, instead looking to the Prince and saying, "There is a pass directly north of here. You will meet sentries who will make certain you are worthy to enter the shadow of the castle. You will know what to do when you arrive there. Stay on your guard and know that not everything you see and hear is completely true. Good fortune to you both." He turned his horse and rode back into the forest.

They watched in silence as he disappeared into the trees, then looked to each other, somehow feeling very alone.

Le'ell raised her chin, letting him know with her eyes that she was with him more in heart and spirit than ever.

He nodded to her, then kicked his horse forward, leading the way toward the pass.

The pass leading to Aalekilk Castle was everything they expected and worse. The air was heavy, cold and damp. Little wind moved and a variety of unpleasant and offensive odors lingered all around them. Only small clumps of scrub brush and struggling grasses grew here. As the dark stone rose around them, fathomless caves reached back into the mountains. An occasional glint of eyes could be seen within them, flashing out of sight as quickly as they were seen.

Le'ell pulled her black mantle from her saddle bag and flung it over her shoulders, pulling it close against the chilly air. Though she suppressed as much fear as she could, her eyes danced around at the caves and scrub brush all around them. Her gaze locked on many long, thin legs that reached out of one of the caves half way up a cliff on her right and grasped the stone around it, stone that was partly covered in a heavy, off-white silk, and she gasped loudly as a wolf sized spider emerged.

Chail glanced up at it, then he looked harder and finally motioned higher, to the web it had begun constructing from its side of the pass toward the other. "It eats birds."

"Its leg span must be three paces!" Le'ell declared.

The Prince nodded. "Three, three and a half or so. It's probably more scared of you than you are of it."

"I really doubt that," she spat. Tearing her eyes away, she looked toward a turn ahead where the walls of the pass grew taller and the road actually narrowed to less than eight paces. "I really have a horrible feeling here."

"I know you do," he assured. "That's how anyone who approaches is supposed to feel. Just stay calm and we'll get through this okay."

"You look calm," she observed, "but inside you're about to soil yourself, aren't you?"

Chail cracked a smile. "Not quite. I'm just staying focused."

She nodded. "Good. Focused is good."

"In your case," he advised, "just remain quiet."

Le'ell shot him an irritated look. "I don't need you telling me what to do like that. You may be the *dominant* half here but just remember—"

"*You* just remember that the spider back there may have much bigger, girl-eating cousins ahead who are attracted to noise."

Her spine stiffening, Le'ell clenched her teeth and turned her eyes forward. A moment later she hissed, "You enjoy scaring me, don't you?"

"Oh, come now," he scoffed. "What kind of man would I be if I didn't?"

The road snaked around to the left and opened up somewhat, and as they got out into the open, Chail's eyes narrowed as they found the two sentries ahead.

Le'ell raised her chin as she saw them, not daring to speak as they drew closer.

From the look of them, they were forest trolls, man sized but not quite man shaped. Shorter legs and slightly longer arms betrayed their species, though they were hidden beneath steel and leather armor. Helmets were worn with the visors down so that their small eyes could not be easily seen.

Only ten paces away, Chail stopped his horse, Le'ell beside him. His eyes narrowed and he slowly pulled his axe from its saddle-strap, then he handed his horse's reins to Le'ell and ordered, "Wait here," as he swung down from his saddle. As he strode toward the forest trolls, he pulled his sword from its sheath with his left hand.

The trolls drew their weapons and went to meet him.

Knowing that trolls were stronger than average men, Le'ell still did not fear for her Prince since she knew that he was also stronger than an average man. Though he wore no armor, he engaged them without fear, yelling a fierce battle cry as he swung the axe at one, then brought his sword up at the other. They tried to retaliate but found this challenger much quicker than he appeared.

Venting a deep sigh and folding her arms, Le'ell watched as he fought bravely against what should have been overwhelming odds. He kicked one hard in the belly and sent him stumbling backward to the ground, then he turned his full attention to the other one, striking hard and fast with both his sword and his axe and hitting the troll's armor many times with both. His assault continued until the troll's weapon was knocked from his hand. Backpedaling away, the troll raised his hands before him, yielding the fight to the Prince.

Chail turned, holding his weapons ready, only to lower them as the first troll held his hands before him as well. With both of his opponents pounded into submission, he raised his chin and sheathed his sword, nodding to them as he informed, "I have won the right to pass. I would speak to the Lord of Aalekilk."

One troll grunted to him and pointed the way.

Nodding to him once more, the Prince turned to his horse.

Le'ell watched him approach, keeping her eyes on him as he took the reins from her and mounted his horse. When he finally turned his eyes to her she raised her brow and asked sweetly, "Did you have fun?"

Ever so slightly winded, he smiled slightly and admitted, "I certainly did."

They rode past the forest trolls and the remaining half league to the castle without further challenges. The landscape changed little, but for outposts built into the mountain walls on both sides, manned by many soldiers who observed their passing warily. The road turned sharply to the left around a steep cliff, and as they steered their horses that way the ominous castle was finally in view.

Constructed of the same dark gray and black stone as the surrounding mountains, it was nestled between mountain slopes and no doubt built into them. There was only one way in; a huge timber gate that was protected by two high towers, each at least seven human's heights tall, and the gate was still a hundred paces away. The defensive wall was an ominous sight in itself, four heights tall and starting at one mountain on one side of the castle and ending on the other, built right into the mountains themselves. It was only interrupted by the two towers flanking the gate that were perhaps twenty paces apart. Movement on the battlements showed they were ready for battle. Fifty or more soldiers were already up there. There were no features outside of the wall, no cover for an attacking army. Everything, every tree and stone, bush and shrub had been removed. This would be an easy killing zone for any invading army to meet its doom.

Chail loosed a deep breath through pursed lips. "Okay, here we go. Are you ready?"

"When did that actually matter?" she countered.

He glanced at her. "Just remember. We're mercenaries looking for work. That's how we must conduct ourselves."

Le'ell nodded. "I wonder if the pay is good."

Glancing at her again, he raised his brow and mumbled, "The pay?"

"I'm not going to risk my life fighting for someone if they pay trifles," she explained.

He smiled slightly as they approached the gate. "You have a point."

The palace was as intimidating a sight as the wall that defended it and built the same way, and bustling with the activity of hundreds of soldiers who trained and tended horses and equipment. The three towers that it was built around were each nine heights tall and twenty paces across all the way up. Positioned in a semi-circle at even intervals of about twenty-five paces, they were joined by stone walls that were five heights high, ending in battlements the same design as the wall. More structures clearly lay beyond and it appeared that much of the palace itself was built right into the mountains. This was a huge castle, though much of it could not even be seen. As with the defensive wall, there was only the one gate, which also stood open.

Swallowing hard as they approached, Le'ell's eyes darted from battlement to battlement, window to window. Everywhere she looked there was an Aalekilk soldier watching them. "Chail, this army must be huge."

He nodded. "Can you hear the smelts within? Look at the smoke to the left. They're still arming. Gnomes are known to be very handy with metal and I have no doubt the mountains around here are full of just what they need."

"Do you think Zondae and Enulam combined could defeat an army this size?"

Hesitantly, he shook his head. "I doubt it, and if they bring us to war we won't have a shadow's chance against them."

Le'ell raised her brow. "So off we go, into the belly of the beast. I hope you have a plan to get us out of here when the time comes."

Chail nodded. "I have it figured out. What we need to decide is how we're going to stop them. I don't think that dragon could even take an army this big."

"We're going to need that Gartner fellow back at Enulam."

The Prince chuckled and stopped his horse at the gate into the palace.

Twenty or more soldiers poured out and took up their positions, looking up at the riders and keeping their hands on their weapons.

Chail raised his chin, looking down at the most decorated of them and announced, "We've come to offer our services to the lord of this castle."

The compound outside the palace had been abuzz with the tasks of war-making. Inside, however, was a place that was lavishly decorated, brightly lit with chandeliers and many lamps. The cavernous main hall was an arch of white painted stone ten heights high and at least as wide. Stone support arches about ten paces apart gave one the impression that they were ribs in a body, but only at a glance. Each had a chandelier hanging from it and there were at least twenty of them. The stone floor in the center of the hall was carpeted in deep red from the entrance to the end. Also on areas of carpet, luxurious furnishings were arranged around fire-pits on both sides like conference areas or just places to relax. But for the escort who led the way through the hall, a tall human in the same armor the rest of them wore, no soldiers were within this hall, but many servants were, cleaning or arranging flowers or tending the many lamps that lit the place.

At the end of the long hall were elaborately carved timber doors flanked by gold oil lamps on tall stands. Suits of armor standing on the outsides of the oil lamps guarded the doorway, each holding a shield and sword at the ready. Only here did weapons actually appear in the room, which was something of a surprise considering the nature of the outside of the castle.

As they reached the door at the end of the hall, the escort stopped and turned to Chail and ordered, "Wait here." Turning back, he opened one of the doors just enough to enter and closed it behind him.

The Prince looked to Le'ell and raised his brow. "Well. I sure hope he can see us today. I would hate to think that we came all this way for nothing."

She nodded. "It would just be plain rude to send us away now. Where else would he find warriors of our caliber who are willing to make such a journey?"

"Especially warriors as pretty as us," he added. He glanced down from her eyes, then reached to her and loosened the laces of her shirt, pulling it apart enough to reveal a good portion of her chest.

Le'ell glanced down at what he was doing and smiled ever so slightly. "I didn't know we came here for that."

"I'm bartering a look at you to win his favor," he informed straightly. "And I like seeing you like this, too."

She laughed under her breath and added, "You like seeing more than this."

Chail turned back to the door. "And I'll never tire of it."

A moment passed.

"How long will he make us wait?" she asked.

"He's testing our patience," the Prince answered.

"That he is," she snarled.

"Just remember that you are not a princess here. You are here to swear your loyalty to the lord of this castle and be ready to kill or die to that end."

"I'll just kill to that end," she said straightly. "Let our enemies die for their loyalty."

He glanced down at her, mumbling, "Savage."

Another long moment passed.

The handle clicked, and slowly turned.

"Here we go," Chail murmured.

It opened fully and the guard exited, pausing only long enough to say, "Lord Poskleer will see you now. Mind your manners and remember your place."

They watched him as he walked by and toward the exit, looked to each other, then turned to enter.

The room on the other side of the doors did not fit the castle at all. Even more elaborately decorated than the hall they had just walked through, this place was clearly designed for comfort, and was huge and spacious. A huge fireplace roared on the far end; two smaller ones built into the center of the walls to the left and right also burned. More oil lamps and suits of armor were right inside of the door, just like outside. Elaborate and expensive furnishings were everywhere, arranged in settings similar to the hall. A long oak table was right in the center of the room, eight plush chairs on one side and identical chairs on the other. A really comfortable chair with a high back and deep cushions sat on the far end. Many bowls of fruit and baskets of bread were distributed evenly on the table, as were flasks and bottles of wine and many waiting goblets and fluted crystal glasses. Gold chandeliers, oil lamps and candles lit this room as well, yet the smoke did not collect, rather it escaped from holes in the ceiling, apparently drawn out somehow.

They only entered a few paces, looking around at the furnishings and decorations with awe. Book cases on the far end of the room, flanking the fireplace, were burdened with many books and trinkets, small statues and other ornaments. They did not span the full wall, rather they stopped two paces short on either side. A stag head hung above the fireplace, staring into the room with lifeless eyes.

Le'ell commented in a low voice, "This is the most comfortable room I've ever seen."

Chail nodded.

From behind the bookcase to the right of the fireplace appeared a man in white flowing robes that were clearly of a light material and made for comfort. His light blond hair was below his shoulders and flowed behind him as he walked much as his robes did. He had no hair on his face, wearing only a pleasant smile as he saw them.

As he approached, extending his arms, four servants followed him, also dressed in white. Two were women who wore light clothing similar to the slave girls at Enulam. The other two were men, dressed similarly but not wearing shirts. None of them wore shoes or sandals and they all kept their eyes on the floor before them as they walked.

"Be welcome," the man in the robes greeted, extending his hands to Chail first. As the Prince extended his hand, the man took it in both of his and offered a broad smile. "I've already heard of your encounter with my sentries. Absolutely splendid! Please, come in and make yourselves comfortable." He extended his hand to three comfortable chairs near the fireplace on a side wall and led the way.

Each of the blue cushioned chairs had a table beside it.

The servants hurried to the long table to collect some of the food and wine there.

Chail and Le'ell noticed quickly that their host was a slight man, both thin and lacking in stature. As he looked to Le'ell, she noticed he was considerably shorter than she was, the top of his head coming up maybe to her nose, and she tried to disguise her smile as politeness rather than amusement. All of his servants, even the women, were also taller than him and much better built, but curiously submissive.

Waiting for his guests to sit, the slight man sat down himself, lounging in his chair and absently holding his hand out to the side, which was quickly filled with a goblet of wine.

"Thank you for coming," he said to them, holding his goblet to them.

Servants offered them goblets as well and they all drank to this strange enthusiasm to their presence.

"So," Chail started, "you know why we've come."

"Of course I do," he informed. "Might I say I have no swords of your status here at Aalekilk Castle. I trust you've come looking to be employed?"

The Prince nodded. "We have. Word got to me in Border that you pay well."

"I pay my soldiers very well," he assured. "But, I pay my bodyguards much better."

Chail raised his chin. "Bodyguards?"

"Why, yes. A man in my position needs to be properly protected, don't you think? With what's coming in the next months I will no doubt have many attempts on my life and I will need loyal and worthy guards to keep me safe. The second best way to buy loyalty is with gold, and I have enough gold to buy a hearty lot of loyalty."

Le'ell asked, "What is coming in the next months?"

He waved his hand to her and scoffed, "Oh, I don't want to bore you with such details. Suffice to say I have enemies that need to be dealt with and you two are here at a very opportune time."

Nodding, Chail agreed, "It seems so. You look like you are preparing for quite a war, and I want to be on the winning side with a generous rank, perhaps some of the spoils."

"I'm sure you do," Poskleer drawled. He glanced at one of the servants who brought them food on gold plates, then he glanced at Le'ell and observed, "I guess you have no use for a slave girl."

He shook his head. "Haven't found one worthy enough to replace this woman. I don't think I will. She more than satisfies my appetites in my bed and she has among the best sword arms I've ever seen."

"I can see that," Poskleer said straightly. "I suppose you wish to keep her at your side?"

"Of course," Chail answered, then took a drink of his wine.

Smiling slightly, Poskleer countered, "I can clearly see why. I wouldn't part with her at any cost. Sadly, you are going to have to, Prince Chail."

Chail's neck stiffened and his grip on his goblet tightened as he stared back at the smaller man sitting across from him.

"Yes, I know who you are," Poskleer casually went on. "Actually, I've been expecting you. I wasn't entirely sure you would meet all of the challenges presented to you on your journey, but I'm glad to see you've braved them well and gotten here on time. More wine?"

Le'ell turned anxious eyes on the Prince.

Setting his jaw, Chail accepted, "Please." As he held his goblet up to be filled, he looked the Castle Lord square in the eye and asked, "How is it you knew to expect us?"

Poskleer sighed. "I know a great many things. You see, I'm considered somewhat clairvoyant. I know the thoughts of those around me and I express my wishes to those who serve me in the same way. I also make them feel compelled to serve me in any way I wish by many different means."

Chail nodded. "I see. That would explain how you got trolls and gnomes and men to all work together so."

Looking to his plate of food, which had been set on the table beside him, Poskleer picked at the cheese and rolls absently as he admitted, "That was quite an undertaking, and some time putting together. They really don't get along well so maintaining discipline was something of a chore at first. But, with the proper motivations and formulas everything fell into place and now I've massed the largest standing army on the continent." He finally chose an apple and looked back to Le'ell. "So tell me, Princess. How is it you and the son of your enemy get along so well?"

Her eyes narrowed.

Taking a bite from his apple, Poskleer looked to Chail and observed, "I don't think she likes me. No matter. You will both serve me in the roles I have chosen for you."

"What makes you think that?" the Prince asked in a challenging tone.

He motioned toward Le'ell with his head and answered, "It starts with her. You see, your loyalty to each other will most certainly be the undoing of everything you have worked so hard to achieve."

Le'ell leaned forward slightly, her eyes boring into him as she challenged, "Or it will be *your* undoing instead."

Holding a finger up, Poskleer corrected, "I really don't think so. Shall I demonstrate?" He turned his eyes behind them.

A red haired woman approached, dressed just like the other slave women but for the silver bracelets she wore.

Seeing her, Le'ell slowly stood, facing the slave girl as she declared, "Jan'ka!"

Unable to meet her eyes, the red haired woman drew her shoulders up slightly and just stared at the floor when she reached Poskleer's chair.

"Sit," he ordered, watching as she sank to the floor beside his chair.

He stroked her head as if she was a pet dog. "She fears a great many things. I helped her face them. Believe me she does not want to face them again, which she never will so long as she is my loyal servant."

Le'ell's hand found her dagger, her eyes locked on him.

"You should reconsider what you're thinking," he advised. "You see, what dear Jan'ka fears the most is being burned alive. I think it has something to do with a little incident when she was just a wee girl. Up until now I have kept her from having to experience that even in her little mind, but *right* now only you two keep that horrible fate from her."

The red haired woman cringed and appeared to weep softly.

Poskleer looked to her, stroking her hair ever so gently as he assured, "There, there, my dear. She won't let that happen to you again." He looked to Le'ell and finished, "Will she?"

These words gave Le'ell pause and she turned her eyes to Jan'ka, fearful about what might happen to her. Still she saw a way to get her out and glared at the Castle Lord again, assuring, "I can kill you before you can reach that lamp."

"I don't need the lamp," he informed. "But, I challenge you to do so. Go ahead. Throw your dagger. Kill me and you are all three free to go. Fail and I burn her alive."

"Please, Master," Jan'ka wept.

He simply patted her head and looked to Chail. "You too. Come now, I haven't the entire day to dance around like this. Things to do."

The Prince glanced at Le'ell.

She snarled, "I don't, either." Her hand moved swiftly, almost too fast for anyone to see and her dagger flew with a true aim right at his heart, through him and his chair without even touching him and slid point-first across the floor behind him. Her eyes widening, she took a step back.

Shaking his head, Poskleer raised his brow and observed, "You aimed so carefully, too. No worries, for you anyway. But I'm afraid little Jan'ka has a problem now."

"Please, Master," Jan'ka implored. "Please. I've served you so well. Please don't do this to me."

He shrugged and lifted his hand from her, looking back to Le'ell as it burst into flames. "Do you feel foolish yet?"

Breathing came very hard and she just slowly shook her head.

"When I touch her she will burn to death, and you will watch and hear her cries of agony. I can make it last seconds or hours."

"Don't," was all Le'ell could manage.

"We had a bargain, remember?"

Desperately, she looked to Chail.

He somehow maintained his composure and leaned back in his chair. "You put on an impressive display, but I don't see how burning her to death will serve you."

Poskleer turned a mischievous look to the Prince. "It may, or it may not. Or, sparing her for now could serve me better." His eyes were hard and commanding when they found Le'ell again. "On your knees or she burns."

Jan'ka looked up to her and begged, "Please!"

Slowly, Le'ell sank to her knees, her eyes on Poskleer's.

The fire around his hand vanished and he stroked Jan'ka's head once again. "You see? Now, be a good girl and just stay right like you are while Prince Chail and I have a little chat, okay?"

"I'm involved in this, too," she insisted.

"You were," he corrected. "My scouts returned a day ahead of you. Zondae is no more."

The Prince and Princess exchanged glances.

Poskleer continued, "The first strike against your people went as planned. My soldiers attacked and withdrew. Your mother foolishly followed them out, and wouldn't you know, they ran head long into an entire legion from Enulam that was already marching on the castle. A second legion laid siege to Zondae Castle itself while most of their troops were in the field and their gates were wide open. It wasn't really even a battle. Your mother and her remaining army surrendered within an hour."

"You're lying," Le'ell hissed.

Looking to her with pitiable eyes, Jan'ka slowly shook her head.

The Princess' gaze shot to Chail, who met hers with eyes she had never seen before. He did not seem to know where to go from here.

"My second thrust reached your northern keep two days ago," Poskleer went on. "With most of those troops in the field it fell easily. My armies will march on Enulam in the morning and finish your people off."

Chail glared at him, demanding, "And then what?"

Poskleer shrugged. "Then we move on. Your people were merely an obstacle. Believe me we have much bigger game to hunt south of you."

"So you mean to conquer the entire land by yourself?" the Prince questioned.

"Oh, no. Not alone. I have allies who have similar goals. By the end of summer we will be as far south as Trostan."

Chail huffed a laugh. "You didn't think things through, you and these allies. Only a couple of leagues away from Trostan is the lair of the biggest dragon in the land, perhaps in the world, and he has no patience for conquering invaders."

Poskleer laughed back. "Oh, we have a plan for him as well. In fact, he's the biggest part of our plan. Dragons aren't exactly invulnerable and my ally at Red Stone Castle will deal with him. Word is that this dragon near Trostan has the biggest hoard of gold anywhere in the world, large enough to raise an army so massive as to allow us overrun the entire continent."

"Huge aspirations for such a small man," the Prince snarled.

Shrugging, Poskleer countered, "Some men grow big, some of us think big." He patted the red haired woman's head and ordered, "Run along, now." As she stood and hurried from sight, he looked back to Chail and observed, "You want to know what you do now. I suppose it would only be fair to tell you."

Not answering, the Prince sipped his wine, his steely eyes locked on his host.

Poskleer smiled slightly. "Oh, how you hate being in a position you can't control. It must be horrible for you."

"I would thank you to get to your point," Chail prodded.

Looking to Le'ell, the Castle Lord smiled and said, "And he's still so polite. Most men in his position would be hurling insults at me by now." He turned his eyes to Chail and continued, "I always like to reward good manners. I feel there just aren't enough people in the world who use them. I assume you would like to live through the day?"

The Prince shrugged. "I suppose so."

"And you want her back?"

"Do I really need to answer that?"

"I suppose not. I'll tell you what, hero. Complete three tasks for me and you are both free to go."

Chail's expression did not change as he said, "I'm listening."

"First, I want you to go to Enulam Castle and convince your father to surrender. Tell him I will grant quarter to all who will and all who don't will be put to death."

The Prince's eyes turned down to his wine goblet.

"Second," Poskleer went on, "since someone else clearly knows of my plans for the land, bring me the head of the one who sent you to find me."

Setting his jaw, Chail's gaze snapped back to the Castle Lord. He clearly and unsuccessfully attempted to hide the fear and uneasiness of this task.

"And third," Poskleer finished, "return here within three days."

"And if I don't?" the Prince asked in a hard voice.

A slight smile touched the Castle Lord's lips. "Let's just say your princess' life depends upon it. She will remain here as my guest until you come back. Fail or betray me in the slightest and she is mine to do with as I wish."

"You will kill her if I fail?"

"Perhaps, or I may make her long for death. Or I could make her forget you ever lived and simply replace you in her mind and heart. Either way, you will decide her fate. Her suffering or joy will be in your hands."

Chail found himself unable to respond or even look Le'ell's way.

"Let's not forget about poor Jan'ka," Poskleer added. "She so fears what can happen to her since you arrived. You could probably live with her horrible death, but could your Le'ell live with it? Perhaps her fate lies in your hands as well."

"I can't promise that I'll complete all of this in three days," the Prince growled.

Poskleer raised his brow sympathetically. "There are fates worse than death, Prince Chail. It would be a shame if you were to find one or more in your future. Perhaps that should be the driving force in your life from now on." He held his goblet up and a slave girl immediately filled it. "It always comes back to selfish need. You cannot imagine life without her nor could you live with the agony of the death she will experience should you fail. You're a smart boy, so I'm sure you can figure out how to avoid that."

When Chail finally turned his eyes on the Castle Lord, his brow was low between them and that predatory look was there as he informed, "If I succeed or fail, I *will* be back for her, and if she is harmed in any way I will kill my way through your entire army to get to you and show you how many ways a tiny mouse with big thoughts can die."

His eyes hardening, Poskleer warned, "It is never wise to threaten a wizard."

The two men glared across the three paces between them for long seconds.

"Your time is already running out," the Castle Lord informed.

"As is yours," the Prince countered. He slammed his goblet onto the table beside him and stood, making sure that this wizard got a good look at his true height and bulk, then he turned to Le'ell and stepped toward her.

As she reached for him, Poskleer warned, "Do not touch her."

Le'ell hesitated, but Chail defiantly took her hand anyway and assured, "I will be back for you. I promise." Without another word or look, he turned and strode out the door, slamming it shut as he left.

The sound echoed through the room for some time.

Her eyes on the floor before her, Le'ell slowly shook her head, fighting back tears as she whimpered, "Why?"

"Why did I send him to his death?" the wizard asked, "Or why do I want the head of the dragon that sent you?"

Her gaze snapped to him.

"Yes, I know about the dragon," he told her. "The image is still vivid in both your minds. I don't know where the beast came from or why he made a pact with you, but it will cost him or your prince his life, perhaps both." He leaned back in his chair, staring down at her. "You know, you should really think about your future."

"According to you I have none," she countered, looking back to the floor.

Poskleer smiled. "Oh, don't let my threats to your man-toy harden your heart. You could have quite a prosperous future here with me. Good to my word, once he fails, your life as his ornament will end. That doesn't mean you can't start a new life here with me as mine."

"May I get up yet?" she asked.

"That all depends," was his answer. "What do you intend to do once you are standing?"

"This hurts my knees," she complained.

The wizard sipped his wine.

"I won't cooperate with anyone who enjoys watching me suffer," she added.

"You will cooperate with me regardless," he assured. "Remember poor Jan'ka."

Le'ell loosed a shallow breath. "Promise you will not harm her, or me, and I'm yours willingly in three days if Prince Chail fails."

"Is that *your* promise?" he asked hopefully. "If so, why must I wait?"

She finally turned her eyes to him. "I will not assume that he will fail. Unlike you I believe in him. He still owns my heart and he has my faith."

"How about a new pact," he suggested.

She raised her chin.

"You will not be my prisoner here," he explained, "you will be my guest for the next three days. At high sun on the third day we will drink a toast with a special wine I will give you, one that will wash him from your heart forever. After, you will belong to me for the rest of your life. But, you must drink the potion—uh, the wine—of your own will."

Looking away from him, Le'ell considered hard what this would mean.

"It won't hurt," he assured. "Once you drink the wine then any pain that you ever knew him will be gone. You will have a new life with me."

"As long as I'm your mindless slave," she added for him, a tear rolling down her cheek.

He stood and walked to her, offering her his hands. When she took them, he helped her to her feet, looking up into her eyes for long seconds before assuring, "That is not what I want at all. I am surrounded by mindless slaves. I want conversation with someone who is not afraid of me, someone with her own voice. I can literally offer you the whole world and pleasures you have not even dreamed about."

"Why are you offering me this?" she demanded, staring coldly down at him.

"Look in the mirror," he ordered, then motioned to the wall behind her.

She looked over her shoulder as the stone of the wall parted to reveal a gold framed mirror over a height tall. In it she saw her reflection, but not one she recognized. Her reflection was in a long silk dress, one that fit her body tightly as the long skirts belled out ever so slightly over her legs. Gold lace layered over the skirts. It was low in the back and her shoulders were bare, and as she turned she saw that the front was also cut low and was held in position by a single gold strap over her left shoulder, leaving her sword arm naked and free. Her long hair was restrained neatly behind her by a gold ribbon. When she blinked, a gold and diamond necklace appeared and long elegant earrings dangled from her ears.

She watched her reflection as she slowly raised a hand to her neck, gasping as she felt the necklace there and she stepped back and looked down at herself, seeing that she was really dressed so!

"It's how you really are," Poskleer explained. "At Zondae you were not the heir to your throne. You can be here."

Astonishment still ruled her as she looked back to him.

"This is the princess every girl wishes to be," he went on, "but your wishes get to finally start coming true. You won't have an older sister to compete with here. In fact, I can arrange for her to be your servant if you like."

She turned back to the mirror, quickly growing to like what she saw, yet feeling something about it was so unnatural. "But this isn't real."

"Of course it is," he assured. "Everything here is as real as I wish it to be, but for one thing. I'm a man who gets what I want from everyone around me, but for once I would like for something to be offered freely."

"You want me," she said.

"What man wouldn't?" he almost laughed. "What you see in the mirror is the beautiful young woman you are on the inside; you've just never been told that before."

His words made sense to her. He was telling her everything she had always wanted to hear, and yet it conflicted with what clung stubbornly to her heart. Closing her eyes, she begged, "Please make it stop." When she opened her eyes again the mirror was gone and the stone wall was as it had been. Slowly turning back to him, she realized she was still in the white gown and plead with him, "I can't have this life."

"Not yet," he assured, "but in three days you can. I will care for you and keep you safe and comfortable until then."

"And Jan'ka?"

"Her fate is up to you, Le'ell. She says you were playmates as little girls. You can be here if you wish. Just understand that I will do what I must to retain control here."

She nodded.

He continued, "I will force nothing from you and demand nothing so long as you behave and do not leave here. I will uphold my end of the bargain so long as you uphold yours and drink the wine with me in three days as agreed."

"Only if he fails," she added.

He smiled slightly. "Of course. And if he succeeds, you are free to go with him. If he can truly bring me the head of the black dragon, then I still win, even if I have to let the three of you go. So, is it a bargain?"

This wizard Poskleer was a very persuasive man and she found herself almost feeling trust for him. Staring down at him, she simply answered, "Yes."

—

CHAPTER 16

Perhaps the big wizard at Border was a man of habit.

There had simply been no time for sleep and a two day journey was finished in less than half that time. As it had been before, the Dragon's Talon was a busy place. High sun seemed to be the time of day when this place was the most crowded and finding any one man in here would be a problem, but Chail seemed to know right where to go.

As hoped, the big wizard was indeed a man of habit and was found where he had been found before with a feast for four people in front of him and his tall, red haired wench sitting across from him.

Finding him had been easy. The meeting would not be.

Not quite half an hour later the big wizard sat in front of Chail with his face resting in his hands as he digested what he had heard. Chail sat across from him, beside the red haired woman as he stared with blank eyes down at the table.

Long moments passed and the wizard finally drew a breath and leaned back in his seat, exasperated eyes on the Prince as he reviewed, "Okay, let me see if I have your story straight in my mind. You went to the castle posing as mercenaries. He took you to his meeting hall, wined and dined you as if you were visiting dignitaries and then finally revealed his plan to you as well as his knowledge of your true identities, and instead of killing you both, he sent you to bring him back the head of whoever sent you to find him and then to talk the King of Enulam into surrendering to the armies that have lain siege to that kingdom. Does that sound right so far?"

Chail nodded.

"And he kept my woman with him to make certain you would not fail, even though we all know you probably will," the wizard continued.

Chail nodded again.

"And if by some miracle you complete these tasks he wants you to, you think he will actually give her back to you and let you just walk away."

The Prince glanced at him. "I have no reason to believe he won't."

Raising his bushy eyebrows, the big wizard just stared at him for a moment, then asked, "Were you born an imbecile or have you had a sharp blow to the head recently? He has no intention of giving her back no matter what! Didn't you consider that you might encounter such an obstacle when you went in?"

"I suppose I should have," Chail admitted.

"That you should," the wizard agreed. "Now explain to me how this whole experience of yours was anything but a smoldering cauldron of impending disaster for us both."

The Prince finally turned his eyes to him and did not answer.

Loosing a frustrated breath, the wizard looked away, then back to the Prince and asked, "Does he know about your pact with me?"

Chail shook his head. "I don't think so. I think he wants me to go after the dragon specifically. That's the impression I got, anyway."

Rubbing his lips with his fingertips, the wizard simply stared back for a time, then nodded. "He figures if you can slay a dragon then you are as formidable as he hopes. Your tasks aren't the end for you in his eyes. Survive, and he will have more awaiting you. Clearly, you should do exactly what he wants."

"So how do we kill this dragon?" the Prince asked straightly.

Raising his eyebrows, the wizard exclaimed, "We? There is no we in this matter and I'll not involve myself in a conflict with another wizard."

"Afraid he's more powerful than you?" the Prince asked in a challenging tone.

"The power of the *wizaridi* is clearly not something you have a great deal of knowledge about. I'm beginning to think you don't have much knowledge about anything, especially planning ahead."

"I had hoped you would be of more help."

"Only a fool locks horns with a dragon. Of course, you've more than proven that status today so you are the best qualified of us."

"I was beginning to think you were the powerful wizard you wanted me to think you were." Chail stood, finishing, "My mistake."

As he turned to walk away, the wizard summoned, "Prince."

Chail stopped and turned, much annoyance in his eyes.

Shaking his head, the wizard leaned over and reached into a pouch, then another, then checked another, then checked his pockets.

The red haired woman reached into her cape and produced a black vial about the length of her finger and twice as thick with a faded cork shoved in the opening. Holding it up where the wizard could see it, she raised her brow and smiled ever so slightly.

He snatched it from her hand and turned back to the Prince, offering him the vial as he instructed, "Pour this on the edge of the blade you intend to use on the beast."

Taking the vial, Chail examined it closely, then asked, "What does it do?"

"It's supposed to kill dragons," was the wizard's answer. "Your blade alone will not penetrate his armor so it will need the help of such a potion. Just make sure you catch the beast asleep. Heroics and pride will do nothing more than get you killed, so approach unnoticed and strike the killing blow quickly at his neck. Sever his head and you might just walk away. And you might pray to whatever gods you believe in first and make sure you relieve yourself before you attack him."

"So you aren't coming," the Prince guessed.

"You botched this up, you fix it."

"At least your courage hasn't failed you today," Chail growled as he turned and walked away.

Outside, he reached his horse and took the reins, leading the weary beast down the semi-crowded main street of Border. His destiny was a day's ride ahead, or his death.

❦

Somehow, Prince Chail knew he would find the dragon at the hot springs. Sunrise was an hour behind him, and as he rode into the open around the pool, an enormous black predator lay sprawled beside the water ahead of him. A few days ago he was right where he wanted to be with his princess in his arms. That thought drove him.

Keeping his horse near the trees, he swung down from the saddle and pulled the axe slowly from the strap. Patting his horse's neck, he bade, "Wish me luck."

As he slowly strode toward the slumbering beast, he removed the vial from his pocket, pulled the cork out with his teeth and poured the glowing sky blue liquid on the edges of his axe, then he tossed the vial away, spat the cork the other direction and took the axe with both hands, his gaze locked on his huge opponent, on his neck two paces behind his head.

With his snout turned toward the pond, the dragon lay on the hard stone looking almost like a huge lounging cat. The end of his long tail twitched as he slept. With the sunlight just over the trees, his scales

❦ 277 ❦

shined with many dark blues and even darker greens as the light hit them just right.

Twenty paces away, Chail froze as the dragon shifted slightly and he watched for many long, anxious moments as the great beast settled back into his nap.

Glancing around, the Prince noticed that the red dragon was absent, and hoped she would remain so. This black dragon's head alone was the size of Chail's horse and he prayed that his first blow would be the killing blow. Le'ell needed him to win this fight. Swallowing back his fear, he hesitantly started forward again, his eyes fixed on a spot between the armor-like dorsal scales, and he poised his axe to deliver the blow.

Ten paces away and his heart thundered. Five paces and it felt as if it was going to burst from his chest. Three paces, then two, and he finally swung the axe with all of his strength.

The gap between the scales was a shadow and the enchanted axe slammed into thick dragon armor with a metallic clank—and bounced off!

Chail stumbled backward a step, his wide eyes looking for at least a blemish on the scale he had struck but not finding it. Looking toward the dragon's head, he was relieved to see that the beast had not moved. He had not even awakened.

With a mighty yell, the Prince struck again, with the same results, then again, this time nearly losing his grip on the axe. Turning his eyes to it, he reset it in his hands, gripping it tightly toward the end to maximize his swing. He simply *had* to succeed! As he set himself to swing again, he looked back to the dragon's neck, then turned his eyes up and froze.

The dragon had raised his head and was staring down at him.

Chail stared back, not knowing what to do now.

Neither of them moved for long seconds.

"What are you doing?" the dragon finally thundered with half open eyes, his voice more exasperated than angry.

The Prince swallowed hard again and stepped back, then loosed a battle cry and charged, swinging his weapon hard at the dragon's head, only to have it plucked from his hands from behind.

He swung around, then turned back as the dragon stood with his axe.

Examining the axe, the dragon growled softly, then sniffed the blade. He turned his eyes on the Prince again and asked, "Where did you get the potion?"

"It doesn't matter," was Chail's reply.

The dragon tossed the axe to the ground before the Prince, then turned away from him, saying as he laid back down, "You paid way too much for it."

Chail found himself perplexed at first. The potion to kill the dragon did not work. He had been disarmed and would have been easy to kill, and yet the dragon just turned away. This had suddenly gone from terrifying to humiliating and he found himself in a rare moment where his temper got the better of him. His lip curled in rage, he picked the axe up and struck the dragon lower on the neck, then again, and again.

As the Prince hacked away at his armor, the dragon growled a sigh and asked, "Don't you have someone else to annoy?"

A little winded, Chail backed away a few steps, holding his axe at the ready as he announced, "Someone has demanded your head!"

"Let me guess," the dragon said dryly. "You reached the castle and whatever plan you came up with fell apart right away."

Clenching his teeth, the Prince yelled, "Are we going to fight or should I just behead you?"

"Your blade's already dull," the dragon pointed out.

Chail threw the axe from him and drew his sword, demanding, "Fight me, damn you!"

Slowly, the dragon raised his head and turned to look at the big human who dared to challenge him. "By the way, where is that female you owe me?"

His lips tightening, the Prince replied, "She's being held prisoner at Aalekilk Castle."

The dragon nodded. "I see. And whoever has her insisted that you bring him my head, or was that your brilliant idea?"

"To free her I must bring him the head of the one who sent me there. That would be you." He poised his sword, glaring up at the dragon.

"Does he know I'm a dragon?"

"I believe he does."

"So…" The dragon looked away, then back to the Prince. "Does he know that you *aren't* a dragon slayer?"

"I'm not yet," Chail growled back.

"Nor will you be today," the dragon countered. "What happens if… Okay, *when* you fail to bring my head to him?"

"I can't fail," the Prince insisted.

"Nor can you succeed. Put your sword down and listen carefully. You aren't killing me today and I have no wish to kill you. I have a belly full of Grawrdox that I'm busy digesting, so run along and get back to the castle like a good prince." The dragon turned away again, laying his head back down.

Chail's frustration began to mount, but he complied and sheathed his sword.

Raising his head again, the dragon looked back to him and asked, "Just out of curiosity, where did you get that so-called potion?"

The Prince met the dragon's eyes and answered, "A wizard at Border gave it to me, one who has also laid claim to her."

"Wizard, huh? Why didn't he come to kill me himself?"

"He says killing you is my problem, not his."

The dragon nodded. "Is it? Okay, go back to Border." He raised a hand, made a fist and held it in front of the Prince, ordering, "Hold your hands out."

Hesitantly, Chail complied, and as the dragon opened his hand, a heavy gold coin as big as the Prince's palm dropped into his hands. In the center was the image of a dragon. On the edges were words scribed in an ancient language, words that Chail could not read. Looking up at the dragon, he asked, "What is this for?"

"Your wizard at Border," was the dragon's answer. "Give that to him. He'll know what to do."

"I only have a day and a half left to get back to Aalekilk," the Prince informed. "If I don't make it in time he'll kill her."

"Then perhaps you'd better hope your wizard in Border is better at planning what to do than you are. Now, if you will excuse me." He turned away and lay back down.

As the dragon drifted back to sleep, Chail turned his eyes back to the huge coin he held, then finally picked up his axe and turned back toward his horse.

Anger and frustration mounted the whole journey back to Border. He felt like a pawn in a three way game of chess. Everyone held overwhelming advantage over him and used him at their whim for their own desires, and yet the fate of the land and the princess he loved rested entirely on his shoulders. That burden alone offered no end of discouragement, but he would not be daunted.

A league from Border, he stopped his horse, staring blankly at the two unicorns who stood in the road before him. Weary from almost two days with no sleep, he stared blankly back at them, not sure what he was feeling. At least they had not used him for something.

Slowly, they paced toward him, each going to a different side of his horse.

The big bay whickered something to him, something he wished he could understand.

Chail turned his eyes down, saying absently, "Things aren't going well. Le'ell is being held prisoner at Aalekilk, I have already failed in my quest to free her... I'm not sure what I'm doing anymore."

The image of Traman flashed into his mind and he looked to the little white mare, somehow knowing she had sent it to him. "You want me to find him?"

She shook her head and whickered to him, then another image flashed into his mind, one of the northern road out of Border and south of the imps, then Traman again.

"He's waiting for me?" the Prince asked.

The white unicorn barked a short whinny.

Nodding, Chail said, "I have someone else to find first." He looked to the bay and asked, "Would you wait with Traman north of Border?"

The bay glanced at the mare, then seemed to reluctantly agree.

They followed him nearly all the way to Border, then as more and more people came and went, he looked behind him and found them gone. Feeling more alone, he continued on.

Back to the Dragon's Talon. For once the wizard was not eating. Chail reasoned that he was probably in his suite.

He banged on the door twice, then twice more. When no one answered, he turned to leave, seeing the wizard coming up on him.

"Well," the big wizard greeted. "No missing body parts, no profuse bleeding, no signs you've been gnawed on... I'd say the battle went in your favor." He waved his hand and the door opened. "Inside. Tell me how you did it."

Chail entered ahead of the wizard and sat on the love seat where he had before. He glanced at the empty place where Le'ell had passed out beside him only a few days before, then he looked to the wizard as he sat down in the same chair he had before.

"Don't keep me in suspense, boy," the wizard ordered with a smile. "How did you kill the beast? One mighty blow from your enchanted axe?"

The Prince turned his eyes down, softly admitting, "Not exactly."

"Well out with it! What happened?"

Looking out the window, Chail set his jaw and growled, "You're potion was useless. His armor wasn't even scratched."

The wizard puzzled. "You didn't kill the dragon? But here you sit. Dragon's won't just lie there and let you hack away at them. He would have killed you."

"He just laid there," the Prince corrected, "and he didn't kill me."

His eyes narrowing, the wizard half turned his head and asked with a tone of suspicion, "Did you actually find this dragon?"

"Of course I did," the Prince growled back.

"Prove it."

Chail removed the heavy coin from his pocket and tossed it to the wizard, who caught it with one hand.

The wizard stared down at the dragon in the center of it for a moment, then read the words along the edge, his features going blank as he did.

"He said you would know what to do with it," Chail said dryly.

Slowly nodding, the wizard confirmed, "I do. This is a price for *my* head. Apparently my life belongs to the beast you failed to kill, as does yours." He loosed a deep breath, still staring at the coin. "He wants your woman back, and apparently this is my problem as well now."

The Prince raised his chin slightly. "Well, it looks as if you've involved yourself more deeply than you intended."

Glaring at him, the wizard growled back, "That's what I get for my charity. If not for trying to help you to begin with I would still be distant from this matter." He closed his fist around the coin and it disappeared, then he stood. "We'll barter with the dragon later. Right now we have to go for the girl."

"Why don't you just go and kill this dragon yourself?" Chail asked, almost taunting.

"You don't know the beast you're dealing with, do you?" The wizard shook his head. "You've chosen to tangle with the Desert Lord."

"We found him in the hot springs a few leagues from here."

"That's probably only one of his haunts. Aside from being one of the strongest dragons in the land, this dragon is wizard trained and is said to control power of few limits, so it's best not to be on his bad side."

Chail slowly stood, rubbing his eyes. Many days of not sleeping was steadily catching up to him.

"You look like hell," the wizard observed.

"I'm fine," the Prince assured. "Just haven't slept in a while."

"Hmm," the wizard growled. He strode to the Prince, raising a hand to his forehead.

Chail flinched away at first.

"Hold still," the wizard ordered, grasping the Prince's forehead.

In a moment the weariness drained away and Chail felt as if he had just awakened from a long sleep. Energy poured back into him.

"I need you alert," the wizard informed harshly. "Now let's go. We've a long ride and a short time and I have much preparation ahead of me."

As they turned to the door, Chail hesitated and looked around the room, asking, "Where is your Hallaf?"

"She's running an errand for me. Don't concern yourself with that."

"You aren't concerned with her out there alone?"

"Of course not," the wizard scoffed. "Quit worrying over her and let's go. We've much to do and little time."

Within the hour they were riding north out of Border. The wizard's horse was an enormous white beast with large tufts of silver hair around his hooves and a long silver mane and tail. The huge horse seemed to fit the big wizard nicely and hardly seemed burdened by the wizard's weight.

Another league of quiet riding and they found themselves joined by the black haired man, who awaited them at a crossroad. As they passed, he rode abreast of them. He also did not speak for some time, but finally looked to the wizard and said, "You look good."

The wizard's eyes slid to him and he growled back.

Traman smiled slightly.

"Did the unicorns not find you?" Chail asked.

Glancing at him, the black haired man replied, "They're nearby. Many horses were heading south this morning."

"Perhaps an occupation force," the Prince guessed.

"More likely reinforcements," the black haired man corrected. "They were heavily armed and appeared to be ready for a long siege."

"Probably to take the southern keeps," Chail snarled.

Traman looked to him. "How big are these keeps?"

"About a thousand men each," he replied.

"That was an awfully large force for such small holdings. I'm thinking they were moving on Enulam Castle itself."

"I heard Enulam had already fallen."

The wizard looked hard at Chail, informing, "I think this Poskleer's information is not entirely accurate, or he fed misinformation to a gullible boy who was in over his head."

Chail snarled back, "I'm growing tired of your insults, wizard."

Smiling unexpectedly, the wizard reached across and slapped the Prince's shoulder. "I'll give you some new ones, then."

CHAPTER 17

Standing atop one of the battlements of Aalekilk Castle, Le'ell watched grimly as the sun plunged toward the horizon. The third day was almost over and still no word from her Chail. Her long flowing yellow gown rippled in the little bit of wind in the canyon, as did her hair which she wore loosely behind her.

Jan'ka, still in the attire Poskleer had chosen for her, approached quietly from behind, pausing to let three soldiers pass in front of her, before she reached the Princess. Hesitantly, she asked, "Are you okay, Ell?"

Turning her head ever so slightly, the Princess barely acknowledged her, then looked out over the activity in the common area below. The soldiers there continued to train and prepare to overrun her homeland and she knew there was nothing she could do about it. She finally answered, "You know, Jan'ka. Under different circumstances we would be standing together to fight off these invaders. I know I would fight to the death to defend Zondae. I used to think you would."

Lowering her eyes, Jan'ka could not respond.

"What is a fitting punishment for betraying your people? In some places you would be put to death. In other places you would be burned alive."

The red haired woman cringed.

Le'ell finally turned toward her, leaning back against the battlement wall. "Three days now and you still haven't told me why you betrayed Zondae."

Jan'ka was a long time in answering, simply staring at the stone before her, but finally managed, "I didn't betray anyone."

"We were friends once," Le'ell reminded.

"I want to still be," Jan'ka whimpered.

"No friend of mine is a traitor," Le'ell snarled. "You've been following me around like a loyal puppy for three days even after I've told you to leave me alone."

"He told me to," Jan'ka replied. "Don't you understand? I have to obey him."

"Why?"

"There is no why. I just have to."

"Because you're afraid? There are worse things than dying, Ka, much worse."

Jan'ka looked aside, then back to Le'ell and informed, "He wants you. Come on." She turned and strode toward the stairs that led into the palace.

"I'm not his loyal dog," Le'ell barked. "You just tell him I'll be there when I'm ready."

Jan'ka stopped. Slowly, she turned, her eyes betraying terror as she whispered, "Don't defy him!"

"Or what?" Le'ell challenged. "Do you think I'm afraid of him? I can snap him in half like a rotted arrow!"

"I'm sure you can," Jan'ka said in the wizard's voice. "I'm hoping you won't, though. It is time to seal our bargain, and since I know you are a woman of your word, I will await you in my meeting hall."

Le'ell's eyes widened, her lips parting as she took a step back. She did not realize that he could do this and a chill swept through her.

"You look startled," the wizard's voice said through Jan'ka again. "If you need a few moments then take them. And please don't blame poor Jan'ka for what has happened. It really wasn't her fault. She simply underestimated my power, as do you."

"I will never become what you have made her," Le'ell hissed.

"I know," the wizard assured, "and I don't want you to. You are much stronger than this girl, stronger than you realize. And I know your displaced anger toward her is not truly how you feel about her, otherwise you would have let me burn her alive. Be friends with her again. Light the fire within her anew. I would consider it a personal favor."

"I'm sure you would," Le'ell grumbled. "Very well. Can you release her so that we can talk for a moment?"

"Of course," he replied.

Jan'ka blinked and rubbed her eyes. She stepped back to keep her balance and shook her head, finally turning her eyes to Le'ell. She still looked dazed and rather out of sorts and long second passed before she seemed to get her wits about her.

Le'ell approached and took her hands, asking, "Are you in there?"

Nodding, Jan'ka smiled slightly and informed, "He told me to come up here and get you, but I don't remember getting here."

The wizard's power truly took quite a toll on her and Le'ell finally realized that he was right. This fire haired friend of hers no longer controlled her own destiny, much less her own thoughts and actions.

Pursing her lips, the Princess asked, "Ka, do you remember when I was ten and you were twelve, that time we filled Sesh's bathtub with fresh horse dung?"

Smiles overpowered them both and they shared quite a hearty laugh over the memory.

Some time later they made it to Poskleer's meeting hall and Le'ell's heart suddenly felt very grim. He wanted to erase Chail from her forever. He had said it would be painless, though the thought hurt more than anything she could imagine.

He stood from his plush chair as they approached, his eyes on Le'ell and a smile on his lips as he greeted, "My, but you look lovely."

She looked away and nodded.

"Are you ready to complete our bargain?" he asked.

"He's just a little late," she assured.

"The bargain was three days. If he's late—"

"I know. I gave you my word and I'll keep it. Just know that he will always have my heart no matter what you do to me."

He just offered a smile and a nod, then he looked to Jan'ka and ordered, "The wine over there."

The red haired woman hurried about her task.

Approaching to within a pace, the wizard took Le'ell's hands and looked up into her eyes, assuring, "I'm going to give you everything in the world you could possibly want."

"Except Chail," she reminded.

"You won't want him in a moment," he assured. He looked to Jan'ka as she brought him two crystal goblets and took them from her, offering one to Le'ell. When she took it, he held his glass up to her and said, "To you, my dear. May you find the world I offer as appealing and beautiful as I find you."

Refusing to touch her goblet to his, she raised the wine to her lips and took a sip. She stared down into it, stubbornly clinging to her prince, but a distraction intervened, the sweet wine itself, and she looked to the wizard, asking, "Is this strawberry?"

He nodded. "It is. I thought you might like it."

"I do," she confirmed, taking another sip.

Poskleer held his goblet to her again. "To you, my sweet. You may like the taste of a sweet wine, but they are all bitter compared to your heart."

She smiled and touched her goblet to his, responding with, "You are the sweetest man in the world." She sipped her wine, then bent to give him a kiss.

He stroked her cheek, looking possessively up at her.

Jan'ka turned her eyes down, knowing that part of Le'ell was gone forever.

Le'ell finished her wine and handed the goblet absently to Jan'ka, then she looked to Poskleer and folded her arms. "We never did decide what to do with the Zondaen prisoners at Enulam."

Poskleer also finished his wine, handing his goblet to Jan'ka as he took Le'ell's arm and turned with her toward the door. "No, we did not. I'm assuming you want control of that?"

"Of course," she confirmed. "You know I'm going to want them treated well. If we play our cards right we may even integrate them into our army, perhaps even reestablish Zondae under our rule."

"Do you think that's a wise idea? Why not just finish them all and have done with it?"

"Now, Poskleer, they're still my people and I do wish to protect them."

"And should your mother resist us?"

She playfully tugged on his arm and informed, "Oh, I think you can persuade her to go along with us. Just think about how much stronger our army will be with my people on our side, especially once we liberate them from Enulam."

"My sweet, you do have a mind for strategy. Do you think they would help us with the overthrow of Enulam?"

"Of course!" she scolded. "We've been enemies for generations. Between the two of us those barbarians won't know what hit them!"

"Oh, I'm sure they'll know. We want them to know exactly who brought them down."

"I suppose," she sighed. "I'm hungry. Lets talk more about it over dinner."

"I'd rather talk about you," he countered.

Her eyes slid to him. "Quit being sweet. I have important things to discuss with you."

"Le'ell, whatever you want is yours. There should be no reason to discuss it."

"You're going to spoil me."

"Of course I am. You deserve to be spoiled."

She rolled her eyes. "And I suppose I should spoil you in return."

"I'm thinking so."

"Well, you'd better get some more of that wine in me."

He hesitated and looked up at her, a little fearful that his spell had failed.

She turned her eyes down to him and smiled slightly. "How else are you going to handle me? We don't want me hurting you, do we?"

He smiled back. "No, I suppose we don't."

They left the meeting hall, toward the private dining room of the Castle Lord. There, a hearty meal already awaited them. More wine and foods from all over the land were spread out on the table and many servants attended them. They talked at length and shared many a good laugh over different matters. Poskleer would usually have a guest sitting across from him, but this one sat right beside him, close enough to touch at his whim. She pushed away his advances at first, but slowly found herself succumbing to him. Once dinner was finished and night darkened the windows of the castle, the wizard led the Princess of Zondae by the hand to his bed chamber. Her protests were playful and meant more to tantalize him, but as the evening wore she found herself ensnared in the web of his pretty words, the candle light, and his soft caresses.

She was finally his.

True to her word, he would feel the aches and muscle pulls, the bites and ferocity of this beautiful, savage young woman he had wanted for some days.

The coming of the sun would find Poskleer awakening alone. Before opening his eyes, he groped for her, but she was not to be found. Finally looking around for her, he smiled as he saw her standing at the window, staring out over the castle and the entrance to the kingdom. She had not yet dressed and leaned seductively on the window shelf.

As silently as he could, he slid from the bed and stood, then groaned softly and grasped his aching back, then stretched his neck and raised his hand to a bruise there that was in the shape of a human mouth. She was indeed as brutal in his bed as he had both hoped and feared. Pulling a blanket from the bed, he wrapped it around himself, walking stiffly on sore legs as he approached her from behind and laid half of the blanket around her shoulders.

She turned her head and offered him a warm smile as she greeted, "Good morning. I'm glad to see you are still alive."

"Most of me is," he confessed.

Le'ell laughed under her breath and asked, "Did you expect me to take it easy on you last night?"

He raised his brow, admitting, "Well, I was hoping you would."

"Will you *make* me be gentle tonight?"

"Perhaps I will."

She turned and slid her arms around him, pulling him to her with what felt like the grip of a bear. "Well, then. I should have my fun with you now." She lowered her mouth to his neck, kissing at first, then she bit him right under his ear.

He cringed and tried to back away, protesting, "Now, my lamb. I still hurt there from last night. Kiss all you want but don't bite for a while."

She drew back and smiled, hissing, "But you're so chewable!"

He laughed under his breath. "Okay, I may have to start restraining you."

"I thought you were going to spoil me."

Raising a hand to her neck, he pulled her down to him for a kiss. He had been with many women and knew how to control them all, but this one was more wild forest cat than any he had ever experienced.

A knock on the door interrupted them and he looked to it and impatiently shouted, "What do you want?"

A guard on the other side answered, "The Prince of Enulam has returned and insists on an audience with you."

"What does *he* want," Le'ell snarled.

"Tell him to leave," the wizard ordered. "He should have come yesterday."

"He says he is here to take the girl or bring the castle down around you," the guard informed. "He also says he has information you need."

"Is he alone?" Poskleer demanded.

"Yes, my Lord, he is."

The wizard sighed and looked up into Le'ell's eyes. "Very well. Take him to the meeting hall and have him wait there. I'll be along as soon as it is convenient for me."

Le'ell raised a brow. "I hope he has a couple of hours. You aren't leaving until it's convenient for *me*."

"You're insatiable," he whispered to her.

"I'm Zondaen," she whispered back. "What did you expect?"

He stroked her hair and said back, "Let me attend to this matter, my sweet, then we can spend the entire day together."

She turned her eyes up, then looked down at him and agreed, "Oh, very well. But don't think you are out of reach of my claws yet."

"Never," he assured.

"Should I go with you?" she asked.

"No, my pet. I'll be fine."

"Let me know if he gets out of line and I'll fillet him like a fish."

"I'll be fine," he assured again.

Chail was not a man who liked to be kept waiting, but he was a man of great patience and felt that patience being tested, and quickly running out.

After almost an hour of waiting the door finally opened and he stood and faced the wizard as he strode in. The two burly guards behind him were forest trolls, clearly there just in case the Prince became unruly.

No matter.

Folding his arms, Chail raised his chin and informed, "You shouldn't keep your guests waiting, Poskleer."

The castle lord smiled back at him, stopping two paces away as he countered, "My guests announce their visits; they don't storm my castle a day late and make demands. So, did you bring me the head of the one who sent you?"

Chail shook his head.

"And the King of Enulam? I suppose he is not with you either?"

Again, Chail shook his head.

Poskleer raised his brow. "Then why did you come here?"

"I want Le'ell back," the Prince answered straightly.

"She is mine now," the wizard informed straightly, "and now you are as well. I gave you three easy things to do and you failed at all three. Tell me why I should let you live."

"The girl's rightful owner has come for her," Chail answered. "I escorted him here so that he could negotiate her release and deal with you should you give me any problems."

Slowly, Poskleer nodded. "I see. So where is he?"

"Waiting for us at the mouth of the canyon."

"I'll simply have my soldiers deal with him."

"Your guards out there are already dead," the Prince reported. "Any others you send will end up the same way. He made it clear that if he has to come to the castle he will destroy it and all inside. I at least want Le'ell spared that."

The wizard sighed impatiently and rolled his eyes. "Why I should indulge you is beyond me, but I suppose I could use some time away from the castle. Return to your horse and wait for me there. I'll be along shortly."

"See to it you make it quick," Chail growled as he strode past. "This wizard is not as patient as I am."

As the door slammed, Poskleer raised his chin and observed, "Wizard, huh? I think preparations are in order for our meeting."

Chail expected a few escorts but not two hundred armed soldiers. Clearly, Poskleer did not intend to underestimate the other wizard. Poskleer himself wore brightly polished armor, high black boots and a white cape. He had a sword at his side in a golden sheath decorated with many gems.

They did not speak much, but the wizard seemed a little too smug. He expected a confrontation and expected to win easily.

The ride to the mouth of the canyon was a slow one and as they rounded the last turn they could see the big wizard standing in the center of the road, his black and green robes fluttering slightly on the breeze.

Riding to about forty paces, Poskleer finally stopped his horse and waited for his large compliment of soldiers to line up evenly abreast on both sides.

The standoff lasted a couple of moments. It was the big wizard who finally broke the silence.

"You must be Poskleer," he greeted in a loud voice just below a yell. "The horse makes you look even smaller."

Poskleer laughed and responded in almost as loud of a voice. "Small man, perhaps, but huge mind and vast power. Prince Chail here tells me that you want my new woman."

"I've come to reclaim her," the big wizard informed straightly, "and, before you tell me something asinine like 'over my dead body' I'm ready for just that."

"I was thinking over *your* dead body. Perhaps you should tell me why I should just hand her over to you and not kill you where you stand."

"Get off your horse and come closer so that we aren't yelling back and forth," the big wizard suggested.

Poskleer looked to Chail and smiled ever so slightly. "He just doesn't seem to understand. We'll go closer, but keep your distance. I have plans for you and I don't want you reduced to a pile of ash during our exchange."

As they dismounted, the Prince advised, "You shouldn't underestimate him."

The wizard's eyes slid to him. "Looking out for my welfare?"

"The first law of battle: Never underestimate your opponent."

They walked side by side toward the big wizard and Poskleer replied, "I'll try to remember that." He raised a hand and ordered, "Wait here. This won't take long."

Chail stopped where he was and watched Poskleer, who did not look at all comfortable in all that armor, walk ten more paces and stop about eight paces away.

Raising his chin, Poskleer demanded, "Convince me. Tell me why I should just give my new woman to you and not destroy you where you stand."

The big wizard cleared his throat. His eyes showed annoyance and he cocked an eyebrow up. "You aren't destroying anyone today. I can sense you have considerable power, but I also sense that you have little experience compared to me and far less intelligence. What makes you think you are even a wizard?"

"I could ask you the same, stranger." Poskleer sighed. "Listen. We can stand here and hurl insults at each other all day but I simply don't have the time or the patience. I can also sense your power. It isn't quite mine, but I could use a wizard of your talents. So do you intend to fight or can we simply join forces?"

Folding his arms, the big wizard informed, "I see no profit in joining you. Now bring my woman to me or I'll go through you and your little toy soldiers to get her."

Poskleer laughed. "What makes you think you can?"

"If I show you, it will already be too late. Now bring me my woman or be prepared to fight and die."

"I'm not bringing you the girl and you clearly will not join me. I'm afraid I am going to have to kill you. A pity, really." Raising his arms, a bright blue light enveloped his hands and white discharges of power randomly shot from his fingers and cracked like miniature lightning. He smiled as the wind picked up from behind him, as the pop and crackle of his power grew louder, and he shouted over the wind and noise, "This will be extremely painful. Enjoy." He thrust his hands and the power converged from his fingers and lanced toward his enemy.

The big wizard raised his hand quickly yet casually and caught the attack on a bright green cushion of light from his palm. As the powers met, a mighty explosion roared forth and shattered into hundreds of tiny bolts of light which pelted the ground and canyon walls all around.

Silence followed.

Staring back at the smaller wizard, the big wizard simply snarled, "Ouch."

Poskleer set his jaw, glaring back at his opponent.

The big wizard folded his arms. "Not familiar with the first law of combat, are you?"

"Prince Chail here filled me in. Now that I know what you're capable of, let's end this little confrontation and your life." His power roared to life in his hands once again and he thrust them at the big wizard with all of the force he could muster.

Once again the big wizard defended against the attack almost easily, but this time he struck back, forcing Poskleer to suddenly wave his arm to defend himself.

An exchange of lightning, fire and ice followed and Chail watched in awe. Strong wind whirled around them and clouds seemed to roll in above from nowhere. Lightning flashed in a blinding spectacle above and occasionally the ground would shake as a discharge of two combating powers burst forth. The powers of wind, fire and lightning were used by both in a deadly game of strike and parry. Poskleer actually seemed to be tiring while the big wizard he fought remained calm and focused.

The battle was not very old, perhaps only a few moments, and the big wizard stretched his arms out, then brought them together and slapped his palms together. A wave of an unknown emerald force rolled from him and toward his enemy and his forces, too fast for any to react to. Poskleer and all two hundred of his soldiers were flattened. Only Chail and the horses remained standing and he was bewildered as he glanced around him and behind at the men, gnomes and trolls who lay moaning on the ground.

Struggling to his feet, Poskleer held a sore arm as he glared at his big opponent, then he looked to the cliffs around him and shouted, "Kill him!"

Archers emerged from the caves and hiding places all around and sent a volley of arrows at the big wizard, all of which disappeared into puffs of smoke only a few paces from him.

Never taking his eyes from his slight opponent, the big wizard smiled slightly, then he slowly shook his head. "You've still much to learn, haven't you?" Lightning flashed in the sky all around and his eyes began to glow red. "You've found the secret to unlocking great power, boy, but you never took the time to find the wisdom to use it properly. Allow me to teach you."

The lightning in the sky intensified, deafening cracks and booms echoing through the canyon behind Poskleer. Without warning, a bolt reached down and found the opening of a cave where an archer was hiding. The whole cave exploded with a frightening sound. Another bolt found another archer, then another. They came faster and faster in a terrifying volley that pelted the cliff sides almost like rain. A few bolts found some of the soldiers guarding the smaller wizard, and one found Poskleer, blasting into his shoulder. He hit the ground almost where he had been standing. Much of his armor was blasted away from him and landed not far away.

As quickly as it began, the storm of lightning ended and only distant thunder remained of it.

Two of Poskleer's soldiers helped him to his feet and once standing he pulled away from them, rubbing his burnt shoulder as he glared at the opponent who had now downed him twice.

The big wizard raised his chin and taunted, "Are we learning yet?"

Clenching his teeth, Poskleer raised his hands and the clouds responded with roaring thunder and lightning, and as he thrust his hands down the lightning lanced forth toward the big wizard, who simply and casually waved his hand and diverted the strike to the ground some fifty paces away.

Slowly, the rumble of the lightning fled.

"Poskleer," the big wizard sighed, "while I've enjoyed our little game, I find I haven't the time or the patience to continue. Now just bring the woman to me so that I can be on my way."

Raising his chin, Poskleer observed, "You seem to have me at a disadvantage."

"Long before you were born," the big wizard chided. "Fetch me the woman."

"And who makes such demands?" the smaller wizard asked. He was clearly stalling, and clearly had one more trick in his hands. "Give me your name!"

His eyes narrowing, the big wizard simply answered, "Ralligor."

Poskleer's eyes widened and he took many steps back, as did his soldiers.

Chail looked over his shoulder at their retreat, then looked to the big wizard.

A stout wind seemed to blow hard in all directions from under the big wizard's feet, kicking up dust and blowing pebbles and stones from him.

Seeing the bright red glow in the wizard's eyes, Chail took a step back, himself.

The wind grew stronger and burst into flames right beneath the big wizard, reaching outward at first. In a moment they consumed him. Seconds later the inferno that had once been a powerful wizard exploded upward and all present shielded their eyes against the intense heat of the flames.

Feeling the heat burn out, Chail slowly lowered his arm, looking to the wizard and then up—five men's heights into the sky!

His eyes still glowing crimson, the black dragon stared down at the slight wizard, and a deep growl rolled from his throat.

Poskleer stared back for long seconds, then shouted up at the beast before him, "Do you think I came unprepared?"

"Of course you did," the dragon thundered.

"You are clearly not as wise as you would have one believe," the wizard sneered back. "I have allies not even you can stand against."

Nodding, the dragon sighed, "I'm sure you think so. Just bring the girl out here so we can all get on with our lives. And be quick about it. I have things to do."

"She's mine now," Poskleer shouted.

The dragon turned his eyes up, exasperation in his voice as he asked, "Do I *really* have to take her by force?"

"Try," the wizard challenged.

A deep roar—a warning—sounded over the mountains and everyone turned and looked. The dragon even looked, though he seemed to remain perfectly calm.

Chail's eyes darted around the mountaintops and finally fixed on a huge winged form that floated over them. He raised his eyes, his heart pounding with fear as the huge beast drew closer and descended on a broad wingspan.

The scales on his throat and belly were a dark bronze; those on his sides and back were more of a copper. His wing webbing was almost black. Bronze horns were thick and curled outward from his head, similar to those of a ram. Eyes of amber were locked on the Desert Lord as he descended. Landing hard right behind Poskleer and his men, he swept his wings forward right before slamming onto the ground.

His arms folded, Ralligor stared back calmly. Standing, this other dragon was nearly two heights taller than him, yet he did not seem to be concerned.

Prince Chail backed away from the bigger dragon, angling away from the black one.

Poskleer's army marched in both directions toward the cliffs, the wizard following with a very smug grin.

Spreading his wings, the other dragon raised himself up and roared at the black dragon again, baring many murderous teeth of white and ivory.

Ralligor looked to his right and up, raising that brow as he turned his eyes to the cliff top to see the scarlet dragon just landing there. Turning his attention back to the copper, he did not take a challenging posture, nor did he cower from this much larger dragon. Quite the contrary. He did not seem worried at all. Lifting his snout slightly, he greeted, "Mettegrawr. It's been many long seasons since I saw you last." He spoke deliberately in a language the humans present would recognize.

The bigger dragon replied through bared teeth, "Not many seasons long enough, Ralligor." His voice was very deep and somewhat raspy. "Did you think my last warning to you was merely a suggestion?"

"Oh, no," the black dragon answered. "I took you seriously. This isn't a matter you should concern yourself with. In fact, you should be concerned that you aren't exactly in your own territory at this time."

The bigger dragon took many long strides toward the Desert Lord, growling, "And you intend to do what about it?"

Ralligor did not even flinch as the larger dragon drew closer. "Well, since you aren't in the Hard Lands, I don't intend to do anything about it. However, I still recommend you leave and leave quickly."

Taking two more long strides to the black dragon, Mettegrawr was almost upon him and challenged, "Perhaps you would challenge me again since you've forgotten the last time we tangled."

"I haven't forgotten," Ralligor assured, "nor have I forgotten what happened right after that. Your time is running out."

Something roared loud and deep, something big!

Mettegrawr retreated a few steps and looked skyward, his eyes darting around and finally fixing on something, and he retreated further.

Ralligor dropped to all fours and backed away.

Chail's eyes widened and he backed away further himself.

Soaring over the trees was a dragon of truly gargantuan proportions. His bulk cast a shadow of frightening size. When his massive wings swept forward they kicked up a blinding storm of dust.

Mettegrawr backed away further as an old rival slammed onto the ground right in front of him.

Ralligor stood.

When the newly arrived dragon stood, he was far taller than either of the others: His massive head was over ten heights above the ground. His scales were a very dark, metallic green. The scales on his belly were even darker. The dorsal scales that ran from between his thick, bull-like black horns were obsidian black. When he spread his wings, the webbing was a dark blue. His features were not pleasant, even by dragon standards. Very dark green eyes glistened beneath a thick, scaly brow. Tusks protruded from his heavy lower jaw, half way up his upper jaw. As he bared his teeth—many of them the length of a broadsword—powerful muscles tensed beneath the armor that was his scales. Black claws curled and his jaws parted as a thunderous growl rolled from him.

No longer feeling so invulnerable, Mettegrawr backed away a step more and opened his own wings, growling back as his scaly lips curled from his teeth.

Easily twice Ralligor's girth, the massive dragon gaped his jaws and roared at his smaller foe.

Mettegrawr roared back.

The black dragon approached a few steps, saying, "I'd say your time's run out."

The massive dragon looked over his shoulder and growled, "Stay out of this!" then he turned his attention back to the business at hand, bared his teeth further and roared in a very deep, growling voice, "I see you have crossed the dark mountains again."

His eyes narrowing, Mettegrawr snapped, "Why is *he* so close to my territory again?"

"I don't see where that is any concern of yours," the massive dragon bellowed. "I don't see him *in* your territory nor do I think you chased him out."

"I have an alliance with these humans, Agarxus," the dark copper dragon informed. "That means when your *subordinate* tries to raid their holding he involves me!"

"These humans are in *my* territory," the massive dragon observed. "That means their fate is at my discretion, and since they are allied to my enemy they will be exterminated!"

Chail's heart jumped. Le'ell was still in there!

Glaring up at his foe, the dark copper dragon roared, then he belched fire into his huge enemy's face. Agarxus roared back and turned his face from the flames, and when he did the other dragon charged and was upon him before he could react. Now was a battle of titans. So close, they would not use fire, but teeth, claws and horns would be just as deadly.

Mettegrawr's jaws went right for Agarxus' throat. Agarxus' claws found his first. As much as anything, this was a contest of strength, a test of power between the most powerful dragons in the land. Truly, battles between Landmasters were the most awesome spectacles any human would see in his lifetime, and today awed humans looked on as this rare event occurred before their very eyes.

The outcome of this fight was easy for even an imbecile to see and ended with Agarxus' jaws slamming shut around the shoulder of his smaller foe. Mettegrawr shrieked and as the murderous teeth plunged through his armor he responded with his horns, but to no avail. Slamming his horns into the bigger Landmaster's thick neck twice more, he finally clawed at Agarxus' armored chest and struggled to back away.

Releasing his enemy at last, the massive dragon roared again as he lowered his head and rammed his horns into the smaller dragon's chest, the point of one penetrating the copper dragon's armor and drawing more blood.

Stumbling backward, Mettegrawr took the only survivable option he had: He opened his wings and swept himself into the sky, stroking his broad wings hard to grab air and lift himself over the mountains.

Mighty Agarxus did not pursue. He had made his point and tasted the blood of this rival once again. Barely winded, he slowly turned to Ralligor and folded his thick arms.

Looking back up at him, the black dragon raised his brow.

"Well?" the Landmaster thundered.

"I didn't challenge him again," the Desert Lord assured, "and at no time did I cross into his territory. I was simply attending some business—"

"Conveniently right on the border at the Dark Mountains," Agarxus finished for him, "and conveniently Falloah had to come and tell me where and when Mettegrawr would cross into my territory."

The black dragon shrugged. "I felt he would cross here when I approached that castle. He does have an alliance with them, after all."

"And I'm sure you knew that in advance," the Landmaster snarled. "Your schemes are wearing thin my patience."

The black dragon's eyes widened and he placed a hand on his chest. "Whatever do you mean?"

Agarxus lowered his head until his snout was a pace away from his subordinate's and he rammed a clawed digit into the black dragon's chest as he warned, "I tolerate this wizard training of yours just barely, Ralligor, and I tolerate all of the trouble that seems to come with it even less." He looked toward the canyon, then back to the black dragon and ordered, "I don't want yet another human colony in my territory. Destroy the settlement and all within, then get back to the desert where you belong." With an irritated grunt, he turned and strode away, opening his wings and lifting himself into the air. Seconds later he disappeared over the treetops.

The scarlet dragon extended her wings and gracefully drifted down to the black dragon's side.

Poskleer slowly emerged from his hiding place among the boulders at the base of the cliff, his eyes still locked on where the Landmaster had disappeared. Finally, he turned toward the black dragon and froze as he saw the beast staring down at him.

Raising a brow, Ralligor growled, "You got me in trouble."

The wizard's hands were surrounded in a blue glow as he slowly raised them and he shouted back, "You were in trouble when you challenged me, dragon. Now die as you should!" He thrust his hands at the dragon and loosed a massive blast of all of his power, striking the dragon squarely in the chest.

The explosion of lightning and fire spun the dragon half around and he stumbled to keep his footing. When he turned back, his teeth gleamed as his scaly lips curled away from them and he growled, "It's time to end this foolish little duel of yours." He raised his hand and an emerald glow enveloped it. A bright green beam of light lanced from his palm and pierced the wizard's chest, then emerged with a struggling blue mass of light and retreated into the dragon's hand. As his fingers closed around it, the blue light flashed and spat lightning and sparks, then died in his grip.

Poskleer tried to call upon his power for another strike but found it gone. He looked down at his hands, then fearfully turned his eyes up to the dragon's. Slowly shaking his head, he sneered, "I'll recover my power by sunup, dragon."

"But right now you stand there without it," Ralligor pointed out. He looked down at Chail and said, "You heard Agarxus. We have a castle to destroy. Find your horse."

The Prince nodded and looked around for his mount.

Turning his eyes back to the wizard, the dragon advised, "I'll give you an hour's head start. Leave the woman outside of your walls for me and clear your castle. I'll be along shortly to destroy it and any left within."

"And if I choose not to leave the woman with you?" the wizard asked.

"I'll not pursue you if I find her," was the dragon's answer. "Otherwise, you will not live through the day." He glanced up at the sky. "Your time is running short, human, as is my patience."

Pointing a finger up at the dragon, Poskleer warned, "This isn't over, Desert Lord. In time I'll have your broken carcass as my trophy."

The black dragon rolled his eyes and nodded. "Of course you will, rodent. Now get out of here before I change my mind and finish you now."

Quickly mounting their horses, the wizard and his men rode toward the castle, Poskleer pausing to shout one last thing at Ralligor. "Mark my words, dragon. This isn't over."

As the wizard turned and fled, Ralligor nodded again and grumbled, "You just keep thinking that." He looked down at Chail, noticing that he had no mount with him. "You still need to find your horse, Prince of Enulam. We've only an hour."

"Why all of this?" Chail asked. "You could have killed him at any time and saved us all this trouble. Why the charade?"

"Not everything is as it appears," the dragon replied, looking down the canyon. He sat catlike before the Prince and finally turned his eyes down to him, continuing, "There is more happening than what you can see in your meager perception of the world. The whys of what I do are not something you should be concerned with. When you return to Enulam, tell your king he may come and sack the remains of the castle at his leisure, but I will expect the hoards of gold you find in chambers dug into the mountain to be taken to my lair in the desert. Any other booty you find you may have."

"And what about Le'ell," the Prince growled.

"What about her?"

"How do I get her back?"

The dragon raised a brow. "That's for you to figure out. She'll be waiting for you outside of their castle within the hour." He stood again and turned toward the forest.

"I'm to save her just so that she can end up in your belly?" the Prince shouted.

Hesitating, the dragon answered, "If that's her destiny."

"I don't accept that!"

Ralligor stopped and slowly turned. "What?"

Glaring up at the dragon, Chail demanded, "I want her free of you."

"And if I refuse?"

The Prince had no answer for him.

"I thought so," the dragon growled. "Stick to our bargain and you may just live a long, fruitful life."

"How fruitful will it be without her?" Chail snapped. "How fruitful would yours be without that red dragon? My gut tells me not very."

"As it probably tells you not to challenge me further on this matter. You have two choices, Prince of Enulam: Trust your guts or see them spilled before you."

Chail's lips tightened, his hands clenching into tight fists.

CHAPTER 18

Le'ell could only watch as the riders paraded by, leaving the gate four abreast on their long retreat away from Aalekilk Castle. Moments ago she had been drug from Poskleer's chamber by a human and four trolls and chained by the wrists to the perimeter wall right outside the gate. With her arms held high above her, she watched desperately as the castle was abandoned. Her thin yellow gown, low cut and again with her sword arm bare, was little protection against the chill that still lingered in the air. Struggling against the iron cuffs that held her firmly had left her wrists sore, so now she just watched, praying that this was merely a test of her loyalty.

The last riders out were Poskleer himself with Jan'ka at his side. He paused and looked down at her with hollow eyes.

"You're taking me with you, right?" she asked with a hint of whimper in her voice.

He half smiled and shook his head. "I'm afraid not, my dear. Here you must stay."

"But you'll be back for me?"

Again he shook his head. Reaching into a pouch on his belt, he removed a key and tossed it toward her.

Le'ell watched it land at her feet and a pace away, knowing it was the key that would unlock her, then she slowly raised her eyes to him, her mouth ajar as she shook her head and insisted, "You can't do this. We have plans together, remember?"

"Plans change," he sighed, "and you are now among the spoils of war. I'm glad we at least had last night. Alas, now we must part ways. Fair thee well, my Princess." He kicked his horse forward without even a glance back.

Jan'ka gave her a pitiable look, then turned around and rode on to her master's side.

Her lips curling away from her teeth, Le'ell shouted after him, "You bastard! *Nobody* betrays me! I'm going to hunt you down like an animal and tear your heart from your chest and make you watch its final beats. Do you hear me? I'm going to castrate you like a pig and make you eat them!"

He ignored her, and in a few moments had ridden out of sight.

"I will find you no matter where you hide!" she screamed after him. Alone now, she finally felt the cold air nibbling at her and a shiver finally had her. Loneliness took her just as quickly. A long, unknown time passed and the chill began to penetrate. She slowly shook her head, trying not to weep, trying to cling to what dignity she had left. Poskleer was not coming back for her. She looked down at the key before her, the key that meant freedom for her, the very key that was just out of reach. Perhaps she was meant to be found dead where she was. Perhaps she was simply part of the spoils of war as Poskleer had said. Either way his betrayal would sting for some time.

Distant hoof beats caught her attention and she turned hopeful eyes up the canyon, praying she would see the wizard riding back to collect her.

It was not to be. She did not recognize the big man who rode into view and she raised her head as he drew closer, meeting his eyes coldly. Behind him he led another horse, one that had once been ridden by one of Poskleer's soldiers. Perhaps the tide had indeed turned against the wizard. Her eyes narrowed as he stopped only about three paces away.

At a look, Chail knew something was wrong. He was slow to dismount and approach, a feeling in his gut telling him that things were somehow much different.

Le'ell raised her chin, glaring back defiantly. He was a big man, well made and very appealing to the eye, but she could not allow herself to be taken in by his appearance. If he meant to take her as his prize then he was in for a costly battle.

The look on her face told the Prince that something was horribly amiss and he struggled for the right words after four days apart from her, finally managing, "Are you all right?"

She did not answer right away, but finally snarled, "It's cold out here, I'm not dressed for it, I've been abandoned and I'm chained to a wall. What do you think?"

"I think you sound cranky again," he observed

"What is it you want exactly," she snapped.

He glanced at her chains and reached for his dagger. "Well, we can start by getting you down from there."

As he stepped toward her and reached up with his dagger to work on the cuffs that held her, she cruelly pointed out, "You're standing on the key, genius."

He hesitated, then looked down and moved his foot. Once again she had made him feel a little foolish but now was not the time to engage in yet another fight with her. He simply picked the key up and unlocked her left hand, then stepped back and looked down at her again.

"What are you waiting for?" she barked. "Free my other hand."

Chail stared down into her eyes for long seconds, then softly asked, "What did he do to you?"

She could not know what he meant. Her eyes narrowing again, she half turned her head and suspiciously asked, "What do you mean? What did who do to me?"

"Poskleer," he growled. "What did he do to you? You look at me as if you don't even know me."

"Should I know you?"

His heart sank. He backed away a step, slowly shaking his head. "Le'ell, this isn't funny. I've come to take you home."

"What makes you think I want you taking me anywhere? The only reason you're here is because Poskleer somehow lost to you and now you think that I'm yours for the taking. Well you're wrong about that. You may take me but you'll never own me, I promise you that."

"He erased me from you," Chail breathed, "just as he said he would."

"You're speaking madness. Now would you mind releasing my other hand?"

The Prince's lips tightened and tears blurred his vision. He finally stepped toward her again and unlocked her other hand, then he turned away and threw the key as hard as he could. Everything they had done, everything they had been through had come to this. He had even challenged a dragon to get her back. Now she was there to be his again, yet she was gone forever.

"So where are you taking me?" she demanded.

"Nowhere," was his answer. "I'll not have you as my prisoner."

Le'ell stared at his back for some time, more curious about him than hating him as an enemy. She folded her arms against the cold and finally asked, "What is your name?"

The very question burned horribly and he tightly closed his eyes, bowing his head as he replied, "Chail."

"Chail?" she confirmed. "The Prince of Enulam?"

He nodded.

She looked away. "Why did you come for me? I had heard that you demanded an audience with Poskleer, but I didn't know I was in any way involved."

"You were always at the center," he told her. "I came here to rescue you."

"From what?" she barked. "We were planning to free my people from Enulam. Why am I suddenly so important?"

He loosed a deep breath, then he answered, "You have been for three seasons. You just don't remember."

"I think I would remember you in my life," she corrected. "I don't have a yob at Zondae but here at Aalekilk I had Poskleer, and he's nowhere near your stature."

"So you don't remember me at all."

"I think I would remember having the Prince of Enulam," she almost laughed, "especially such a prince who looks like you do. Now are we going to leave or should we wait for nightfall and just freeze to death?"

"Your horse is over there," he answered. "As I said, I won't have you as a prisoner."

She glanced at the horse, then suspiciously asked, "You are just releasing me?"

"Yes. Just go, please."

Still wary of a trick, she raised her chin, then looked to the horse again, back at the Prince, back to the horse. "Okay, well, I'll be off then." She strode to the horse and hesitantly mounted. Turning to him one last time, she called back, "I suppose you expect me to thank you for freeing me."

Shaking his head, he corrected, "No, I expect nothing. If I never see you again, have a nice life. Just leave knowing I'll always love you."

His words gave her pause, but she turned the horse and charged away from the abandoned castle.

Not quite out of the canyon, as she saw the forest and the road through it before her, an arrow whizzed by, then another. She kicked her horse faster and looked up at the canyon wall, seeing a half-dozen archers on her left and even more to her right. Stopping to turn would mean certain death, as would charging through their volley of arrows. This ambush was clearly meant for her and the Prince of Enulam, one last, morbid gift from her former lord Poskleer.

She steered her horse left, then right, kicking it faster and trying to weave through the shower of arrows that grew thicker as she rode toward the middle of the archers. More of them undoubtedly waited ahead. She had no way out and prayed the archers who ambushed her were poor shots.

As she looked up at the canyon wall to the left, bursts of flames lanced at them from overhead and slammed into the positions the archers hid behind and exploded. Six explosions killed six archers.

The volley stopped and Le'ell turned her eyes up as an enormous black dragon swept overhead toward the castle about ten heights above her. The canyon was not quite big enough for this dragon to turn, but he banked over and kicked off of the canyon wall, stroking his wings as he directed his deadly fire on the other archers. Seven bursts of fire hit the canyon wall and exploded even more violently than the first.

Le'ell stopped her horse and shielded herself as best she could from the debris that pelted the canyon floor, turning her face away. With tightly closed eyes, she waited until she heard the last of the stones and pebbles hit the canyon before opening them again. Something big hit the canyon floor right in front of her and she was hesitant to look, praying it was a boulder that had been jarred loose in the dragon's attack. Since her horse did not react, that is what it had to be. Slowly turning her eyes ahead, she lost her breath as she found herself facing the enormous black dragon that had saved her.

Crouched on all fours, he held his head low, intense eyes locked on her.

A lost memory stirred. She remembered this beast.

Forcing herself to breathe again, she managed, "You've come for me, haven't you?"

"Perhaps I have," he boomed. "Perhaps I'm wondering why you've come this way without the Prince of Enulam."

"Did—Did you send him to fetch me?" she nervously asked.

He raised a brow and a red glow overtook the pale blue of his eyes. The glow went to green and Le'ell found herself enveloped in a glow the same color. Then it was gone.

The dragon grunted, then nodded. "I see you've been made to forget the Prince of Enulam. That's unfortunate for him. You seem to remember me, though."

She hesitantly nodded. "I remember you."

"Our first encounter in the forest?" he asked.

She nodded again.

"And at the hot springs?" he prodded.

Again she nodded.

"But you don't remember the Prince of Enulam at all." He raised himself up and sat before her, wrapping his tail around him on the ground. "Well, that's none of my concern. You need to go to Border."

"You want me to find that big wizard who bought me," she guessed.

"You won't find him," the dragon informed. "Just go there."

Le'ell nodded. "What do you want me to do once I'm there?"

He stood and opened his wings. "Just go. Everything should fall into place once you are there. The imps will let you pass without bothering you. I'll find you another time."

Watching him stroke his wings and lift himself into the air, she kept her eyes on him until he was out of sight. As her heart slowed, she kicked her horse forward, no longer concerned about ambush as much as her fate with that dragon.

Many hours of riding through the forest gave her too much time to think. She kept her pace as fast as her horse could go over that distance, stopping half the day later at a stream to allow her horse to drink and eat some of the lush grass on the banks.

She sat on a boulder near the water, trying to remember, trying to piece fractured memories together. Since leaving Aalekilk, nothing made sense and she doubted her every thought and memory. She knew she had to get to shelter before nightfall and something distant and elusive in her mind told her to look for a castle another hour ahead of her, yet the thought of that castle was somehow frightening.

A feeling overtook her, a feeling that she was being watched. With no weapons, her mind scrambled with thoughts of how to defend herself should she need to.

Movement in the grass behind her drew her attention and she tensed up, preparing to spring up and fight off whatever was there, or flee to her horse and run for her life.

It stepped closer and she jumped up and spun around.

The white unicorn flinched back and snorted.

Le'ell's mouth fell open, her eyes locked wide on the little unicorn. Moving slowly, she held her palms to the little unicorn and offered, "I'm sorry. I—I didn't mean to startle you so. Had I known it was you back there, I..."

Leaning her head, the little unicorn whickered back.

An image flashed into Le'ell's mind, the image of a tall man with long black hair, bronze skin and deeply chiseled features. She had seen him before and yet another sleeping memory stirred.

Almost as if summoned by her thoughts, the black haired man rode into the clearing across from the spring, his eyes on Le'ell as he guided his horse across the shallow water, stopping only a few paces from her where he swung down from his saddle.

Somehow, although she did not at any time truly know him, she did not feel fear of him, even as he approached, even as he reached to her and took her shoulder. His steely eyes did not betray any emotion, rather they seemed to scrutinize her, examine her. He finally nodded, saying, "It is good to see you are well."

She raised her chin, trying to remember more of him. "Thank you."

"You barely remember me," he observed, "and Chail not at all." A whicker from the unicorn drew his attention and he looked to her and nodded, then he turned his eyes to Le'ell. "She cannot help you with that. Many of the memories he took from you are gone and cannot be found again, nor can the power of this unicorn bring them back to you. The false memories put there by the wizard at Aalekilk will fade in time as he is absent from you, but the memories of your true love will not return."

Backing away from him, Le'ell shook her head, not wanting to believe what she was hearing. "My true love? I have no such feelings for anyone."

The unicorn whickered to her, then barked a short whinny, and Le'ell glanced at the her.

"She says the feelings will survive the loss of the memories," the black haired man explained.

Her lips parting in surprise, Le'ell breathed, "You can understand her?"

"Of course," was his answer. "You do not hear the unicorn with your ears, you hear her with your heart." He motioned to the unicorn with his head and said. "Speak to her at last. Tell her what you've wanted to your whole life."

An important moment in Le'ell's life was to come, something she had never known she thought to be impossible. She looked to the little unicorn and took a couple of steps to her, for the first time in her life believing the impossible. Something within her changed, and her heart opened. Everything she had ever been taught seemed distant and tears blurred her vision as she softly admitted, "I want to hear you, since I was a little girl. I want to believe."

The unicorn seemed different to her now, not a mystical beast of legend, but something of her world she had never known. As the unicorn looked to the black haired man and whickered, Le'ell heard in her heart and mind, "Traman, are you sure this is going to work? I've been trying to talk to her for days and she just doesn't understand."

Le'ell gasped and covered her mouth, her wide eyes locked on the little unicorn.

The black haired man smiled as he looked from Le'ell to the unicorn and simply said, "She only has to believe. Talk to her."

With a look of exasperation, the unicorn turned to Le'ell and whickered, "Sometimes humans are so difficult to figure out. I wish she could understand—"

"I can," Le'ell breathed. "I can hear you!"

The unicorn's ears perked. "You can?"

Nodding, the Princess sank to her knees, her jaw quivering as tears rolled from her eyes. "I can hear you."

With a look at the black haired man, the unicorn seemed to grumble, "I'll bet the big man still can't."

He shrugged.

Looking back to the Princess, the unicorn straightly said, "Okay, there isn't much time. Ralligor says he wants you back at Border as soon as possible and you will know what to do when you get there."

Le'ell nodded, confirming, "The dragon, you mean. He found me as I was leaving Aalekilk and told me that."

"You also have something else you have to do," the unicorn informed.

The Princess could tell that she spoke of the big man who had released her, the Prince of Enulam. "I just don't know what to do."

"What does your heart tell you?" Traman asked.

Turning her eyes down, Le'ell shook her head and admitted, "I don't know anymore."

The unicorn butted her with her nose. "What do you feel when you see him? I'll bet you have feelings then, don't you?"

Le'ell shrugged. "He's very easy to look at. There was something in the pit of my stomach when I saw him that I could not... I don't know."

"Feelings can survive memories," the unicorn informed, "especially if that feeling is love. You don't remember him, but you will always love him. He hurts without you and you will hurt without him."

"But he's my enemy," the Princess tried to explain.

"Ralligor is supposed to be my enemy," the unicorn explained, "but he is one of my dearest friends. I have friends who are human, too, and humans are supposed to be the enemies of unicorns. You and Chail are the same species, so there is one line you don't even have to cross."

Le'ell finally looked up to the unicorn.

"He told me how you met," Traman said. "I suppose you don't remember that either?"

She shook her head.

"It was many seasons ago," he told her. "You had left your castle to ride in solitude. Apparently you had something to prove to your mother or something of the like. You were brazen enough to cross the border into Enulam territory. When Prince Chail happened upon you allowing your horse to drink and graze, you challenged him."

Le'ell turned her eyes to the black haired man, trying to remember.

He continued. "When he got off of his horse and approached you, you drew your sword and scratched a line in the sand before you. You told him that he would have to go through you to get into Zondaen territory."

The Princess' lips tightened.

"He met your challenge," Traman went on. "Your first encounter with each other was with steel. He was taken with you from his first sight of you and did his best not to hurt you but finally surrendered himself to you when he realized you were tiring."

A slight smile touched her lips and she breathed, "That is so romantic."

The black haired man nodded. "You probably thought so at the time, too." He offered her his hand and helped her to her feet. "You are no longer truly complete without him or him without you. You can choose to move on without him and find another, or you can find the path you once walked with him." He looked to the unicorn and announced, "I should go. I will look forward to seeing you again." The unicorn whickered to him as he walked to his horse, and as he mounted, he looked back to her and assured, "I will. Be well, Shahly." He nodded to Le'ell once more, then rode into the forest, back the way he had come.

When he was beyond sight or sound, Le'ell looked to the unicorn and said, "He called you Shahly?"

She looked back and confirmed, "That is my name, or as close as your language gets to it. It is what my friends call me."

"May I call you that?"

"Of course you can. We'd better go. There's a long journey ahead but I know some shortcuts that will get us there faster."

"You're coming with me?"

The unicorn leaned her head. "I will unless you don't want me to."

Shaking her head, Le'ell assured, "No, I want you to!"

"I thought you might like some company. Your horse is rested and only wants to eat more if he can't run."

"You're coming all the way to Border with me?"

"Well, I won't go into Border but as far as I can without being seen by too many humans. The humans there make me nervous."

"I understand," Le'ell said, mounting her horse. "Some of them make me nervous, too."

They looked to each other, then shared a good laugh.

CHAPTER 19

A long journey was only made longer by the horrible solitude that went with him. The road back to border was as empty as Prince Chail's heart felt. He had stopped to sleep that night, but a restful sleep was not to find him, so his lonely journey continued before sunup.

Many long hours passed and before high sun and only an hour from Border he encountered another group of riders coming toward him. Many horses carried many armored soldiers who escorted almost a score of empty wagons toward Aalekilk. His curiosity finally distracted him from his lonely thoughts as something about this caravan seemed terribly amiss. The riders were a mix of Enulam men and Zondaen women. He stopped five or six paces away and they stopped in turn. Captain Trehtar led them, as did a familiar Zondaen officer, one he was actually glad to see.

Pa'lesh swung down from her horse, striding to Prince Chail with just the hint of a smile on her face as she greeted, "Well here comes Chail of Enulam."

He dismounted and met her half way, his eyes strained and unable to meet hers. "Le'ell. She... She doesn't—"

"We passed her early this morning," Pa'lesh interrupted. "She borrowed a sword and had a message for you should we see you."

Chail slowly turned his eyes to her. "A message for me?"

One of Pa'lesh's eyebrows cocked up and she slowly nodded. "She said if you are going to Border then you will have to go through her to enter."

His eyes widened and his lips parted ever so slightly.

"She sounded pretty serious," the Field Captain warned, "so I hope you've rested."

"Why aren't we moving?" a familiar voice shouted from the center of the convoy.

Turning his eyes from Pa'lesh, a smile touched Chail's face as he saw another familiar face drawing closer.

Noorain strode to the front of the line, rambling, "I've a schedule to keep and much work to do! Let's go! We just rested yesterday!" Stopping as he saw the Prince, he smiled broadly and shouted, "Chail!" The merchant ran to him and took his shoulders, laughing as he greeted, "It is so good to see you again, my friend!"

Taking his shoulders in return, Chail smiled and replied, "I'm glad to see you as well. How is everything? Did they treat you well at Enulam?"

Throwing his head back in a hearty laugh, Noorain finally answered, "My friend, you have no idea. I sold out of almost everything! Your gracious father and pretty Le'ell's young and beautiful mother are even having me escorted to the fallen castle to collect more stock for my shop once the battle ends. It's almost one hundred percent profit! My worthless brother is watching the shop now and what little is left there while I'm on this venture."

Chail nodded. "Well, at least things are looking up for one of us."

"Oh, if you only knew. I'll be making monthly journeys to Enulam and Zondae with my best wares. I may even expand into cooking wares, I don't know yet. Oh, my friend, meeting you has come with great fortune. I'll be naming my next son after you!"

Smiling a strained smile, the Prince simply offered, "I'm honored, thank you."

"No no no. Thank *you*!"

Captain Trehtar approached and took Pa'lesh's side, extending his hand to the Prince. "Good to see you again, Highness."

As Chail shook his hand, Pa'lesh slapped his shoulder and scolded, "Don't call him that out here. Do you want to make a target for the raiders?"

The Prince glanced at her, then admitted, "I must say that I'm a little confused. The last I heard was that Zondae had been attacked by Aalekilk and then fell the next day to Enulam and most were captured."

Pa'lesh met Trehtar's eyes and observed, "He's a little behind."

Nodding, Trehtar looked back to Prince Chail and informed, "The battle between Zondae and Enulam was a ruse, as was the mass surrender."

Chail folded his arms, his eyes narrow as he raised his chin. "Aalekilk never attacked?"

"Oh, they attacked," Pa'lesh corrected, "but their second strike had a nasty surprise awaiting them two leagues north of the castle. It seems your father had a force of garrison strength waiting for them. A third force was ambushed by the garrison that you advised Queen Le'errin to send north. Those laying siege to Castle Zondae were set upon by yet another garrison sent by Enulam."

Trehtar continued, "When the Zondaens saw the raiders turning to defend against us they poured out of their castle and hit them from the other side. After that the fight only lasted a few moments."

"No prisoners were taken," Pa'lesh went on, "not from Zondae and not from Aalekilk. Your father and Queen Le'errin came up with a scheme to make them think their plan had succeeded. We wiped out their unsuspecting occupation forces and overwhelmed two garrisons that were on their way to attack your northern keep."

"They sent more troops toward the Southern keeps," Trehtar added. "They didn't make it past Castle Enulam."

Chail nodded. "So, what happens now?"

Trehtar and Pa'lesh exchanged glances again, and Pa'lesh answered, "It's time for Castle Aalekilk to have its turn. I understand that—"

"Don't bother," Chail advised. "The castle's been abandoned and the other half of their army has fled north along with their leader. I will recommend to King Donwarr and Queen Le'errin that the castle be occupied indefinitely."

"Way ahead of you," Pa'lesh informed.

"Also," the Prince continued, "All of the gold in the vaults there is to be taken to this dragon in the desert. Don't ask why; let's just say we're repaying a debt for his services."

Hesitantly, they both nodded, and Trehtar asked, "What should we tell King Donwarr?"

"I'll handle it," Chail said softly.

Noorain pursed his lips and nodded. "Just as long as I can fill my shelves, I don't care what the dragon has, but if Aalekilk left some barrels of ale behind I say we don't tell anyone."

Someone else approached, a huge presence with huge footsteps who shouted, "What the hell is the holdup? Some of us have lives beyond this journey!" As the big stablemaster grew closer, he saw Chail and folded his arms. "I might have known you were holding me up again."

Raising his brow, the Prince greeted, "Good morning, Gartner."

"It's past morning," the stable master growled. He turned around and shouted, "All right, get yourselves dismounted and tend to those animals. Give 'em a chance to rest or you'll all be walking."

Watching the huge man depart, Pa'lesh approached the Prince and grasped his arm, asking, "Where did you find him?"

"A land of giants, I'll bet," Noorain answered for him. Looking back to the Prince, Noorain declared, "You have somewhere to be! You'd better get yourself going. Go on, get on that horse and get out of here." He waved the Prince away with his hands and repeated, "Get on out of here!"

Pa'lesh motioned to the Prince's horse with her head and assured, "I'll be seeing you later. Go on, now. She's waiting."

An excitement Chail had not felt for some time overwhelmed him and he turned and jumped on his horse, riding fast through the convoy.

Time seemed to pass slowly for him and the journey seemed very long, but before he realized he was almost to Border and abruptly stopped his horse.

Standing in the road ahead of him was a tall, well made warrior, a princess of Zondae. She was still dressed as she had been when he had freed her, but this time she was brandishing a sword, slowly tamping the flat of the blade into her free hand as she glared at him with challenging eyes.

He just stared at her for a time, then he slowly got down from his horse and hesitantly approached. Not quite four paces away, he stopped as she raised her blade before her.

Stepping back, she drew a line in the dirt before her, then held her weapon ready.

Slowly pulling his own blade, Chail locked his eyes on hers and hopefully asked, "Do you remember me?"

Le'ell shook her head. "No, I don't."

His lips tightened and he lowered his weapon.

"I don't remember you Prince of Enulam," she continued, "and you aren't coming this way." One of her eyebrows lifted ever so slightly. "That is, unless you think you can come through me."

His eyes narrowed and he raised the tip of his sword, striding cautiously toward her and pausing only when she smiled slightly and winked at him.

The lives they knew had ended, and would begin anew.